THE CHRISTMAS CASTLE IN SCOTLAND

JULIE CAPLIN

One More Chapter
a division of HarperCollins*Publishers* Ltd
1 London Bridge Street
London SE1 9GF
www.harpercollins.co.uk

HarperCollins*Publishers*
1st Floor, Watermarque Building, Ringsend Road
Dublin 4, Ireland

This paperback edition 2022
1
First published in Great Britain in ebook format
by HarperCollins*Publishers* 2022

A catalogue record of this book is available from the British Library

ISBN: 978-0-00-843126-6

This novel is entirely a work of fiction. The names, characters and incidents
portrayed in it are the work of the author's imagination. Any resemblance to
actual persons, living or dead, events or localities is entirely coincidental.

Printed and bound in the UK using 100% Renewable Electricity
by CPI Group (UK) Ltd

For Donna – for too many reasons to count.

October

Chapter One

As she unloaded her case from the boot of the car, Izzy could hear the ragged flapping of a flag – a Jolly Roger, for some reason – accompanied by the chorus of clinking metal flagpole clips and the mewling cry of a buzzard gliding through the thermals high above her.

She stared at the flag flying half-mast and shook her head. Because a castle needed a pirate flag. Of course, it did. Her mother was a law unto herself.

Hauling her case up the stone steps, worn smooth in the middle from decades of use, she pushed open the heavy, studded wooden door, laced across with iron fittings, and stepped onto the uneven flagstone floor that she felt sure vibrated with the echo of hundreds of ancient stories. A huge smile lit up her face. She, Izzy McBride, was the official owner of Kinlochleven Castle. Her! What on earth had possessed Great Uncle Bill? It had certainly been a shocker. The expectation had always been that it was to go to his cousin on the East Coast, although there'd been no rancour from him when she'd met him at Bill's funeral.

Right now though, she needed tea. She'd been travelling for the last twenty-four hours back from Ireland where she'd spent the last six weeks at the famous Killorgally Cookery School. She needed a big mug of tea and one of the ridiculously overpriced shortbread biscuits she'd picked up at Edinburgh Airport. Knowing Xanthe, the cupboards would be bare. Her mother was not a cook and had no interest in food. She lived on fags, gin and lettuce.

To Izzy's surprise, foody smells were emanating from the big kitchen, which was down through a long, wainscoted corridor as she entered the castle. Perhaps she'd underestimated her mother after all.

'Hi, Xan...' The words died on her lips at the sight of a broad back leaning over the big black Rayburn. The man turned around and Izzy was confronted with over six foot of rather dishevelled male, dressed in faded jeans and a thick, cable knit sweater, a woollen scarf wrapped several times around his neck. Wow! He had the bluest eyes she'd ever seen outside of a TV screen.

'Hello,' he said, pushing back the fringe of a wild mop of hair with one hand while holding a wooden spoon and stirring something in a pan with the other.

'You got it working,' she said, nodding at the beast of a cooker that she had never been able to light previously.

'Yes,' he said with a smile. 'Although I had to resort to YouTube and the purchase of firelighters definitely helped.'

Izzy nodded, wishing she'd done that before, but somehow it had felt like cheating. Surely the owner of a Scottish castle should be able to light her own woodburning oven?

'I'm sorry, who are you?' she asked, perhaps a little too directly but it wasn't every day you came home and found, quite frankly – despite the scruffy almost-beard – a film-star-gorgeous stranger in your kitchen. She blamed those mesmerising blue eyes for making her sound so blunt.

He raised an eyebrow. Of course he could do that. Just looking at him, you could tell he was the sort of man that could do that.

'I'm Ross Strathallan, and you?'

A little put out she stared at him for a minute, trying to figure out how to take back control of the situation while her brain, still discombobulated from travel weariness and those blue eyes, dissolved into mush. 'I'm McBride ... I mean McBride Izzy.'

He stared at her, his eyebrows doing that I'm-not-sure-what-we-have-here-but-I'll-play-along thing. 'Nice to meet you, McBride.' He turned back to the pan on the cooker.

'Er, excuse me,' Izzy spluttered, nonplussed by this complete disinterest in who she was. She might have been away for a while but this was *her* home and she still had no idea what Ross Strathallan, whoever he was, was doing in *her* kitchen.

'Yes?' he replied, as if he were offering to help her. He was totally at ease, both in the situation and with himself. One of those supremely confident, calm-without-being-arrogant-and-full-of-themselves men who were comfortable in their own skin. At the same time, there was a certain reserve about him, as if he were holding himself apart from the world.

She didn't want to sound rude again but what was he doing here? In *her* kitchen. She had so many plans that centred on this room, the heart of the castle. She didn't want people in

5

her kitchen. This was her space. The whole time she'd been on her cookery course in Ireland, she'd been itching to get home and take charge of her domain and start practising in preparation for when they were ready to entertain paying guests. Having some stranger here, in her home ... well, it wasn't right.

'What are you doing here?' The words came out in an un-Izzy-like challenge. She was normally a lot more patient than this – with a mother like hers, she had to be.

He raised that bloody irritating eyebrow again and stared at her. 'I'm about to have dinner.' He raised the spoon to reveal baked beans.

She decided against snorting – where she'd been for the last few weeks, baked beans did not qualify as dinner. Her cooking mentor back in Ireland, Adrienne Byrne, would have been horrified.

'Why?' she asked.

'Because I'm hungry,' he said slowly and carefully, as if he were speaking to a complete idiot.

She glared at him. Was he trying to be funny? Blowing out a deliberately irritated sigh, she gave him a saccharine sweet smile in response. 'Yes, but why are you cooking in this kitchen? This house? What are you doing here?'

'I live here,' he said, as if it were completely obvious.

'No, you don't,' she said.

'I do.'

'You can't.'

'I can.'

'Since when? No.' She held up her hand. 'Don't answer that. You can't stay here.' Although under different circumstances she definitely wouldn't kick him out. There was something solid and reliable and unflappable about him and that was even without the good looks and rugby player build, not that she normally went for that sort of man. Well, not in real life at least. Secretly, she'd had more than her fair share of hot fantasies about Jamie Fraser from *Outlander*.

'I beg to differ. Why don't you talk to my landlady, Xanthe? The owner of the place.'

'Landlady?' Izzy's voice pitched. 'You've moved in? When? How?'

'The way most people move in. I carried a few boxes and a couple of suitcases. Oh, and a house plant, as I recall.' His mouth twitched in misplaced amusement that made her want to punch him, although she suspected her hand would bounce off that granite-hard chest like some wimpy cartoon character. Not that she'd ever punched anyone in her life, nor felt the need to apart from that one time when Philip announced he was engaged. But she was so not going there right now.

'I might have known,' she muttered. 'How long exactly are you planning to stay?'

'Three months, possibly longer. Although that was on the basis that I'd be paying for peace and quiet.' His eyes narrowed with this pointed barb and he turned back to the saucepan, gathering up one of the two slices of toast browning on top of the Rayburn's hotplate and sliding them onto a dish before tipping what looked like nearly a full tin of beans over them. Picking up his dinner, he pulled out a chair and sat to eat, propping a Kindle up against a mug of tea.

She stared at him. 'Three months? You can't. I'm not being rude but you really can't stay here. We're nowhere near ready for guests. You're going to have to leave.'

'Again, I suggest you take it up with Xanthe,' he said with

the most irritating calmness. He reached forward to turn on his Kindle and began reading, ignoring her.

'I will,' she said, sounding like a petulant toddler.

She was going to kill her mother. What on earth had she been thinking? They weren't ready for paying guests and certainly not ones that did their own cooking. This wasn't a bloody youth hostel or a doss house or lodgings. There was an awful lot of work that needed doing before then, but in her head, she'd planned that the kitchen – once she'd worked out how to work the Rayburn – would be her cosy space, separate from the rest of the house. A place for respite, especially from her mother. Now this man seemed to have made himself comfortable here and Izzy wasn't very happy about it at all.

But she was hungry and despite everything the beans smelled good. With a sniff she moved past him and got a plate, helped herself to the remaining slice of toast and the last of the beans in the pan. Ignoring his sudden stare, she sat opposite him and began to eat. This was her kitchen and she wasn't going to be forced out.

'Help yourself,' he said, with an outraged stare at her plate.

'Thank you.'

'Would you like another tin? I brought plenty with me and I can knock them off the bill if you like.'

Izzy dropped her fork with a rattle on the plate. Oh God. How embarrassing. She'd assumed at the very least that whatever he was paying her mother would have covered food. Was Xanthe really that shameless?

While her temper was fizzing, there was no point confronting Xanthe as that really would push her blood pressure into the danger zone. Instead, she stormed back into the hallway, past the sets of antlers and fishing rods that decorated the walls, to the porch where she grabbed one of the waxed jackets hanging there. She needed fresh air. Tugging it on, she shouldered her way through the heavy wooden door and stalked out onto the gravel drive, stopping briefly to take a calming breath before striding through the ornamental plantings of trees and shrubs in the parkland, heading towards the slopes of the nearby moorland.

The sun was low in the sky, there was probably only another hour of daylight and the clouds were already tinted with pink in readiness for sunset but she didn't care, she needed to be outside. Since her stay in Ireland, she'd learned that while food might nourish the body, being outdoors in the countryside, at one with nature, nourished the soul. And she needed that right now. After twenty minutes' brisk walking, she finally stopped to catch her breath and turned to look back down the slope at the way she'd come.

The early evening light bathed the scene in gold, harmonising with the autumn rainbow of russets, auburns, burnt oranges and ruby reds. A sharp scythe of joy stabbed at her heart, pushing aside her earlier irritation. She stared down with a mixture of pride, excitement and terror at the rough-hewn walls of Kinlochleven Castle, rising up from the umber, yellow and pale rose of the autumn-clad trees crowded around its walls. Beyond it, rust-coloured, bracken-strewn hills guarded the skyline – the impact of the scene doubled by the perfect mirror image reflected in the glassy stillness of Loch Leven.

With its striking, shingle-covered, conical roofs, tourelles and battlements, the nineteenth-century Scottish Baronial castle was majestic and owed its splendour to a bygone age of romanticism and wealth. It was also now her home – at least for as long as she could keep the roof from falling in on their heads, even if it took her last penny and/or breath.

She sank down onto a fallen tree trunk, propped her chin in her hand and stared at the beautiful legacy of which she was now guardian. She needed to preserve the building for future generations but she also had to make the castle pay its way. Her great uncle had been adamant he didn't want any of the estate sold off, which is why he'd left it to her instead of her mother or the cousin on the East Coast, and turning it into a small, private hotel was the only way she could think of bringing in an income.

There was a lot to do and one of the trickiest jobs would be keeping Xanthe in check. Clearly she'd already got carried away and offered a complete stranger a room. Izzy's mother was the sort of person who wanted to sprint before she could walk, preferably at Olympic record-breaking speeds. It was a complete mystery to nearly everyone as to where Izzy had inherited her common sense, as it appeared her long-dead father hadn't been much better. He'd died in a fatal accident, tractor racing on the lane outside their house, when Izzy was five.

Enough of the introspection. She glanced down at her phone. The WhatsApp message group that they'd started during her cookery course in Ireland had been busy in response to her earlier message.

Izzy: *I'm home. Hellish journey but it's good to be back.*

Jason: *I'm back at work, my boss already cracking the whip. Can't believe I'm missing Killorgally already.*

Fliss: *Hope your new venture goes well, Izzy. Good luck.*

Jason: *Let us know when we can visit, I've never stayed in a castle.*

Hannah: *Good luck with the cooking!*

She smiled down at her phone. She was going to miss them all but especially Hannah, Fliss and Jason, who were closest to her in age.

Izzy rose to her feet, blowing out a breath. Now she'd calmed down, it was time to find her mother and find out what the deal with Ross Strathallan was and how quickly she could get rid of him and reclaim her kitchen.

Chapter Two

She was relieved to find the kitchen empty when she returned but just as she was taking her first grateful sip of tea, the door opened and a wiry man strode in, his salt and pepper hair still containing a few strands of faded red.

'Ah, lassie, you're back. I saw the car coming along the road earlier.'

'Duncan, how are you?' She smiled at the man who had worked at the castle for over twenty years. He was supposed to be retired, but he'd offered to help her with any information she might need about the estate and its history.

'Not so bad, not so bad. How d'ye get on in Ireland?'

'Well enough,' she said. 'I'll no be embarrassing myself with my cooking.' Her accent always became stronger whenever she spoke to Duncan. 'Do you want a cup of tea?'

'Aye. I've got plenty to update you with.' He shook his head and clicked his teeth.

'Right,' she said, busying herself with making him a cuppa.

'I got that quote frae the builders about the roof repairs.'

'That's brilliant; thanks, Duncan.' She gave him a grateful smile. They'd talked about it six weeks ago and she was impressed he'd remembered to fix it for her return.

He gave her a terse smile in return. 'I dinna think you'll be thanking me when you see the size of the estimate. Yon roof's a bit worse than we thought.'

'How much worse?' asked Izzy, wrapping her fingers around her cup as if its warmth might offer some solace.

Duncan pulled his mouth into a variety of comical shapes.

'You'd better spit it out.'

'Yer looking at twenty thousand as a minimum.'

The tea swirled in her stomach in a nauseous wave. 'That's a lot of money.'

'They might be able to do a bit of patching in the short term but the whole lot over the east wing needs replacing.'

Izzy nodded dully, trying not to feel sick.

'On the good side, the hens are still laying so at least we won't go hungry.'

'Great,' she said with a weak smile.

'It's good to have ye back, lassie.' He gave her a cheerful grin before his face darkened for a moment. 'Verra good to have you back. Xanthe's had me running about the place like a loon for the last couple of weeks. I'll be glad of a rest, that I will.'

Izzy gave him a gentle smile, wondering what on earth her mother had been up to.

'I'd best go find her. I haven't seen her yet.'

'She's no changed,' said Duncan, his mouth firming into a straight line.

When she walked out into the main hallway a few minutes later, she was hailed from the floor above by a voice as loud as a foghorn. 'Izzy, darling! You're home!'

Her mother leaned over the wooden balustrade and waved as if she were Her Majesty the Queen on the Royal Yacht Britannia as it came in to dock.

'Yes, Xanthe, I'm home,' Izzy muttered as her mother skipped down the stairs, almost getting tangled in the layers of lilac chiffon floating around her legs. At the bottom of the stairs, she clutched Izzy's shoulders and the feathery plume of a matching lilac fascinator, perched like an exotic bird on her mother's fire-engine red curls, almost took out Izzy's eye. 'Darling, look at those dark circles. We need to get you some cucumber.'

'Why was there a strange man in the kitchen?'

Her mother took a haughty puff of a cigarette in a diamante holder and shot Izzy a wicked grin. 'Nice, isn't he? Those shoulders. He's got a touch of the Jamie Fraser about him. I thought we might keep him.'

Izzy burst out laughing. Her mother was completely bonkers but there was no point trying to argue with her. She'd learned long ago that it was counterproductive. 'You're incorrigible. What's he doing here? He thinks he's staying for three months.'

'Yes,' said Xanthe, looking very pleased with herself. 'Mrs McPherson, the woman that runs the post office – you know, the one with the teeth? By the way, do you think they have dentists round here? I've got a filling which feels a bit loose...'

Izzy sighed. Her mother was a great one for going off on nonsensical tangents.

'What is this about Mrs McPherson?'

'Well, she was the one that sent him up here a few weeks ago. She knew … well, of course she knew. She's the post mistress and they always know everything, don't they? Anyway she told him about how we're planning to open as a hotel and he wanted somewhere to stay with complete quiet – he's writing a book – and as we haven't got any other guests at present, I thought we fitted the bill perfectly.'

Izzy gritted her teeth. 'We haven't got any other guests because we're not ready for guests.'

'Pish, sweetie. We have rooms. You should see what I've done with the drawing room while you've been away. And he's quite happy to fend for himself. In fact, I barely see him. More's the pity, he's very easy on the eye.'

'That's not the point.' Izzy swallowed.

'He said we won't even know he's here.' Her mother's voice, loud already, went up another couple of decibels. 'He's a writer. A history professor on sabbatical. Honestly, darling, he spends all day in his room, goes for walks and then spends all night up there. Terribly boring, actually, although I'm hoping he's one of those tall, dark and brooding types. Still waters and all that. Do you think there's some passion bubbling under that laid-back exterior? Anyway, he really is no trouble. Now come see what I've done.'

Before Izzy could say another word, her mother wafted away in her cloud of purple. With an exasperated sigh, she followed her across the hall to the north corridor and down another hallway covered in a very threadbare tartan carpet, bits of which were stuck down with glossy grey gaffer tape. It obviously needed to be replaced before someone tripped on one of the ragged edges and broke their neck. Another reason why they couldn't have a guest yet. Health and safety would have a field day here.

'Oh, and one more thing. Why is there a skull and srossbones flying from the tower?'

'Isn't it fun? I found it in one of the trunks in the attic and I thought, why not. It will let the neighbours know we're in residence.'

Izzy smiled. Typical Xanthe.

'Tah-da.' Xanthe announced in her booming voice, throwing open a door at the end of the hallway.

Izzy stepped into the drawing room, which had four large windows overlooking the loch and a further two windows at the end. The light in here had always been wonderful, so much so that it had unfortunately highlighted the faded paint on the walls, the exuberant collection of cobwebs around the dusty plasterwork ceiling and the sun-bleached upholstery of the furniture – but all that had gone.

'Oh my goodness,' exclaimed Izzy. 'This is gorgeous.'

Her mother had completely overhauled the room. Tasteful mid-green paint – which probably had some name like 'forest sage' or 'deepening grass' – covered the walls, the ceiling had been whitened and the windows were dressed with drapes on either side of Roman blinds in familiar-looking sumptuous fabrics. Izzy also recognised some of the pictures and antiques, which had been brought in from other parts of the castle to create this cosy, stylish lounge.

'I know,' Xanthe said smugly.

'How did you...?' While her mother was extremely creative, she wasn't that practical. However, when she set her mind to something she could also be extremely pig-headed and determined, especially if she wanted to prove someone wrong.

'I winkled Duncan out of the estate office and he helped me move the furniture about.' Izzy stared at her. 'Don't you love the throws? Feel them; they're so soft. I made them from some old blankets I found in the trunks up in the attics. Such fun searching through them. I must say they did proper housekeeping in those days; everything was wrapped up with mothballs, and I also made the blinds out of a couple of pairs of curtains from one of the bedrooms. They'd only faded around the edges, so I was able to use almost all of the fabric. And then the drapes are for decoration but I made them from the originals and cut off all the sun damage. Pretty, aren't they?'

Izzy had to admit they were. 'Very resourceful. You've done a brilliant job, Mum.'

'Resourceful is my middle name and it's "Xanthe", darling,' her mother corrected.

'This room looks brand new.' Izzy paused looking again at the pristine walls. 'Did you do this painting?'

Xanthe laughed. 'Good lord, no. I got a man in, darling.' She waved her glossy nails. 'There's no one for miles to do my nails. He did a jolly good job although I had to get someone in to replaster the walls first.'

Izzy gulped. 'How much did that cost?'

She rammed her hands into her jeans' pockets and gritted her teeth in a facsimile of a smile. They'd talked about this. Izzy was going to do that sort of work herself to save money – well, not plastering, of course, but filling cracks, making do.

Her mother smiled a touch too smugly for Izzy's liking. 'I

know what you're thinking. We can't afford it but...' She tapped her nose.

'We agreed we'd do as much of the work as we can ourselves.' Painting was definitely one thing that Izzy could do herself.

'You're forgetting something.'

Izzy eyed her mother. 'What?'

'Professor Strathallan paid for the first month in advance.'

What happened to tweedy jacketed men with elbow patches? Wasn't that what professors were supposed to look like? Not like Thor on a day off.

'His money more than covered the painting and plastering.' Xanthe tipped her nose in the air with snooty superiority. Izzy was surprised she didn't add a sniff to punctuate her point. 'And there's more coming.'

Izzy closed her eyes. She dreaded to think how little her mother had asked for rent. She didn't have a clue about money; it slipped through her fingers faster than water. Knowing Xanthe, it probably wouldn't cover the cost of heating his room. Which was all the more reason to ask him to leave. They'd be losing money.

'How much have you charged him?' she asked, as if she were only mildly interested instead of fearing the answer.

'Five hundred pounds.'

'Five hundred pounds for three months?'

'Don't be silly, darling. What do think I am? Stupid? That's for a week.'

'What!' Izzy squeaked, her eyes widening in shock.

'Yes, two thousand up front for the first month. I thought that was fair. To have a castle to yourself. And,' Xanthe

19

preened for a moment, 'we need the money, remember? And I've also—'

'But we're not even feeding him!' Izzy's blood heated in sudden mortification.

Xanthe shrugged. 'He doesn't seem to mind. As long as he gets his peace and quiet. He was most insistent about that, which is why I've stuck him at the end of the west corridor. You know, the room with that awful painting of rutting stags.'

Izzy's mouth stopped working for a moment and then she started to laugh. Her mother never failed to surprise her and if the man had agreed to pay that much, she wasn't currently in a position to turn it down. Damn, she was going to have to apologise to him and let him stay at least until the end of this month. She had too much to do to let him stay any longer than that. He'd get in the way and there was no way there would be peace and quiet with all the building work going on.

'Honestly, Izzy, I don't know why you think I'm so hopeless.' The feather in her fascinator moved back and forth, mirroring her outrage.

Izzy linked her arm through her mother's. 'I think you're brilliant and this room looks amazing. Where do you think we should start next?'

'Ah,' she said with a sly, smug smile. 'Come see the dining room. I have something else to show you. I got rid of that awful stuffed weasel.'

'Wow, just wow,' said Izzy staring around at the magnificence of the newly decorated dining room a little later.

Xanthe grinned and preened with the smug satisfaction of a peacock displaying its glorious feathers. 'Good, isn't it?'

Xanthe had not only brought together a fine selection of polished, glossy furniture but had also set the long table with twenty place settings featuring an array of sparkling crystal, shiny silver cutlery and delicate china, along with crisp damask napkins and a matching tablecloth. Bold green drapes framed the big casement windows and Xanthe had made new window seat cushions for each of them.

In the centre of the table, she'd created a garland of golden fir cones and candles that wove its way down the middle, culminating at each end with two enormous golden stag candelabras, small white candles placed in their antlers.

'Wow, Xanthe, it looks amazing. Christmas has come early.'

'I know, I've had so many likes on my Instagram page. We're all set for Christmas bookings.'

Izzy nodded. 'Next year, maybe. It's far too soon this year. There's so much to do. Think of how many bedrooms we need to prepare.'

'Isabel Margaret Mary McBride! I sometimes think you inherited too many genes from my granny, she was a crabbit old bat.'

'Or perhaps she had some common sense,' said Izzy, rolling her eyes.

'Where's your sense of adventure?'

'Xanthe, we're not ready to host a Christmas party; not unless they're prepared to pay a ridiculous sum of money.'

Xanthe flounced across the room and fiddled with one of the candles in the stag candelabra before lighting it and then proceeded to light all the candles in the votives hidden amongst the trail of ivy and greenery lining the centre of the table. 'What if they were going to pay twenty-five?'

'Twenty-five what?'

'Thousand,' spat Xanthe with haughty exasperation.

'I'd say they were barking mad.' For that sort of money people would expect Cordon Bleu standard catering and expensive booze.

'Mad or not' – she turned with a dramatic flourish, waving a match dangerously in the air – 'I've got some brilliant news.'

Izzy was still examining the freshly painted walls and paintwork.

'Don't you want to know?' trilled Xanthe, her eyes bird bright with almost fevered excitement.

'Want to know what?' asked Izzy, still distracted by the sums in her head. There couldn't be much left of Professor Strathallan's money.

Xanthe folded her arms and looked excessively pleased with herself, which immediately filled Izzy with a sense of foreboding.

'I have let the castle for Christmas.'

'What?' Izzy straightened. 'You can't.'

'I have.'

Izzy rolled her eyes and stared at her mother. 'Don't tell me, some billionaire has spotted your post on Instagram and has offered us twenty thousand pounds to come for Christmas?'

Irritation warred with triumphant superiority on her mother's face.

'Actually, Miss Smarty Pants, they have.'

Izzy narrowed her eyes.

'It's true. An assistant of a Mr Carter-Jones messaged me and said that Kinlochleven Castle was exactly the place they were looking for. So I said…' Her mouth twisted momentarily in remembered glee. 'I said that it was very exclusive and not available for anything less than five figures for a week. He asked if we'd do it for twenty-five, so I said yes.'

Izzy's stared at her. 'T-t-twenty-five … th-thousand pounds. You're … you're kidding.'

'No I'm not.'

'But there's no way we can—'

'Honestly, Izzy, there's no pleasing some people. You say we need money so I've arranged for us to get it and now you've got a problem with it. What is wrong with you?'

'M… Xanthe, for that sort of money, they're going to want a fancy six-star, superior, de-luxe stay.' Izzy shook her head. 'And are you sure it's not a wind-up?'

'Izzy, even you must have heard of the Carter-Jones fortune. He's in boxer shorts, you know. Rather fitting in Scotland, the home of the kilt and where most men I know let everything hang free underneath them… Anyway, apparently, his wife has Scottish ancestry and it's always been a dream of hers. I've already told him we need a deposit of seven thousand pounds to secure the booking and he transferred it to the bank account this morning.'

'What!' Izzy blinked at her mother. 'Seriously?'

'Oh ye of little faith. Yes.' She paused. 'We can spend it on getting the rooms ready. I've seen the most darling wallpaper.'

'Mum, Christmas is only six weeks away. That's not enough time.'

'Pish, don't be silly. Where there's a will there's a way. I'm sure we can hire someone from the village to help with the decorating and cleaning, if we need to.'

Izzy caught her lip between her teeth, tugging anxiously.

'How many people are coming?' Already her mind was racing, thinking of what needed to be done.

'Four at the moment, but he said there might be one or two more. I'll leave you to it. Toodle pip.'

Izzy sat staring at the door for a while after her mother wafted out on a cloud of perfume and satisfaction. Twenty-five thousand pounds. That was a lot of money. Enough to patch the roof and pay for renovations and repairs, providing Xanthe didn't spend it all on wallpaper. They had six weeks. She shook her head. They could do this.

With the Carter-Joneses' money and Professor Strathallan's rent she might just pull it off...

Chapter Three

I zzy tapped her foot and checked the clock. She'd hoped to catch Professor Strathallan first thing but alas the only sign of him was a warm kettle and a clean cereal bowl on the draining board, leaving her to deduce that he was clearly an early riser. He also seemed to be quiet, unobtrusive and self-reliant as her mother had not been providing bed making or cleaning services in Izzy's absence, which made the exorbitant sum Xanthe had charged him quite embarrassing and yet another reason as to why he couldn't stay. For that price they ought to be providing a better service and although waiting on one guest wouldn't be too onerous, she needed to focus on getting the castle updated and redecorated without worrying or having to work around him.

For a moment Izzy dithered, then, with a sudden fit of resolve, she put down her notepad and pen and darted out of the kitchen, running lightly up the stairs past lots of gilt-edged framed portraits of stiff-necked men and their wives looking sternly down at her. It reminded her of all the people that had inhabited the castle before her. As she walked down the hallway to Ross's room, she slowed and at the door she hesitated for a moment, nerves getting the better of her before she told herself firmly that the man was obviously already up, so she wouldn't be waking him or disturbing him.

With a touch more confidence, she knocked on the door with a firm tap, her knuckles rapping the polished wood. She waited but there was no answer. Was he in there? Maybe he'd gone for a walk. She knocked a second time and again waited for a response. When none was forthcoming, she called, 'Mr Strathallan?' Still no answer. She knocked for a third time and was about to open the door when she heard a distinct crash and a loud, 'For the love of God.'

Oops. He didn't sound very happy.

Now she regretted bothering him, especially as she was about to tell him they wouldn't be able to guarantee his peace for much longer and so he couldn't stay. The solid wood door was thrown open and rocked on its considerable hinges. Ross Strathallan stood scowling in front of her, tension vibrating from him and his dark brows drawn together in two angry slashes. She very nearly backed up.

'What do you want?' he demanded, the words running together so fast it took her a second to pick them apart and make sense of them. She was so surprised she was lost for words.

'I... Er...'

His dark blue eyes bored into her and she felt awkward, crossing one leg behind the other and feeling like a teenager again, not knowing what to do with her limbs.

'I'm working. Is it urgent?'

'Er, no,' she squeaked with all the aplomb of a strangled

guinea pig, a blush tinting her cheeks in a hot rush of embarrassment and humiliation.

'I made it quite clear, Ms McBride, that I'm not to be disturbed. That is why I came here and why I'm paying a fortune. For *peace* and *quiet*.' There was no mistaking the fierce emphasis he placed on the two words. With a glare, he shook his head as if he were doomed to deal with idiots and Izzy could only stand there as he closed the door in her face.

'Well, of all the…' she muttered when she finally came to her senses. How rude!

***

Ten minutes later, she stomped across the cobbled courtyard, carrying a thermos mug of tea to the grandly titled 'estate office'. Duncan never said no to a cup of tea and she needed to get out of the house. Punctuated by each exasperated step, she dictated a coldly polite eviction letter in her head, which she would take great delight in pushing beneath the professor's door before the day was out.

Dear Sir

It is with regret… No, she didn't regret it at all.

Dear Sir, I must ask you to vacate your room at the end of the month.

No again. She wasn't asking him, she was telling him.

Dear Sir, Please take this as notice to vacate your room by the end of the month. Actually, she should make it 'with immediate effect', but that wouldn't be very professional. In fact, it might sound a bit hysterical.

Perhaps, *Dear Sir, please take this as notice for you to vacate your room by Friday.*

There, that was better. Pleased that she'd got it all worked out in her head, she pushed open the door to the estate office and stepped inside, taking in the faintly musty smell. The room was a delightful muddle of papers, old photographs and bits of unidentifiable equipment and ironmongery, the original uses of which she could only guess at. Although this was very much Duncan's domain, she loved the sense of history and things being passed on from generation to generation that pervaded the room. Although Izzy had only met him in those initial weeks before she'd gone to Ireland, she'd quickly developed a fondness for the man. In return, he seemed to appreciate her keenness to learn and to do what she could to maintain the estate for as long as she could. He was in receipt of a pension from the estate which thankfully was all taken care of and could live in his estate cottage for as long as he wanted.

'Morning, Duncan.'

'Ah, Isabel, lassie.' He looked up from the old-fashioned ledger he was peering at through a magnifying glass. Izzy had noticed on her previous visit that he needed glasses to read but he flatly refused, saying he could see well enough, and to be fair he had extraordinary long sight. He could see a deer camouflaged in the bracken on the hillside from almost a mile away.

'I got the farm shop to bring up a delivery for ye.' He nudged a box on the table, which was spilling over with groceries and vegetables. 'I didn't think your mother would remember.'

'Thanks, Duncan, that's so helpful. I must take a trip down there at some point to see what they've got.' She cast a quick glance at the vegetables. With a quick prick of pride, she realised she could put some of her cookery skills into practice. She was itching to get started. 'I can make a soup for lunch. If you'd like some, I'll leave the saucepan on the cooker and you can help yourself, whenever you want it.'

She had a feeling that no one had looked after Duncan for a very long time and she rather liked the idea of being able to do something for him.

'Thanks, lassie. That's very kind of you. I have nae had a home-cooked soup for a long while.' He beamed at her and she was glad she'd suggested it. 'Now, where d'ye want to start?'

'At the beginning?' Izzy offered him a tentative smile. 'I know it's not going to be good news.' She looked at the stack of papers by his elbow. 'But I need to get cracking on refurbishing the place. Did you know that Xanthe has already taken a booking?'

'Ah, dinna fash yourself, we'll get by.'

Duncan patiently took her through everything, including the outstanding feed bills for the Highland cattle, which had now all gone apart from two that Duncan had been unable to part with. He'd hand reared Dolly and Reba (who knew he was a country music fan?) from calves and they were more like pets to him. When he'd asked to keep them, Izzy had seen beyond his unemotional stoicism and realised how important to him they were. Xanthe had joked that it was probably a good job to keep two as they could always have steak if all else failed. Izzy winced at the memory and the scorching look of horror Duncan had sent Xanthe's way. As always, her mother had been totally oblivious to her inappropriate comment.

As Izzy made to return to the house carrying the box of groceries, Duncan called, 'One last thing I forgot to mention. There's a couple of wild campers taken up residence on the edge of the loch. They seem nice enough and tidy. They've no left any litter and are not doing any harm but I thought you should know.'

'Right, thanks, Duncan. Maybe I'll pop down and see them.' Unlike in the rest of the United Kingdom, wild camping in Scotland was legal and people had open access to any unenclosed land. Izzy thought it was rather nice – the one thing she didn't feel comfortable about, in inheriting the castle, was being a landowner. Land belonged to everyone, didn't it, as well as the creatures that roamed over it? For her, owning it seemed a human arrogance, the idea of stewardship felt much better. A privilege that she would never take for granted.

Chapter Four

'There you are.' The minute Izzy stepped out of the little study she'd appropriated, Xanthe pounced on her, as if she'd been lying in wait for her to emerge. In truth, Izzy had been in hiding for most of the morning. She looked down at her phone, which had just buzzed with a response to her last message to the Killorgally Cookery group. *I've got a ton of carrots. Any recipe suggestions?*

Fliss: *Here's a carrot and ginger soup recipe. Perfect for an autumn day.*

Izzy couldn't wait to get back in the kitchen.

'I've decided to start on the morning room, guests will need more than one sitting room,' Xanthe announced, as if making a great proclamation to an audience in a packed auditorium rather than to her daughter in a corridor. 'And I've decided which room can be the master bedroom for the Carter-Joneses.'

'Great,' said Izzy, not really paying attention; she was still thinking about food.

Following Fliss's recipe, she selected a handful of carrots to make soup. There wasn't time to make proper stock so a vegetable stock cube would have to suffice until she'd got herself more organised. The easy to make carrot and ginger soup would be warming and go well with the bread she'd made the day before. She still couldn't get over how easy bread was to make from scratch. Before going on the cookery course, it had been something that came from the supermarket. Home-made bread tasted so much better and she was going to buy some different flours to experiment with. When the hotel was open, she planned to offer a seasonal soup of the day along with home-made bread and local cheese for the guests' lunch or provide packed lunches for hikers going out for the day.

Putting on the radio, she hummed along to a Proclaimers song about walking five hundred miles as she peeled and chopped carrots, inhaling the fragrant, herby scent of the stock cube she'd poured boiling water over.

Lost in her thoughts, she pottered around the kitchen, moving easily around the big, scrubbed pine table that took up one half of the room.

'Something smells good.'

Izzy whirled around; she'd not heard anyone come in.

'Professor Strathallan,' she said with a reserved nod of her head, not sure how to treat him after this morning's grumpy encounter. He was a paying guest so – unfortunately – she couldn't be rude to him. Not when she needed his money so badly.

He winced. 'It's Ross. "Professor Strathallan" sounds like a relic from the Victorian age.'

'As you wish,' she said, she too sounding horribly like a servant in *Downton Abbey*. She'd never said, 'as you wish' before in her life!

Ross raised that expressive eyebrow of his. 'That's very formal.'

'No more formal than *Ms McBride*.'

'Ah, yes. You wanted to talk to me earlier.'

Izzy turned her back on him, pretending to stir the soup mix while she tried to gather her thoughts. Being sensible, there was no way she could ask him to leave because she needed his money, but she was finding it very hard to be civil to him. She took a deep breath and plastered a smile on her face.

'Actually, *I* wanted to apologise for yesterday. Xanthe hadn't told me that she'd let a room to anyone. I had no idea who you were.'

'Ah, that explains things, Ms McBride.'

She glared at him and once again her tongue tangled as she tried to correct her name. 'It's McBride … it's McBride, Izzy. I mean Izzy McBride.' Why did he have this effect on her?

'Okay, McBride Izzy. I'll accept you didn't know who I was or what I was doing in your kitchen.'

Izzy held back the words, 'big of you,' as he continued.

'Xanthe strikes me as an impulsive lady.'

'Mmm, you could say that.' Izzy pursed her lips at his circumspect observation. She was supposed to be trying to get on his good side and regain control here. 'Look, I wondered if you'd like food preparing now that I'm back. I'll have to cook each day anyway and' – she paused and shot him a quick forced smile – 'my repertoire is a slight step up from baked beans on toast.'

'That is not difficult. No offence but I don't want to dance to someone else's timetable. I came here to work so I don't want to have to break off at specific times for meals.' His smile was equally forced. 'But I am very grateful for the offer. Eating spaghetti hoops and baked beans is a bit too much of a return to student days for my liking but they're quick and easy.'

'I noticed there were a few tins in the recycling bin.'

He grimaced and shrugged.

Izzy frowned. Although he was fairly unobtrusive and tidied up after himself, it didn't sit right with her that he was eating such basics when she could cook and needed to practise her skills.

'Okay,' said Izzy. 'How about I leave you things you can help yourself to when it suits you? There'll be a pot of soup on the Rayburn for lunch, which I'm making anyway, and you can help yourself to that and bread. And for dinner, I'll leave you something to reheat in the microwave or in the Rayburn.'

'Now you're talking.'

'They say the way to a man's heart is through his stomach,' Izzy quipped easily.

'Not mine,' he said, his face going blank as he drew a wallet from his pocket. 'How much do you want for the meals?'

The offer irked her but she couldn't say why, after all the only reason he was staying was because she did need his money. 'I'm not completely mercenary. I think you're paying enough already,' she said a touch primly.

'Tell me about it. Xanthe drives a hard bargain but she guaranteed me absolute peace and quiet. I don't like being disturbed when I'm working.'

'So I gathered,' she said.

He quirked that dark eyebrow again. 'I'm not going to apologise. I'm paying for the privilege.'

Izzy nodded, wondering whether he'd want to stay once they got started on the renovation work. Some of it was bound to be a bit noisy.

'Although that view from my window… It's worth every penny.'

She turned and smiled at him. 'Isn't it? This is such a beautiful spot, there seems to be a gorgeous view from every window. I can't wait to see what all the different seasons bring.'

He nodded and Izzy felt her pulse misstep as his blue eyes crinkled into a warm smile.

'Yes, although the light is … a bit too distracting sometimes when I'm supposed to be working.'

'Xanthe says you're writing a book.'

'Yes.'

Despite the tone of his voice not inviting any more questions, she asked anyway, telling herself she was being friendly. 'What sort of thing are you writing?'

'Nothing very interesting,' he said, his face adopting a bland look that immediately made Izzy think he wasn't telling the truth. 'A history book. I teach at Edinburgh University but I'm taking a sabbatical to get this book written.'

'What period of history?' she asked, her eyes sharpening at his evasive and rather vague answer.

'Jacobite Scotland, of course,' he said with a wry smile.

'Bonnie Prince Charlie and all that.'

'That's the one.'

'I'm sure my great uncle said that he stayed here once. Is that why you wanted to come here?'

Ross snorted. 'If local legend is to be believed the man stayed in every castle in Scotland.'

'A bit like Mary, Queen of Scots, then.'

'Aye. The pair of them were a right set of gadabouts.'

'Is that a historical term?' asked Izzy.

'Not officially. And I wanted to stay here because the lady at the post office said it was empty. I knew I wouldn't get asked lots of questions about what I was writing.'

'Well, that's told me,' said Izzy.

'No, I'm just explaining, McBride Izzy.' He gave her a rare grin, which lit up his face and made him – disturbingly – even more attractive. Damn, when his eyes sparkled like that, crinkling around the edges, her hormones jumped to attention.

'When you're staying somewhere and people know you're a writer, they ask what you're writing, tell you they've always thought they should write a book and then proceed to tell you that you can write it for them and they'll split the proceeds. If I'm really lucky they don't ask me to read their work. Telling them I write dusty history books tends to put most people off.'

'Clever,' said Izzy. 'This soup will be ready in a few minutes. Do you want to wait or come back later?' She was waiting for the carrots to soften before she blitzed the mix in the blender. 'And do you want a cup of tea or anything in the meantime?'

He stood for a moment as if weighing the question up. 'Tell you what, McBride Izzy. Why don't I make it while I wait for the soup? I know my way around.'

She smiled, deciding that this was as close to a truce as she was going to get and she should make the most of it.

'So when you're not here, where do you stay?'

'Edinburgh,' he said as he pulled mugs from the cupboard.

She felt she'd be prying if she asked whereabouts in Edinburgh and he wasn't very forthcoming about anything personal anyway. Although she wasn't a naturally nosy person, she herself was quite open. 'I lived in Edinburgh for a while. I worked at the Festival last summer.'

He winced. 'That must have been interesting.'

'That's one way of putting it,' she said with an involuntary sigh, thinking of all the time she'd wasted waiting for Philip to notice her. Deliberately she smiled. 'I love the Festival though, there's nothing quite like it. There's such a buzz in the city. And I love walking down the Royal Mile when everyone is giving you leaflets and trying to persuade you to see their shows.'

'Yes, some of the shows are brilliant. I dip in and out, and it is a hotbed of creativity.'

'It's also a wonderful city. I loved living there.'

'Did you leave to come here?'

'No.' She turned her back on him and reached for the blender. She didn't want to unburden herself to him and tell him that she'd left three months ago after three years of unrequited love, when she'd finally realised that she was a handy crutch for Philip who was never going to commit to her. The sound of the blender meant that any further conversation was forgone and Duncan soon trooped through the door, distracting them both.

'Smells like I'm here in the nick of time,' he said. 'That woman will be the death of me. I've carried umpteen chairs down three flights of stairs for her. Afternoon, Ross.'

'Duncan.'

'You two have met then?'

'The man's been here for two weeks,' said Duncan. 'He's quite the explorer.'

'I like walking, it helps with the plot … clears my mind.'

Izzy had assumed the man sat in his room all day writing.

Just then a phone buzzed and Ross glared at his mobile as he rescued it from his pocket. 'Bethany. Hi. Yes.'

He cocked his head, cushioning the phone between his neck and his ear as he opened a drawer and took out three spoons.

The conversation was very one-sided, with Ross saying the occasional, 'yes', 'no' and 'I'll do my best'. He finally hung up with a scowl and a heavy sigh, placing table mats from the dresser on the table and finding the butter dish to put in the centre, all without being asked.

Izzy and Duncan exchanged a glance, but neither said anything. There was a degree of tension in the air that hadn't been there five minutes earlier. In silence Izzy dished up the soup into three bowls and carried them over to the table, sitting down opposite Ross and next to Duncan. 'Sorry about that,' said Ross suddenly, as if realising he'd put a damper on the atmosphere. 'Just my editor chasing me. Isn't Xanthe eating?' he asked, warily glancing at the door. Izzy was amused to see that Duncan followed suit. Her mother had that effect on people.

'No, she doesn't like routine. She'll eat when she's ready,' said Izzy, knowing that when distracted her mother could quite happily go several days without eating a proper meal. She was rather like a demanding Persian cat, completely self-contained and aloof when it came to food, expecting it to be left out for her, but if it wasn't fresh enough when she finally deigned to eat it, she'd turn her nose up.

After a surprisingly companionable lunch, during which Ross seemed to cheer up a little, he rose to wash the dishes while Duncan disappeared out the door, grumbling slightly about her ladyship as he headed upstairs to carry down the last of the chairs. Izzy put the rest of the soup in the freezer – she'd made a double batch, planning to stock up for those days when she was busy with other things – and when she returned to the kitchen, Ross had gone, leaving the dishes draining.

Keen to get some fresh air before she started cleaning the paintwork in the morning room, and drawn to the stillness of the loch, she pulled on her Converse and set off through the trees down to the water's edge. A grey wispy mist had come down over the moorland beyond the castle, the tendrils seeping across the ruddy brown bracken and patches of gold and russet bilberry plants. It deadened the cries of the birds who appeared almost wraith-like when they loomed like shadows out of the sky.

The only other sound she could hear was the coarse rustle of her coat and the swish of her feet through the crisp, curling leaves on the ground. Around her the trees were silent and still and she felt as if she were the only person around for miles. Izzy took in a deep breath. Much as she'd enjoyed living in Edinburgh, she loved this intense quietness and the sense of peace and being at one with the world.

When she emerged from the quiet shadow of the woodland, she saw a little red tent perched in a sheltered spot surrounded by gorse bushes on the edge of the loch.

'Hello,' she called, as someone with a woolly hat jammed over a flurry of dark curls came into view.

'Hi, there,' came the friendly response from a small pixie of a woman who jumped up from the log she was sitting on. She was wrapped in dozens of layers and brought to mind a small Christmas pudding on legs.

'Gosh you're brave. Isn't it a bit cold for camping this time of year?' Izzy asked with a small internal shudder. She certainly didn't fancy it but then she was more of a camping by Marriott type of girl.

The woman shrugged and suddenly looked wary. 'S'all right.'

'Are you staying long?' asked Izzy.

'We're allowed, you know.'

'I know.' Izzy gave her a careful, non-threatening smile. 'It's fine, I don't mind at all. I mean, if you wanted to build a fire down here, it wouldn't be a problem.'

'Oh, really?' There was a wealth of relief in the woman's words. 'Oh God that would be fantastic. It's so cold at night. Are you sure it'll be all right with the owners? I don't want us to get turfed off.'

Izzy paused, feeling a little self-conscious. She wasn't that much older than this girl and it felt a bit pretentious to declare that she was the owner. 'They won't mind. I know them well.'

'Thank you, that's very kind of you. I'll tell Jim when he gets back. He's my husband.'

'I'm Izzy.'

'I'm Jeanette.' The girl didn't look old enough to be married and from the infinitesimal pause and slightly self-conscious use of the word 'husband' Izzy wondered how long they'd been married.

'Are you on your honeymoon?' she asked.

The wary look filled the woman's eyes. 'Yes … well, sort of.' Hurriedly, she added, 'Would you like a cup of tea?'

Surprised by the unexpected invitation, Izzy was about to say no but there was something almost like pleading in the other woman's expression. 'That would be lovely if you can spare one.' She wondered how long the other woman had been here on her own and where her husband was and what he was doing. Izzy felt a little sorry for her; she seemed a bit lost and forlorn.

'It's only a teabag and some milk.' Her chin lifted and Izzy realised that she'd pricked Jeanette's pride. 'I keep it in the loch to keep it cold.'

'That's a great idea. So how long are you on holiday for?' Though as far as Izzy was concerned, this was too hard core for her to consider it a holiday. She'd miss her creature comforts after one night.

'Not long,' said the woman, her eyes shifting from Izzy's gaze as she busied herself with a small camping stove and a little tin kettle. Despite Jeanette's open, honest and youthful face, Izzy felt there was an undertone there.

'You've picked a lovely spot,' she said, trying to be encouraging and hoping to set the woman at her ease as she seemed quite tense and jumpy.

Jeanette frowned and looked around her as if she'd never really noticed the scenery. 'Yeah, I s'pose so.'

'Where are you from? Glasgow?' Izzy had picked up a strong hint of a Glaswegian accent.

'Yes.' Now her voice was filled with suspicion and a definite thread of alarm. 'How did you know?'

Izzy smiled trying to put her at ease. 'I grew up in Glasgow; you've got the accent.'

'Oh.'

'How did you get here? Surely you haven't walked all the way from Glasgow.'

'Jim's got a motorbike. He's taken it into Fort William this morning.'

'And you didn't fancy going with him?'

'He's working, casual like.'

'Ah, I see,' said Izzy, not seeing at all. It seemed a strange time of year to take an extended wild camping trip.

'Mmm,' said Jeanette, not paying much attention.

Just then a man came running out of the trees towards them.

Jeanette went to intercept him and Izzy watched as they held a quickly muttered conversation before they approached her. There was tension in the air now and the man held himself stiffly.

'Who's this?' he asked, gesturing with one thumb.

'Jim, this is Izzy. She knows the owners of the castle.'

Jim sneered slightly. 'Nice work if you can get it. I bet they're rich bastards.'

'Lucky inheritance,' said Izzy, pricked by his unexpectedly snide comment. 'It's mine, actually.'

'Jim,' Jeanette remonstrated, her eyes widening as if trying to remind him of something.

'Sorry, that was rude. Didn't mean it.' He gave an apologetic smile that was more aimed at his wife than Izzy but she could see that he genuinely meant it.

'That's all right,' she said. 'I am very lucky and I don't take it for granted. If it's any consolation, I wasn't born with a silver spoon in my mouth and lived in Glasgow for most of my life in a two-bedroom flat with my mum.'

'What part of Glasgow?' asked Jim, quickly sending a worried look towards Jeanette.

Izzy frowned, wondering which bank the two of them had robbed, although it was difficult to believe either of them had been up to no good with their round, innocent, wholesome faces.

'I grew up in Langside,' said Izzy, knowing it was now one of the nicer areas of Glasgow but it hadn't always been. When her mother had been widowed so young, the two-bedroom flat was all she could afford after the insurance money paid out. Luckily Izzy's dad had worked for a small local firm who paid out a death benefit.

Both of the campers visibly relaxed.

'How long have you lived here?' asked Jim.

'Just a couple of months, although I've been away for most of that time and only came back yesterday. We're planning to turn it into a hotel.'

'Oh.' They both straightened.

'Have you got any jobs going?' asked Jim.

Izzy shook her head. 'Not at the moment. I might have inherited a castle but I didn't inherit any money. I can't afford staff yet.'

'Right.'

Jim's mouth pursed and tightened in disappointment.

'Here you go.' Jeanette pushed an enamel mug of tea into Izzy's hand. 'You'll have to share with me,' she said to her husband. 'We've only got a mug each.'

Izzy warmed her hands on the mug, starting to feel chilly. It must be freezing sleeping out here. 'There's plenty of firewood up at the castle if you need any logs for a fire. It's all stacked in the courtyard. And there's loads of kindling in the woods. Help yourselves.'

Jim beamed at her. 'That would be brilliant, cheers.'

'No problem.' Izzy smiled, wondering if she ought to offer them a bed for the night but they were clearly keeping secrets and she couldn't take in every waif and stray that crossed her lands.

She stayed and chatted for a few minutes until she'd finished her tea and then left them to walk around the western side of the loch, wondering who they were hiding from. There was definitely a mystery there but they weren't doing any harm and no doubt they'd be gone in a day or so.

Chapter Five

'What do you think? Isn't it gorgeous?' crowed Xanthe, throwing open the huge door to the morning room as outside the daylight faded.

The two coats of soft primrose paint contrasted beautifully against the white plasterwork ceiling and the golden woodwork now shone with a gentle lustre.

'Can you turn the lights on? I want to take some pictures for Insta.' As always, Xanthe had already moved on to the next thing.

'Yes, then I need to go and sort dinner out.'

'We could eat in here,' trilled Xanthe, pointing to a small, round dining table in the corner.

Izzy looked at the beautifully laid Instagram-ready table. It did look gorgeous and in that moment, she could hardly believe that she lived here. 'I think it's a bit grand for mushroom risotto and salad.'

'You have no soul, Isabel.' Her mother tossed her head and sighed, looking positively tragic.

Izzy went over to her and gave her a quick peck on the cheek. 'Nope, but I do know my mother is a decorating genius. And besides, I wouldn't want to spoil this lovely set-up. Why don't you take some pictures and I'll start cooking? Dinner's at seven.'

'Excellent. I'm quite peckish and I think we should open a bottle of Prosecco to celebrate.'

Izzy returned to the kitchen, popped the radio on and began to potter, enjoying having the time to herself. She'd discovered that cooking was much better when she took her time as things tended to go wrong when she rushed. There was something soothing and reassuring about the process of making a dish. Chopping onions and knowing they would turn golden brown if you cooked them long and slow, frying spices over a gentle heat to add depth of flavour or stirring in cream to provide additional richness. Everything was better when it was done with care and attention. She loved being able to immerse herself in the ritual and not have to think about anything else. It was her time. It had begun to rain outside and the wind had risen, hurling the raindrops at the kitchen windows with alarming ferocity, but with the Rayburn, it was warm and cosy in the kitchen. Despite that, Izzy gave a small shiver as she looked out at the inky blackness of the early evening sky. There wasn't a single light for miles to break up the darkness and it brought a sense of being marooned in the night.

It was quite a relief when Xanthe marched into the kitchen clutching two slender Champagne flutes. 'Look at these. Aren't they perfect?' Without waiting for Izzy to comment, she bustled to the fridge and yanked out a bottle. 'Bubbles.'

While Izzy fried onions and chopped garlic, Xanthe opened the bottle and poured two generous glasses.

'What shall we toast to?' she asked. 'I think I shall start on the master bedroom tomorrow. I've seen the most stunning wallpaper from a wonderful Glasgow-based company, Timorous Beasties. Look, isn't it stunning?' She held out her mobile.

Izzy took the phone and enlarged the picture. It was typical Xanthe – dramatic and bold – but she could imagine it in that room. 'It'll look stunning.' Then she scrolled down to check the price and gasped.

'Three hundred and fifty pounds a roll! Mum!'

Her mother snatched the phone back. 'It's an investment,' she said blithely before glancing up at the door and trilling, 'Oh, Ross, you're just in time. Come and have a glass of Prosecco. We're celebrating finishing the morning room. Izzy's done a marvellous job on the painting.'

It was rare to see him at this time of day. He still kept himself to himself and the only sign of his occupation was the occasional washed-up soup bowl on the draining rack.

Izzy glared at her mother who beamed back, knowing that Izzy wouldn't say anything in front of him.

'Sorry to bother you but I think there might be a leak upstairs.'

'Oh shit,' said Izzy. 'Whereabouts?'

'Along the corridor from my room. There's water dripping through the ceiling.'

Grabbing a bucket and a pile of old towels from beneath the sink she dashed out of the kitchen and had ascended two flights of stairs before realising that Ross was close behind her.

Sure enough there was water pooling and dropping onto

the threadbare carpet a few metres along the corridor from his room.

'I really don't need this,' said Izzy, glaring up at the ceiling, studying the crack through which the water seeped. If there was this much water here, how much was there upstairs?

'Here.' Ross held out a hand and took one of the towels, folding it several times before putting it down to soak up the water, and at the same time placing the bucket underneath the steady drip. 'There must be a bigger leak coming in upstairs.'

'Aye, Sherlock,' she muttered, shaking her head as she squinted upwards, following the line of the ceiling down the corridor trying to work out where the leak might be coming from on the next floor. 'I'll go up.'

'I'll come with you.'

'You don't need to do that.'

'No, I don't, but I'm going to.' He smiled as he grabbed the bucket. 'Two heads are better than one and all that.'

'I'm not sure heads are going to solve this,' she said, weakly returning his smile.

The two of them moved quickly down the corridor to the smaller servants' stairs leading up to the attic immediately under the roof. Together they found the ominous bulge in the ceiling with a crooked crack running through it from which a small torrent poured, spilling water onto the floor and sending dusty splashes bouncing along the floorboards.

Her heart nose-dived in her chest. Glancing anxiously up at the distended plaster, puffed up like an angry spot, she had visions of the whole thing bursting and bringing the ceiling down.

'Damn,' she said, staring up at the water, paralysed by the

knowledge that there was absolutely nothing she could do at this time of night and that things were only going to get worse.

Ross didn't say anything but took the bucket from her hand and placed it strategically below the leak before tugging a towel from her limp hands to mop up the puddle on the floor, which was trickling away through the floorboards.

'Sorry,' she said, suddenly realising what he was doing. 'I should be doing that.' But she didn't seem capable of rallying herself. Instead, she stared around the room while Ross went down on his knees at her feet to spread the towel to soak up the worst of the water.

'Have you got anything bigger?' he asked, as the bucket began to fill at an alarming rate.

Hysteria – that must have been what it was – made her giggle, even though the situation was far from funny. 'Aren't I supposed to say that?'

A small smile tugged at the corners of his mouth. 'I was thinking *Jaws*. You're going to need a bigger boat ... or rather bucket. Have you got anything suitable?'

She bit her lip and thought. 'Not up here. There might be something down in the cellar or the scullery.'

'Come on then, let's take a look. This'll do for the minute. We might have to do shifts tonight to keep checking and emptying the bucket if this rain doesn't let up. Then you can get someone out in the morning.'

She swallowed. Did builders take credit cards? Or a deposit? She closed her eyes because if she didn't, she might cry. Suddenly all her blithe confidence that everything would work out sank, torpedoed by the reality of water streaming through the roof.

'Come on, Izzy,' he said, touching her arm as she stared

worriedly at the bulging ceiling. 'You can't control this now. It will be fine and things will look much better in the morning.'

She looked at him dolefully, despair getting the better of her. 'You shouldn't even be here. You're a guest.' Her voice faltered.

'Hey,' he said, shooting her a reassuring look. 'I don't mind. Think of me as a lodger and don't worry about it. Besides, what sort of person would I be if I didn't help?' He gave her a quick squeeze. 'Come on, let's go find a bigger … thing.'

She sniffed. 'Sorry. I'm not normally such a wimp.'

'You don't strike me as a wimp at all. I think it's impressive you've decided to take all this on. Some people would be making a drama out of a crisis. You seem quite cool about it.'

'Thank you,' she said, reassured by his quiet praise. 'Xanthe creates enough drama in my life so I try and avoid it wherever possible. In truth I don't feel calm, but I need to get on with it.'

'Come on.' He gave another of those comforting smiles. 'Let's go on a scavenger hunt and see what we can find. I've got a horrible feeling that pimple is going to burst.'

'That's exactly what I thought it looked like!' She smiled up into his face, inexplicably delighted by his mirroring of her thoughts, and received a sudden jolt, like a quick burst of electricity that fizzed as it rushed through her chest, when she realised how near he was and how his blue eyes narrowed into crinkles at the corners. She pulled away suddenly. *Not going down that road, Izzy,* she told herself firmly. And certainly not now.

'We'd better get a move on,' she said, 'before this bucket gets too fool … I mean too full.' She was the fool. She had enough going on in her life, she didn't need any emotional entanglements and certainly not with a guest. Even if he was a very gorgeous guest.

'Is everything all right?' asked Xanthe brightly, Prosecco in hand as she looked up from her phone when Izzy and Ross returned to the kitchen. There was a strong smell of burning and Izzy screwed up her face. Dashing over to the Rayburn she removed the pan of burned congealed mess and counted to three under her breath. Had her mother not smelled it?

'No, it isn't,' said Izzy, wanting to strangle her mother who seemed totally unperturbed. 'There's water coming in through the roof and I don't suppose you noticed that dinner was burning.'

'Oh dear. I thought there was a funny smell.'

Luckily before Izzy could say anything, Ross emerged from the scullery at the back of the kitchen, carrying a large tin bath.

'Ta-dah.' He held it up in both arms in triumph, like a gold medal winning weightlifter.

'My hero,' said Izzy. 'That's perfect.'

'Until we have to empty it but we'll worry about that later.'

'Thank you,' she said again, touched by his use of 'we' and his unconditional help.

'I'll take it up in a bit.'

'Thank—' Izzy started to say as the door banged open and Duncan came in. His hair was plastered to his head, rivulets of water ran down off his coat onto the floor and his shoes squelched as he walked. The wind gusted in behind him, bringing the damp night air into the kitchen.

'Duncan!' squealed Xanthe. 'Close the door and take that coat off. You're soaked and you're making the floor wet.'

He looked down at the puddle around his feet and pursed his lips, shaking off the coat and hanging it up. 'It's just a bit of wet.'

'Is everything all right, Duncan?' asked Izzy.

'Aye, lass. I wanted to let you know I put Dolly and Reba into the old stables.' He looked hopefully at the Rayburn and then wrinkled his nose. 'I was wondering if you might have some of that soup on the go. I'm cold to the bone.'

'It will have to be soup,' said Izzy, a touch bitterly, glancing at her mother who was bent over her phone.

He beamed. 'Perfect. Rain's set in for the night, I'm afraid.'

'Great.' Izzy groaned. 'I'm going to be up all night checking the water doesn't overflow.'

'Don't be daft, McBride,' Ross said. 'There's no point you being up all night. Like I said, we'll do shifts. I'll check at midnight so you can get a good few hours sleep and then do a middle of the night check, say about three. Then I'll do one at six. And you can do one at nine.'

'But you're a—'

'I'm willing and able,' he said with a hard stare that made her smile.

'Well, you're all very noble,' said Xanthe. 'Some of us need our beauty sleep and I'm not sure I want to be messing about with water in the middle of the night.'

'I'm not sure any of us do,' said Izzy, a trifle tartly.

'Don't be like that, darling. You know that once I'm asleep I'm out for the count.' Which was true. Even if Xanthe had offered to help, Izzy wouldn't have been able to rely on her mother to get up or remember what she was supposed to be doing. 'Why don't I do the washing up?' she asked with a magnanimous air, as if that was some sort of compromise.

'Done and you can clean up the pan that got burned.'

'Right, I think I'll turn in now so I'm rested for the midnight check,' said Ross.

'Thank you so much, Ross,' said Izzy. 'I appreciate your help.'

'Not a problem. Better than having the ceiling come down on me in the middle of the night.' He smiled at her.

'God, don't even joke. I hope it stops raining soon.'

He looked out of the window where the rain lashed the glass panes like hail stones. 'Not much chance of that, I'm afraid.'

'I know.' She sighed heavily. She hated not being able to do anything more practical.

'Hey.' He gave her a quick, kind smile that softened his already too handsome face and she found herself praying that she wasn't giving away how lovely she found him. 'Try not to worry; you've done all you can for now. I'll see you all in the morning. Night, McBride.' He leaned in and to her utter surprise kissed her on the cheek. To be fair it was a casual, matey goodnight sort of kiss, but a zing of awareness shot through her and as their eyes met he froze as if he'd walked into the wrong room and needed to leave immediately. Without another word he turned and walked out of the kitchen.

Izzy stood staring after him for a moment, her skin tingling where his lips had brushed so softly. It might have been the barest, almost there, kiss but it felt as if she'd been burned.

'Well, that was interesting,' said Xanthe with a cat-like grin while Duncan's gaze was glued to his feet.

'He was just being friendly and offering a bit of solidarity, unlike some,' snapped Izzy.

Xanthe merely raised her eyebrows and sauntered out of the kitchen, leaving Izzy trying not to press her hand to her cheek.

Chapter Six

When her alarm went off at three o'clock in the morning, Izzy clawed her way back to consciousness, shivering in the cold night at the sound of the rain hurling itself against the window. Still raining then. She bundled herself into joggers and a sweatshirt over her PJs and plodded up to the attic.

Despite hoping for some sort of miracle, the bathtub was almost full. And by the time she'd wrestled it to the bathroom to empty it, water slopping everywhere, she was soaked through, and wide awake. She might as well change into dry clothes, go downstairs and make herself a cup of tea.

Outside the gale howled, battering at the building with quick, punching gusts, making her grateful for the thick walls of the castle that protected her as she warmed her hands in the latent heat of the Rayburn. Through the window she could see the kitchen light reflected on the slick of water on the ground outside and the fierce slashing lines of the rain cutting down through the sky. She sat in the rocking chair by the big oven nursing her tea, her chin tucked into the thick wool of a polo neck jumper.

Bang. Bang. Bang.

Having dozed off, she jerked awake, her heart pounding in tandem with the hammering on the door. The heavy rapping came again and she jumped to her feet. Was it Duncan? At this time of night? Who else would be out there?

When she opened the door, she was barely able to hang on to the handle against the gust of icy wind that burst its way into the kitchen. It quickly scurried into every nook and cranny, making the crockery on the dresser rattle and the old light fixture swing, sending light and shadow helter-skeltering around the room. She peered out, the inside light spotlighting two bedraggled figures in cagoules slick with rain, hoods up, the drawstring puckered around pinched, pale faces.

'Please can we come in? Our tent has blown away,' pleaded a tearful voice and Izzy realised they were the wild campers, Jeanette and Jim.

'Oh my goodness, of course, come in.' She widened the opening and the two of them stumbled inside, each clutching a soggy sleeping bag that trailed over their arms like drowned caterpillars. 'Oh, you poor things. You're soaking.'

She quickly closed the door, firmly shutting out the raging wind and rain.

'Thank you. Thank you,' said the girl with a sob, dropping her things to the floor. 'I'm so cold.' She held out blue hands.

'Come over to the Rayburn. Let me make you a hot drink.'

'Thanks,' said Jim in a gruff voice as he eased a rucksack off his back.

'Everything's wet,' sniffled Jeanette, dropping hers with a defeated thud.

'I'll get you some dry things.' Izzy looked at Jim. 'Not sure I've got anything your size.'

'Don't worry, love. Just get something for Jeanie.' He reached out and kissed his wife on the forehead. 'It's okay, babe.'

'No, it's not. Everything's gone. What are we going to do?' Her voice rose in a distraught wail.

'You can stay here tonight,' said Izzy, her heart going out to them. They looked like a pair of bedraggled puppies and she was convinced more than ever that they couldn't be any older than twenty, if that.

Half an hour later, with Jeanette wearing a pair of Izzy's tracksuit bottoms, a sweat shirt and a pair of fluffy socks, and Jim wearing an old silk dressing gown of Great Uncle Bill's and a big bath sheet wrapped around his lower half, the two of them were looking a little more human as they sat at the table with big mugs of hot chocolate and a plate of toast each.

'Mmm, this is so good,' said Jeanette, in between sips of her drink. 'Thank you so much. We haven't eaten since lunch time because we couldn't get the camping gas stove lit. Jim was going to walk down to the village to get fish and chips but by then it was too wet and windy. We've been hanging on to the tent for hours hoping the storm would die away but then … those last gusts… Sorry, Jim, my hands were too cold.' Throughout the recital of the litany of woes, Jim had held her hand enclosed in his much bigger one.

'That sounds awful,' said Izzy, picturing the two of them

57

huddled in their tent. 'There's a spare bedroom made up, whenever you're ready.'

'It's so good of you,' said Jim for the thousandth time, his hand rubbing Jeanette's back in reassurance but with a slightly downcast expression on his face, as if he'd let her down. 'Sorry to wake you.'

Izzy smiled. 'I was up anyway.' She explained the roof situation.

'I could take a look at it in the morning if you like. I bet there's access from the battlements.'

'That would be great. Thank you.' She realised his pride meant he needed to be able to do something to help and to repay her for her kindness.

While they drank their hot drinks, Izzy put a clothes airer in front of the Rayburn.

'You can dry the damp things from your rucksacks on here.' She'd already scooped up the rain-soaked and mud-splashed clothes that they'd been wearing and they were now in the washing machine in the scullery.

'Can I get you anything else?' she asked.

'No, you've been so kind. We really appreciate it,' said Jeanette.

What else would anyone have done? No one could have turned them away. Izzy was just grateful that she had the room to put them up. She showed them to a bedroom on the first floor and left them to it before trotting up to the attic to see how the water was going. The water coming through had slowed slightly but the bulge looked near bursting point. Eying it anxiously, she decided to empty the tin bath again now and then come back first thing to check on the leak.

When she finally collapsed back into bed, she was

extremely grateful that Ross had said he'd take the six o'clock shift. So much for thinking she'd have a quiet life in the country.

———

'Wakey, wakey. I've brought you a cup of tea.' Her mother's voice sounded horribly loud.

Izzy lifted her head and then threw it back against her pillow. It felt as if she'd only just gone to sleep.

'Did you know there are some strange people sleeping in the tartan room?' Indignation was clear in her voice.

'Mmm,' mumbled Izzy, trying to open her eyes and failing.

'Where did they come from? I went in there this morning and got such a fright.'

'What time is it?' Izzy groaned, peering at Xanthe.

'It's half past seven. I was up so I thought I'd make you a nice cup of tea.'

Her mother never made her a cup of tea in the mornings let alone brought it up to her bedside.

Xanthe put the tea down on the small table, switched on the lamp and perched like an expectant robin on the edge of Izzy's bed.

'Muuum. Been up … most … the night.' It was an effort to get the words out. She felt shattered.

'These people. Do you know them? How did they get there?'

'Camping. By the loch.'

'And you let them stay? We could all have been murdered in our beds.'

'You're still here,' mumbled Izzy.

'That's not the point. What if they helped themselves to the silver? Like the man in *Les Misérables*. Jean Valjean. He stole the candlesticks from the vicar.'

'We have silver? Who knew?'

Xanthe gave her a tart smile. 'Here, drink your tea. That will make you feel better.'

Izzy frowned. 'Why were you in the tartan room so early?'

'Because I've heard from the Carter-Joneses. They're bringing at least two more people with them.'

Izzy threw her head back against the pillows.

———

Izzy was kneading bread when Duncan tapped on the door and let himself in later that morning. He went straight over to the Rayburn and held out his hands to warm them.

'Mind if I make myself a cuppa? The bluidy pilot light has gone out on the furnace for the heating. It's pure Baltic in my place.'

'Oh no,' said Izzy. 'Can you get someone to fix it?'

'Huh! I can try but every other bugger's heating's gubbed this morning. I canna even get through to the plumbing boys; the line is permanently engaged.'

Izzy smiled ruefully. What was one more? Suddenly the size of the household had doubled but soon there'd be even more guests, so she might as well start getting used to feeding them all. 'You're welcome to stay here until it's fixed.'

'Lass, that would be very kind of you. By the way, looks like the wild campers've gone.'

'Hmm, not very far,' said Izzy, but before she could explain further Ross walked into the room, carrying his coffee mug obviously in need of a refill.

'How was the night shift?' he asked. 'Morning, Duncan.'

'Eventful. I picked up a waif and a stray. I was telling Duncan. The wild campers' tent was blown away. They've taken refuge here.'

'Have they now?' Ross eyed her with concern.

'Don't you start about them stealing the silver,' she said.

'I'm not worried about that, more about them making a noise. I came here for peace and quiet, remember? How long will they be here? Would you like a cup of tea?'

'They'll probably be gone today,' she said, turning the dough and working it. 'And yes, please. This is thirsty work.'

He pulled out a fresh mug for her and filled the teapot as she finished off the dough and popped it into an oiled bowl, covered it with a damp tea towel and left it beside the Rayburn to prove.

'Come sit down and drink your tea,' he said. 'You look tired.'

Though it wasn't exactly complimentary, it was hard to take offence at the comment when he was urging her to rest. 'It was a very long night.'

'You need to rest lass. I'm just away to check the cows,' said Duncan, 'I'll be back in a minute for my tea.

Ross squinted down the table, which was filled with her handwritten notes scribbled on several sheets of A4 paper. 'What's all this?'

She paused before answering.

'Christmas,' she finally said. Xanthe's news that morning about extra guests had galvanised her into action. 'I don't know what your plans are but we've taken a booking for a few days over Christmas.' She gave him a direct look. 'Sorry. I know you want peace and quiet but I'll be totally honest with you...' Her teeth grazed her lip before she ripped the plaster off. 'They've offered to pay a fortune and we need the money to pay for the roof. I can reimburse you for that last week in December, if you want to leave before the Christmas break.' She assumed he'd be going home to family then anyway.

He frowned for a moment and then stared out of the window, a stillness to his body that spoke of his self-containment. 'I haven't thought that far ahead. I'm hoping to have got my first draft done by then and was thinking about taking a couple of days off. I'm not sure of my plans, yet.' Pushing his hands into his pockets and hunching his shoulders he asked, 'How many are coming and for how long?'

'At the moment it's a party of six and I'm not sure of the exact dates.' She winced. 'Xanthe is liaising with the family.'

'God help us,' joked Ross. 'I can envisage a sleigh with a full complement of reindeer in the hall, Christmas trees in every room in the house and more glitter than a primary school.'

Izzy pursed her mouth. She ought to be disapproving – after all he was talking about her mother – but she was biting back a smile because he'd nailed it. Xanthe's enthusiasm and excitement for the project were likely to reach delirium levels until it came to the actual hard work.

'I'll understand if you want to leave.' As she said it, she realised that she really didn't want him to.

'I'll think about it. Like I said, I haven't made any plans for Christmas.'

'Haven't you got any family?' she blurted.

He stared at her for a moment before nodding. 'Yes, I've got family. Mum, Dad, two sisters.'

'Won't you see them over Christmas?' Now she was bordering on nosy but she wanted to keep him talking, his presence calmed her and also delayed the moment she actually had to start addressing her lists.

He shrugged. 'Not sure yet. I wouldn't mind staying here.'

'What aren't you sure about?' Xanthe strolled into the room still looking extraordinarily pleased with herself.

'We were talking about Ross's plans for Christmas.'

'Aren't you going to stay with your family?' asked Xanthe with a frown.

'I hadn't planned to,' said Ross.

'Do they live a long way away?' Xanthe gave him a kind smile.

'No. Callandar.'

'Well, you should go and see them— Oh my goodness. Callandar. You're not related to Alicia Strathallan, are you?'

Ross's face froze. 'Yes,' he said, his voice full of wary distrust.

'Oh. My. God!' Xanthe clapped her hands and began dancing around the table. 'Alicia Strathallan. Hear that, Izzy? Remember that gorgeous glass exhibition we went to at the Dovecot in Edinburgh, where I drooled for a full day?'

Izzy nodded.

'That was Alicia Strathallan! Is she really, really, really your mother?' Xanthe hopped up and down on the spot, quite overcome.

Ross nodded. 'One and the same.'

Xanthe fanned herself. 'She. Is. My. Absolute. Favourite. Artist. Isn't she, Izzy? I'm not just saying it, am I? I simply adore her work. Her use of colour is extraordinary.' She stopped and laughed before adding, with her usual tact, 'Imagine. You're her son. That's so funny. You don't seem very creative at all.'

Izzy was relieved to see that rather than take offence, a small flicker of mischief lit Ross's eyes. He nodded gravely. 'No. Not a creative bone in my body. It's a sore trial to my mother.'

Across the table, he gave Izzy a crooked smile.

'We can't all be creative, I suppose,' said Xanthe, throwing her arms wide as if to demonstrate her own creative genius. 'Izzy's very practical. It's quite disappointing.'

'Thanks.' Izzy's voice was dry. She'd long since stopped taking umbrage at her mother's blunt assessments.

'You know what I mean. Now…' With her usual lightning change of direction, she turned to Izzy. 'I'm thinking of inviting a friend to come and stay.'

'A friend?' asked Izzy, wrong-footed by the sudden about turn of the conversation. 'Who?'

'No one you know.' Xanthe waved an airy hand. 'An old friend.'

Izzy narrowed her eyes with suspicion. 'What old friend?'

'I told you, no one you know. You don't mind, do you?'

The pointed question was Xanthe's way of taking a dig at the fact that Izzy had been left the castle instead of her, and the unspoken accusation, that Xanthe wasn't allowed to invite her friends, stung.

'It'll only be a few days. You won't even know he's here.'

Izzy thought that was unlikely.

'Now that the blue room is finished, he can stay in there.' Xanthe gave her a slightly patronising smile. 'He'll be gone before Christmas and I'm sure you'll find him utterly charming. I've known him for aeons. He's very well connected. He's related to the Highland Sinclairs, you know.'

Xanthe's verbal flood was a definite sign that she was hiding something.

'Which reminds me.' Xanthe's eyes brightened as her enthusiasm for something else ping-ponged back into life. 'Now that we're having a proper Christmas party staying, we need at least three Christmas trees. I do love the smell of a real tree. There's nothing like it, is there, Izzy? And this year we can get everyone to decorate the tree together. What fun!'

Izzy smiled as the memories of Christmases past bloomed in her head like popcorn bursting out of their shells. They'd always had a real tree, even when money was tight, and it was a tradition to gift each other a new ornament every year. When Izzy was younger they'd been handmade at school and no matter how rubbish they were – the little mouse in a walnut shell, the tufts of cotton wool on a string or the fairy made out of a doily and wooden peg – Xanthe would exclaim in delight over them and insist they went in a prime spot. Decorating the tree had always been a big deal and when Izzy had got older they'd always opened a bottle of fizz to celebrate and have an official toast to switching on the lights.

'As I said, I'm thinking we're going to need at least three trees: one for the hall, one in the dining room and one in the lounge. And it won't cost us anything because Duncan says we can cut some down from the forest on the edge of the loch, although we'll need to buy some new decorations. I wonder if there are any up in the attic.'

'You're going to cut a tree down?' asked Izzy with a teasing smile.

'Well, not me, obviously. I'm sure we can persuade this strapping young man to help us,' said Xanthe, giving Ross a coy smile. 'Don't men love to swing their axes about and play He-Man?'

'All the time,' agreed Ross, his mouth quirking as he glanced at Izzy who shook her head. Xanthe really was the end.

'That's all sorted, then.' She beamed at Ross. 'Alicia Strathallan's son under my roof. How marvellous. I must tell my sewing WhatsApp group – Sewing for Glory.' With a skip in her step, she left the kitchen, humming loudly.

Looking rather bemused, Ross watched her go before taking his own coffee and leaving the room.

With the kitchen to herself once more, Izzy sat with a notebook and marked the first page, writing: *To do list*. She underlined the words twice, thinking about all the lovely things they could do to make this Christmas one to remember.

Marking out several pages in her notebook, excitement bubbled as she broke things down into manageable portions.

'Hi, Izzy,' said a small, tentative voice and she looked up to find Jeanette and Jim hovering in the doorway.

'Come in.'

'Sorry we slept so late. I haven't had such a good night's sleep in weeks. I always worry a sheep or a deer's going to start eating the tent. Thank you so much for letting us stay.'

Izzy smiled gently at her. Despite the extra sleep, the poor girl's eyes were shadowed and filled with anxiety. 'It isn't a problem. I'm glad you slept well. Would you like some breakfast?'

Jeanette looked uncertainly at her husband.

'If it's no bother,' he said, urging her forward into the kitchen.

'Would you like some bacon and eggs?'

'No, it's fine,' said Jeanette, but Izzy saw the droop to Jim's mouth.

'Honestly it's no trouble and there are plenty of eggs. Duncan is a bit of a hen whisperer and they're still laying. I don't think they've realised winter's arrived.'

'We certainly have,' said Jeanette, looking out of the window and wrapping her arms around herself.

'That would be grand,' said Jim hurriedly and Jeanette nudged him.

'He's always hungry.'

'Take a seat,' suggested Izzy.

'No!' said Jeanette almost jumping forward. 'Let me help. You've been so kind letting us stay last night.'

'I could hardly throw you out,' replied Izzy with a kind smile.

'Maybe not but you made us feel welcome and not as if we were a burden. We're very grateful.'

Izzy shrugged. 'Like I said, it wasn't a problem. What are you going to do now? Go home?'

Jeanette and Jim exchanged a guarded glance. 'What can I do?' Jeanette asked, changing the subject.

'You could lay the table. Cutlery's there.' She nodded to a nearby drawer.

'It's dried out nice,' said Jim, crossing to the kitchen window. 'Do you want me to take a look at the roof?'

'That would be amazing. Are you sure?'

'Let him, he's very good with his… He's very practical,' she amended quickly with a slight blush.

67

Jim sent her an intimate, sweet smile that made Izzy unexpectedly envious. What would it be like to have that wholehearted connection with another person? To have someone that cared that much about you? Was it weak to want someone to look out for you occasionally?

'If you wait a minute, Duncan will be in. He knows the castle inside and out and he'll be able to take you up to the battlements.'

Right on cue, Duncan came through the back door and Izzy made quick introductions.

'I'll take you up now,' he said. 'And hopefully my coffee will be waiting for me when I get back.'

Izzy grinned at him. 'Right you are.'

'You'll be all right, love?' Jim asked, addressing Jeanette and suddenly sounding wary. 'I won't be long.' He snagged his fleece from the drying rack by the Rayburn and gave her a quick peck on the cheek, followed by a reassuring hug as if fortifying both of them before he left.

'Okay,' she said, watching him go, sighing a little, a dreamy expression in her eyes that made Izzy hide her smile.

'How long have you two been married?' she asked.

Jeanette's face sharpened and she stiffened, her mouth pinching tightly closed before she said, 'Not long.' She turned her back as Izzy broke the eggs into the frying pan and Izzy frowned to herself, wondering why the younger woman was so uncomfortable.

'It's here!' Xanthe's voice trilled and Izzy turned to find her mother waving a long, slender parcel, almost taking out a row of plates on the dresser in the process.

'What's here?' Izzy asked, confused.

'The wallpaper, darling!' Xanthe exclaimed.

'The world's most expensive wallpaper? But you only showed it to me last night! You ... you'd already ordered it days ago, hadn't you?' commented Izzy dryly as she realised her mother had not actually been seeking her approval when they discussed the wallpaper yesterday.

'Don't be like that, darling. Besides, people like the Carter-Joneses expect the best, if they're going to pay twenty-five grand for a week in a Scottish Castle.'

'That's what I'm worried about,' said Izzy quite truthfully.

'Twenty-five grand,' echoed Jeanette, her eyes so wide they'd exceeded saucers.

'Mmm.' Izzy nodded wishing her mother knew the meaning of discretion.

'That's a lot of money.'

'We need a lot of money,' sang Xanthe, turning to beam at Jeanette. 'You must be one of our lost puppies.'

'Xanthe,' Izzy ground out as she gritted her teeth.

'Sorry?' Jeanette looked understandably confused.

'Ignore her, most sensible people do,' said Izzy. 'This is Xanthe.'

Xanthe sniffed and bestowed a tight smile on Jeanette before turning to Izzy. 'Don't you want to see the wallpaper?' She was already tearing into the brown paper wrapping.

A gust of wind announced the arrival of Jim as he slammed the door behind him.

'Puppy number two,' said Xanthe gaily, as she wrestled with the packaging. 'Oh look, look ... isn't it divine?' She held up the picture on the front of the roll.

'One hell of a repeat on that,' said Jim.

'I know,' said Xanthe, 'but isn't it gorgeous.'

Jim stepped forward and picked up one of the rolls, studying it. 'Beautiful quality.'

'It bloody should be at that price,' said Izzy. 'I'd be terrified of messing it up.'

'Oh, Jim's brilliant at wallpapering,' said Jeanette.

'Are you?' squealed Xanthe, as if that was the most exciting thing she'd ever heard.

'I can turn my hand to most things,' he said. 'I think we can patch that roof and get it fixed up today, if you don't mind Duncan running me to the builder's merchants.'

'Did you hear that, Izzy?' Xanthe's eyes bored into her. 'Roof repairs and decorating.'

'I heard,' said Izzy, hating the way that her mother assumed she had all the answers.

Xanthe turned to Jim. 'Izzy says you've been camping down by the loch. Are you on holiday?'

Jim and Jeanette did what Izzy was now thinking of as their *Midwich Cuckoo* act, as they glanced uneasily at each other.

'No,' said Jeanette, as Jim said, 'yes.'

'Well, what is it?' asked Xanthe with her trademark impatience.

'We're…' started Jeanette, as Jim said, 'We've…'

'Are you planning to stay in the area?' Xanthe looked from one to the other with bright-eyed animation.

'We were,' said Jim, 'but we've lost the tent.'

'And you've got nowhere to stay,' said Xanthe, giving Izzy a look full of meaning.

'Mmm,' mumbled Jim as Jeanette ducked her head in what looked to Izzy like embarrassment.

'Mum,' Izzy snapped, seeing where this was going.

'Well, it's obvious to me.' Xanthe tilted her nose up in regal style. 'You should both stay here. We need extra help. Many hands make light work and all that.'

Jeanette twisted her hands and looked at her husband, hope shining in her eyes, and how could Izzy resist.

Izzy glared at her mother, although it was a very good idea. 'First you have to explain what's going on. Can I trust you? Have you robbed a bank? Murdered someone? Burned a house down?'

Jeanette shook her head vehemently. 'No!' she protested. 'Nothing like that.' Her face creased into a sudden, spontaneous smile and she laughed. 'When you put it like that, it's nothing bad.'

Jim put an arm across her shoulder. 'It's not that bad.' He dropped a kiss on Jeanette's hair.

'We got married,' explained Jeanette. 'Our families don't approve, so we ran away.'

'We thought we'd live as cheaply as possible. Find casual jobs, but it turns out no one wants to employ you without a proper address.'

Izzy refrained from suggesting that was quite obvious to anyone with half a brain. The pair of them were clearly besotted with each other and seemed to have had a complete lapse of common sense. 'And do your parents know where you are?'

'No! And we don't want them to. They know we're well and safe but that's all. They'll only try and split us up, again. And I can't bear it.'

'We got married on Jeanette's eighteenth birthday,' said Jim, as if that explained everything.

'Ahhh, young love.' Xanthe beamed at the couple. 'I was only eighteen when I married Izzy's father. Unfortunately, he died when I was twenty-three but he was the love of my life.'

'Mmm,' said Izzy, ducking her head and reading some of her notes. He died at twenty-three because he was still a child, racing tractors, for God's sake. From what her nan had said, Izzy doubted the two of them would have stayed together. Her mother was still, in many ways, a toddler – constantly seeking instant self-gratification. In comparison, Jim and Jeanette seemed quite a steady pair and clearly devoted to one another.

'So?' asked Xanthe, an arch look on her face as she nudged Izzy with a sharp elbow.

Izzy sighed. She didn't like being backed into a corner but given the volume of work that was needed between now and Christmas, two extra pairs of hands would be a real bonus.

'I can't afford to pay you very much.'

'That's fine. How about free board and lodging in exchange for working in the house?' suggested Jim.

Izzy gnawed at her lip. That sounded a bit too good to be true and also, her conscience pointed out, taking advantage. The two of them would never gain any independence if they didn't start earning any money.

'And a reference,' said Jeanette. 'That way, with an address as well, we can get another job.'

'Yes,' said Jim. 'See, it works for everyone.'

'How about we do a week's trial?' suggested Izzy. 'To see if it will work. And I'll pay you a small amount.'

'Done,' said Jim, raising his coffee mug as if in a toast. 'You won't regret it, we promise.'

Izzy hoped not, she seemed to be gathering occupants of the house at an alarming speed.

Chapter Seven

'Deliveries for I McBride,' said the woman standing on the doorstep with a large, well taped box and a couple of parcels a week and a half later. 'Someone's been busy online shopping. You need to sign for that one. Is that you? Do you want me to bring them in? I'm Mrs McPherson from the post office, by the way. There's been a lot of these boxes of late.'

Had there? Izzy hadn't realised, probably because Xanthe was very good at intercepting the post.

'Hello,' said Izzy. 'I'm "I McBride" – but please call me Izzy.'

'Ah, the new owner!' She gave Izzy a quick, appraising look. 'I heard you were young.' She sounded as if she hadn't believed it. 'You're turning the place into a hotel, I believe.' She peered behind Izzy into the hallway of the castle. 'Paint, is it?'

'Yes,' she replied, grinning at this blatant curiosity. 'My mother's ordered it. I don't even know what colour she decided upon.'

'Shall I bring it in for you? Farrow and Ball. That's the posh stuff. I've always favoured Dulux myself.'

'Yes, please. That's very kind of you.' Amused, Izzy stepped aside and let her in.

'It's no bother.' She walked in and stopped, taking a good look around at the hallway. 'Where do you want it? Shall I take it through to the kitchen?'

'Er … yes,' she replied, surprised, but the woman had already begun walking in the right direction.

'It's all right, I often used to stop awhile and have a wee cup of tea with Bill when he was alive.'

She elbowed her way through the door into the warm kitchen, currently filled with the homely smell of fresh bread, and set the box down on the table, looking around the room with an approving nod. 'You've not made any changes in here then. Something smells good. You been baking? It's been a wee while since breakfast.'

'No, not yet,' agreed Izzy. 'Would you like a cup of tea?' She glanced at the clock. Duncan, a creature of habit, would be up for his morning brew any minute.

'Aye, lass.' She gave an approving smile. 'I thought you'd never ask. And perhaps a piece of toast. That bread looks good, did you make it yourself?'

'I did.' She was rather proud of today's batch as it had been an experiment. The course in Ireland had touched on some of the science behind bread making and how different flours reacted, which had fascinated her and made her desperate to try new recipes. She shot a quick fond glance at the small Kilner jar on the side, which contained her sourdough starter that she'd brought home with her, and went by the name of 'Wee McBride'. 'I'm planning to try some others.'

'They sell good flour in the farm shop from the local mill

over the hill. You should try it. Have you been there yet?'

'No I haven't. I must.' She'd been a bit lazy and had relied on a big shop at the nearest supermarket in Fort William, which went against all she'd learned in Ireland about sourcing and using local food, but she just hadn't had time. As she put the kettle on to boil and sliced the fresh loaf, she was aware of Mrs Macpherson's subtle interrogation into her plans for the castle and wondered if the whole village would be updated by the end of the day.

'So the paint … where you painting it?' she asked with blatant nosiness.

Izzy eyed her and decided to tease the prim woman a little. 'You really want to know?' She filled her voice with a hint of suggestive breathiness.

'Aye.' She widened his eyes as though an unpleasant thought had struck her. 'You're no planning on turning this place into a brothel, are you?'

Izzy let out a shout of laughter. 'No, nothing that interesting. The paint is for the morning room.'

'I dunno, Bill had a fair few wild parties back in the day.' Her prune-like mouth pursed with disapproval. 'I ken some of the rooms have seen a bit of action. He was one for the ladies, was Bill, although he never married. I'm guessing you know that though.'

'I don't know much about him, to be honest. He was my grandfather's brother, so my great uncle, and he was always very respectable the few times I ever met him.'

'Hmm, well, there's a few tales about him. But he was a good enough sort. He always liked a party.'

'Who's having a party?' asked Xanthe, sweeping in wearing a jaunty red beret, a blue and white striped T-shirt and wide-legged white culottes. 'I love a party. Hello, Mrs McP. Ooh, are you making tea, Izzy? I could murder a cup; I haven't stopped all morning.'

'Morning, Mrs McBride,' replied Mrs McPherson in a frosty tone. 'How ye going?'

'Busy, busy. There's so much to do. Is that my paint? Look, Izzy, the paint's arrived.'

'Really?' teased Izzy, wide-eyed, glancing at the parcel as she poured hot water over the tea-bags in the tea pot she'd decided to use in honour of the post mistress's rather uptight demeanour.

'Young Ronald Braid could come back and do some more painting if you need it,' said Mrs McPherson. 'I'm guessing you'll be needing a fair bit of decorating. Would you like me to put in a word for you? See if he's free?'

'That's very kind of you but I'm going to do it myself.'

Izzy caught sight of Xanthe's mouth wrinkling slightly.

Mrs McPherson gave Izzy a frank, assessing glance. 'Aye, I can see you'll be all right. You'll no blow away in a puff of wind.'

Xanthe squealed with laughter. 'She takes after her father's side of the family.'

'No, I won't,' said Izzy gravely, figuring that the woman was being practical about her five foot eleven, sturdy build, rather than insulting. 'But I've also taken on a couple of people.'

'You have. Who?' Mrs McPherson sounded quite put out.

'A couple who were wild camping around here.'

'Those two. They've been hanging around for a while. Very suspicious.' She frowned. 'Strange time of the year to be camping.' Her expression suggested she expected Izzy to explain more but Izzy felt it was none of her business. There was a measured silence before the other woman accepted defeat and asked, 'And what about food? Will you be wanting a chef?'

'No, I'll be doing the cooking too.'

'You're going to be a busy lass. All work and no play will make you miserable. You ought to come down to the village. There's a ceilidh on Friday.'

'A ceilidh!' Xanthe clapped her hands together. 'We have to go. I love a Dashing White Sergeant.' She let out an extremely dirty laugh and began skipping around the kitchen with her arms above her head, kicking her feet. Izzy decided not to mention that she was doing a Highland Fling rather than a ceilidh dance. 'Do you know, I'd love to learn to play the bagpipes.'

Izzy shuddered but not before Mrs McPherson said, 'My son has a set of pipes but he won't be playing them at the ceilidh as he'll be doing the calling.'

Izzy glared at her – that sounded a terrible idea – but the woman was already saying with a malicious twist to her mouth, 'You're welcome to give them a try.'

Dear God, the potential noise didn't bear thinking about. That would drive their current guest away for sure. Thinking about the professor she realised he'd been very quiet himself. In fact, she'd barely seen him over the last few days.

'There'll be a few young people there,' said Mrs McPherson with an encouraging nod at Izzy. 'What are ye, about twenty-nine? Have you a young man of your own?'

Her eyes were suddenly beady bright and Izzy had to bite back a smile at the unsubtle probing.

'No, not at the moment.'

Thankfully Xanthe's attention was diverted at present as she was busy attacking the box holding the newly arrived paint with Izzy's brand new vegetable paring knife.

'That's a proper shame but don't you worry yourself, lassie. We've plenty of fine young men roundabout here. A bonny lass like you will have them buzzing round like bees among the heather.'

'Thank you,' she murmured. Finding a man was at the very bottom of her agenda at the moment.

'Have ye thought about suppliers? You should talk to John Stewart down at the farm shop. He's a handsome man.'

'I've been planning to visit since I arrived,' said Izzy, ignoring Mrs McPherson's steady stare. She had a feeling that by nightfall the news that she was single would have been relayed to the whole village. 'I plan to design seasonal menus and use locally sourced ingredients when we have guests. If he can help that would be perfect.'

'We've some grand local foods round here. John Stewart will definitely see you right. And don't forget the whisky – *uisge beatha* – the water of life. You'll be wanting some of that for your guests. I can get you a good discount on a case if you're interested. I also stock a fine line in heather soap in the post office. That'd be good for your guests. I'll bring some up for ye to try.'

'Er, thank you,' said Izzy. 'I haven't got around to thinking about that sort of thing yet and I'm on a tight budget.'

'Yous not found the sapphires then?' Mrs McPherson's mouth tightened as if it was information she hadn't wanted to release but felt duty-bound to do so.

'Sorry?'

Xanthe dropped her knife with a clatter. 'Sapphires? Now

that sounds interesting.'

'Lady Isabella's sapphires,' said Mrs McPherson, lowering her voice as though to add an air of authority. 'You've no heard the story then? Old Bill always said he didn' ken where they were but they'd reveal themselves when they were needed. Auld fool.'

Izzy shook her head, wondering if this was just local folklore.

'Legend has it that her ladyship had a fine dowry of rare sapphires when she married the laird in 1724 but when the laird died, a rival clan stormed the castle to marry Isabella off to their laird. She refused to reveal where the sapphires were and they burned the original castle down, so Isabella built this one and according to the story, put the sapphires somewhere safe. They've never been seen since.' Her eyes widened in suggestion.

'Ooh.' Xanthe's eyes brightened with fervent enthusiasm. 'That would solve all our problems. Think what we could do if we found them.'

'Given they've been missing all this time, I suspect they were either lost in the fire or if they did keep them, they've probably been sold,' said Izzy. 'If they even existed.'

'Pish. Izzy McBride, have you no romance in your soul?' Her mother shook her head so vigorously she dislodged the beret and it fell down over one eye.

Mrs McPherson stared at her in horrified fascination. 'Or they may have been well-hidden.'

'Aw, Maggie. You're not telling that old fairytale, are ye?' asked Duncan, coming through the back door into the kitchen. 'Och, it's dreich out there this morning.' He shook off his heavy tweed jacket.

Mrs McPherson's back stiffened. 'No one's ever found the sapphires.'

'With guid reason, woman,' said Duncan, rolling his eyes. 'They don't exist. Don't you think they'd have turned up in the last three hundred years?'

Xanthe folded her arms, lifting her chin with a touch of belligerence. 'What if they did exist?'

'I ken you might be right, Duncan.' Mrs McPherson turned to Izzy, with a begrudging smile. 'But it's a grand story.'

Duncan shook his head. 'There's a rare thing, Maggie McPherson admitting she doesna ken everything. I suppose you do ken there's talk of a bad storm brewing in the next few days?'

'I love a good storm. So dramatic,' declared Xanthe, clutching her hand to her chest. Duncan shot her an acidic look and ignored her, turning to Izzy.

'Aye, a south westerly. We'll be having a fair few wet nights ahead of us,' said Mrs McPherson.

Izzy automatically looked up at the ceiling, worrying about the roof again.

'Dinna fret, lass,' said Duncan. 'Young Jim says he can patch up a few places. Worse comes to the worst, we'll set some buckets down.'

That wasn't exactly reassuring, Izzy thought, catching her lip between her teeth as she handed over two steaming mugs of tea.

'Did Maggie tell you about the ceilidh, lass? You and your' – he nodded towards Xanthe – 'should call in.' He'd clearly been warned by Xanthe that she preferred not to be called 'mum', 'ma' or 'mother'. 'And you can give me a lift down to the village. It's been a while since I've been. It'll be a grand affair. Raising money for the Mountain Rescue. I used to go out wi them back in the day. It's a verra good cause and you'll meet a few people.'

'That sounds fun. I'll definitely think about it,' said Izzy, her blood already pumping at the thought of the joy of a ceilidh. It would be a great way of meeting some local people but could she really spare the time? Just the thought of leaving the castle for more than a few hours made her feel uncharacteristically anxious.

'You should ask Ross to come too. He's no been anywhere for weeks. I reckon the local lassies would like a bit of new blood, and the lads, of course.' He winked at her.

'I can't imagine Mr Peace and Quiet would be seen dead at a ceilidh,' replied Izzy.

'No, he wouldn't.'

Izzy whirled round, horrified to see Ross standing in the doorway as he added, 'He has better things to be doing, like working.'

'Morning, lad,' said Duncan cheerfully, ignoring the sudden fizz of tension in the air. 'You ought to come; you've no left this place for weeks. Bit of dancing and a few bevvies would do you good.'

Ross gave him a tight smile. 'I'll bear it in mind.' Izzy was pretty sure from his stern expression and taut body language, those words actually translated as 'when hell freezes over'.

'It's for a very guid cause,' said Mrs McPherson, her hands folded on her lap, suddenly channelling a very prim Queen Victoria. 'They're raising money for the mountain rescue.'

Izzy glanced at Ross as he helped himself to a coffee and wondered for a moment what he'd look like in a kilt. And what did he look like under that big chunky sweater? She tamped the irreverent and wholly inappropriate thought down. What was the matter with her, for god's sake?

Encouraged by Mrs McPherson's rather obvious plug for the local business people and the need to start finding local suppliers, Izzy decided to pay the farm shop a visit a few days later before she got stuck into more painting for the afternoon. It was only a ten-minute drive and when she pulled up outside the big, converted barn to park in a very full car park, she had a good feeling about the place. While Izzy was on her cookery course, Adrienne had stressed, over and over, the importance of good food ingredients, not only for their taste but also to support sustainability and the environment. While there were a few chickens that Duncan looked after, ultimately Izzy would like to run a smallholding so that she could be sure of the provenance of her food. One of the things she also wanted to do was to plant a herb garden. But as the climate wasn't exactly Mediterranean, that was a project for the future when she'd have a hot house built to grow basil, oregano and marjoram, as well as chillies, tomatoes and peppers. In the meantime, there was no reason why she couldn't start planting onions, potatoes and beetroot.

'Hello, can I help you? Do you need a basket?'

Izzy realised she was daydreaming and looked up to find herself under careful scrutiny. 'You must be the new owner of the castle. Bill's niece. You look a lot younger than I was expecting, although Maggie said you were a bonnie lass.'

'Great niece,' she corrected, smiling at the compliment as she wondered what else Mrs McPherson had said.

'Ah that would explain it then. I'm John Stewart.' He held out a big hand, which engulfed hers when she shook it. He was about the same height as her with a stocky build and a pugnacious boxer's chin along with inquisitive eyes, which gave the impression they didn't miss a thing.

'Izzy McBride.'

'Welcome to Stewart's farm shop. Word is that you're turning the castle into a luxury hotel.'

Izzy smiled. 'I'm not sure about the luxury. But we're definitely going to be offering rooms.'

'And you're looking for local suppliers.' His eyes twinkled down at her. 'That is music to my ears.'

'Gosh, the jungle drums round here work fast.'

'You've met Maggie McPherson – she's the next best thing to the local paper,' he said. 'Why don't we sit down and have a coffee in the café and you can tell me what you need?'

'That sounds good,' said Izzy, impressed by his friendly enthusiasm and his obvious business acumen. He wasn't about to let this opportunity get away.

A few minutes later they were sitting on a mezzanine floor at the far end of the barn with the most wonderful view out over the sunshine-dappled valley with the loch in the distance. Rocky crags crowded the skyline to the west while rolling bracken-topped moorland softened the skyline to the east.

'This is lovely,' said Izzy, waving a hand at the large picture window through which the weak autumn sunshine shone.

'Brings in a lot of passers-by who stop for a coffee, some cake and a comfort break, and they're always keen to spend money in the shop. We also get a lot of walkers as there's a great circular walk that starts and finishes here.'

'Handy,' observed Izzy.

'Very. I'll give you a few maps, if you like, for your guests.'

Izzy laughed. It seemed John Stewart didn't miss a trick. 'And I'll need some leaflets about your award-winning jams and home-smoked salmon as well, I assume.'

He let out a bellow of laughter.

'I'll take them but only if you're going to give me some samples of the aforementioned goodies?'

'You drive a hard bargain. Aye, I'll give you a wee taster. Shall we talk business?'

Ten minutes later, there was an array of dishes in front of her.

'This is a Tain cheddar, a caboc and that's Morangie Brie. All made at the Highland Fine Cheese farm up at Tain. This is venison carpaccio, here we've got Scotch Bonnet chilli and mustard ketchup.'

As Izzy sampled her way through the different foods, John told her where they came from and a little about the ethos and values of the companies that made them.

'It's important to know where your food comes from,' he said at one point. She nodded and grinned at him.

'Exactly,' she said, and proceeded to tell him all about attending the cookery course in Ireland and what she'd learned there about the Slow Food Movement.

'We're on the same page,' said John, holding out his hand and shaking hers vigorously. 'You're a woman after my own heart. I've been banging on about organic sustainability and slow food for years. You need to speak to…'

For the next ten minutes he reeled off names and wrote down contact numbers and email addresses. And just like that,

Izzy found herself with suppliers for all her meat and fish, vegetables and condiments.

'You'll do well, I think. There's a chap opened a restaurant in the town and he's got a fancy menu but he canna get half the produce half the year, so it's all shipped in. Madness when there's so much great produce right on his doorstep.'

'I suppose with a smaller operation like mine, I can afford to offer seasonal dishes,' said Izzy diplomatically. 'I'm not planning to have a menu. There'll be a dish of the day for guests. If they don't fancy it, they can go out.'

'Excellent. What I can do is call you when I get anything special in, like a couple of rabbits or some grouse. And Kenny the fish guy, he'll do the same if they get something unexpected in the nets.' There was a pause and then he said, 'I'd love to sample some of your cooking.' His eyes twinkled with charming mischief. 'It sounds like you've had an excellent teacher and I do love my food. We could make quite a partnership.'

Izzy raised an eyebrow, unsure if he were flirting with her or whether he was very hot on customer service. 'You move fast, Mr Stewart.'

'John. And round here you have to. Most of the bonnie lasses are spoken for.'

When she went to leave half an hour later, she was laden with smoked salmon that had been smoked on the premises, two jars of Finlay Sisters Jam – made where the sisters lived just a couple of miles away – a pack of Cumberland sausages made by an organic farm at the other side of the loch and a vegan haggis, of all things.

'I've been trying to get rid of the haggis for months now,'

John said with a cheerful grin, as he packed it into the top of a brown paper bag.

'This is really kind of you,' she said as he handed the bulging bag over.

'Rubbish,' he said. 'It's good business. And...' He paused, his eyebrows rising. 'Perhaps you'll come to the ceilidh with me?'

Izzy stared at him. He really did move fast. 'I'm ... I'm not sure if I'm going.'

'Despite the size twelves' – he gave his feet a self-deprecating glance – 'I'm no such a bad dancer. And I can introduce you to a few folk.'

Izzy smiled at him. He wasn't bad looking, with his mop of dirty blond hair and steely grey eyes. She made a snap decision. 'Okay.' It had been a long time since she'd been on a date; perhaps this was the fresh start she needed.

He beamed at her. 'Excellent. I've written my phone number down for you. You text me and I'll text you. I'll even come pick you up if you like.'

'Let me see. Duncan is talking about going and he might want a lift,' said Izzy,

'I don't mind taking Duncan along. He doesn't get out to see his old cronies very often.'

Izzy's heart softened and she smiled up at John, admiring his kindness.

'Just ring' – he smiled at her again – 'whenever you want ... to place an order or something. I'm always happy to come up and deliver. And perhaps we can fix up a date for you to cook me that meal.'

November

Chapter Eight

Izzy hadn't been on a date in a very long time and she couldn't help the nerves that jangled through her system as she tidied up the kitchen on the day of the ceilidh.

'Isabel McBride, will you stop fussing around this kitchen and go get yourself ready,' Xanthe cried when Izzy started wiping the front of the fridge down.

'Yes, go, Izzy. Me and Jim will clean up,' said Jeanette.

Izzy put down her cloth and smiled at her mother, Duncan, Jim and Jeanette, who were all at the kitchen table finishing off a fish pie she'd made with the local smoked haddock, which had turned a distinctive saffron yellow in the smoking process. Jeanette and Jim had decided to duck out of the dance and were taking the estate Land Rover to Fort William to go to the cinema.

'I've got plenty of time,' said Izzy. John had arranged to pick her up at seven.

She huffed out a half-laugh to herself. Could it even be

called a date when her mother and Duncan had scrounged a lift with them?

'Go now,' said Jim, standing up. 'Otherwise, I'll carry ye up there.'

She grinned even though inside she felt a little sick, and held up her hands. 'Okay, okay, I'm going.'

Once upstairs in her room, having showered and washed her hair quickly, she stared at herself in the mirror. If she were being practical, she'd tie her hair up but vanity dictated otherwise. Normally she left her hair to dry naturally, or scrunched it up in a ponytail, but if she was vain about anything, it was her auburn curls, so she spent some time blow-drying her hair into soft, feminine waves.

She wasn't one for make-up but tonight she wanted to make a good impression. With a big, fat blusher brush, she dusted pale bronze powder over her cheeks, adding a touch of highlighter to define the bones. She picked neutral shades of eye shadow that emphasised the hue of her green eyes and a smoky green eyeliner that made them pop a little. When she came to apply her mascara with a slightly shaky hand, she smiled at herself, pleased with the transformation. For once she looked pretty and feminine. Xanthe would approve. She had a feeling that John Stewart might too. She definitely hadn't mistaken those flirty vibes from him and they'd given her a much-needed boost after Philip taking her for granted for so long.

Although she opted to wear a flouncy, tiered dress – it could get very warm at a ceilidh – she still wore her faithful

Converse because she knew from experience that they also got very energetic and some people could be very enthusiastic about flinging their partners around. With a final glance in the mirror, she gave herself a nod of approval. The deep green of her dress was perfect with her colouring.

A half hour before John was due, she went downstairs into the living room rather than the kitchen. Given her slightly jittery state, she'd likely find something to do and end up splashing her dress and ruining her make-up.

Someone had lit the lamps in there – probably Xanthe – and the room glowed with the patina of the love and care that had been recently bestowed on it. Her mother really had done a wonderful job.

Izzy had walked into the room planning to pick up a book, but she realised there was already someone else in one of the armchairs by the fire, which was burning low in the grate.

'Ross, I didn't see you, there.'

'No,' he said, rising slowly to his feet. His voice was soft and he looked a little confused … or even lost. She couldn't quite fathom the expression in his eyes but there was a gentleness she'd not seen before in them.

'You look…' She saw him swallow as his pause lingered in the air. As she waited for him to finish the sentence there was an odd bursting sensation in her chest.

He was still staring back at her and then with a start, as if coming to, he said, 'You look very nice, McBride.'

Her mouth twitched. It sounded as if the compliment had been forced from him. 'Thank you.'

He nodded and shifted awkwardly on his feet. 'What time are you off?'

'Seven.'

JULIE CAPLIN

'Well I hope you have a nice time.' He made to make a move and suddenly Izzy didn't want him to go, not when he looked at her like that.

'Have you eaten?' she asked.

'Not yet. I was just about to.'

'I made a smoked haddock fish pie. There's plenty left if you want it.'

Now his mouth twisted in wry amusement. They both knew she was talking for the sake of it – there was always plenty for him.

'Duncan said it was very good. Just like his mother used to make. I believe that's high praise indeed.'

Izzy laughed. 'Apparently so, but's that's usually what he says when he wants seconds. Why don't I heat a plate up for you?'

'Not in that pretty dress but you can supervise, if it makes you feel a better hostess.' He winked at her and she followed him into the kitchen, where they found Xanthe and Duncan lightly bickering about tartans.

Her phone pinged as she pulled the pie from the fridge and she took it from her pocket, giving the message a cursory glance and then winced as the words sank in.

Huge apologies Izzy. Something has come up, I can't make it this evening. But why don't I take you out to dinner tomorrow to make up for it? John.

Damn. She looked at Duncan's ruddy face. He was already wearing his kilt in anticipation of the night out and Xanthe had been primping for the whole afternoon.

'Change of plan, folks. John has had to cancel.' Both their faces registered disappointment and she put on a brave smile. Somehow she didn't think suggesting an evening of Scrabble or a card game was going to cut it but going to a ceilidh with her mother and their geriatric estate manager – lovely as he was – wasn't terribly appealing. Now it had been snatched from her, she realised how much she'd been looking forward to this evening.

Duncan's mouth folded in an uncharacteristic straight line as he sat poker-straight in his seat. Guilt nipped at Izzy. He'd been so looking forward to the evening. She caught Ross's eye and couldn't quite tell if it was disapproval or sympathy in his expression. Either way, it made her feel worse about letting Duncan down.

'Tell you what,' she said overbrightly. 'I'll drive us there. We'll go in ten minutes. I just need the loo.'

She dashed off before she gave herself away and ran up the stairs cursing herself. Fool. John's flirtation and attention at the farm shop had been a welcome sop and she'd actually been looking forward to their date. Since Philip she'd avoided going on dates and this was the first time she'd let down the barrier, but look what had happened. He'd cancelled on her at the very last minute, which had also been Philip's favourite MO. The number of times she'd been all dressed up with nowhere to go... She sighed. She couldn't let Duncan down. Nor her mother who had been dancing around the house all day; quite a few ornaments had come to grief as she'd flung her arms about.

When she returned to the kitchen ten minutes later, her teeth gritted and her hands clenching and unclenching, it was empty and for a minute she wondered hopefully if both Xanthe and

Duncan had changed their minds about going. A sound behind her had her turning.

All the blood drained from her head.

'R-Ross,' she managed. She stared at him because, well ... there was nowhere else to look. He'd changed out of his usual chunky sweater into a torso-hugging black T-shirt that left absolutely nothing to the imagination. Someone might as well have drawn arrows – abs here, pecs here and deltoids here. He was also wearing a kilt! And man, did he make a kilt look sexy. The sudden flutters in the bottom of her stomach made her realise that every nerve ending had gone on red alert and she was very aware of him, her body responding to him in an unseemly, totally inappropriate manner. She also had a feeling her tongue had stuck to the roof of her mouth in classic cartoon manner.

'I thought I'd come to the ceilidh with you,' he said in a soft voice that set off flutters in her chest.

'I-I thought you were here for peace and quiet,' she stuttered, still stunned by the sight of him.

'It's not very nice being stood up,' he said. 'I thought you might like some moral support.'

'That's very kind of you,' she said faintly because she still couldn't quite believe what she was seeing.

'I couldn't bear to see Duncan's disappointment.' He smiled at her. 'Neither could you. I decided if you could man up, then so could I.'

She looked at him, touched and surprised by his perceptive observation. She'd never really understood the term 'heart-melting' until that moment because despite his words, she knew that he was also doing this to help her save face.

'He has been looking forward to it,' she agreed.

'And so have you.'

'Thank you.' She stepped forward and placed a quick kiss on his smooth cheek. 'You're a very nice man, Ross Strathallan.'

He smiled at her. 'Don't tell everyone.'

Again. That heart-melting thing. She lifted her shoulders in a wary shrug, not willing to admit how much it had hurt to be stood up. Not because she especially liked John but just being dumped at the last minute brought back a few too many memories. Ross appeared to have seen that too but was, it appeared, too kind to point it out.

'Come on, let's round up the others before Mr Peace and Quiet changes his mind,' he said with a quick grin. 'Would you like me to drive?'

———

They could hear the rousing music of an accordion and fiddles as they approached Balacluish Village Hall. Xanthe, rocking the Flora MacDonald look draped in a tartan scarf over a taffeta dress, began dancing as she walked up the path to the front door. Next to her, Duncan's face was alight with anticipation, which made Izzy doubly glad she'd come. 'I have nae been to a ceilidh for a long while,' he said, rubbing his hands together.

Izzy glanced at Ross, still a little tongue-tied. The man scrubbed up well and was just too handsome for his own good. Her mouth a little dry, she swallowed as she watched the heavy pleats of his kilt flare out, revealing strong, muscular legs covered in dark, silky hair as he strode along beside her. Who knew well-defined calves could be so sexy?

'You came,' said Mrs McPherson, who was collecting the ticket money.

'Aye,' said Duncan, as Xanthe hooked her arm through his and dragged him through the door, leaving Izzy to sort out payment.

'Nice to see you here, Miss McBride, and you too, Professor Strathallan. You make a fine pair.' She nodded with satisfaction, almost as if she'd organised this turn of events.

'Thank you, Mrs McPherson,' Ross replied with sweet-voiced charm as if she'd paid them the greatest compliment, instead of assuming they were a couple when they were no such thing.

Impressed by his aplomb, Izzy shot him a grateful smile as they headed into the main hall where a dozen couples were already dancing.

Duncan was at the bar while Xanthe was watching the dancing, tapping her feet, whooping enthusiastically and clapping along to the music, drawing quite a few openly curious stares. *Perhaps it was the hat*, thought Izzy, with a wry twist to her mouth. A blue velvet affair, the tiny top hat was perched on top of her bright crimson curls.

'Oh this is such fun,' she screeched as Izzy approached her. 'It's been so long since I've been out.'

'Do you want a drink?' asked Izzy with a benign smile. She was quite used to Xanthe drawing attention to herself, although her mother always seemed blithely oblivious.

'No, darling. I want to dance.' She looked around the room and over at Duncan who visibly shrank as if he were trying to merge into the bar. But it was no use.

'Duncan,' she called in her piping tone that made all heads whip her way like compass points drawn to due north. 'Come and dance,' she said as she waded through the group of men surrounding him.

Izzy could see him duck his head. Luckily one of his braver friends stepped forward and offered his arm in a gallant gesture that had Xanthe cooing all over the man.

Izzy heaved a sigh and sent a smile Duncan's way. He shot a scowl back and turned back to his beer, clearly grateful for his reprieve.

She felt Ross's presence next to her. 'Does the poor sod know what he's let himself in for?' he muttered, watching Xanthe tug the man into the group of dancers waiting for the next song to strike up as the caller – Mrs McPherson's son, Izzy recalled – put down his drink, got up onto the makeshift stage with the three musicians and began to call out the instructions for a trial run.

'Join right hands on the lady's shoulder, left hands in front.' Most people knew exactly what he meant and got into position. 'Four steps forward and then pivot, so that the gentleman's hand is on the lady's left shoulder and the right is in front. That's right, you've got it. Then four steps backward.'

The caller talked the dancers through the set moves once more and then the music began.

With an outrageously loud whoop Xanthe set off, immediately turning the wrong way and barging into another couple. She gave a riotous laugh, grinned at her partner and danced a few steps on the spot, humming to herself. With a slightly bewildered grin back, her partner steered her in the right direction. The couples separated then, each going in the opposite direction in a circle so that they passed their partners. It was a simple skipping step but Xanthe was throwing her arms up in the air as if she were doing the Highland Fling again.

Izzy rolled her eyes to herself and muttered, 'Oh dear God.'

'She certainly knows how to enjoy herself,' said Ross, surprising her. He generally went out of his way to avoid Xanthe.

'Do you know how to enjoy yourself?' she asked, suddenly feeling mischievous.

He looked a little taken aback. 'Of course, I do.'

'Have you done much ceilidh dancing?' She shot him a quick grin. 'Or are you the sort that has to look down at their feet all the time?'

'Are you implying I need to concentrate on the steps?' There was a hint of teasing amusement in his eyes as he looked at her. 'Do you?'

She raised imperious eyebrows. 'You're looking at the winner of the Bute and Argyll Country Dance Championships under sixteens, seventeens and eighteens in 2007, 2008 and 2009.'

'Impressive.' The music stopped.

'Come on, ladies and gentlemen. Take your partners.'

'That's our cue,' said Ross, nudging her and stepping onto the dance floor, murmuring in her ear, 'I was voted most likely to break my partner's ankle at a ceilidh when I left school.'

Izzy spat out a laugh. 'Now you tell me.'

'You didn't ask,' he said, his eyes crinkling in that way that made butterflies stir in the bottom of her stomach.

'Okay folks, it's the Gay Gordons. And I warn ye, it's going to be a fast one. You'll be earning your drinks.'

Everyone around the room laughed as the music began and the dancers all took up their positions.

'Ready?' asked Ross, linking one hand with hers over one shoulder and the other in front. She straightened in readiness, trying not to dwell on the warmth of his hand holding hers or the closeness of his big, broad body.

'Aye,' she said. She knew the moves well but with the frequent turns and changes of direction, there were invariably collisions when people forgot to turn in time. The first set of steps was fairly decorous and Ross was much better than he'd claimed; surprisingly light on his feet and well-versed in the moves.

'You've done this before,' teased Izzy as they turned in perfect synchronicity, dancing forward for four steps before turning again.

'I've had a wee bit of practice since I left school and I'm not so tongue-tied with the lassies anymore.' His eyes twinkled as he said it. Izzy found it difficult to believe he'd ever been shy; he had such a commanding air of confidence and self-assurance about him. In her teens she'd been staunchly independent and something of a novelty among her peers as she had far more freedom than any of them. They were all impressed that she called her mum by her name and they liked coming to her home because of the lack of rules and routine. To them, it seemed perfect parenting, but Izzy knew otherwise, not that she ever let on. She'd quite enjoyed the notoriety of being the girl who could do whatever she wanted.

She twirled under his arm, suddenly nervous about the next step when they'd be face to face in a close hold. Her heart skipped when they moved smoothly into the move, Ross's hand around her waist, the other holding her hand, and she tried hard not to stiffen and to maintain eye contact with a pleasant smile. It was ridiculously difficult to be this close when all her senses were clamouring at the touch of his fingers, the slight smell of musky man, the sight of the smooth skin over his jawline and the need to let her gaze rove over his face at will. *Don't look at his lips. Don't look at his lips*, she chanted in her head. And then, mercifully, they were back to being side by side and starting the cycle of steps over again. She eased out a breath. She could do this. It was just dancing. She loved dancing.

They skipped through another circuit of the dance floor and then the pace of the fiddle increased. The fingers of the accordion player flew over the keys as footsteps thumped on the worn, wooden floorboards. The dance steps grew faster and faster and Izzy skipped, almost breathless, her hand clutched in Ross's. He swung her round, the heavy weight of the folds of his kilt brushing her legs, and they moved into a hold again. Dancing at a furious pace their eyes met, and suddenly it was just the two of them whirling around the floor. Everything else blurred until there was just Ross. Those blue eyes holding hers. Her heart pitter-pattered in her chest and her cheeks flushed as she looked at his lips. His quirked in response and his hold on her back tightened. Neither of them spoke. Then they separated again and Izzy didn't dare look at him. The thump, thump of her heart resounded in her chest as she tried to catch her breath, and it was almost a relief when she was back in his arms and his blue eyes settled on hers again, solemn and watchful but with that slight smile. She wasn't imagining the spark between them. Despite the speed of the dance, their gaze held slow and steady and it was the most erotic thing Izzy had ever felt. His fingers squeezed hers, his hand flat and firm against the small of her back, as if anchoring her to him.

It was a shock when the music finally stopped and the rest of the world intruded.

She opened her mouth but the words deserted her. He seemed equally lost for words and for a moment the two of them stood there looking at each other.

'What fun! And what a gorgeous pair you make,' shrieked Xanthe, coming up and throwing her arms around both of them. 'You're both such good dancers. Especially you, Ross. A big fella like you. Who'd have thought you'd be so light on your feet? And did you see Gregory? My, he's some dancer. I'm quite worn out. I think I need refreshment.'

Ross tightened his jaw and turned to her. 'Would you like a drink, Xanthe?'

She beamed up at him. 'I thought you'd never ask.'

Izzy shook her head at her mother's blithe assumption that Ross should pay for her drink and the sudden frostiness on his face. 'You do know it's the twenty-first century and women are quite capable of buying their own drinks,' she said sternly to her mother. She touched Ross's arm. 'I'll get them.'

With a charming smile completely at odds with his earlier expression, he said, 'It would be my pleasure. I'm in need of a drink myself after all that' – there was the most infinitesimal pause – 'excitement.' His eyes met Izzy's again and his gaze softened.

'I'll have a G&T and don't let them drown it with the tonic,' Xanthe said, oblivious to the tension between them.

'Izzy?'

'I'd love a River Leven Pilsner. John told me all about it when I was at the farm shop.'

Did she imagine it, or had Ross's eye's narrowed ever so slightly when she mentioned John's name?

'River Leven is the microbrewery,' she explained. 'I'm planning to stock some of their bottled ales for guests.'

'Excellent, I enjoy a good Scottish ale.'

'I hope his wallet's in his sporran,' said Xanthe with a wicked laugh as he strode away.

'What are you like?' Izzy rolled her eyes, although she did find herself watching the sway of his kilt.

'Oh darling, he's a big boy. He can look after himself. I should nip in quick if I were you. There are quite a few ladies here eyeing him up.'

'Xanthe, he's a guest.'

'Pish, he's a good-looking man and by my reckoning you've got first dibs. Although I've noticed a few other men here keeping a close eye on you. You could take your pick.'

Izzy shook her head, laughing. It was impossible to stay cross with Xanthe. 'I'll keep it in mind. Are you having a good time?'

'I'm having the most wonderful time. Although I don't think Mrs McPherson likes me very much. Probably to do with her teeth.'

Izzy blinked. 'Her teeth?'

'Yes, I only asked her which dentist she frequented. So I can avoid them.'

Izzy literally goggled at her mother, who let out a peal of ringing laughter.

'I didn't tell her that bit. That would have been rude.'

'Phew.'

'Honestly, Izzy, you don't trust me.'

With good reason, thought Izzy, as she asked, 'And what did she say?'

'Said she hadn't been to a dentist for years.'

Izzy swallowed before asking, 'And what did you say?' She didn't trust her mother not to have put her foot in it.

'Nothing bad. I just said that I could see that. What's wrong with that? It was an observation. People can be so sensitive. If she's so bothered, she could go to a dentist, couldn't she?' Xanthe shrugged her shoulders, dismissing the subject. 'Oh look, here's Ross with our drinks.'

Xanthe cooed all over him as he handed her a drink, which he pretty much ignored as he supped his pint and looked around the room. It had filled up since they'd first arrived and the noise was a cheerful cacophony of chatter punctuated with gales of laughter. Everyone was smiling with the possible exception of Mrs MacPherson who seemed to be keeping a watchful eye on everyone as if she were taking notes, ready to spill the beans to the next person that stepped foot in the post office.

'Ooh, there's Gregory,' said Xanthe, and made a beeline for the man standing on the other side of the room. Suddenly Izzy stiffened. 'I don't believe it,' she muttered, unable to stop the words spilling out.

Ross followed her gaze towards the man who'd just walked into the hall, his hand resting gently on the small of the back of a very pretty blonde girl who was laughing up at him.

With acute insight, Ross said, 'John?'

Izzy nodded, her stomach contracting in embarrassment. How bloody humiliating. The guy had clearly stood her up because he got a better offer.

Her face flushed bright red.

'You don't need to feel bad about this, Izzy,' Ross murmured in her ear as he stepped closer to her, almost as if he were protecting her.

Despite his words, Izzy's mortification deepened when involuntary tears started to well up in her eyes. Why did this keep happening to her? She didn't care about John, she didn't know him well enough to care, but it hurt that once again she'd been tossed aside in favour of someone else.

'Hey,' said Ross, one finger gently swiping away the tear.

She swallowed hard and looked up into his concerned blue eyes. 'It's fine. It's just a bit of a pisser being dumped before you've even been on a date with someone.'

'His loss,' said Ross, his mouth narrowing with fierce disapproval. He slid an arm across her shoulder, his fingers caressing the bare skin at the nape of her neck, his lips brushing across the side of her forehead as he pulled her in for a hug. 'The man's an idiot. Come on, put your drink down. We're going to dance.' He took the glass from her and took her hand, leading her straight towards John who was making his way to the bar.

'Of course, being an award-winning dancer, you'll be wanting to dance with the best,' said Ross in a suddenly conversational tone, apropos of absolutely nothing. He tightened his hold on her hand as their paths crossed with the other couple and he gave John and the woman with him a friendly nod. 'Evening,' he said, and carried on, chatting away to Izzy as if nothing untoward had happened but quite clearly staking his claim. Izzy could have kissed him right then and there.

John's eyes had widened at the sight of her and Izzy was rather pleased that she was able to give him a blithe smile and turn her face up to Ross as if she were hanging on his every word.

Before she could say anything, they were on the dance floor

and the caller was explaining the next dance. Ross's fingers interlaced with hers and those blue eyes never left her face as they marked the steps. She couldn't look away. There was something mesmerising about his gaze and she wondered what he was thinking.

When the music started, they danced the first refrain together and she smiled up at him, his face softening as he smiled back. Then, to her disappointment, they were separated. Her new partner took her in his knuckle-crunching grip, his stride much bigger than hers, and she had to try hard to concentrate. Then she was with a new partner, and then another, as the women moved one way around the circle and the men the other. Halfway round she glanced over at Ross to find that he was looking at her. He nodded, his face set in an expression that gave little away. A second later she looked over at him again to find he was still watching her. A small smile tugged at his lips. She couldn't look away and neither, it seemed, could he.

At last they were facing each other. 'Fancy meeting you here,' he murmured in a low voice that thrummed through her as they stepped forward to meet each other.

'Fancy that,' she whispered back.

Once again their eyes were drawn to each other and neither of them looked away as they danced together. When they had to move on again, Izzy turned her head to look back over her shoulder at the same time Ross looked back. They both gave each other a wistful smile.

'Izzy, isn't this fun?' said Xanthe, grabbing her arm as she walked past a little later in the evening. Before she could respond, her mother whirled away calling, 'I'm having such a good time. Oh look, there's Fraser.' And away she disappeared into the throng of people.

For a while Izzy watched her mother throwing herself quite literally into the dance. Her unfettered enthusiasm had proved popular with men and women alike and she was quickly surrounded. In contrast, Izzy felt a bit like a wallflower. She tried hard not to watch Ross, his kilt flaring as he danced, his head nodding as he talked to his partner, but it was impossible. She didn't seem to be able to help herself. Thankfully the dance soon came to an end and he came to stand beside her.

'Xanthe's a hit,' he said.

'So are you,' said Izzy, hoping she didn't sound bothered by it.

'I'm a novelty, that's all. And you've not exactly been short of dance partners.'

She grinned at him. 'New blood, that's all.'

'I think it's a bit more than that. The stocky chap seems quite enamoured.'

'He's a carpet fitter. I'm potentially a very good customer.'

'You keep thinking that, sweetheart,' said Ross with a teasing smile.

Izzy was about to say something when she noticed the crowd around her mother dispersing slightly.

A man in a black and yellow kilt with a bald head, a perfect pot belly and a bushy white moustache had dropped to his knees in front of Xanthe, reaching for her hand. In a loud plummy and very English accent he said, 'Fair lady, please take pity on a poor miserable wretch and lend me your hand for a dance.'

Xanthe's eyes glittered with delight and she smiled regally down at him.

'Oh dear God,' muttered Ross. 'Why do people insist on making such spectacles? Don't they know they're making an utter fool of themselves and embarrassing everyone around them? And poor Xanthe can hardly say no now, can she? It's so bloody manipulative.'

Izzy shot a quick glance at Ross's face, which had tightened with disapproval.

'I loathe grand gestures like that,' he added.

'Sometimes, it's nice,' said Izzy, although she had to admit this was a bit much.

'I can't think of a single circumstance where I'd want to make a complete prat of myself in front of scores of people.'

'He's making a point so she's not left with any doubt that a dance with her is what he wants. I think it's quite sweet.'

'You don't think it's slightly coercive? Being forced into it.'

Izzy shook her head. 'She can always say no.'

'Can she?' asked Ross, his mouth turning downwards and it was obvious he was thinking of something else.

Meanwhile, Xanthe, who wasn't the least bit embarrassed by the man's display, had smiled prettily down at her suitor, helped him to his feet and accepted his offer to dance with absolute delight. Izzy turned to Ross to say, 'see', but he'd disappeared and she caught sight of him shouldering his way through the fire exit and out of the hall.

Izzy stared after him, tempted to follow, but something about the expression in his eyes suggested that he wouldn't welcome company right now.

Not long after that, the final dance was called. When Izzy returned to the car, having rounded up Duncan and Xanthe, she found Ross already sitting in the driver's seat. Xanthe, who was slightly tipsy, insisted on sitting up front with him so Izzy climbed into the back with Duncan who promptly fell asleep. Meanwhile, Xanthe prattled on about the evening for the whole ride home, reminding Izzy horribly of a post-ball Mrs Bennet. When they arrived back at the castle, Ross dropped them outside the front door before taking the car round the back. By the time Izzy had helped her mother up the stairs, listened to her giggling observations on all the attendees, urged her to bed and then returned downstairs, Ross had retired for the night. She sighed as she switched out the lights, feeling a little bit like a Cinderella who'd been to the ball but struck out big time.

December

Chapter Nine

'You look very fierce. Everything okay?'

Izzy jumped and almost toppled off her ladder, where she was cleaning the ceiling in one of the bedrooms. She pulled out her earphones. 'Ross. Hi. Just trying to work out how I'm going to get everything done in time for Christmas.' She'd barely seen him the last two weeks since the ceilidh.

He grabbed the ladder to steady it and stood there looking up at her, his dark blue eyes dancing with amusement. 'And here I thought those cobwebs had upset you somehow.'

'I don't think anyone's been up here in years.' She sighed.

'Where do you want me to put this?' He held yet another large box. 'I found Xanthe wrestling with it, trying to get it down the stairs. I was worried she might break her neck.'

'Oh god,' said Izzy. 'She's got the bit between her teeth. Can you put it down over there? It feels like no sooner do I empty the room, she brings more stuff down.' There was no stopping her mother; it would be easier to a halt a stampede of rhinos.

'Mmm, she was being a bit ambitious.' He hefted the box.

'Although the minute she offloaded this she skipped back upstairs. She's been making quite a racket up there but I needed a break.' He rubbed the back of his neck and shoulders and looked around the bedroom. 'Looks like a big project.'

'It is,' said Izzy, a touch glumly. 'But Xanthe wants to get it all done yesterday. She's filling the place up with antiques and finishing touches before I've completed the painting.'

'She's very, er … enthusiastic.'

'Except when it comes to the hard physical labour,' replied Izzy. This was the third bedroom she'd painted this week. Even with Jim and Jeanette's help, it was a race against time as they now had just a few weeks to get everything prepared. The amount of work felt never ending.

'I could help with some of the painting if you'd like. I've got a spare half hour.'

Izzy looked at him. 'Are you sure? I thought you were really busy.'

One shoulder lifted in a laconic shrug. 'I am but I can't get much done at the moment as my agent keeps plaguing me about publicity stuff. Mindless work like painting helps me pl… Helps my thought process. Gives my brain a rest. Besides, there's so much noise today, it's difficult to concentrate.'

'Sorry, I know you wanted peace and quiet. Jim's had to get the work done in the bathroom next door to you but he'll be finishing this week.'

'It's all right. If I'm honest I find the view is inspiring, it's sent my thoughts in a different direction and funnily enough so is being around people,' he paused, 'as long as no one specifically interrupts me when I am working.'

'Jim will be done soon, I promise. All he has to do is take

the tiles off the walls and instal a new shower and he'll be done in that room.'

'He's quite the handyman.'

'He certainly is.'

'You got a spare paint brush, then?' he asked.

Realising he was serious, she grinned at him. 'Over there. Thanks, I'm not going to turn down free labour.'

'You haven't seen my painting yet.'

'It's not me you have to answer to, it'll be Jim— No, it will likely be Xanthe who'll have final say and she's quite fussy.' And she wasn't the sort of person to hold back if she didn't like something. This had made Izzy a lot more circumspect and less inclined to welcome intense emotion.

It was probably the reason why she'd let Philip get away with being so reticent with her for so long. Having become used to Xanthe's effusive heart-on-sleeve attitude, which could sometimes be quite wearing, she'd mistaken his reserve for deep emotion. He'd even used the words 'let's not rush into anything' and from that she'd taken it to read that he was more measured and was taking things seriously. She wasn't going to make that mistake again.

'Nice colour,' said Ross, breaking into her thoughts.

'I'd never have chosen it in a million years – I'd have been scared that it might be too dark – but Xanthe has a real eye.'

'Mmm, she has flair, that's for sure.' The words didn't sound entirely complimentary but then Izzy knew her mother wasn't everyone's cup of tea. Too loud and melodramatic for many people.

'Help yourself to a paint brush. Do you want to do the fiddly bits or a wall?'

'I'm more of a wall man. I don't have the patience for the

corners and skirtings. If you don't mind, I won't talk. This is good thinking time.'

'No problem,' said Izzy. 'I'm listening to an audiobook and it's got to a good bit.'

'Oh? What are you listening to?'

'Just a crime thriller thing. I've only started it today, but it's a good story.'

'There's no *just* about it. People should read what they want to. I can't bear all that literary snobbery. I'm a big fan of Ian Rankin's Rebus.'

'Oh, I like him too but I'm listening to Ross Adair's *Without Bones*. It's a great series, have you read any?'

'Mmm,' he said non-committally and picked up a paintbrush. 'Shall I start here?'

'Yes, thank you. That would be great.'

'You've made good progress in here.' He studied one of the walls, running his hand over its smooth finish.

'Thank you.' She nodded with satisfaction, feeling a touch of pride as she glanced around. Over the last few days, she'd sugar soaped the walls and filled in many holes and cracks as well as sanded the woodwork before waxing and polishing it. The room was starting to come back to life and she couldn't wait to see it when it was finished. Xanthe had also been darting in and out of the space with a tape measure for the last few days, sizing up the windows, measuring the fireplace and making mostly helpful observations along with plenty of constructive criticism about Izzy's work and progress. Hearing praise from someone else was a welcome boost.

She picked up her own paintbrush and began to paint, waiting a few moments to see if he'd say anything else. When it became obvious that he really didn't want to talk, she put her earphones in and began to paint around the skirting board that she'd carefully taped to protect the wood.

They painted in companionable silence and even though he didn't speak his presence was oddly reassuring, especially when he gave her the occasional smile as they would look up and catch each other's eyes.

They'd been painting for an hour – it seemed they'd both lost track of time – and the first coat was almost done when she noticed Ross had come to stand behind her. She pulled out her earphones.

'Do you want a cup of tea?'

'That would be lovely,' she said, stretching out the kink in her back.

'I'll bring you one and then I need to get back to work. Oh blast,' he said as his phone rang from the back pocket of his jeans. He pulled it out. 'Hi, Bethany,' he said in a decidedly weary tone before disappearing through the door.

———

Ten minutes later, when she was absorbed in her book once more, listening to the description of a tense flight by the detective hero, rushing back to his house after a tip off that the officers watching his girlfriend had failed to check in and the villain was closing in, Ross dropped in a mug of tea, gave her a wave with one hand, the phone still clamped to his ear with his other, and left the room again.

Even though they hadn't spoken while they worked, she felt strangely bereft once he'd gone. There was something about someone else being around that had given her comfort, although she couldn't have said exactly why.

Ross already seemed to be an integral part of the house along with Jim, Jeanette and Duncan. How was she going to feel when he eventually left?

'They want stockings,' announced Xanthe the next morning, coming into the bedroom where Jeanette was cleaning windows and Izzy was making up the bed with the crisp white sheets that had arrived the day before.

Izzy plumped a pillow and surveyed her handiwork, very tempted to crawl into the bed herself.

'Who wants stockings?' She tweaked the duvet cover and then bent down to pick up the soft cashmere throw in a rich, emerald-green colour, which Xanthe had selected to go with the accents in the phenomenally expensive wallpaper. Even Izzy had to admit the cost had been worth it and the room looked spectacularly opulent, with three painted walls that set off the striking wallpaper and roman blinds that Xanthe had made.

'The Carter-Joneses,' said her mother, doing a very odd crab-like sidle up to the wooden panelling around the fireplace.

Izzy blinked at Xanthe. 'What do you mean, they want stockings?'

'They want a traditional Christmas in a Scottish castle with all the trimmings and Mrs Carter-Jones has asked that everyone gets a stocking.' Xanthe leaned back against the wall, one hand tapping against one of the panels, which set the white feathers in the boa she sported shivering.

She looks like an agitated swan, thought Izzy.

'I don't even know these people,' she said. How on earth was she supposed to put together stockings for complete strangers? Stockings were personal. Each item had to be chosen with care. Her nan – Xanthe's mother – had always made her a themed one. One year it had been all stationery items, another make-up gifts from nail varnish and eye shadow through to cotton remover pads and blusher brushes. The year she'd gone to university it had been filled with useful things like a set of screwdrivers, a Swiss penknife, a bottle opener and even a pack of condoms.

'It's all right, she's sent me a brief. Oh, and there are two extra people coming now.' Xanthe tapped at another panel, keeping an altogether too bird-bright gaze on Izzy.

'So, eight people total.'

'At the moment.'

Izzy stared at her mother. 'What do you mean, "at the moment"?'

'There may be another two.' Her mother's fingers strayed to another panel and tapped again.

'Another two,' Izzy parroted again and glanced over at Jeanette who was trying and failing to hide a giggle.

'What's another two?' her mother sang gaily.

Izzy rolled her eyes. 'Well it's another four, isn't it?'

'They are paying very handsomely. Which reminds me, I've ordered the most marvellous drinks trolley to go in the library. I thought that would be the perfect place for a pre-dinner whisky or a G and T. It's going to look divine. Don't worry,' Xanthe said in her shrill voice. 'I can see that expression on your face. The trolley was in the antiques shop in the village. It hardly cost anything.'

Xanthe's idea of hardly costing anything was a long way

from Izzy's. The difference between a short hop to Ireland and a flight to Australia.

'Honestly, Izzy, you're such a killjoy.'

Jeanette hastily began to polish the windows again.

Thank goodness the Carter-Joneses were paying so much, although the seven thousand pound deposit was vanishing rapidly.

'Remember we need to make some profit to pay for the roof,' she reminded her mother.

'You could open up to more guests. I've had another enquiry today.'

'No, Xanthe!' said Izzy with a stern wave of her finger. 'As it is we're going to have to prepare another bedroom and don't forget I've got to cook for all these people. They're probably expecting Michelin-star standards. I'm nervous enough as it is.'

'You'll be fine,' said her mother, waving a hand.

'No more guests.' Izzy glared at Xanthe, who was now stretching up with a very unconvincing yawn, her fingers sliding along the wood dividing the flat panels.

'What are you doing?'

'Doing? Me?' echoed her mother.

'Yes. With the panelling?'

'Checking for woodworm, darling. You know these old houses. Dreadful for woodworm.'

'What? You were drumming them out, with the tapping?' Izzy knew when her mother was up to something and she was definitely up to something. She had that fox-scenting-hens look about her, slightly cunning and a bit too blasé.

'You're looking for those sapphires, aren't you?'

'No,' said Xanthe, her eyes widening with faux innocence that didn't fool Izzy for a second.

'What sapphires?' asked Jeanette.

'It's an old legend. There's absolutely no proof they ever existed,' said Izzy, glaring at her mother.

'Pish,' said Xanthe and flounced out of the room.

Thank goodness Jim and Jeanette had worked out so well, as it was going to be all hands on deck. They were both hard workers and after their week's trial, Izzy couldn't imagine how she could do without them. Jim seemed to be able to turn his hand to anything when it came to fixing and mending things, the Dyson vacuum being a case in point – following its transformation, it had sucked up an eyewatering amount of dirt during its maiden voyage. He was also brilliant at hanging wallpaper and could work magic with a paint brush. Jeanette, meanwhile, was willing and extremely capable at anything she was asked to do with the sole exception of cooking. She really couldn't cook. If Izzy had one small further niggle, it was that on occasion they were easily distracted by each other but they were young and in love and what did she know about such things? She'd pined for bloody Philip for so long, she was a dried-up old cynic.

Escaping from the kitchen to the quiet of her little study, Izzy picked up her phone.

Hi all. So the novice cook has been landed with Christmas lunch for...

How many would it be? With the Carter-Jones party of eight – possibly ten – plus Duncan, Xanthe, Jim and Jeanette and perhaps Ross, plus herself.

...for sixteen. As well as gourmet breakfast, lunch and dinner for

eight to ten people for five days. Any suggestions for festive menus, not too complicated but look impressive? My brain has gone completely blank and I'm terrified I've bitten off more than I can chew! Any advice to help me get ahead? Help!!!!!

Hopefully the Killorgally gang would come to her rescue with some brilliant tips because she was totally on her own. Xanthe was useless in the kitchen; her attention span was too short to keep an eye on anything.

There was a quiet knock on the door and then it opened. 'Sorry to disturb you, I just wanted to let you know we're running low on coffee before someone uses the last few spoonfuls and then complains there's none left.'

Izzy lifted her head from her notes and smiled at Ross's thoughtfulness. 'Thanks, there's a secret stash in the pantry for just such eventualities but I'll add a new pack to my list.'

'Brilliant, I need my coffee. I need warming up, it gets cold sitting all day.'

'Oh, I'm sorry. Did you want a fire in your room?'

'God no, I'll doze off then. I just put another jumper on. The cold is good to keep my concentration sharp. Besides, I'll warm up soon enough this afternoon as I said I'd help Jim with a spot of painting.'

'What about your book?'

'I've just sent some stuff off to my editor, Bethany. I'm waiting for feedback. Thought you could use another pair of hands, although Jim seems to be a bit of a whizz on the wallpapering.'

'He's very good at everything,' said Izzy with a quick heaven-sent prayer.

'When he keeps his mind on the job,' said Ross, rolling his eyes. 'He can't seem to keep his hands off the lovely Jeanette.'

'You've noticed that too?' said Izzy with a giggle.

'Hard to miss it. I've taken to whistling before I walk down a corridor these days and I caught them both looking very breathless coming out of one of the bathrooms yesterday.'

Izzy nodded. 'I know but … they're hard workers so I can't complain, and I'm not paying them very much.'

'How are the Christmas plans coming along?' He nodded towards the sheets of paper at her elbow, surprising her by appearing to want to make conversation.

'They're coming along. My main concern is the Carter-Joneses' expectations. Are they expecting Michelin standard cooking and six-star service? I'm hoping that the warmth of the welcome will win them over. They seem quite demanding.'

'You'll be fine.' He leaned back against the wall, studying her.

'Easy for you to say that. Do you know what you'll be doing yet?'

'Actually, that was the other reason for coming to find you, I've decided I'd quite like to stay here.' He paused. 'I can give you a hand.'

'You!'

'Don't sound so surprised. I'll take a couple of days off and I can pitch in. I can also act as maître d'. I worked in quite a few restaurants in Edinburgh when I was a student.'

'What happened to peace and quiet?'

'That's for when I'm working. I can be quite sociable when I want to be, you know.'

'Yes. I suppose you can.' Although she had noticed he tended to beat a hasty retreat whenever Xanthe appeared on the scene, but then her mother was on the loud side for most people. 'Well I'm not going to refuse any help.' She looked up at him, grateful for his support.

Just then his phone rang. Ross glanced down at it and wrinkled his nose. 'I have to take this.' He gave her a quick smile. 'But if all else fails, there's always baked beans on toast.'

She shook her head as he left. 'Spoken like a true man who has absolutely no idea what is involved in Christmas.'

Chapter Ten

'Izzy! Izzy! Izzy!' Xanthe's frantic squawks echoed down the stairs.

What now, wondered Izzy as she looked up from where she was blacking the big iron grate and ornate fire back, covering up tiny spots of rust. The fireplace was enormous but it needed to be to heat the hallway and huge stairwell. The poor thing didn't look as if it had had any attention for centuries and she wanted it to be an immediate welcoming feature when the Carter-Joneses arrived. She'd already planned to have Jim dressed in a kilt (he didn't know that yet) to welcome them with a tray of malt whiskies in front of a roaring log fire.

'Izzy!' Her mother's scream grew louder as she came closer. 'I've found something! I've found proof. The sapphires, they're real.' Xanthe suddenly came into view at the top of the first flight of stairs on the return, carrying a painting nearly the size of herself.

'Careful,' yelled Izzy, jumping to her feet, realising that a catastrophe was about to unfold at any moment. 'Slow down.'

Any moment her crazy mother could fall and break her blasted neck. Xanthe tottered on the top step and Izzy's heart nearly stopped. She raced up the stairs and in the nick of time managed to catch her mother before she over-balanced.

Xanthe, of course, was oblivious to the danger as she danced from foot to foot, vibrating with excitement. 'Look! Look what I found.'

'Mum!' Izzy snapped, her heart now pounding with adrenaline-based fear. 'For God's sake calm down.'

'But don't you see!' Xanthe's eyes were wide and bright, almost manic with delighted anticipation.

Izzy wanted to shake her, but instead she took the weight of the large gilt frame from her mother and set it down on the landing of the stairs. 'You nearly gave me a heart attack.'

'Don't be silly, darling. I was perfectly safe. But look what I've found.' She pointed at the front of the painting. Izzy shuffled the painting forward, astounded that her mother had managed to carry it this far, and pushed it up against the wall, turning it so that she could now see the picture.

'It's Isabella. And she's wearing them. The sapphires.' Xanthe jabbed a finger at the painting. A young woman was pictured seated at a dressing table, a Mona Lisa smile on her face, her neck adorned with a fabulous gold necklace with three rows of cabochon sapphires. The artist had managed to capture the depth of the blue and the glimmer of light bouncing off them.

Izzy had seen the painting before but hadn't registered the necklace or the smooth shapes of the sapphires.

'They're cabochons! You know, the lovely smooth oval shape,' said Xanthe. 'Of course they are. I was expecting them to be cut like modern stones but they're polished. Aren't they beautiful? And now we know they're real.'

'Yes, but this painting is pretty old. They could have been sold or passed on at any time.'

'They're here somewhere. I feel it in my bones.'

Izzy refrained from rolling her eyes. Xanthe's mystical, fortune-telling bones were contrary things that seemed to give out vibes only when it suited them.

'What do you want me to do?' asked Jeanette, drying her hands on a tea towel. Izzy had abandoned the fire grate to get cracking on the mince pies and despite her misgivings had commandeered the younger woman for kitchen duty today.

'Could you roll out the pastry – it's chilling in the fridge – and then start cutting out the rounds for the mince pies?' Izzy suggested as she zested the skin of an orange, inhaling the lovely citrus fragrance. The sprinkling of orange zest on top of the mincemeat in each pie along with a few drops of whisky was going to liven them up and give them an essential Scottish twist. She couldn't claim the credit for the idea though as it had been a tip from Fliss in the WhatsApp group.

When she glanced up a few minutes later, she found Jeanette making heavy weather of rolling the pastry on an unfloured surface. As a result, the pastry was in a sorry state, sticking both to the rolling pin and the surface.

'Sorry, I'm no very good in the kitchen,' Jeanette said, heavy-handedly peeling the pastry away from the counter and promptly leaving half of it stuck to the surface. As she did so, a large tear formed and the rest of the remaining intact pastry dropped onto the floor.

'Oops. Sorry.'

Izzy laughed, knowing everyone had to start somewhere. 'You should have seen me on the cookery course. Me and my friend, Hannah, were useless to start with. It's just practice.'

'I've never done this before. My mam always buys the pies down the supermarket.'

'Then you're in for a treat because these are going to be so much better. Come on, let me show you.'

An hour later the kitchen was filled with the scent of mixed spices and buttery pastry as two batches of mince pies cooled on the side.

'Mmm, looks like I'm just in time,' said Ross, zeroing in on them as he came into the kitchen. With a final glare at his phone he tucked it into his pocket. Izzy couldn't help noticing that he seemed to be getting a lot of phone calls lately.

'You only get one if you make us a cup of tea,' said Izzy, waving the rolling pin at him as she washed up.

'I can do that. I love a mince pie.'

'You're going to like these,' said Jeanette. 'They're dead fancy. Can I take one up to Jim? Or maybe two. I can't wait to tell him that I made mince pies!' She giggled. 'On the second attempt, at least.'

A second later, Xanthe popped in, her favourite feather boa trailing behind her like a plume of white smoke.

'Ooh, mince pies. I don't mind if I do. Your nan always used to make them, brings back so many memories.' She took one and disappeared again, leaving a trail of crumbs behind her.

As Jeanette left to find Jim, who was upstairs painting one of the bedrooms, Ross handed Izzy her mug.

'Another task to tick off your list?' he asked, taking a bite and groaning. 'Wow. These are amazing. So good.' He wrinkled his brow. 'Seriously good.'

Izzy preened a little, delighted with his response. To date her cooking had been fairly basic – everyone liked freshly baked bread, and soup wasn't exactly fancy – and she'd been dying to impress people with her new skills.

'Thank you. Secret ingredients.' But it was also that special ingredient of making food with love. She'd always associated mince pies with Christmas, more than another festive food, and she'd wanted this first Christmas in the castle to be perfect. She wanted the food to be extra special so that it would be memorable as this was the start of something that would live in her and her mother's memories for ever. Christmas had always been the two of them, they'd never missed being together for the holidays.

She sat with her tea and took a bite of one of the mince pies, closing her eyes to savour the hit of citrus, the mellow warmth of the whisky and the crisp, buttery pastry. She smiled, her heart lifting in her chest. Everyone was going to enjoy this Christmas; she was going to make sure of it.

'How's your work going?' she asked as they sat chatting. Ross had taken to coming down for a morning break and despite his earlier avowals that he didn't want to be tied down to a specific time for lunch, he joined Duncan, Jeanette, Jim and her at twelve thirty most days.

'Slow, and I'd get on a lot quicker if my editor didn't keep phoning me every five minutes. Unfortunately, I've to go to Edinburgh on business one day next week.'

'Will you be gone for long?'

'No, I'm planning to go there and back in a day. I'll leave very early and get back late but I don't want to waste any more time.'

'That's a long day,' mused Izzy. Thinking out loud rather than thinking it through, she found herself saying, 'I don't suppose I could scrounge a lift? I've some Christmas shopping to do as I need to buy gifts for the Carter-Joneses' stockings and for Xanthe, Jeanette, Jim and Duncan. If you're only going for the day, that would be perfect.'

Ross didn't say anything for a moment and as the seconds ticked by, Izzy realised she might have assumed too much.

He frowned. 'I still might decide to stay over for the night. My plans aren't finalised yet. And like I said, I'll be leaving very early.'

There was still a slight reserve about him as he took a long slug of coffee. Izzy watched his Adam's apple dip as he stared out of the window.

'Okay,' she said, a little hurt at his obvious reluctance. She had thought they were at the very least friends. 'Sorry I asked. It's obviously a bit of an imposition.' She turned her back on him, her face flaming with sudden embarrassment. Foisting yourself on someone else when they clearly didn't want you was something she'd done with Philip. As he'd candidly said when they'd had that final showdown, she 'was too much'. It had made her worry that she was too much like her mother even though she did her very best to be as likeable and easy-going as possible. It had become a habit to be the easy one when her mother could sometimes be the difficult one.

She turned her back on Ross and busied herself by grabbing a dustpan and brush to sweep up the dusting of flour on the floor. When she stood, Ross frowned and huffed out a long-suffering sigh.

'McBride, you're not an imposition,' he said, but the obvious guilt on his face said otherwise. Still mortified, she muttered something about how much work she had to do and fled.

Chapter Eleven

The cold morning air stung her cheeks and bit at her lungs, leaving her a little breathless as she strode out of the castle, her feet crunching on the gravel drive. As clouds of steam puffed from her mouth, she wrapped a scarf around her neck, tucking the ends into her coat to keep the cold out.

'McBride!'

She turned in surprise.

'Ross.' She greeted him with a forced smile. Thankfully she'd seen very little of him in the last couple of days, although she couldn't shake that sense of deflation she'd felt when he'd refused her a lift to Edinburgh.

'Where are you off to?'

'I'm going down to the village to get a few bits. I thought I'd grab some sausages for dinner; it feels like a sausage and mash sort of day.' And she'd make some nice red wine and onion gravy to go with it.

'Mind if I join you? I'm going to the library. I need a break.'

It would have been downright churlish to refuse but hadn't

he done that himself, just two days ago? He'd made it quite clear he didn't want her company. Well, not on a car journey at least. Was that because in the confines of a car there was no escape?

She silently shrugged, ignoring the quickening of her pulse and her wayward subconsciousness's declaration that he was more than welcome.

He matched her brisk pace stride for stride, but then, it wasn't the sort of morning for dawdling.

A pale, wintry sun glowed eerily through the wraith-grey sky, casting a flat light across the landscape. In the quiet air, their feet crunched across the frosted earth, the only other sound the harsh caw of a lone rook perched in a ragged, sprawling nest, one of many in a clump of ash trees.

Izzy took a deep breath and watched it billow out in front of her. She sighed and rolled her neck, not able to stay quiet and ignore him even though her first instinct was to leave any conversation to him.

'I needed this.'

'Me too.'

'What happened to the writing?'

He scrunched up his face. 'Procrastination. I've got to a sticky part and I'm dancing round it before I go in for the kill.'

'Sounds like you're writing a murder, rather than history.'

Ross almost missed a step but not quite and Izzy smiled to herself as he said, 'History is quite bloody, you know.'

She was now pretty sure he wasn't writing a history book like he'd claimed – he'd made too many near slips when talking about the content – but if he didn't want to tell her, she wasn't going to pry.

'Especially Scottish history,' added Izzy. 'Have you ever been to Culloden?'

'Aye. Eerie place. Haunted by the ghosts of dead clansmen,' said Ross, with a quick shudder. 'A sad end to the clans.'

Izzy nodded. She knew her Scottish history, knew that the Jacobite rebellion, which had ended with the Battle of Culloden in 1746, had wiped out the Highland way of life and that the hereditary rights of the clans to govern their own estates had been lost in the following years.

They skirted the still waters of the loch, following the path down to the village, which cut through a small valley dotted on either side with native trees. Larch, Caledonian pine, birch, ash and oaks had all been battered by the wind into wizened bends and twists rather than the tall, straight pines of the forestry plantations that dotted so much of the Scottish landscape. Izzy loved the wildness of the gnarled shapes and the bent trunks trying to escape the prevailing wind. Here she felt a sense of freedom as the breeze whipped and pulled at their coats, making the needle-clad firs shimmer with life and vitality. Their strength in the face of the storms of nature always renewed her batteries, reminding her that there was more to life than the day-to-day, man-made rhythms.

'It must be wonderful to live out here,' said Ross, as they tramped through the crisp russet bracken, their feet bouncing on the springy, wiry heather and bilberry plants, and their breaths coming in quick, visible pants.

She paused and looked at the loch glimmering like molten silver and then back at the castle standing above the body of water, guarding and protecting the scene. 'It is. Better than I expected. I thought it would be just me and Xanthe rattling around in a big, draughty old castle, feeling a bit out of place, but it feels like home already.'

'You're working miracles, that's for sure. How long have you worked for her? And what's your official title. Business manager? Housekeeper?'

Izzy stumbled and almost fell over, catching her foot in a rabbit hole.

'Steady,' he said, grasping her arm and pulling her upright.

'Xanthe's my…' she began but the words fizzled out when she looked up and saw the strangest expression on his face.

'Are you okay?' he asked, sombre and quiet, his eyes searching her face almost as if he were looking for the answer to a completely different question.

Her heart hitched and she nodded, unable to tear her eyes away from his.

'Yes,' she whispered. He was going to kiss her. She breathed in, anticipating the feel of his lips and waiting for him to close the gap, her heart hammering in her chest.

The disappointment when he turned away and started walking again almost floored her. She stared at his back. Had she made a complete fool of herself, imagining something that wasn't? A quick blush fired its way across her face. Taking a deep breath, she picked up her pace and caught up with him. They walked in silence for a few minutes and Izzy wondered what was going through his mind.

It was a relief when he finally said, 'What was it you said you needed in the village?'

'Sausages,' she said. 'And magazines.' She realised she sounded like an idiot and quickly added, 'I want some inspiration for Christmas recipes as I've got to cook four dinners, three lunches – and of course Christmas lunch – and they all need to be fancy. I'm slightly concerned by how demanding Mrs Carter-Jones is becoming. This morning she sent an email asking for confirmation that the towels will all be at least 600 gsm. I didn't even know what "gsm" was until today.' She was blathering now, anything to avoid not talking and things being uncomfortable.

By the time they arrived on the outskirts of the village, the conversation had thankfully levelled out again and Izzy was laughing at his description of some of his students.

'I'm going to be about twenty minutes in the library. Shall I meet you here to walk back?' asked Ross.

She stared at him. 'Er, sure. Yes.'

She frowned at his back as he walked off. She couldn't figure him out at all.

Hadn't she learned her lesson with Philip? Hankering after a man who wasn't interested was plain ridiculous and only led to heartache. Unfortunately, her heart didn't seem to have read the memo.

'Morning, Mrs McPherson,' said Izzy, handing over the magazines she'd selected.

Mrs McPherson looked at each one carefully before scanning them. 'Is that all you want?'

'Er, at the moment, yes.'

'I hear you've got guests coming. The boxer short man.'

How did she know that?

Izzy nodded.

'It's good to shop local. We've a nice line in jigsaws. Always good to do when it's dreich. You would nae want your guests to be bored.' Her beady eyes bored into Izzy expectantly and Izzy found herself inspecting the display of jigsaws crammed in one corner.

'That's a popular one with visitors,' said Mrs McPherson, materialising at Izzy's elbow and pointing to a kilted bagpipe player on a lonely hillside before handing it to her. 'And Edinburgh Castle is always a favourite.' Somehow Izzy found herself with two jigsaws tucked under one arm.

'And you'll be wanting local soap in the downstairs bathroom, I ken. Wild Nettle and Heather. Handmade, it is. And there's a hand cream too. Make nice stocking fillers. Do you want to take a couple?'

Izzy nodded, feeling as if she'd been hypnotised, and watched as Mrs McPherson put four soaps and four hand creams into a basket for her.

'There you go,' she said, handing the basket over. Thankfully the bell on the door of the post office dinged just then, offering reprieve. 'I'll leave you to browse. We've a nice line in Christmas cards. I'm sure you'll be wanting some of those.' The post mistress gave her a shark-like smile before scurrying off to greet her next victim.

Ross raised an eyebrow at her bulging shopping bag when he met her twenty minutes later. 'Would you like me to take that for you? I thought you only wanted a couple of things.'

'I've been McPhersoned.' Izzy shook her head. 'It's like she puts some sort of spell on you and you have to buy everything she suggests. I couldn't say no as I need to stay on the right side of her.'

'Yes, I get the feeling she's the unofficial linchpin of the village. You upset her, you upset the whole village.'

'I can't afford to do that as I'm hoping that she'll send more guests my way. Did you get what you wanted in the library?'

'Yes. What did she persuade you to buy?' He peered into one of the bags. 'Jigsaws?'

'Yes, apparently my guests are going to love them. I hadn't thought about entertainment. She also made me buy a couple of packs of playing cards and a cribbage set.'

'Made you?' teased Ross.

'Honestly, she's terrifying.' Izzy laughed, relieved that things seemed to be back to normal with him.

The walk home passed in easy conversation and when they turned into the castle drive she gave herself a metaphorical pat on the back. Thank goodness she hadn't let her imagination run away with her and leaned up to kiss him as she would have made a right fool of herself. They were friends, nothing more.

'Izzy.' Ross stopped walking and she turned to face him, puzzled by the sudden uncertainty in his voice. 'I ... I wondered if you still wanted a lift to Edinburgh.'

She blushed slightly, remembering their awkward conversation.

'Er, yes, if that's okay.'

'Of course, it's okay.' He gave her a quick smile. 'I'm sorry if I implied that I didn't want your company the other day, it was just...' His eyes softened as he looked at her. 'Well, I ... I wasn't thinking properly.'

'Well, if you really don't mind, it would be a big help.'

'Great. That's sorted then.' He reached out and touched her hand. 'I really am sorry if I upset you.'

'No, no, not at all,' Izzy said a little too brightly. He stepped towards her and she sucked in a quick breath as their eyes met. But suddenly the engine of a car interrupted and a taxi came past them, bumping its way down the single-track drive.

Izzy frowned and watched the car's red tail lights as they disappeared.

'Visitors? Guests?' asked Ross.

'I've no idea. I'm not expecting anyone.'

Chapter Twelve

There was a battered suitcase sitting in the hallway by the fireplace, along with a laptop bag and a rectangular, black, hard plastic case. Izzy huffed out a breath and hurried towards the sitting room where she could hear voices. Ross followed her, which suddenly seemed completely normal. After all, he was as much a part of the house now as anyone else.

'Izzy, darling. Come and meet Godfrey. You remember, the friend I mentioned.' Xanthe held out an arm with a flourish, indicating a middle-aged, earnest-looking man with rimless glasses that gave him an air of ruthless efficiency. He stroked a neat goatee beard while studying the painting of Isabella wearing the sapphire necklace.

'Godfrey's come to help us. He's an expert in Scottish history and is going to help us find the sapphires. He's a professional treasure hunter. He's going to be staying with us tonight and tomorrow night.'

Izzy pasted a fake smile on her face, shooting daggers with her eyes at her mother.

'Hello.'

As if pulled out of a deep reverie, which Izzy suspected was completely fake, he raised his head, turned and strode forward, the kilt he was wearing flaring around his knees. Coming to a stop in front of her, he clasped her hand between his dry, cold hands in a gesture of over familiarity that could have been interpreted as warm but instead came across as overly manufactured.

'Hello, my dear.' He cast a quick look towards Xanthe. 'The painting is most certainly authentic. I believe the painter is of the George Jamesone school, one of our most pre-eminent portrait painters of the seventeenth century. It could even be an original Jamesone, but I'd need to give it a more thorough examination to ascertain its true provenance.' He turned back to Izzy. 'Pleasure to meet you. This is quite some place you have here. You are a custodian of some fine history.'

His glance moved to Ross, who was standing behind her, and he stiffened, the corners of his mouth turning down in obvious disapproval.

'Ross Strathallan. I might have known I'd find ye here.'

'Godfrey, nice to see you too,' drawled Ross, with a less than amused tilt to his lips.

Godfrey turned to Xanthe. 'I wasn't aware that I'd be in competition with anyone. I usually work alone.'

'Oh, Mr Strathallan isn't here in an official capacity,' twittered Xanthe, patting Godfrey's arm. 'Oh no. He's renting a room to write. He won't disturb you.'

Godfrey pursed his lips, an expression of acute pain on his face.

'Don't you worry, Godfrey,' said Ross. 'I'll leave the treasure hunting to you. If you'll excuse me, I have work to do.' With surprising alacrity, he turned and left the room as if his shirt tails were on fire.

'Hmmph.' Godfrey shook his head. 'These academics. Always think they know better. I've been in this business for over forty years. They seem to think they have a divine right to knowledge. Clearly he hasn't found anything yet.'

'I'm not sure he's been looking,' said Izzy, giving her mother a pointed look. 'Not all of us are convinced the sapphires exist.'

'Oh I'm sure they do exist, my dear girl. There's been talk of them for many years but Bill McBride didn't want anyone here to look for them.' He lifted his chin and shook his shoulders, putting Izzy in mind of an outraged, bustling hen. 'History is the business of everyone, not just the academics.' This was said with a derisive, well-practised sniff, suggesting academics in general were a pet peeve. 'You know what they say about teachers: those that can, do and those that can't, teach.' He followed this little homily with a self-satisfied smile.

Izzy was going to kill her mother. Where on earth had she found this pompous little fart?

'Now, I'm in need of refreshment. May I procure some tea? And I don't suppose you've any biscuits. It's been a long journey from St. Andrews. And then I'll get myself settled. I trust that you've prepared a room for me.'

'Of course, Godfrey,' said Xanthe, rushing forward. 'I thought the blue room – one of our best – and I'm sure Izzy can let you use her little study while you're here.' She shot Izzy a warning glance. 'It's only for a few days.'

Izzy wheeled round and marched out of the room feeling

completely wrongfooted by her mother. Presumably Godfrey wouldn't be paying for his stay.

Her mother hurried after her. 'Izzy, be nice. We're not paying him and he's here as a special favour.'

'A special favour to whom?' asked Izzy in a low voice, fizzing with pent-up frustration as she stopped by Godfrey's luggage in the hall.

'Me, of course.' Xanthe patted her hair and simpered. 'Don't be so difficult. He's not going to be any trouble and when he finds the sapphires, we'll be rich and then you'll change your tune.'

'Yes, Xanthe,' said Izzy. 'In the meantime, I've dinner to cook, so you can sort his lordship's *refreshments* out.'

'That's a very fine Claymore you have on the wall there.' Izzy jumped and turned to find Godfrey behind her.

'Yes,' she said. 'Excuse me, I need to—'

'It's an excellent example of sixteenth-century craftsmanship. Solingen steel from Germany, if I'm not mistaken. They were the greatest swordsmiths in Europe, you know. I'd hazard a guess it's at least one metre, thirty. A very fine example. You ought to think about bequeathing this to a museum for the enjoyment of the whole Scottish nation.'

Izzy shot him a tight smile. 'My great uncle was quite precise in his final wishes, and he was very specific in his instructions that the Claymore should not pass out of the family.' The solicitor had been at great pains to emphasise this. In fact, rather surprisingly, the stipulation about the huge sword was the only one that her great uncle had made.

'Hmph,' said Godfrey, his mouth crumpling like a small prune in obvious displeasure. 'It's a national treasure. It ought to be restored to the nation. I'd like to take a better look at it some time.'

'Mmm,' said Izzy, evasively. 'If you'll excuse me, I have work to do.' With that she hurried down to the kitchen, praying that he wouldn't follow her, although she was reasonably confident in her assessment that despite his proclaimed 'for the people' tendencies, he was unlikely to step into what some might consider the servants' quarters. Having him around was going to be a laugh a minute ... not.

'Who's the pompous windbag?' Jeanette asked, marching into the kitchen and dropping her cleaning box. Her small wiry frame was encased in a baggy sweatshirt covered in dust and leggings striped with cobwebs.

'And what's he doing in the blue room?' Jim asked as he followed her in, with Ross and Duncan bringing up the rear.

'He's a friend of Xanthe's and he's not staying long.'

'Good,' said Ross. 'The man's an idiot.'

Izzy laughed. 'He didn't seem to like you too much either.'

'He's one step down from a conspiracy theorist. Thinks all historic artefacts should belong to the people and that everyone has a right to go digging them up wherever they like. He and a couple of his friends completely wrecked an archaeological site by randomly digging all over the place with their metal detectors in the middle of the night. He calls himself a "historian of the people" and is into every legend and half-truth going whether or not there's evidence to back things up. Like I said, the man's a complete idiot. He wouldn't know an antique from something found at TK Maxx.'

'Well, he's very rude,' said Jeanette, brushing a cobweb from her leggings.

'Let's hope he tires quickly of the wild goose chase and… Where've you been anyway?' Izzy couldn't help blurting as she eyed Jeanette's dirty clothes.

'I made a start on one of the attic rooms. I thought maybe' – Jim stepped closer to her as though showing his allegiance – 'me and Jim could move up there when the guests come. There's a bedroom and a sitting room with a fireplace and a bathroom. If you wouldn't mind us decorating it a bit, we could make our own little staff suite.'

Izzy was amused and touched at the same time. 'That's very thoughtful of you. You and Jim planning on staying then?'

'Aye,' said Jeanette, adding with a sudden cheeky grin, 'You need us and I'm sure you had no plans to put us up in one of the guest rooms for ever, did you? Of course, that's if you'll have us?'

'I'd love you to stay but I don't want you to feel you've been thrown out of the room you're in. Although I was considering moving to a different room myself.'

'Don't you dare, Izzy McBride,' said Duncan. 'This is your home now. You've every right to stay in a nice room. Xanthe won't be moving, will she?'

Ross folded his arms and leaned against the edge of the table. 'He's right, you know.'

'We'll see,' said Izzy, a little overwhelmed by their support.

'You must.' Jeanette put her hands on her hips and gave her what was likely supposed to be a threatening glare. She thrust her chin forward. 'You're one of the kindest people I've met.

You do everything for everyone else. You do all the work and so you should be able to enjoy living here.'

Touched, Izzy leaned forward and gave Jeanette a quick hug. 'That's very sweet of you but I'm perfectly happy. And if I have to move rooms it's not the end of the world.'

'Hmmph.' Jeanette sniffed but gave her a hug back. 'You really are the best. Thanks so much for letting us stay here.'

'You're working.'

'Yeah, but not as hard as you,' said Jim.

'You're working yourself to a wee frazzle,' butted in Duncan.

'Do you think we'll get everything done in time for Christmas?' asked Jeanette.

Izzy swallowed. 'I certainly hope so.' It wasn't so much being ready in time for the arrival of the Christmas party group, but more how she was going to make sure they were well looked after while they were here, and living up to their no doubt high expectations.

'I was wondering about uniforms,' said Jeanette.

'What?'

'Me and Jim. We could dress up while they're here. I was thinking I could wear a sash and Jim could wear a kilt – there are some tartans up in the attic – and we can help with serving the food and what not.'

Izzy laughed. 'You've got it all figured out. But I don't expect you to do that. Don't you want to go home to your family at Christmas?'

Jeanette put her hands on her hips again. 'Yeah, right. I don't think so.'

'Shouldn't you let your mother know where you are?' Izzy had asked this question before, hoping that Jeanette might get in touch with her mother and start to heal the rift between them.

'She knows I'm safe.' Jeanette's mouth firmed into a mulish line. 'And that I'm with Jim. So we're staying for Christmas and we'll pitch in.'

'You don't have to do that. It's not as if I'm paying you very much.' Although once she'd had the Carter-Joneses' money and paid for everything, she planned to give them a bonus.

'We've been talking upstairs, all of us, and as we'll all be here we're going to help, so that's the end of it. I'll no have any argument from you about it. And Ross and Duncan are both going to dust their kilts off too.'

'Aye, lass,' agreed Duncan, nodding his head. 'And Ross says he's going to be wine waiter extraordinaire.'

Ross raised an imaginary glass and nodded.

For most of her life, Izzy had done the looking after and supporting and though a big part of her was proud of her independence and capability, sometimes it felt lonely and the responsibility wearing. Always being in charge had become the default setting for so long. It would be so lovely to share some of the load for a change. She couldn't find the words for a moment, instead she stared down at the table, tears shimmering in her eyes.

'That's very kind of you. All of you,' she finally squeaked out.

'Away with you, you big Jessie,' said Jeanette, putting her arms around her. 'You'll set me off. Literally I don't know what Jim and I would ha' done without you giving us a roof over our heads. And you've never made us feel beholden or that we're employees. You've always been so nice.'

Izzy sniffed.

'So we want to do something nice for you.'

'Thank you.' It was all Izzy could say.

'Why don't I put the kettle on? And perhaps we could heat up a couple of those mince pies from the freezer?' Ross looked hopeful, a bit too much like a friendly Labrador who was trying to convince everyone he hadn't been fed for a week.

'Away with you,' said Izzy, shaking her head. 'At this rate there won't be any left for Christmas.'

Izzy rose to retrieve a batch of mince pies. She ought to be paying him as well.

With everyone's help, Izzy was beginning to think she might just pull Christmas off.

Chapter Thirteen

'What time will dinner be served, this evening?' asked Xanthe, sweeping into the kitchen in a floor length, dusky-pink velvet cape. 'I think as it's Godfrey's last night we should eat in the dining room and make a night of it.'

'How about seven?' suggested Izzy.

'Perfect, I'll lay the dining room table, make it look nice.' Xanthe glanced round the kitchen where Jim, Jeanette, Duncan and Ross were assembled, having their usual morning coffee break. 'I expect you all to dress for dinner.'

With that, she departed, her cape flapping behind in a flurry of velvet folds.

'Seriously?' said Jeanette. 'He's a right old windbag. Always under my feet and asking stupid questions. Banging and tapping, determined to find those sapphires.'

'Bluidy fool,' said Duncan. 'Doesn't know his arse from his elbow, that fella. He came sniffing round before and Bill sent him packing. Bill always said they were in plain sight and would be found by the sharp-eyed.'

'You didn't say that before. You said they didn't exist,' said Izzy, sharply turning to look at Duncan.

He assumed an innocent expression. 'Didn't I?' He shut his mouth with clam-like implacability. Did he know something?

'Well, me and Jeanette work here,' said Jim, 'so we'll go to the pub. Save you cooking for extra mouths.'

'Don't even try that one,' said Izzy. 'If I have to suffer, I think you should too.'

'I don't see why I should,' said Ross. 'I'm a guest here.'

'All the more reason,' said Izzy. 'You should be getting the guest treatment. Dinner in the dining room. Please, Ross.' She gave him a beseeching smile. 'As soon as you've had dinner, you can skedaddle. And it will be a nice dinner.'

'Will it now?' asked Ross, narrowing his eyes with suspicion. 'And what makes you think I'm the sort of man that responds to bribes?'

Izzy frantically thought of what there was in the freezer and what she might get from the farm shop.

'Venison,' she said, 'with roast potatoes, crispy kale and mixed greens.'

He gave her an assessing look. 'I do like a nice piece of venison. You're on, but don't blame me if we come to blows over his ridiculous views. If he starts to suggest you sign the castle over to the nation, ignore him.'

After trawling through some of the Scottish recipe books in the kitchen, Izzy had pulled together a menu and made a hasty visit to the farm shop. As she brought in the first course in a big ironstone soup tureen, complete with matching ladle, which Xanthe had unearthed in the wooden sideboard in the dining room and insisted they use, Izzy had to admit it did look rather wonderful, especially with the matching Victorian crockery.

With its new paint, polished wooden panels and the carefully laid table, the room looked absolutely stunning and it made Izzy feel a lot better about the amount of money they were going to be charging their Christmas guests. Everything looked very stylish with a touch of authenticity thanks to all the original silverware, china and glasses that Jeanette had painstakingly cleaned and polished under Xanthe's supervision.

'What do we have here?' asked Godfrey.

'It's a partan bree,' said Izzy with a breezy air, as if she'd been making the dish all her life. Thanks to Adrienne's training at the cookery school making the fish stock for the crab bisque had been quite simple and she was extremely chuffed with the results.

'Ah, excellent,' said Godfrey, rubbing his hands together as if he were bestowing some great compliment on her.

Next, she served up the pale orange soup dressed with slivers of pickled fennel, which tasted deliciously tart against the creaminess of the soup, and for once she was pleased with her presentation, never her strong point. The little touch looked impressive and was surprisingly easy to make. Thank you, Jason, for that little tip. She hoped that he and Fliss would have their phones switched on over Christmas.

'Oh this is delicious, Izzy. I take it all back. It was worth going on that cookery course.' Xanthe tapped her soup bowl with her spoon in approval.

Izzy rolled her eyes. She'd been doing most of the cooking

since she'd been about fourteen as Xanthe had a habit of losing interest in the process and wandering away from the kitchen, which inevitably led to the smoke alarm being set off and another pan being destroyed.

'I'd love to take a look at the Claymore,' said Godfrey, as he slurped his soup. Of course, he slurped; he was that kind of man – irritating in the extreme. Izzy heartily wished her mother hadn't invited him to stay.

Izzy wasn't sure she wanted it in Godfrey's hands but before she could say anything, Xanthe piped up. 'Of course you can. It's so good of you to come all this way and help us look for the sapphires. I'm sorry it's been a fruitless task.' Godfrey had spent the whole day searching the castle, tapping at walls, examining shelves and panelling and peering up chimneys, all to no avail, which Izzy was secretly pleased about.

'Ah, it takes persistence, fair lady. Always the way with these family treasures. Of course, they'll be well hidden out of sight in a place only the family knew, so it was always going to be difficult. I'd like to come back again, bring another expert with me.'

I bet you would, thought Izzy a touch resentfully, and who would be footing the bill for that? In fact, it was embarrassing that Godfrey was staying for free given how much Ross was paying.

'That would be lovely,' said Xanthe.

Izzy rose, the serene smile on her face hiding her inner irritation. 'Let me help,' said Jeanette, who immediately began gathering plates and cutlery with a practised hand. Leaving her to it, Izzy took the soup tureen out and went to check on the main course in the kitchen. She'd left the venison steaks to rest and they were oozing meat juices nicely and the roast potatoes looked wonderfully golden, with crisp skins. The kale glistened with olive oil, salt and the tiny bit of sugar that she'd sprinkled over. The carrots, cooked in butter and star anise, smelled wonderfully aromatic. Quickly transferring the meat juices to a pan, which already contained meat stock, fried shallots, port, red wine and a bay leaf, she set it to boil to reduce the liquid, while she plated up the meat and vegetables. Right on cue, Jeanette appeared.

'Is it me or is that man a complete lavvy heid?'

Izzy laughed. 'He's full of crap, that's for sure.'

The main course went down extremely well and Izzy was rather thrilled with all the compliments that came her way. Maybe she could do this after all.

After she'd served the loganberry and apple pie – a cheat from the farm shop because she hadn't had time to think about a dessert let alone make one – she nipped off to the loo before going to face the devastation in the kitchen and make coffee. It was going to take her a while to tidy up but when she went back to the kitchen, she found Jeanette had brought through the plates, Ross had tidied up the pans and utensils she'd used and was stacking the dishwasher, while Jim was wiping down the surfaces and cleaning the cooker and had already made a big cafetière of coffee.

'Wow,' she said, coming to a halt and looking around the kitchen. 'Thank you. You really didn't—'

'Teamwork,' said Ross. 'It's much easier if we all pitch in.'

'But you're supposed to be a guest,' Izzy said for the umpteenth time, with a slight wail of panic in her voice.

He shrugged. 'I'd be bored sitting around. Besides, there's only so much of that windbag I can take.'

'And we work here, remember?' said Jim.

'Yes, but I'm hardly paying you.' Izzy's stomach cramped in guilt. They were both so lovely and willing. Nothing was ever too much trouble.

'Board and lodgings is enough.'

Izzy shook her head, suddenly overcome. Her throat closed up and she couldn't say anything so she just stood there, tears glistening in her eyes.

'Hey,' said Ross, sliding an arm around her shoulder.

'Sorry.' She sniffed. 'You're all so kind.'

'We're a team,' said Jeanette, coming up and putting an arm through hers.

'Group hug,' said Jim, bundling in and encircling them all with his long, gangly arms. He was like a puppy with a lot of growing to do.

Izzy sniffed again. 'I'm not sure what I'd do without you.'

'Well, you don't have to worry because we're all here and we're not going anywhere,' Jim said.

'Don't you worry, Izzy,' said Jeanette. 'This is going to be one heck of a Christmas. The Carter-Joneses won't know what's hit them.'

She served the coffee in the hall by the fire that Jim had lit earlier, the logs spitting slightly and the flames licking around glowing embers. Izzy had hoped that Godfrey had forgotten he wanted to examine the Claymore, but she was to be disappointed.

'Now that...' Godfrey stopped dead in front of the fire and threw an arm up towards the sword hanging on the wall. 'It's magnificent but it really should be in a museum. May I take a look?' Despite the question he was already moving forwards.

Ross, who'd been loitering by the stairs as if he were heading up at any moment, stopped and turned back.

'It's just an old sword,' said Xanthe. 'I don't know what all the fuss is about. It's not even very shiny.'

Godfrey went to the wall but wasn't quite tall enough to reach the sword, which, for some petty reason she wasn't that proud of, pleased Izzy no end.

Ross stepped forward as if to help.

'No,' snapped the other man. 'I can manage.' He overturned the coal scuttle beside the fireplace, scattering crumbs of black coaldust everywhere, and climbed on top of it. With one hand, which even Izzy knew was foolish – a Claymore was a two-handed sword – he grasped the hilt and lifted upwards, away from the two sturdy hooks that held it in place. For a moment, as the full weight settled into his hand, he staggered back, swaying about in a situation comedy moment that had everyone stepping back out of range.

'Whoa!' cried Duncan who was the closest and was a hair's breadth from having his ear removed.

Godfrey managed to grasp the sword with his other hand and stood there, rocking on the spot for a moment before he regained his equilibrium.

'Ah,' he said with a long exhale, his eyes glazed with wonder. 'So well balanced. This would have been a very expensive sword. Solingen steel from Germany, if I'm not mistaken. They were the greatest swordsmiths in Europe, you know.'

'So you said before,' drawled Ross.

Godfrey glared at him and swished the sword experimentally, almost falling over with the weight of it.

'Steady,' said Ross, as Godfrey's arms gave way and the tip of the sword thunked to the floor, the metal ringing out against the stone. He reeled on the spot, his arms dead straight, clutching the hilt of the sword, reminiscent of a small boy trying out his dad's wellies for size.

With a shake of his head, Ross strode over and removed the sword from Godfrey's hands, lifting it with apparent ease, although Izzy saw the way the muscles in his arms bunched. She'd got used to his size and bulk but this was a reminder that Ross wouldn't have looked the least bit out of place on a battlefield, his kilt flaring around him, hefting that very sword. Izzy wanted to cheer as much for his casual display of masculine strength, which set her hormones buzzing in the most unseemly fashion, as for the matter-of-fact way he picked the sword up without a speck of drama, flair or showmanship. He put it down on the long oak table by the wall.

Godfrey glared at him with an audible sniff and stalked over to the table.

'As I was saying,' he sneered, 'It's an excellent example of seventeenth-century craftmanship. A blade forged hundreds of years ago and as sharp as the day it left the blacksmith.'

'I doubt it,' said Ross. 'Judging from the nicks in the blade. It's been well used and it doesn't look as if it's been sharpened for a while. Although it could still do some damage.'

Godfrey ignored him and turned to Xanthe who was pretending to be spellbound. History bored the pants off her, as Izzy well knew. 'It's so fascinating to hear an expert's opinion on it,' she gushed.

'Yes. This Claymore would have been used to protect the castle from all sorts of invaders, such as the Sassenachs.'

'I doubt that,' said Ross. 'The laird and Lady Isabella were loyal to George II as Lady Isabella's brother, Richard, was married to one of the king's favourite envoys' daughter.'

'That's hearsay,' blustered Godfrey. 'And the family probably promulgated that story in later years to stay on side with the English government.'

'Promulgated,' whispered Jeanette to Izzy. 'What does that even mean?'

Ross's mouth firmed. 'According to the family bible, the family tree is quite clear and the parish register at St John's Kirk in Perth clearly records the wedding of Sir Richard to Lady Henrietta, daughter of Edmund Poley, envoy to Hanover.'

'I've not heard that,' dismissed Godfrey.

'Just because you're not aware of it doesn't mean it's not true. It's historical fact backed up with evidence from a primary source.'

Xanthe shot Ross a look of dislike and Godfrey allowed himself a small smirk and patted her on the hand.

'See here? The long handle and the unusual decorative pattern on the hilt are typical of the region.'

Ross leaned forward and frowned at the rows of crude lumps on the hilt. 'They're not typical,' he said, looking genuinely puzzled. 'I've never seen anything like them before.'

Godfrey tutted. 'What was it you were saying? Just because you've not seen something before doesn't mean it doesn't exist.' He turned to Xanthe with an oily smile. 'These have been added to aid the grip on the hilt. It was quite common in battle, when blades were slicked with blood, that a sword might slip out of a warrior's hands, so they customised their grip, rather like tennis or squash players put towelling grips on their racquets these days.'

Izzy heard Ross cough, with a distinct 'bollocks' contained within the cough.

Xanthe tucked a hand through Godfrey's arm. 'Would you like to come through to the drawing room and you can tell me all about it? Bill left a fine selection of malt whiskies and I'm sure you'd love to try one.' She drew him away, shooting Izzy and Ross an admonishing glare as she left.

'Pompous arse,' said Ross as soon as they were out of earshot.

Izzy began to giggle. 'I thought he was going to fall flat on his back when he first picked it up.'

'I thought he was going to take my heid off,' said Duncan.

'It was close,' agreed Jim.

'Silly sod had obviously never held a Claymore in his life. They weigh a ton and were designed to be held two-handed. God, he talks some nonsense. I've never heard such rubbish. A Claymore like this would have a plain leather grip.' He indicated the hilt. 'I'm not sure what's going on with this but it's a much later addition and whoever did it wants shooting. They've potentially devalued a fine piece. No wonder your uncle didn't want it leaving the family.'

He picked the sword up and returned it to its rightful place above the fire. 'Still, you could probably frighten off a potential burglar with it.'

'I'll bear that in mind,' Izzy said with a grave smile.

'I must go and do some work. Thanks for dinner.'

'Thanks for the help.'

'Night, Izzy.'

She watched him climb the stairs, stopping halfway up to stare at the Claymore with a puzzled frown. He saw her studying him and raised a hand in farewell before disappearing from view.

Izzy sighed, her heart fluttering a little too much. The more time she spent with him, the more she liked him. He was a steadying ballast in a choppy sea. Calm, sensible and solid … while they didn't sound like terribly attractive characteristics, after a lifetime of living with Xanthe's mercurial barometer they were a welcome relief. But then she was again reminded of that hot thrust of physical attraction, which was bad news. After all, she knew better than most that physical attraction didn't always end well.

Chapter Fourteen

Izzy's feet crunched through the heavy frost to where Ross's smart green Range Rover was parked, the engine running with exhaust fumes billowing out in the cold, early morning air. Behind her the castle was dark and silent beyond a solitary light beside the front door. Six thirty was far too early to be up but it would give them a whole day in Edinburgh before the drive back this evening.

'Morning,' she whispered, conscious that the rest of the house was probably still sleeping. 'I've brought you a coffee.'

'You angel. Are you all set?'

She ignored the quick buzz that the word 'angel' gave her. He was being complimentary; it didn't mean anything.

'Yes.'

'Hop in then. It should be nice and warm.'

It was and she sighed as she nestled her bottom into the heated leather seat. This was a very swish car, in fact it might be the poshest one she'd ever been in. Who knew they paid history professors so well?

The drive took them down into the valley through Kinlochleven, which was just stirring, lights appearing in windows here and there. Then they were pitched into blackness again as the car headlights sent their light sweeping through the night, occasionally catching glowing, yellow eyes of some rabbit or vole scurrying away to safety. Izzy leaned back into the seat, warm and content. It was a very comfortable car and it was nice to let her brain switch off for a while. She let out a small sigh.

'This was a good idea,' she said, feeling the tension draining from her shoulders.

'Good,' said Ross. 'Without being rude, you look like you need a rest. Why don't you have a bit of sleep? Then I could look after you for a change?' He brushed his knuckles across her cheek in the most unexpected gesture. 'Give yourself a break, you've taken on quite a lot, recently.'

She nodded, feeling a little punch drunk. She had been doing everything in the castle and this was the first proper time away she'd had in ages. She realised he was looking at her intently and she felt her breath catch in her throat at the concern she could read in his eyes.

'Thank you,' she said, her voice soft with unexpected emotion. It was a long time since someone else had worried about *her*.

———

'There's going to be a glorious sunrise,' she observed when they crested the top of a hill two hours later. The sky spread out before them, glowing pink with shades of peach, indigo and cobalt dispersed across the horizon, promising a whole new day.

'Shall we stop for a moment? There's a parking place up ahead and I could do with some of that coffee you promised.'

They pulled in at a layby on the edge of Lochan Lairig Cheile and both got out of the car. Without saying anything, as if equally drawn to the water, they walked through the sparse pine trees to stand by the loch. Izzy took in a deep breath, feeling the cold air filling her lungs as she looked up at the craggy hills surrounding them and the wisps of mist that danced above the pine trees packed in together along the water's edge. Izzy poured them each a strong dark coffee. 'There's milk in the cool bag, if you'd like some.' She indicated the small bag at her feet.

'You are organised. Have you a packet of sandwiches wrapped in greaseproof paper like my granny always used to make?'

She tapped him with her hand. 'You cheeky wee beggar. No sandwiches but you can have an apple if you're good. I've done this drive a few times now so I know there's no handy Starbucks or Costa. But it is beautiful. I can never decide which is my favourite bit.' She smiled and sighed, looking at the range of hills in the distance silhouetted in purple and greys against the skyline. 'Every time I do this drive, my heart sings at the beauty of the scenery. The landscape is so much bigger than us and it's endured so much more than we can imagine. It was here before we were and will be long after we've gone. It puts all our puny problems into perspective, don't you think? It never fails to fill me with awe.'

He turned, a slow smile spreading across his face. 'That's

exactly how I feel. I'm not sure I can go back and live in the city again.'

They shared a smile, the sort of smile when two people are completely in accord, and Izzy felt her heart quicken. She took a quick sip of coffee, deliberately breaking their gaze to scan the waves rippling in the light wind.

'Only an hour to Edinburgh. What time does your meeting start?'

'I've to be there at ten.' His eyes assessed her in that careful way of his, as if he knew or suspected what was going on in her head, but he followed her lead with the deliberate change of subject. 'According to the sat nav, there's been an accident on the M9, so we'll take a diversion over the Kincardine Bridge, which will take us via Dunfermline. Not ideal, but I've left plenty of time.'

As they crossed the Forth Road Bridge, the familiar sight of the dull red painted trusses of the Forth Bridge came into view. It wasn't the prettiest bridge but it was a testament to the ingenuity and engineering of a bygone age that had created a beautiful city and it always signalled coming home to Izzy whenever she'd been further north.

'Where do you live in Edinburgh?'

'Morningside,' said Ross, glancing at his watch.

'I love Morningside. All the lovely terraced houses. My friends live on Braid Hill and have a beautiful place. There are some great cafés there.'

'Mmm.'

She glanced at Ross's profile. He seemed focused, his gaze

fixed on the road, his movements clipped and precise; even the way he flipped the indicator control seemed to be sharp and snappy.

'Does it take you long to get into the city in the mornings?' she asked.

'Not too bad.' He shrugged.

'How long does it take?'

'Twenty to fifty minutes. Depends on traffic.' This time his words were definitely brusque. It was like pulling teeth. Why had he suddenly become so uncommunicative?

'Big meeting today?' she asked with a touch of sympathy. Maybe he was stressed about it now they were nearly there.

'What?' He sounded preoccupied.

'The faculty meeting you're going to.'

'Erm … yes. Sort of.'

'I'm sure it will be fine,' said Izzy, trying to be reassuring.

'I'm sure it will.' He gave her a vacant smile but he was clearly miles away.

Izzy decided not to bother him with inane chatter but he was the one to ask the next question.

'Where shall I drop you off?'

'Are you parking at the university?'

'Mmm.'

'Which part? I don't mind walking from there. I've got all day.'

Ross turned to her. 'I was planning to park in St James Quarter. There's a multi-storey there.'

'Great, although isn't it away from the university buildings?'

'It's an away day. We're meeting away from the faculty offices.'

She frowned, sure that he was being evasive. Why was he being so secretive? Unless … could he be meeting a married lover or something like that? If he were having a clandestine meeting, that might explain it, although from what she'd seen of Ross, he didn't seem the type. But then what did she know about how men thought? She'd got it so painfully wrong with Philip.

'That suits me.'

'Are you sure? I don't mind dropping you off somewhere.'

'That's pretty central to the main shops.'

'Okay, if you're sure. I don't mind driving you somewhere else. Did you want to go to the Old Town?'

Izzy had an insane desire to laugh and was tempted to ask him to drop her on the Royal Mile. She knew, like everyone in Edinburgh, that the Royal Mile would be crowded with tourists spilling onto the road and coaches gravitating to Holyrood Palace, causing the traffic to back up behind them.

'I'll come with you to the car park. As I said, that suits me perfectly. Thanks to Jeanette, I've got a list of who's coming for Christmas, so I can put together stockings, and I thought some touristy gifts would be cute. I also thought I'd get everyone some genuine Scottish fudge and some shortbread. And a fridge magnet from one of the wee tourist shops.'

'Good call.'

'And maybe a miniature whisky and some tinned haggis.'

'Where are these people from?'

'Mr Carter-Jones is from the Midlands and his wife is from Canada but she apparently has Scottish ancestors from way back who left Scotland in 1747, not long after the Jacobite uprising.'

'Hence her wanting to revisit her roots.'

'Exactly. I'm slightly nervous about her expectations, although Jeanette said she was lovely in her email.' Although how you could tell what someone was like from an email, Izzy had no idea.

Mrs Carter-Jones had given an additional budget for the stockings of £50 per person and a brief description of everyone. Mr Carter-Jones and his brother-in-law were both keen golfers, both sons were whisky fans, the daughter into beauty, the niece was a bookworm, and Mrs Carter-Jones and her sister were keen cooks.

Izzy rubbed her hands together. It had been a while since she'd been properly shopping and she was looking forward to the day. She just hoped she had enough time to fit everything in and that her arms were long and strong enough to carry all the bags.

'I can almost hear your brain whirring,' said Ross. It was the first time he'd spoken voluntarily for a few minutes. Izzy couldn't decide whether she was being paranoid or not but there seemed to be an odd tension in the car, like a coil that had been wound tighter and tighter.

'Is everything all right?' she burst out, finally succumbing to her anxiety and hating the feeling of impotence that came with giving in to the temptation to ask him about the tension.

His jaw tensed and he didn't turn her way.

'It's fine,' he said with an enunciated snap that clearly meant it was anything but.

'Fine?' she echoed, deciding they were so close to the car park now that she had nothing to lose. 'When people say "fine", they usually mean the opposite.'

'Well, I don't,' he said, in the sort of terse tone that would normally shut a conversation down. But Izzy was made of sterner stuff.

'So I'm imagining the heavy frost that seems to have taken up residence in the car?'

'You are,' said Ross.

Well, that told her. It felt like the sort of argument she'd had with Philip when he'd been blowing hot and cold. He could be her best friend in front of everyone, making her feel like the centre of his world, and then in the blink of an eye he could grow distant. Izzy gritted her teeth and turned to stare out of the passenger window. Ross could suit himself. She wasn't going to let it bother her, although it did. She'd begun to think of him as a friend – and, stupidly, perhaps a bit more – but clearly away from the castle he didn't want to know her.

When he pulled up outside the entrance of the car park and offered to let her out there rather than stay until he'd parked the car, she immediately agreed.

'I'll meet you back here at seven this evening.'

'Great,' said Izzy in a clipped voice, adding a forced smile.

For a moment she thought she saw regret shimmer in his eyes but then it disappeared, leaving her thinking that perhaps she'd imagined it. This was the cool, distant, self-possessed Ross Strathallan she'd first met in the castle and she'd do well to remember it. Why did she get the impression he was trying to get rid of her?

'See you later,' she said and with a jauntiness she was far from feeling, she waved and turned to stride away as quickly as she could. Bugger Ross bloody Strathallan. She'd had enough of vacillating men to last her a lifetime. She was not treading that treacherous path again.

Having been cooped in the car for three hours, she decided

to walk for a while and set out across town to the old part, ignoring the lure of the Christmas market on Princes Street. She'd come back to that later.

Her first port of call was Fabhatrix, a gorgeous hat shop on Grassmarket. They sold the most wonderful selection of stylish hats and quirky fascinators and she was confident she'd find exactly the right thing there for Xanthe.

From there she walked up the steep, cobbled hill of Candlemakers Row, stopping in many shops to browse and pick up the odd gift. Everyone seemed full of Christmas spirit as they weaved along the crowded pavements and Izzy smiled, relishing the wonderful atmosphere and the displays in the windows. Lights twinkled, tinsel sparkled and the strains of festive songs floated out of shop doorways. At the top of the street she crossed to the churchyard to say a quick hello to the statue of Greyfriars Bobby, the legendary dog buried there, before grabbing herself a takeaway coffee.

Stopping on the bridge and looking down at Cowgate, she paused to reflect on the ancient buildings, the tenements rubbing shoulders with the grander architecture. There was nowhere quite like Edinburgh but her home was the castle now and for the first time in a long time she felt truly settled. She'd found her place in the world. While she loved the bustle, creativity and history that the city was steeped in, she didn't need to live here anymore. She'd moved on and now that she had a place to call home, she could view the city with fondness rather than the lovelorn hope that she'd so long associated with it.

She smiled, feeling refreshed and renewed. She had moved on and made a new life for herself, and it felt good to cast off the final ties that had held her to Philip for so long. With a definite skip in her step, she doubled back, down into the touristy shops of the Royal Mile and Canongate, stopping in the aptly named Thistle Do Nicely to buy a few stocking fillers including a couple of fridge magnets, a few miniature bottles of whisky, some Aran Aromatics soaps and several small jars of heather honey. With her bag already feeling heavy she treated herself to a reviving cuppa and a fruit scone with jam and cream in Clarinda's Tearoom. The quiet charm of the café with its mismatched vintage tea cups and saucers felt like an oasis after the rugby scrum outside and she studied the walls crammed with knick-knacks, embroidered pictures, blue and white Lochs of Scotland plates and shelves of tiny thimbles before girding her loins for round two.

Revived by the sugar hit, she felt ready for the gaudy, busy spectacle of the Christmas market on Princes Street and the enchanting little wooden huts sparkling with fairy lights and thronged with people wrapped up in cosy hats and long scarves against the chill in the air.

As she browsed the stalls, looking at hand-made jewellery, paintings, pretty bookmarks and pottery, she caught the scent of mulled wine here and hot mince pies there, while candles on the stalls perfumed the air with pine and cranberry.

With so many beautiful crafts on display, she was spoiled for choice and bought Jeanette a pretty dish to keep her jewellery in, a jazzy pair of earrings for Xanthe and bookmarks for all the stockings. She also bought a couple of lacy linen handkerchiefs for the ladies and a couple of jars of whisky marmalade from a local company in Leith.

Deciding she was ready for a bite she decided to head for the slightly quieter George Street area beyond the main drag of Princes Street. After a quick lunch of a cheese toastie in one of the many cafés there, she popped into Jenners, the big department store, to make her annual pilgrimage to buy Xanthe's Christmas decoration and spent some time dithering between a little felt mouse playing the bagpipes and a fat, jolly Santa with a cloud of white fuzzy cotton for his beard.

By now her arms were beginning to ache with all the shopping bags but she'd had a successful day. All she needed were a few more bits for the stockings, in particular for the bookworm niece of Mrs Carter-Jones.

Waterstones on Princes Street was a good-sized bookshop and she knew they sold lots of book-related gift items. As she entered the teeming store, she noticed a queue of people stretching around the racks of books. Must be a book signing. More out of curiosity than any great interest Izzy sought out the poster with the details of the author and found that Ross Adair was signing copies of his new hardback book today. She peered through the crowds to catch a glimpse of the man himself. Much as she loved his books, buying a hardback was a bit out of her price range at the moment.

Craning her neck to find a gap in the queue, she finally caught a glimpse of the man himself, head bent as he signed a book. A funny frisson went through her, like a hand grabbing her heart in her chest. It couldn't... No! But it was! It was Ross Strathallan. Her mouth opened and an odd, strangled squeak came out, making the woman next to her turn in surprise. At that exact moment Ross lifted his head and as if drawn by the strength of her shock, looked right at her. A horrified expression crossed his face before he immediately turned to the lady whose book he was signing and moved slightly so that her bright red coat obscured him from Izzy's sightline.

Ross was Ross Adair! For a moment, she stood there like a startled rabbit, frozen with indecision as to what to do.

How was that possible? But now, it all made sense. The half-finished sentences about his work, his evasiveness about how the writing was going…

She crept away consumed by a mix of mortification and regret. And anger, actually. Anger that he hadn't confided in her. Anger at her own disappointment.

She felt as if she'd barged in on something that she shouldn't. Was that why he'd withdrawn this morning? Had he regretted bringing her to Edinburgh with him and increasing the risk of her finding out who he was? And why was he so keen to remain anonymous? The questions raced around her head like speeding go karts on a track, buzzing irritants that made her scratchy and restless. Did she leave? Did she stay? Did she wait for Ross to acknowledge her? Or was he going to pretend he didn't know her?

She walked over to the gift section and tried to focus on looking for items for stockings, all the while wanting to sneak another peek at Ross but she didn't dare in case he caught her.

'Izzy?'

She whirled round at the familiar voice. 'Philip!' Her voice pitched unbecomingly in an embarrassing squeak as she came face to face with the man she'd loved so hopelessly for so many years.

'Hello,' she said, desperately trying to appear cool. She'd made such a fool of herself over him, it was quite humiliating to see him now.

'How have you been?' He paused and then added in a low voice, his eyes meeting hers, 'I've missed you.'

She swallowed, frozen by the unexpected comment.

And just like that she was back on the roller coaster, her stomach churning with that same old adrenaline thrill as her heart did that stupid leap of hope. Philip missed her. After all this time, he missed her. Part of her wanted to whoop with triumph and vindication, while another part of her despaired.

'Fine,' she managed. 'How are you?'

'God, it's so good to see you, Izzy.' He grinned at her, his warm, brown eyes roving over her face, as if drinking in the very sight of her. 'You look ... you look wonderful. Are you back in Edinburgh? I heard you'd moved to the Highlands.' He shook his head as if he didn't want to believe it.

'I'm just here for the day. And yes, I have moved to the Highlands.'

'No!' he wailed. 'For how long? You're coming back to Edinburgh, aren't you?' The horrified look on his face did strange things to her insides, her stomach knotting in confusion and dizzy regret.

'It's fairly permanent at the moment. Me and Xanthe have moved there.'

His face fell and for a moment Izzy could've sworn he genuinely looked agonised as he lowered his voice and asked, 'Did I do this?'

Izzy pinched her lips tightly together. Inside her mind, a sensible voice screamed, 'No, you did not, you arrogant prick,' but her head was having a hell of a job fighting against her stupid traitorous heart, which seemed to be lapping this up.

'I'm so sorry, Iz. But this is meant to be. Bumping into you like this. I made a terrible mistake. Antonia and I have split up.'

Her heart did another of those funny little salmon flips against her better judgement while in her head a voice railed, *Here he goes again. Hot. Cold. Hot. Cold.*

'Sorry to hear that.' She was quite proud that she managed to sound indifferent and unmoved by the news, unlike the night when he'd told her he was engaged. Now she was able to appear calm, equable, which was utterly at odds with the maelstrom of emotions bungee jumping their way through her system, erratic and discombobulated.

'Not as sorry as I am, Iz. I miss you terribly.' He reached forward and clasped her hand in both of his, one finger stroking gently over her thumb. 'You were my best friend. I didn't realise until you weren't here anymore.' The insistent slide of skin on skin disconcerted her.

'McBride,' another voice interrupted and she whirled round, tugging her hand from Philip's.

'Ross,' she said, her vocal cords once again being strangled by guinea pig superpowers. 'Hi.' It was all she could say but later she would have to try and analyse why him calling her McBride pleased her so much. Perhaps it was because of the surprise on Philip's face that accompanied it.

She looked up at him and then over to the book signing table. He gave her an odd smile. 'I'll explain later but my plans have changed and I wanted to talk to you quickly. I'm due to finish sooner than planned, do you want to go to dinner before we get back on the road? I've a table booked at the White Horse Oyster Bar on Canongate. I could meet you there…'

His voice trailed away as he glanced at Philip and then

down at all the shopping bags around her feet. 'Successful shopping trip?'

'Yes. Very,' she said. 'Although my arms are killing me. And I still need to do more.'

'Why don't you leave them with me? I'm sure I can ask the manager to pop them in a storeroom.'

Izzy smiled at him, grateful for his thoughtfulness. 'That would be brilliant. Thank you.'

Philip cleared his throat and she turned back to him, about to apologise for ignoring him but then remembered the number of times that he'd suddenly forgotten her existence around other people. 'Ross, this is an old friend, Philip.' Her head was firmly in charge and she was damned if she was going to give in to Philip's blatant curiosity. Leave him guessing for once. 'And dinner sounds great.'

Ross lifted his head and caught a frantic signal from a young lady who Izzy guessed must be the manager or his minder. 'Duty calls. I'll be done in about half an hour. I'll see you at the restaurant.' He bent to pick up her shopping bags and before she could say anything else, he strode off and she saw him depositing the bags into the arms of the bemused woman at the table.

'How do you know Ross Adair?' asked Philip, sounding almost disappointed, as if he'd discovered something about Izzy he didn't know and he didn't like it.

'He's just a friend.' She gave Philip a blithe smile, knowing that he'd described her in exactly those terms when she'd first met Antonia and overheard her fierce whispered question, 'Who is that girl and why's she so familiar with you?' Philip had kissed her cheek and laughed. 'Izzy? Don't be silly. She's just a good friend. We've been friends since we were teenagers. She's more like a sister.'

That's when Izzy's heart had cracked wide open. She gritted her teeth, pushing the painful memory away.

'Have you known him long?' asked Philip.

Izzy shook her head.

'I was going to ask if you wanted to go for a drink. For old times' sake. We could have had dinner together. We still could.'

Izzy caught her lip between her teeth and gave Philip a cursory study. Once upon a time, she'd have dropped everything to be with him.

With a brilliant smile that hid her internal flutterings, she said, 'Another time, maybe. But it's good to see you.'

'Izzy,' he said urgently. 'There's so much we need to talk about. I have made a terrible mistake. I can see it so clearly now. When I saw you... I... It hit me.'

Izzy swallowed, completely confused. She'd told herself she was over him and there was so much else to think about now, like the castle. She had responsibilities and she couldn't let Xanthe down. For all her mother's faults, they were family and they were all each other had.

'I can't. I need to get back home.' Home. The thought brought with it an unexpected warm glow and she smiled. Despite knowing how much there was still to do, she was looking forward to getting back to the castle with all her parcels and packages, decorating the trees and seeing Jim, Jeanette and Duncan, none of whom took her for granted.

'We could go for a quick drink now.'

Izzy could only stare at him. 'I've still got things to buy.'

'I could come with you.'

Now Izzy laughed. 'You will only slow me down because

five minutes in, you'll be trying to persuade me to stop for a coffee.'

He grinned at her. 'And that's why I miss you so much. You know me better than anyone else.'

'I do.' Her heart quivered in sudden recognition. Perhaps a quick coffee. Then his phone beeped and he looked down at the screen, a frown marring his handsome face. 'Damn, I have to go.' He looked at her with evident regret and leaned in to kiss her cheek. 'I'm not giving up on you, Izzy McBride, we've been friends for too long. Like I said, you know me better than anyone else.' His eyes met hers and he smiled with a slow, sad intensity. 'You'll always be my best friend.'

Izzy grabbed a couple of items from the display in front of her. 'I need to pay for these,' she said, now feeling quite flustered. She wished Philip would stop staring at her like that. It was making all her good intentions start to cave. She did not want to get back on the Philip sky train of hope and despair.

'Can I call you, Izzy?' he asked and stood there, staring after her like some tragic romantic hero as she took a few steps backwards before turning to scurry away clutching her purchases like they were tiny life belts keeping her anchored to common sense.

Chapter Fifteen

I zzy's mind whirled during the short walk back across to the Old Town and she barely noticed the icy bite of the wind nipping at her cheeks as it whistled around the corners of the tall stone buildings. Philip wanted to talk. Was she about to fall into the same old pattern?

Determined to push him out of her mind, she focused on her surroundings and the obvious drop in temperature. The odd snowflake had started to fall and it felt a bit like the orchestra tuning up before the main event.

As befitting an age-old celebration that had its origins in bringing cheer to the dead of winter, the darkness of the city was banished by exuberant light displays from giant snowflakes dancing up and down the Scott Monument, a laser show lighting up Edinburgh Castle's walls through to the dazzling tunnel of light outside St Giles on the Royal Mile.

As soon as she walked into the restaurant, she spotted Ross perched on one of the high stools at the rustic wooden tables in the bar area. His size alone made him an imposing presence but there was that self-possession about him that she found so attractive. He was also surrounded by all her shopping bags, which made her smile.

'Hi,' she said, suddenly unaccountably shy and conscious that her face must be glowing and the tip of her nose was probably doing a very good impression of Rudolph.

'Hi,' he said, with a smile that suggested he understood her sudden confusion.

He wasn't Ross Strathallan anymore, her history professor guest, he was Ross Adair, bestselling author with several books under his belt, the first of which had been made into a very successful television series.

'Hi,' she said again, her tongue not so much tying itself in knots but attempting macrame. Why couldn't she think of anything to say? Then her tongue unravelled itself and she blurted, 'Now the Range Rover makes sense.'

If he'd been wearing glasses, the look he gave her now would have been one of those peering over the top of the frames.

Flustered, she tried to explain. 'I didn't think history professors made that much money.'

'Ah.' He nodded.

'So. Ross Adair.'

He winced. 'Sorry. I—'

'Oh god, was I fangirling when I talked about your book that day?' Izzy put her hands up to her face, her eyes widening as she tried to remember what she'd said to him about the audiobook she was listening to when they were decorating the dining room. Had she gushed about how much she loved his books? 'How embarrassing. Of course, I do like your books. I've read them all. Oh, I didn't mean to say that. It's just …

well, I really do love them.' She felt the blush creeping up her neck. 'Sorry, I'm making a dick of myself. I can see why you don't tell people.'

He reached over and put a hand on hers. 'McBride. It's fine. You're fine. Would you like a drink?'

'Oh god, yes, a triple whisky. I need one.'

He raised an eyebrow.

'Okay. Maybe a glass of wine. Yes, a glass of wine.' Why, oh why, was she suddenly so all over the place? It was Ross. He hadn't changed. Except he had. Now he was some kind of distant superstar. She surreptitiously examined him as he spoke to the waiter and ordered a glass of wine for her and a sparkling water for him.

As if he read her mind, he said. 'I'm still the same person.'

She heaved out a sigh. 'I know. Sorry. I'm being ridiculous. It was a… Why don't you tell people?' She paused and slapped her forehead. 'Duh. Because of this. The way I'm behaving.'

'They don't all behave like this,' he teased.

'Just me.'

'It's kind of cute.'

'Urgh. I've never been cute in my life. Always too tall. Clumsy, too. Like I'm being now.'

He laughed and squeezed her hand. 'You're not being clumsy.'

She put a stop on her tongue, preventing herself from saying anything else, and concentrated on breathing. He was holding her hand. Did he realise? The weight of it, warm and strong, was rather lovely, but she shouldn't read anything into it. Then he removed it to hail a passing waiter.

Despite his denial, she felt like she'd made a complete idiot of himself. No wonder he kept what he did quiet. She winced suddenly, imagining Xanthe's reaction. She'd be shouting it from the rooftops. God, she'd have a field day with this juicy titbit and would maximise the drama from it. She could hear it now, her mother's loud voice broadcasting the news to all and sundry. 'Did you know we have the world famous author Ross Adair staying with us at the moment? Writing his new bestseller. Under *our* roof.'

She gave a small shudder as the waiter brought over their drinks.

'Cheers,' she said, lifting her glass and taking a large glug of cold white wine. 'Ooh, that's delicious.' As the chilled New Zealand Sauvignon Blanc slid down her throat, she felt some of her equilibrium start to return.

Ross stared glumly at his glass of fizzy water.

'You could have one,' she said, looking at the bubbles springing their way to the surface.

'Best not. I checked the forecast and though they predicted light snow this morning, it's now changed to heavy snow.'

They both looked out of the window where snowflakes now danced like tiny ballerinas pirouetting through the sky. 'It's not so bad here but I think on higher ground we'll be in for quite a dump. I'm going to need my wits about me. I'd rather not risk it.'

She nodded. 'Good job you've got a big car.'

'That's a bonus.'

He gave her a self-deprecating smile. 'I never dreamed I'd be so successful. That's part of the reason I don't publish under my real name. When I finally got a publishing deal – there are several books in the bottom drawer that will never see the light of day – I kept very quiet about it. The last thing I wanted was to brag that I got that elusive publishing deal and then have the book sink without a trace. Academics are always very competitive about their published work, so I wanted to keep it quiet.

'When the first one did so well, it was difficult to casually drop in the conversation, "Oh, by the way, Ross Adair? That's me."'

Izzy nodded. 'I guess so. And then you get people fangirling all over you.'

'Not everyone is a reader.'

Izzy clutched her throat in horror and he laughed before glancing quickly out of the window.

'We'd better order. The sooner we get on the road, the better, I suspect.'

Izzy picked up the menu and gave a little moan of approval. 'Oh my, I'm spoiled for choice. It all sounds delicious and suddenly I'm starving.'

A few minutes later, having studied the menu in great detail, she said, 'I can't decide between the crab Scotch egg, which sounds divine, or the prawn and lobster toast with yuzu pearls and black sesame. Or there's the monkfish satay or the Scotch Bonnet salmon.' Izzy caught her lip between her teeth with anxiety over the choices.

'Or you could have oysters.'

She wrinkled her nose. 'I know they're supposed to be some wonderful delicacy but,' she lowered her voice, 'I've never tried them. I can't bring myself to.'

Ross leaned forward and lowered his voice too. 'Me neither. They look disgusting and I always got the impression it was a slurp of slimy sea water. I've always thought of them as the Emperor's New Clothes of the sea. A handy by-product after you've nicked the pearls.'

Izzy laughed. 'Let's not have oysters then. I think we have to have the toast and the Scotch egg. Actually, I ought to make traditional Scotch eggs for the Carter-Joneses.' She pulled out her notebook and quickly scribbled a note to herself.

'Do you take that everywhere with you?'

'At the moment, yes. It's my master plan for Christmas. There's so much to do. I've got lists of lists of lists.' She opened the book and showed him one of the pages, covered in writing in different coloured pens. The notebook was full of turned-down corners to remind her where things still needed finalising, arrows and crossed-out bits and yellow Post-it notes stuck to the pages.

'Are you really worried about Christmas?'

Izzy swallowed. 'Only the food side of things. The other night I dreamed the Carter-Joneses all came down to dinner except it wasn't the dining room, it was like the workhouse from Oliver Twist and they were being served gruel with holly leaves and when they pulled the crackers, huge rats jumped out.'

'Well, the only way is up,' teased Ross.

When the delicate prawn and lobster toast arrived, Izzy took a healthy bite and lifted her eyes heavenward as the flavours of rich seafood, tinted with the burst of citrus and balanced by the nutty bitterness of the black sesame, melted with a gentle explosion in her mouth. 'Bliss.' She took a deep breath of pure satisfaction. 'You have to try this.' With ruthless enthusiasm and an uncoordinated lurch, she shoved the square of toast at his mouth as if he were a baby bird that needed feeding. Startled, Ross opened his mouth and took a bite, his lips grazing her fingers. The laugh in both their eyes stilled as they stared at each other for one of those ridiculously long, awkward seconds as Izzy realised that feeding someone like this was perhaps a little up close and personal.

'I need to take a picture,' she said hurriedly, snatching her hand away and grabbing her mobile. 'For my WhatsApp group. My friends from the cookery school. They're all real foodies and they'll love this.' She could feel her freckled cheeks burning even as the last vestiges of tingles ran their course on her skin. *Don't look at his lips*, she told herself. *Don't look. You've a bit of a crush on him because he's kind, nice and good looking.* She stifled a snort. *Puh-lease. Good looking? He's a superstar bestseller hottie and it's messing with your hormones. He's way out of your league.*

There was no denying her hormones had it right, she could feel the low simmer of attraction but she'd been down this road before. Unrequited feelings sucked, especially when you convinced yourself that the feelings were reciprocated.

She took a couple of photos and then put her phone back down. Luckily Ross was either oblivious to her inner turmoil or ignoring it. She prayed it was the former.

Mindful of the weather closing in, they didn't dally over dinner, although Izzy insisted on taking a doggy bag with them when she couldn't finish everything.

As they drove north, the weather worsened. But despite the mesmerising snow that whirled and twirled in the tunnel of the headlights, they were making reasonably good time. The snow ploughs had been through earlier and the roads thus far had been well gritted.

Ross sighed as the car's beams lit up the sign for

Crianlarich just off the main A road. They'd been driving for nearly three hours and still had another forty miles to go.

'You okay?' asked Izzy. It would have been easy for her to fall asleep but she felt that she ought to show moral support and keep Ross company. So far, he didn't seem to have been bored by her inconsequential chat but over the last few miles she'd grown quieter, conscious that he needed to concentrate. Aside from the car engine labouring through the snow, the world outside was completely quiet and they'd passed barely any other cars for a while now. Most people were probably tucked up beside a roaring fire if they had any sense at all.

'Yes.' He yawned and rubbed one eye. 'It's hard when it's like this. You need to focus because you can't quite gauge the depth perception.'

'Do you want to stop?'

'I'd prefer to press on. I've got a shovel and blankets in the boot and you topped your flask up when I filled up with petrol.'

'And don't forget I've got leftover crab Scotch eggs,' said Izzy, shaking the paper bag at him.

'I can't believe you did that.'

'What, ask for a doggy bag?' she asked.

'Yes.' He rolled his eyes and she got the impression he hadn't liked that she'd drawn attention to them in the restaurant. 'Sorry, I don't like to make a fuss when they're busy.'

'Waste not want not.' She put the bag down in the footwell. 'They were delicious and I wasn't leaving them behind. Besides, you might be glad of them if we get stuck.'

'Ye of little faith.'

'It's getting worse though.'

'It is, but my trusty steed has four-wheel drive and this car's designed to cope with extreme conditions. It seems to get a starring role in lots of Bond films and gets driven in some fairly interesting places.'

'Usually by villains,' Izzy protested, laughing.

He pulled what she guessed was supposed to be a villainous face.

'You're not scaring me.'

She folded her arms across her chest and peered out of the window but there wasn't much to see aside from darkness and the feathery flakes like wayward moths fluttering hopelessly into the car's headlights. Even the road signs they passed were now obscured by a layer of snow. Around them the hills loomed like ghostly giants biding their time, their black, craggy faces contoured by snow-filled crevices, creating stern profiles. Ross had reduced his speed as they climbed a particularly steep hill and down in the valley, Izzy could make out a thin, dark ribbon where the river cut through.

Even with four-wheel drive the car slipped sideways as they crawled along at a painful twenty miles an hour, the wheels crunching and squeaking on the fresh snow. When they crested the hill, Ross decreased the speed, maintaining a steady pace down the winding road, his hands holding the steering wheel at exactly ten to two, as if textbook driving would see them through.

Visibility was getting worse and Ross was having to lean forward to see the road properly. Izzy swallowed and pulled the coat on her lap up to her chin. Although the heater was on full blast and her bottom was nice and toasty with the heated seat, looking outside made her feel cold. She might have been born and bred in Scotland but most of her life had been spent in the city and now she was conscious of the sparsity of people in this area. Cocooned in the vortex of snow, it felt claustrophobic and the atmosphere in the car grew heavier as Ross grimly pressed on, neither of them speaking. Drifts began to build up on the road edges, narrowing the dark tarmac strip and increasing the sense of being closed in. The minutes seemed to stretch into hours and every time Izzy surreptitiously checked her watch it felt as if they were as far from home as ever. It was now nearly one in the morning.

'Here we go. Glencoe,' said Ross, peering at the sign. 'After this it's only another five miles.'

They drove at snail's pace into the small town. 'If we weren't so close to home, I'd suggest stopping,' Izzy offered.

'Everywhere is going to be closed at this time of night anyway.'

Ross slowed down, careful, Izzy noted, to avoid using the brakes. But even so, when they took the turn off the main road right onto the smaller road, the car slid sideways for a couple of seconds.

'Don't worry,' said Ross, once the car was straight again, reaching over and patting her hand. 'We're not so far now. If we take it nice and steady, we'll be home soon.'

As they left the lights of the town behind, they plunged into the dark again, the black water of

Loch Leven on their left and the forest that folded down the hills on their right.

If the gritters had been through, any sign was now long gone. The road ahead to Kinlochleven was completely white. Izzy shivered as the car slid sideways again, watching Ross's hands tense on the steering wheel.

'I've never been out in anything this bad before,' said Izzy. 'I suppose I'd better get used to it.'

'Always make sure you've got blankets, a shovel and a torch in the boot, and if you know it's going to snow take a hot flask of something.'

'Hindsight's a wonderful thing,' said Izzy, trying to sound cheerful when she really wanted to be curled up in her own bed rather than out in this weather.

Ross glanced at her quickly. 'We should sing.'

'Sing?'

'Yes. It'll lift our spirits. Choose something on my iPhone.' He gave her his pin and she tapped it in, opening his Spotify account.

'What do you fancy?' she asked, intrigued to see his musical taste. It seemed quite a personal thing to do, like being handed the keys to a locked cupboard.

'Something we can sing along to. Driving through this feels a bit oppressive. Almost otherworldly.'

'Yes, I keep expecting to see Kelpies rising up out of the loch to lure us to our deaths.'

Ross glanced at the cold, black water outlined by the white of the snow and Izzy saw him shiver at the sight of the stark monochromatic landscape. They could have been the only two people in the world.

'Ha! Got something.' She pressed play. 'A bit of Craig and Charlie will chase off the dark spirits.'

As the familiar beat came on, Ross turned up the volume. 'A classic.'

'You can't beat The Proclaimers for a bit of a singalong.'

'You know they were born in Auchtermuchty,' said Ross, shooting her a broad grin. 'It's one of my favourite place names. For some reason it always makes me smile.' He repeated the word, deepening the Scottish vowels. 'Maybe it's because we always stopped for an ice cream in Auchtermuchty on the way to see my gran who lived in St Andrews.'

As the familiar refrain about walking five hundred miles came on, they both joined in at the top of their voices and just raising her voice made Izzy feel a lot better, almost defiant against the elements. She had a sudden thought of her unexpected encounter earlier. Philip would never have done anything this silly.

They sang their way through several songs before she switched to Franz Ferdinand and they belted out the chorus to 'Take Me Out' as the car crept along at no more than thirty miles an hour.

As they came over the top of a slight incline only a mile from the castle, they both spotted the snow drift blocking half the road. Instinctively, Ross rammed on the brakes. The car juddered with the sudden impact and then began to slide sideways towards the edge of the road. Ross wrestled with the wheel, trying to turn into the skid but gravity had other ideas and when the car reached the edge it began to slide backwards towards the loch.

'Brace yourself, Izzy,' yelled Ross, as the car bounced across the rough terrain. He held onto the steering wheel with both hands, trying to wrench back control, pumping the brakes for all he was worth. There was a sudden lurch and the car stopped dead at a slight angle with Izzy and Ross facing downwards.

'You okay?' he said, reaching out to grab her hand. He glanced back over his shoulder. 'We've hit a drift, thank God. I thought we were going to end up in the loch.'

'Me too,' said Izzy, her voice rasping slightly. Her knees had turned to jelly and her heart was trying to beat its way out of her chest like a frightened bird stuck in a chimney.

They both sat there for a moment almost as if they were catching up with themselves, their breathing loud in the quiet car. Outside, the loch seemed unnervingly close.

'Now what?' she asked, as the car rocked slightly, the engine still running.

Ross looked around. 'I think we'd be best abandoning ship and leaving the car here. Even if I can get out of this drift, I'm not sure we'll get back onto the road and I don't want us rolling into the loch.'

Izzy took a few deep breaths. 'You're right and it's not that far to walk.'

He raised an eyebrow. 'Except neither of us are dressed for Arctic exploration.'

'We could stay here but what's the worst that can happen? I don't think we'll develop hypothermia in one mile, will we?'

'We should be okay if we stick to the road. Or I could do the gentlemanly thing and go and get help.'

Izzy laughed. 'Don't be so ridiculous. I'm not some frail little flower. Besides, who's going to come and help at this time of night? Duncan? What's he going to do? Get Dolly and Reba out with a sledge?'

'An interesting picture,' said Ross with a quick laugh.

'It's not that far. Come on.' Izzy wriggled in her seat and grabbed her hat and scarf from the back seat.

'You sure? We could sit it out with the engine and heater on. I've also got blankets in the back.'

'What difference will daylight make? It might still be snowing and we could be snowed inside the car.' Although she could see a possible benefit there. After all, sharing body heat was one of the best ways of staying warm and the thought of snuggling up against Ross's broad chest had a certain appeal.

'True. Okay, I'll have to climb out your side because I won't be able to get this door open.'

Izzy opened the door, wincing at the instant bite of the night air. Her feet sank into the snow right up to her knees and she instantly regretted wearing her favourite Chelsea boots rather than the solid Doc Martens and thick tights she normally charged about in.

Ross wriggled his way over the console and out into the snow.

'Come on then, Captain Scott.'

'I hope we're a bit more successful than him,' said Izzy, starting to flounder through the snow towards the road.

Being taller, Ross found the going a bit easier and he gave her his hand to tug her up the slope.

'Thanks,' she huffed as they reached level ground. 'That was hard going.'

He looked down at her, a wry smile on his face.

'What?'

'You seem very calm about our predicament.'

She lifted her shoulders. 'There's no point worrying and making a fuss about things when you have no control over the situation. You just have to get on with it.'

'Not all women are like that.' His words were softened by his wry smile.

'Not all men are phlegmatic or as practical as they like to believe they are.'

'Touché. I was referring to certain women of my acquaintance.'

'Oh,' said Izzy, strangely warmed by the sudden admiration in his eyes.

'You're independent, practical and you don't give up or let other people take over, but at the same time you see the value of support and teamwork.'

'Thanks, I think. Is that a compliment?' She glanced at him.

He swallowed and she saw his Adam's apple dip. 'It most certainly is, McBride.'

'Oh,' she said quietly, disconcerted by the funny flip low in her belly.

'Come on, we need to keep moving. Keep warm.' He took her hand again and together, heads bowed, they ploughed on, battling against the snow flying into their faces. Izzy kept blinking as flakes landed on her lashes.

Thankfully the drifts of snow blanketing the dark tarmac were easily navigable and they could walk fairly easily, and soon the castle loomed into view.

'We can stick to the road or cut across this field, which will be much shorter but harder going.'

Izzy frowned up at the castle directly ahead and then glanced at the road that curled away in the opposite direction. It followed the lee of the hill while the direct path meant they'd have to cross the field at an awkward camber. All she could think about was getting home to the kitchen, warming up by the Rayburn and having a hot toddy.

'Let's cut across. It's quite open. Hopefully the snow's drifted to the edges and it won't be so deep.'

The field wasn't too bad and they managed to avoid the worst of the drifts, although Izzy could barely feel her feet now. She stamped them down heavily with each step in a vain attempt to warm them up and was so busy doing that she didn't watch where she was going.

'Izzy, watch out.'

But it was too late. She walked straight into a puddle, the water spilling over the top of her boots and filling them. The front door of the castle was only five hundred metres away. 'God, that's cold.' She sucked in a shuddery breath, all her muscles tensing. Despite her feet being so numb, she could still feel the icy water poking at her toes like knives. She gritted her teeth and walked on, the water sloshing with each new step. She closed her eyes, determined not to cry even though every movement was miserable.

Ross stopped. 'Here, lean against this fence and take your boots off.'

'My feet will freeze.'

'No. Take them off, along with the wet socks. I'll wrap your feet in my scarf and carry you the rest of the way.'

'You can't do that. Besides, it's not far now,' she said.

'Just do as you're told for a change.' Before she could protest further he was at her feet, easing her boots and wet socks off. Then he scooped her up in his arms. 'Take my scarf,' he commanded.

Too cold and miserable to do anything but follow his orders she unwrapped his scarf, conscious of his bristled chin and ruddy cheeks within kissing distance, and somehow managed to wrap the warm wool around her bare feet – quite a feat in itself as she was wrapped up in her bulky coat.

Now she was in his arms, she didn't know where to look. He was altogether too close and she felt ridiculously self-conscious but she couldn't resist the opportunity to surreptitiously study his face, trying to work out what components made it so handsome. He was so different from Philip who had delicate, almost pretty, features. Ross's were rough-hewn and she could imagine her fingers running over his face, exploring the strong cheekbones, the hard chin, the glossy, thick eyebrows…

He glanced at her and she ducked her gaze, feeling as if she'd been caught.

'Not far now.'

'Thank goodness.' She tried not to wriggle but staying completely still, especially when she was so cold, was hard. 'I hope you don't put your back out or anything.'

He gave her a weak smile. 'I'll be fine.'

There was the most enticing, heart-shaped freckle to the left of his lower lip, which she'd not noticed before.

Okay, that was a flat out lie. Of course she'd noticed it before. Lots of times. If ever there was an 'X marks the spot', that was it. She caught her breath, forcing herself not to think about kissing him and felt herself tense.

'It's all right, I won't drop you,' he said, looking into her face with a grin, tightening his hold on her.

'I … I didn't think you were going to,' she managed to get out, forcing herself to relax into his hold. She was aware of every bit of him touching her. His arm skimming the underside of her thighs, his chest against the side of her rib cage. Oh God, she was going to come over in a faint like some sort of Southern Belle. There was just something so lovely about a pair of big strong arms cradling your body. She wanted to imagine him carrying her up to bed. Again she stiffened at the thought that had sneaked in, uninvited.

'God, you're like a bloody eel, McBride. I won't drop you.'

The trip to the door seemed to take an eternity but at last he shouldered his way inside. She wanted to wriggle like a child desperate to be put down but managed to retain some dignity until he lowered her to the floor. Her body slipped down his and with her arm still draped around his neck they came body to body.

'Sorry. Thank you.' Their eyes met in another one of those awareness-laden moments and she held her breath, convinced that this time he *was* going to kiss her.

'Ross,' she breathed, unable to help herself. She couldn't help the plea in her eyes. *Kiss me.* She tilted her face up to him. Surely he felt it too.

'Izzy.' He cupped her cheek with his hand. Then he sighed, smiled sadly and stepped back, his hand moving to her waist. 'We need to get your feet warmed up. It won't be helping, standing on this cold floor.'

Her heart squeezed in sudden pain. Seriously she was making all the same mistakes again. What was wrong with her?

'Hot water bottles,' said Izzy, briskly pulling away from him.

His eyes widened.

'We need to get hot water bottles and you probably need to get your wet trousers off. And your wet shoes. Socks too.'

He nodded gravely.

'Do you want a hot drink?' She scurried off down the hall to the kitchen, ignoring the sudden darts of pins and needles in her heels.

Unlike the hall, the kitchen was still warm and someone had left the lights on and a note on the table beside a bottle of whisky.

Hope the journey wasn't too horrendous. Jim (not me) has made soup for tomorrow and there's enough bread so you don't need to get up early. Banked the fires up in your rooms. See you in the morning. Hot chocolate in the flask for you if you fancy it. J & J.

'God, I love those two,' said Izzy with a forced smile, pushing the note so that Ross could see it and immediately crossing to the dresser and grabbing two mugs. 'What sweethearts,' she said with false cheer. 'Hot chocolate and whisky? I think we deserve one, don't you?'

'Izzy...' He reached for her but she pretended she hadn't seen the movement and turned away, busying herself pouring the hot chocolate.

'I suggest you do your own whisky,' she said, pushing a mug towards him and avoiding looking at him. 'Thanks for being such a hero and carrying me back. I hope Duncan knows someone who can get your car tomorrow. He's bound to.' She knew she was blathering but she couldn't bear to hear Ross turn her down gently, which he undoubtedly would. 'There you go. One hot chocolate.'

'Thanks,' said Ross, nodding and looking at her with wary eyes as he sank into the opposite chair. 'I can say that last half hour in the car was pretty hairy. Thanks for...' He looked at her and gave her a weak smile. 'Staying level-headed. Calm in the face of potential disaster.'

'Crying wouldn't have helped.'

'No but you didn't complain or moan once. Some people might have made a complete drama out of it.'

Izzy shrugged.

They lapsed into silence in the cosy warmth of the kitchen, each toying with the drink in front of them, as if they both had things they wanted to say but didn't know how to say them.

'Izzy ... about today...'

197

'Don't worry. I won't tell anyone who you are.'

'Oh, yes. Thanks. If you don't mind.'

'No, not at all. I think I ought to head up now.' She lifted her mug but looked at his neck rather than his face. 'Will you be all right to switch the lights out?'

'Izzy…' he started again.

'Night, Ross. See you tomorrow.' With that she fled from the kitchen. She'd made enough of a fool of herself today. When would she learn?

Chapter Sixteen

When Izzy tugged open the heavy velvet curtains the next morning, she stood for a moment drinking in the magical view. After a good night's sleep with her feet feeling cosy and warm again, she could look more favourably on the snowy scene. She flexed her feet, toasty in thick woollen socks, banishing the memories of yesterday. The clouds had rolled back to reveal a piercing blue sky and bright sunshine, which made the snow glisten and glitter.

From the little turret she could see for miles out over the loch and to the mountain ranges beyond. Like a thick duvet, the snow had softened the features of the landscape, smoothing away the sharp lines and angles. It crept up to the very the edge of the loch, where a mirror double of the brilliant white and blue sky was reflected.

Running downstairs, she was greeted by Jeanette in the hall who was hopping from foot to foot. 'It's snowed! It's snowed! Have you seen it? Of course you have. Sorry.'

Izzy grinned at her and put an arm around her shoulder. 'Do you want to go out and play?'

'Snow day?' she asked hopefully.

Izzy remembered snow days when the school was closed and everyone bunked off for the day and went sledging. Jim and Jeanette both deserved a day off, they worked so hard. 'Snow day,' she confirmed.

'Brilliant,' said Jeanette with a big beam. 'Glad you got back safely. How was the journey?'

'Now I'm home, I'll say it was okay, but we had to abandon the car about half a mile down the road and walking in the snow wasn't that much fun. I can't tell you how grateful we were for the hot chocolate and the fire and the hot water bottle.'

'No problem. To be honest, it was Jim's idea. He's the practical one.'

'Never,' teased Izzy.

'He's made you some porridge, with a touch of cream and brown sugar. His speciality. Hope that's okay.'

'Jeanette, that sounds wonderful. Thank you so much. I was glad of the lie-in this morning. We didn't get back until after one.'

'Izzy! You're back!' Xanthe threw her arms around Izzy, her shrill voice echoing around the hall. 'Where's the car? I thought you'd been stranded somewhere in the snow and had to sleep in the car and get hypothermia. Or had to walk miles to find somewhere to put you up.'

Izzy smiled to herself. Typical Xanthe, focusing on the drama.

For the second time she explained what had happened.

'Good. Did you buy me some decorations?'

'Yes.'

'Where are they?'

Izzy shook her head in disbelief.

'Where do you think they are?'

'You didn't leave them in the car, did you? What if someone stole them in the night?'

'If they went out in that, they're welcome to them.'

'When will you get them?'

Izzy glared at her mother.

'When arrangements can be made to tow the car.'

'Good job then that I ordered some. I was worried you wouldn't get enough. I got more fairy lights, too.'

Izzy raised a brow. 'You mean you didn't trust me to get it right.'

Xanthe linked an arm through hers. 'Now darling, that's not it at all. I just saw some beautiful things online that will supplement the basics I asked you to get. You'll thank me when you see the trees, they're going to be beautiful. You wait and see. In fact, it would be good if we could get the trees today. Duncan has found some tree stands, so we're all set.'

'We'll see, Mum. Ross might not be able to help today as he lost a day yesterday.'

'It's just cutting down a few trees, it won't take very long,' said Xanthe, tossing her head.

Izzy knew there was no point arguing, so she nodded and followed Jeanette to the kitchen.

Jim and Duncan were drinking tea and the promised bowl of porridge was waiting on the top of the Rayburn.

'Smells good, Jim. Maybe you could take over the cooking.'

'Oh no. Porridge is the sum total of my cooking. Me mam taught me how to make it.'

'Well I'm very grateful.'

'Morning, Izzy,' said Duncan, raising his mug to her. 'I'm thinking today would be a good day to cut down some trees. We've a couple of sleds and with this good snow it'll be much easier to transport them back to the castle. Ah, Ross, you up for a tree cutting expedition?'

'When I've had coffee, yes,' said Ross, walking into the room.

'Are you sure?' asked Izzy, worried that she'd already taken enough of his time.

'Yes, my editor is happy with what I've done and has stopped calling me so I have some breathing space ahead of my deadline. Besides, I wouldn't miss it for the world,' he replied. 'Who wants to be shut up inside on a day like this? I can work later this afternoon, although I still need to sort my car out.'

'Don't worry,' said Duncan. 'I've spoken to Alistair over at Highways Farm, and he said he'll get the tractor out and tow your car for ye this afternoon. I'll go wi' ye.'

'Brilliant, thanks, Duncan.'

'No problem. In the meantime, I've to feed the cows but I've sharpened the axes for ye. They're outside the back door along with the sledges. Xanthe wants three trees. Two seven-foot ones for the dining room and the sitting room and at least an eleven-footer for the great hall.'

'I've never chopped a tree down in my life,' said Ross. 'But how hard can it be?'

'You're in luck.' Jim grinned, stroking his beard. 'I worked for a Christmas tree farm last year.'

'Ha! Yes, you did,' said Jeanette. 'And he got a free tree,

though it was the straggliest, runt of the litter tree that you've ever seen.'

'No one wanted it,' said Jim with a gentle shrug. 'I felt sorry for it. It needed a home.'

Jeanette stood on tiptoe and planted a kiss on his cheek. 'You're a right soft touch.'

An hour later they were all wrapped up, ready to brave the icy wastes, and set out on the tree chopping expedition. The only sound, apart from their feet crunching underfoot with squeaky clean virgin footsteps, was the birdsong in the distance. Jim whistled cheerfully, leading the way pulling one of the sledges, Jeanette trotting alongside him chatting away. Izzy fell into step next to Ross and the snow rose in powdery puffs as they kicked their way through the drifts climbing well over their ankles.

'It's better than last night,' he said. 'How are your feet?'

'Warm, thank goodness.'

In some places drifts had accumulated against walls and fences in soft, elegant arches. The four of them skirted the loch and cut across the flat plain towards the woodland. Duncan had directed them to a particular area where there were plenty of Douglas fir trees for them to choose from.

Izzy glanced at the trees, all of which looked pretty similar to her, but she knew that if the tree wasn't right Xanthe would have no compunction about sending them out to get another.

'What about this one, Izzy?' asked Jim, pointing to one of them. 'That's about seven foot.' He stood next to it and reached his hand up above his head to demonstrate the height difference between him and the tree.

'Looks good to me.'

'Come on, Ross. I'll show you how this is done.'

Izzy and Jeanette carried on scouting for trees while Jim gave Ross a lesson in chopping down a tree.

'Cavemen together,' whispered Jeanette with a giggle as Jim handed the axe to Ross after showing where to make the first cut. Jim held the tree while Ross cut through the trunk, swinging the axe with surprising, well-targeted grace.

'You've done this before,' said Jim.

'No, but I've chopped a lot of logs in my time. When he wants some peace and quiet, my dad always goes and chops logs.' Ross's mouth twisted in a rueful smile. 'We would sneak off to the shed when I was younger and he taught me. He has an old armchair and a paraffin heater out in the shed, and always kept a tin of biscuits under the chair. I'm not sure my mum knew about them.' He lapsed into silence, lost in thought.

Izzy wondered if he was close to his dad as there was a slight air of regret to Ross's words as he talked about him.

With a creak and a crack, and one final chop, the tree toppled and Jim caught it as it fell. He and Ross loaded it onto the sledge and Jeanette used a couple of bungee ties to secure it.

'Now you know what you're doing, why don't we split up?' suggested Jim. 'It's cold out here and I've got some painting to finish.' He glanced at Jeanette who was pouting a little. 'Don't worry, we'll build your snowman after lunch.'

She brightened. 'With all this snow, we could build a whole snow family.'

It was agreed that Jim would scout for the bigger tree and that Ross and Izzy would look for the smaller one.

'You'll need to go up the hill, to the next plantation. These trees were all planted at the same time, so they're much the same size,' said Jim, so Izzy and Ross headed off in the opposite direction.

As Jeanette and Jim's voices faded, there was utter silence apart from the soft crunch of snow underfoot and the rustle of their heavy coats.

'Difficult to believe that yesterday we were in the bright lights of Edinburgh,' said Ross. 'I enjoyed going to the city but I much prefer this. Calm and quiet.'

'It's energising in a way,' said Izzy taking in a deep breath of the clean, crisp air. 'The snow makes everything feel new again. I feel like a kid when I take that first step out into fresh snow. Leaving that first footprint. Like I'm making my mark on the world. Even if it's only temporary, I'm the only person that has stepped there. In the city the snow will be grey by now and churned up.' She wrinkled her nose.

'I know exactly what you mean. Come on, we've got a tree to hunt down and catch.' Ross hefted the axe.

'You're enjoying this. I can see an axe murderer coming in a future book.'

He grinned. 'Now there's a thought. A bloody murder in the snow, in a churchyard in Edinburgh. A medieval axe … or maybe a Claymore.'

'Are you often thinking about murder?' asked Izzy semi-seriously.

'A lot of the time. My Google search history makes for interesting reading. And if someone's pissed me off, they often become my next murder victim.'

Izzy laughed. 'I'll try and be on my best behaviour.'

They walked up the slope to the next set of plantings.

'Here we go. What do you reckon?' asked Ross. 'I wouldn't want to get on the wrong side of Xanthe.'

'The castle's going to look so wonderful.' She imagined the tree in the room and suddenly felt a shiver of excitement. She turned to Ross, grinning. 'I can't wait for Christmas.'

'I can tell.'

'Come on then, do your thing. Let's fell this beast.'

Izzy watched him while he chopped the tree down, wondering about the wisdom of throwing a snowball at him while he was wielding an axe. Deciding it probably wasn't that sensible she waited until he'd put it down and loaded the tree onto the sledge. Taking quick aim she fired a shot and was delighted to see it hit the target, right on his bottom. When he whirled round, she was innocently regarding another tree, her snow-dusted gloved hands hidden behind her back. His eyes narrowed but he didn't say anything and bent to his task again. It was too much of a temptation a second time, and so again Izzy scooped up another ball of snow and fired it off. For a second time, she hit the target. Ross straightened but didn't say anything. Feeling mischievous and egged on by his cool indifference, she took another shot … but that was her mistake. This time, Ross levelled a look at her that promised a world of retribution and suddenly she felt a frisson of fear.

'McBride, once, I might have thought it was a passing squirrel, twice, a lucky fluke on the part of said squirrel but three times…' He shook his head, bent quickly and scooped up a ball of snow and stepped towards her.

'You wouldn't,' she said, doing her best to look demure and

totally undeserving of any retribution he might be tempted to dole out.

'Wouldn't I?' He took another step and with a shriek of laughter she turned and ran as the snowball he launched went sailing past her head.

'Missed,' she called with a distinct note of triumph, ducking quickly to scoop up her own ball of snow, which she sent flying his way. With smug satisfaction she watched it smack him on the shoulder, exploding into a powdery flurry. She let loose a shout of glee and dodged behind a tree as he picked up a handful of snow in retaliation, his eyes narrowing and his steps full of purpose. This was war. Izzy realised her mistake when he kept coming towards her, not the least perturbed by her makeshift barrier. With his steady progress, he kept patting the snowball between his hands with mock threat. He meant business and she took off running between the trees, zig zagging out of aim. He launched his snowball and she ducked just in time but as soon as she'd straightened, he was already moulding the next ball. She turned to run again, floundering through the deep snow, her muscles starting to protest at the unfamiliar gait. Then disaster struck. Her foot snagged on a hidden tree branch beneath the snow and she went flying forward. The icy burn of snow crystals scoured her face and she got a mouthful of snow, which set her front teeth tingling with cold. Scrabbling about to gain purchase in the snow, she rolled over to find Ross towering over her, a grin of triumph on his face, the snowball held high in his hand.

'You wouldn't,' she said breathlessly, slightly winded from the fall, looking up at him with a plaintive expression on her face.

'I'm sorely tempted but it wouldn't be very gentlemanly to take advantage of you in this position now, would it?' His lopsided smile suggested that he wasn't considering being a gentleman very seriously.

'No, it would not,' she said, sucking in a breath and doing her best to appear dignified in the face of the ignominy of lying on her back like a stranded beetle.

He extended a hand to pull her up and she grasped it gratefully. As she stood, he mashed the snowball into her head and she shrieked as the cold snow slid down her neck. 'That was...' She pushed him, laughing at him as she did deserve it. He caught her arms as he toppled backwards taking her with him. She landed on top of him with an oomph and finished with a gasped '...mean.'

Her eyes met his and suddenly all the breath wheezed out of her chest as they stared at each other in one of those moments of complete awareness. She was so close she could see the navy blue flecks in his eyes, the curl of his dark lashes and the spark of interest that danced below the surface. There wasn't a sound around them apart from their own breaths, their chests lifting and falling in quiet unison.

Izzy's gaze strayed to his lips. She wanted him to kiss her but conscious of the previous evening when she'd been so sure he'd kiss her and then he'd turned away, she wasn't about to humiliate herself again. Even though the words, 'are you going to kiss me?' danced on her tongue, she refused to give them life. It was his move.

Her heart hammered, the blood racing through her veins as she waited, watching him with hopeful anticipation and absolute stillness.

She almost sighed with relief when, still holding her gaze,

those blue eyes steady and calm, he raised his lips to hers. A punch of adrenaline exploded in her stomach at the soft touch of his mouth. She kept perfectly still, terrified that he might still pull back, not daring to believe that he was actually kissing her. Then he rolled both of them onto their sides and this time he took charge, caressing her lips with slow, gentle touches, sending tiny shivers radiating out through her body. She softened against him, moving her mouth against his. It had been worth the wait. He kissed with a leisurely but consummate confidence, as if she was worth taking time with and nothing was going to distract him. The man certainly knew how to kiss – there was nothing tentative or hesitant about his touch, it was typical Ross, totally in command, in that calm, measured way he had.

His single-minded attention was utterly intoxicating and Izzy sank into the kiss, her body so boneless in the snow that it took every effort to lift her arms to wrap one hand around his neck and thread her fingers into his soft hair, the other clutching his broad back as if trying to anchor herself to reality. She opened her lips as the kiss deepened, him propped on his elbows as his hands cradled her face. There was no hurry, no race to the finish, just a careful, thorough kiss. As if he planned on tasting every last drop of her.

Inside her head, fireworks with bells and whistles were exploding and when he finally pulled away, there was a knowing twinkle in his eye.

'Well, that was nice,' he murmured, stroking her cheek.

'Nice!' she squeaked indignantly. It had been flipping earthshattering, knee wobbling and she wasn't convinced her knickers weren't about to catch fire. She'd been on the receiving end of far more passionate, enthusiastic, lust-driven kisses but none of them compared to this slow, languid takeover of her senses. Regaining her equilibrium as the coldness of the snow on the back of her head began to make itself known, she added, 'For someone who's supposed to be a writer, that's pretty lame.'

A slow grin lit up his face. 'Are you accusing me of being lame?'

'No, the description.'

'Well, there's nice and there's *nice*.' He lowered his voice, the intimate tone almost reverberating through her chest. 'And that was *nice*.'

'Hmm,' said Izzy, slightly mollified.

'I'm not sure our particular location is that conducive to kissing. I'm slightly concerned I might look up to find a grizzly bear looking down at me.'

'Last time I looked there were no grizzlies roaming the Highlands.' She shivered, the cold starting to penetrate.

'Come on, let's take our prize home. I feel like I'm a proper hunter-gatherer now.' He rose and pulled her up, giving her a final kiss before leaning down to take the rope of the sledge.

Dragging it behind them, each pulling one of the ropes on either side of the sled rails, they made their way through the glistening snow, which looked like a plump layer of icing on top of a Christmas cake. Tiny bird footprints made lacy delicate trails on the surface of the snow as they neared the loch, and the only sound was their breathing accompanied by the slide of the sledge on the snow behind them. When the castle came into view they both paused, moved by the sight of the golden stone burnished by the low sunlight and the diamond sparkles glinting from the blanket of snow draping the roof.

'It's so beautiful.' Izzy sighed, feeling that familiar thrill of ownership. She wasn't sure she'd ever get tired of the sight of her castle.

'Aye,' said Ross. 'It is.'

She glanced at him and they smiled at each other in a shared moment of awe, revelling in the fact that they were a tiny part of this. Inside her a golden glow of happiness swelled. Perhaps, just perhaps, she'd finally got it right and Ross was as attracted to her as she was to him.

Chapter Seventeen

Izzy had barely eased her boots off when Xanthe came skipping towards her.

'Let's see,' she said, peering through the window to where the three trees were propped up against the wall of one of the outbuildings.

'Give us a chance,' said Izzy, rubbing her hands together. She wanted a large mug of tea and a hot mince pie. Ignoring her mother, who was exclaiming over the size of the trees and their bushiness and exhorting Jim to put the tree into the waiting heavy duty stand, she put a tray of mince pies into the Rayburn. They all deserved a reward after their efforts this morning and she had a feeling they were going to need sustenance to survive Xanthe's pursuit of perfectionism. It had once taken her over an hour to select a suitable tree.

'Bloody hell,' said Jim, slumping into one of the kitchen chairs ten minutes later. 'The woman's a termagant. We've done our bit, it's all over.'

Ross didn't say a word, just grabbed a mince pie.

Izzy grinned. 'Not yet, it isn't.'

Both men narrowed their eyes and stared at her. 'What do you mean?' asked Jim. 'Three trees is plenty, isn't it?'

'They need to be decorated,' said Izzy. 'There'll be the decorating party later.'

Jim shrugged as if to say he'd made his contribution and was now out of it.

'No, you don't understand,' said Izzy, with a smile. Her mother wouldn't let anyone off the hook. 'It's a McBride tradition.' She lifted her chin, remembering past Christmases. She and her mother had always been together to do the tree. There might only have been two of them but they had their family rituals and she decided there and then from now on, it was going to be a Kinlochleven Castle tradition. 'Everyone is to meet at six in the hall to decorate the tree. There'll be whisky cocktails to help make an occasion of it.' She gave them all a stern look to emphasise that she meant it and there'd be no abstentions, although her eyes softened when they met Ross's. 'It's the official start of Christmas and everyone in the house has to join in.'

'That sounds like fun.' Jeanette looked at Jim. 'We need to start making traditions of our own now we're married.'

'I quite like the one where we cut down a tree in the woods and…'

Jeanette blushed a rosy red, snatched up the nearest tea towel, and slapped him with it.

'Too much information,' said Ross with the air of a man who was entirely innocent. Only Izzy saw the wicked smile he shot her way.

'I'll never go walking in the woods again,' said Duncan with a visible shudder.

Jim helped himself to a third mince pie and Jeanette shook her head in disapproval.

'A man's got to keep his strength up,' he said with a big grin.

At six o'clock, with everyone assembled in the hall, Izzy handed round a tray of Edinburgh Crystal glasses filled with a winter whisky sour.

'Izzy, these look amazing! So festive. I love the gold.' As always, Xanthe's voice was at full volume. She wore a scarlet satin dress with a plunging neckline and a long skirt trimmed along the hem with a froth of white marabou feathers. It was Mary Claus meets festive tart with a heart.

'They do look very pretty,' said Jeanette, noticeably forcing her attention from Xanthe's dress to focus on the edible gold glitter that circled the top of the glass.

Thanks to a well-timed piece of advice from Fliss a few weeks ago on the WhatsApp chat, Izzy had ordered in the glitter, which she attached to the glass by first dipping the rim of each glass into honey. The cocktail itself was very easy to make, a tablespoon each of fresh orange and lemon juice, some whisky and half a tablespoon of sugar syrup, which she'd boiled up in two minutes.

'Mmm, that's good,' said Ross, taking a mouthful, the tone of his voice suggesting a little more as his eyes lingered on Izzy's face. A fizz of emotion flashed inside her as she remembered their kiss.

She sent him a private smile, hoping they might get a moment together again soon. She'd caught herself dreamily touching her lips four times since they'd returned to the castle.

He smiled back, the sight of the quick curve of his lips warming her as much as her first sip of whisky.

'Right,' Xanthe announced. 'Lights first. Ross, I want you up the ladder, here. Duncan, you'd better go halfway up the stairs, we don't want you falling.' With the exacting demands and bark of a sergeant major she launched into delivering orders, thrusting a long string of fairy lights into Jim's hands. 'No higher than that. No, Duncan, not there. On that branch, Ross. This way. No! No, don't put them there.'

Jeanette and Izzy exchanged amused looks as Xanthe chided, cajoled and yelled at the three men as if they were small boys in kindergarten that needed organising. She'd have made a fearsome commander because when she wanted something done, she was nothing if not single-minded about it.

As Izzy watched Ross stretch and lean this way and that, she itched to feel his warm skin under her fingers, to feel his muscles relax and contract beneath her hands. She prayed that no one could read her thoughts or saw how often her eyes strayed his way.

After a good twenty minutes, Xanthe finally deemed that Izzy could switch the lights on. Everyone turned to look at Xanthe as the lights flickered into life. She took a couple of steps back to inspect the tree, tilting her head this way and then that way, her lips as pursed as a small prune.

The tension in the room grew as her guarded gaze roved over the tree.

'Izzy,' her mother snapped. 'What do you think?' There was a petulance to her tone, which Izzy knew from long experience did not bode well.

'It looks great,' she said with a healthy helping of fake enthusiasm. As far as she was concerned it looked absolutely fine but then she didn't have Xanthe's picky standards. For good measure, she added. 'Really great.'

'Hmm,' said Xanthe, prowling around the tree and looking it up and down like some haute couture designer eying up their creation before the model is sent down the catwalk.

There was a silence in the room and Izzy almost felt the collective will pushed Xanthe's way, desperate for it to be all right.

'Those middle lights aren't right,' Xanthe suddenly declared, like the leading actress finding a dead body. 'They're all bunched together. They need to be more evenly spread.'

'They look all right to me,' grumbled Duncan.

'No, no, no. We'll have to start again.'

Jim, Duncan and Ross looked at each other incredulously but before they had managed to say anything Xanthe stepped forward clapping her hands, shooing them back towards the tree as if she were guiding chickens back into their coop. 'Come on, chop, chop. Ross, you undo the top and pass the wire down to Jim, gently now.'

Xanthe hopped about. 'Not that way. Higher. Next branch. Back again.'

Even from her place at the other side of the tree, Izzy could see that Ross's teeth were firmly gritted.

'Up a bit. That's better. No, Duncan! No, on that branch.'

Jeanette giggled under her breath but Izzy shook her head

to herself. Xanthe was enough to try the patience of a dozen saints.

Eventually the lights were arranged to her satisfaction and she clapped her hands. 'Izzy, turn the lights on.'

Ross, Jim and Duncan began to shuffle away, and Ross looked as if he might make a bolt for the door, with Jim not far behind him. Xanthe fixed them with a piercing stare. 'You're not going anywhere until this tree is finished.'

Izzy switched on the lights and everyone held their breath watching Xanthe, except Jeanette who was still laughing to herself. 'They look like three schoolboys outside the headmaster's office,' she whispered to Izzy.

Xanthe studied the tree. 'What do you think, Izzy? And change the setting of the lights, I prefer the one that fades on and off, not all this flashing; it's like a disco and we don't want that.'

Izzy obliged, pressing the control switch to a setting that had the lights behaving in a less migraine-inducing pattern. She shot a look towards the three men, their faces mutinous in the glow of the lights. There would be a walkout if Xanthe suggested redoing the lights again.

'It looks fabulous,' gushed Jeanette, clearly reading the glint in her husband's eye.

'Really lovely,' agreed Izzy, her mouth twisting as she tried not to laugh.

'Now the real work can start,' said Xanthe with a gay wave of her hand towards the boxes of decorations stacked at the bottom of the stairs. She raised her glass. 'Let's have a toast. To Christmas at the castle, which I hereby declare open. Now, Izzy, open that box of decorations. We'll start with those.'

'I'll watch,' said Duncan, plumping himself down in one of

the leather chesterfields by the fire. 'I've no skill for this sort of thing.' Ross perched on the arm next to him, showing solidarity.

Xanthe pouted for a moment and then said with a touch of cattiness, 'I suppose you couldn't be trusted to do it properly anyway. Jeanette, Izzy, this needs a woman's touch.' Jeanette giggled again while Izzy rolled her eyes and Xanthe was all smiles as she dug into the box and pulled out a couple of paper-tissue-wrapped parcels, which she dispensed as though she were bestowing royal favours.

Xanthe unwrapped hers quickly. 'Look, Iz!' With a whoop of laughter, she held up a sparkly glass unicorn with a decidedly out of proportion horn. 'It's Inappropriate Una. Remember when Gran gave us this? When you were fifteen and she couldn't understand why we thought it so funny.' She broke off and said in an aside to Jeanette, 'Very phallic, although my mother never understood.' Izzy took it from her with a fond smile, the memory flooding back. The she realised her mother was looking at her with the expectant eyes of a Labrador at one minute to tea time.

'What?' she asked, deliberately teasing her mother.

Xanthe arched one of her perfectly pencilled eyebrows and Izzy relented, pulling a paper bag from beneath one of the armchairs and dangled it in front of her. 'This, you mean?'

Her mother jumped up and took a similar bag from her handbag where it was hanging on the newel post at the base of the stairs.

'Here you go, darling.'

Izzy unwrapped a pretty ice skater in a glittery tulle skirt, white boots and a red Santa hat, performing a delicate one-legged manoeuvre while Xanthe peeled back the tissue paper around the little felt mouse playing the bagpipes that Izzy had bought in Edinburgh.

'Oh, darling, he is gorgeous. I'm going to call him Mousetro and this year is going to be the "Christmas of the Scottish Castle".'

Jeanette wrinkled her forehead in puzzlement and Izzy explained. 'Every year we name our Christmases according to something that happened.' She laughed. 'One year it was "The Christmas of the Farting Dog".'

'Oh, Iz. Why do you have to bring that up? Revolting creature.' Xanthe twisted her mouth in disgust. 'Our neighbour came for lunch and insisted on bringing his smelly pug, who slept under the table and broke wind for the whole of the meal.' Xanthe exploded into raucous laughter. 'We never invited him again, did we?'

Izzy looked over at Ross, to find his forehead furrowed into deep creases. He was staring at her with a sort of sudden spooked recognition, as if she'd sprouted horns from her head.

Xanthe held up a new decoration from the box, a little wooden nutcracker. 'This one is from "The Christmas Gran Left The Presents Behind". She was mortified, wasn't she, darling?'

Izzy nodded.

'Although it wasn't as bad as the Christmas I forgot to put the turkey in the oven.' Xanthe hooted with laughter. 'What a disaster. We had to have baked beans on toast and after that Izzy took over the cooking.'

Izzy giggled and shook her head at the memory. At the time her mother had roared with laughter at her own stupidity and none of them had minded what they ate, they were just happy to be together. She'd always remember sitting by the

Christmas tree in the warm glow of the open fire with Mum and Gran, their plates on their knees. It was a good memory. Her mother might be a little bit unconventional, utterly self-absorbed and a lot scatty, but Izzy knew despite everything she was loved.

As Xanthe unpacked the treasures from the box, along with nuggets of family history, she directed Izzy and Jeanette as to where they should go on the tree.

'No, Jeanette, dear. Higher up.'

Duncan and Jim were enjoying the show, mock chiding her by teasing, 'Jeanette! What were you thinking?'

Each time they hung a bauble on the tree, Xanthe would inch forward, peer over their shoulders before picking it up and saying, 'Perhaps here would be better, don't you think, darling?'

Ross had grown quieter and quieter, receding into the background with a puzzled expression on his face. There were no more sparkly smiles or discreet glances between them. Izzy wondered what was troubling him.

'Turn out the lights,' said Xanthe when the tree was finally completed. 'Ross, you're nearest.'

He dutifully rose to his feet and snapped off the wall lights.

In the corner of the room the tree shimmered and sparkled, making Izzy smile. It was perfect. Christmas had started. This was the beginning of the real countdown and she didn't have long before the Carter-Jones family arrived. Six days to get the last of the rooms ready and to finalise her Christmas plans.

'Time to crack open the Prosecco,' cried Xanthe, her voice hitting the high notes with her enthusiasm. 'I officially declare this Christmas open. Ross, you can do the honours. Glasses are over there.'

With a polite smile, Ross popped open the cork on the Prosecco and poured Jeanette and Xanthe a glass each with his usual calm, good grace but Izzy could tell from the set of his jaw that her mother's high-pitched squeals and dramatic declarations were grating. It wasn't anything Izzy hadn't seen before. Xanthe was an acquired taste; even Izzy found her boundless enthusiasm and high-octane delivery wearing at times and she was used to it. For someone like Ross, who relished peace and quiet, it must be quite jarring. Over the years Izzy had become adept at acting as an intermediary, and soothing situations when Xanthe rubbed others the wrong way because she knew her mother wasn't unkind, malicious or mean spirited. She might be loud but she was essentially harmless and Izzy loved her.

'Good job, Mum,' said Izzy, lifting her glass and going over to give her a hug. The tree really did look fantastic and was quite the centrepiece of the panelled hall. It exuded cosiness with the burnished leather chairs glowing in the light of the fire, the flames leaping and dancing in the big grate and the garland of cinnamon sticks and dried orange slices strung along the mantelpiece.

'It's a super tree and it's the heart of our Christmas castle. May all who stay here be merry and bright, enjoying health and happiness for the whole of the festive season.'

'That's a lovely sentiment, Mrs McBride,' said Jeanette, holding up her glass, the light refracted through the pale golden liquid.

'Oooh, lovely, don't call me that. I sound like I'm a hundred and three and a crabbit old bat. That's why I never let Izzy call me "Mum". It's terribly aging and I was a child bride, you know. I'm nowhere near old enough to have a daughter in her mid-twenties.'

Izzy regarded her mother with a rueful smile. Mid-twenties. Ha! If only. She was far closer to thirty than Xanthe cared to be reminded. Izzy glanced over at Ross. He was looking thoughtful as he mouthed the word. *Mum.*

Had he really not known? She thought of all the times Xanthe had come up in conversation and the time when he'd asked if she worked for Xanthe. She realised she'd never answered him. Had he really thought Izzy was her business manager?

As Xanthe cooed over her tree, Izzy cleared up the empty decoration boxes and piles of abandoned tissue paper and bubble wrap, putting them all neatly in one crate. Duncan was busy stoking the fire and adding a couple more logs and, as was their habit, Jim and Jeanette had vanished down one of the corridors, although Izzy could hear the echo of a faint giggle. She scooped up her box and put it on the wide bottom stair, ready to take up later. Ross was holding the newel post staring thoughtfully into the fire.

'Ready for dinner?' asked Izzy.

He started and looked at her briefly before returning his gaze to the flames licking at the logs in the grate.

'I didn't realise Xanthe was your mother. Not sure how I missed that.' He gave a rueful smile.

Izzy frowned, surprised he really hadn't realised. 'Well, who did you think she was?'

'I thought she was your employer and that you acted as her housekeeper cum business manager. You never specifically said she was your mother.'

'I never said she wasn't either.' Izzy lifted her shoulders in a quick shrug.

'But you call her Xanthe. How was I supposed to know she was your mother?'

Izzy shook her head, trying to clear the cloud of confusion fogging her brain. 'It's not a secret. She doesn't like being called "Mum" and when I was a teenager I thought it was quite cool to call her by her name. It's stuck ever since.' Now, if she were honest, Izzy thought it was a terrible affectation that spoke of ridiculous vanity on her mother's part, but she wasn't going to admit this to Ross, who was being a bit weird right now.

'So you're her daughter.'

'That's usually the relationship when someone is your mother,' said Izzy.

'Mmm,' muttered Ross, shaking his head slightly as if trying to dislodge an unwelcome thought. 'I need to go and do some work. Don't worry about dinner for me; I'll eat later.'

She watched as he climbed the stairs without a backward glance. She wondered what had changed between them.

Chapter Eighteen

'Where's Ross?' asked Jim, tucking into a slice of freshly made coffee and walnut cake. 'He won't want to miss this. It's his favourite. You've got a great hand with a sponge, Izzy.'

Jeanette's shoulders lifted shaking with her perennial giggles. 'I bet you say that to all the girls.'

'There's only one girl for me,' he said, snagging her wrist and pulling her onto his lap.

'Pack it in, the pair of yous,' grumbled Duncan. 'It's enough to make my porridge curdle in my belly.'

The couple grinned at him, and Jim placed a quick kiss on his young wife's lips to wind Duncan up even more. Duncan groaned and picked up his tea. 'Where's the lad?' he asked. 'I haven't laid eyes on him since Tuesday evening when we did the trees.'

'I think he's working,' said Izzy. 'I'll take him some coffee and cake in a minute.' She hadn't seen Ross either for the last two days, but she assumed that was the way with writers and that he was consumed by inspiration.

When the others had disappeared back to work, she loaded up a tray with a thermos of black coffee, a jug of milk and a large slab of cake and ignored the shiver of unease that danced down her spine. She'd relived that kiss in the forest a dozen times. Had he decided it was a mistake or something?

Steeling herself and ignoring the flutter of anticipation at seeing him again, she lifted a hand and rapped on his door. Silence. She waited. Still no response. Izzy caught her lip between her teeth. If he was in full flow, she didn't want to disturb him. Perhaps if she slipped in and discreetly popped the tray on his desk?

Knocking again, she called softly, 'Ross. I've brought you some coffee.'

Was that a sound? A muttered expletive? She strained to hear, now a complete mess of indecision. What if he didn't want to be disturbed? What if he were ill? He might be asleep.

But she was just being kind bringing him coffee and cake. She straightened her back, knocked again and turned the door knob, immediately hit with a slap of déjà vu.

Ross was at his desk wearing earphones. She swallowed now in a complete dilemma, not wanting to make him jump but she was here now.

'Er, hello,' she said, raising her voice.

He turned round. Several expressions flitted across his face, including surprise and irritation, before he narrowed his eyes in careful assessment, as if he were making some important decision.

'McBride.' He nodded. 'Can I help?'

Stung by the dispassion in his voice, she took a second to find her voice.

'I brought you cake and coffee. I thought you might like them.'

The sudden chagrin in his eyes appeased her a little but despite it she knew something had changed. It was as if a light had gone out or a wall had gone up.

'That's very kind of you, thanks. Sorry, I'm up against it. My editor sent through some changes. Big changes. Structural. Things that need a lot of unpicking. Do you want to leave it here?' He cleared a space on his desk and turned back to his computer, his fingers tapping at the keys with a sure touch, his eyes rigidly focused on the screen.

It was obvious he didn't want to talk to her.

She was being dismissed and it hurt.

She dropped the tray with a clatter, irritated that he'd got to her.

'You're welcome,' she said with all the warmth of a robot. Then she turned and marched out, slamming the door behind. It felt good. Childish but good.

Bloody man.

After lunch, she took Jeanette with her to Fort William.

'It's Christmas!' yelled Jeanette, doing a fair impersonation of Noddy Holder as she turned up the radio when Slade's 'Merry Christmas Everybody' came on and proceeded to sing along, word perfect. Izzy joined in, determined to revive her own spirits. She refused to brood over Ross's behaviour, there was too much to do. At the supermarket they did the final big shop for food, battling their way through the vegetable aisles, which were brimming with bags of sprouts, piles of potatoes, carrots and parsnips, and shelf upon shelf of tins of chocolates, chocolate reindeer and Santas, before hitting the wine section.

Izzy looked blankly at the shelves, intimidated by the rows of bottles and then at Jeanette. 'The Carter-Joneses are going to want the good stuff.'

'Don't ask me. I always grab the cheapest Prosecco.'

Izzy sighed. 'I don't know where to start.'

'I thought Ross said he'd help.'

'He's busy writing. I didn't like to ask.' And she wasn't going to. She had her pride.

'Why don't you ask your mate Jason? Didn't you say he works in a posh restaurant? Won't he know someone who knows something about wine?' Jeanette suggested.

'Brilliant idea.' He'd been so helpful already, she was sure he wouldn't mind. What was one more request? Although it would mean coming back again but both trolleys were already full and she'd had enough for one day. They also still had to stop at the farm shop on the way back.

'Come on.' She glanced at her list, satisfied that everything was ticked off. 'We'll leave the wine for today.'

As they stood in the queue to pay, she rattled off a quick message.

Me again. Sorry, this one is for you, Jason, and any of you that know anything about wine. Can you recommend wines to go with this menu?

She attached the ambitious menu plan that she'd put together for Christmas Eve, Christmas Day and Boxing Day.

Thirty-five minutes later they pulled into the car park of the farm shop in high spirits, having sung their way through an entire medley of festive songs.

'Do you know what?' asked Izzy as they got out of the car and crossed the gravel surface to the old barn. 'I'm starting to feel like it's—'

'Chriiiiiistmas,' yelled Jeanette in another gravelly Noddy Holder impersonation.

Izzy laughed. 'Exactly.' She linked arms with Jeanette. 'We're going to have a great time. Even if the Carter-Joneses are hideous, behind the scenes we'll still manage to have fun.'

'It'll be like *Downton Abbey*. We'll be the servants below stairs having a good time. It'll be nice to have lots of people around.' Her mouth drooped a little. 'We always had everyone at home for Christmas.'

'Do you miss your mum?'

'A little.' She lifted her shoulders in a small, sad shrug. 'You know there's so many times in a day when I think, I must tell Mum that. We were' – Izzy heard the break in her voice – 'always quite close.'

'I'm sorry, I didn't mean to upset you.' Izzy put her arms around the younger woman as she began to cry.

'You didn't. I miss her and I feel bad because I know she'll miss me but I love Jim and she wouldn't see it. Said he wasn't good enough and he had no prospects. He wants to make furniture and he had an apprenticeship. He's good but the company went bust and he lost his job.'

Izzy could see Jeanette's mum's point of view. On paper he had no qualifications beyond his Highers, although he'd proved to be a fantastic asset to the castle and he seemed to be able to turn his hand to anything. And they were both so young.'

'I'm sure she wants the best for you.' Izzy said diplomatically, giving Jeanette another hug. 'Why don't you give her a call? She'll have had time to think and perhaps emotions will be a bit calmer. You might be able to have a good talk. I'm sure she's worried about you.'

'I think I might,' replied Jeanette with a sniff. 'Thanks, Izzy. It must be nice living with your mum but her letting you get on with things. And she's not like a proper mum, is she? That must be great. She doesn't judge you, she takes you as you are. And she's done a lovely job on our sitting room even though she's got loads of other stuff to do. It looks like a proper home up there in the attic. It's so cosy.'

'Mmm,' Izzy muttered with a vague smile. Yes, she had put a lot of thought into making Jeanette and Jim's attic quarters warm and cosy, even getting a chimney sweep in so that they could use the fire, but Jim had done all the heavy lifting and Jeanette the cleaning. All Xanthe had really done was boss them about.

'Good morning, ladies,' said John as they pushed through the glass doors of the barn. 'Can I interest you in some mistletoe?'

He held up a large sprig with a cheeky grin as Izzy snatched up one of the fancy wicker baskets at the front of the store.

'I don't need mistletoe,' said Jeanette with a grin. 'But you, Izzy, definitely should. I reckon a Christmas kiss from Ross is well overdue. Honestly, you're both single, I don't know why he hasn't made a move on you. I'm sure he fancies you. I've seen him looking at you. A lot.'

Izzy glared at her, aware of John's guilty, wary expression. Served him right. Another man that had messed her about. And talking of which, what of Philip? He'd seemed so sincere and desperate to see her again when she'd seen him in Edinburgh but she'd not heard from him.

'I'm sure he doesn't. We're just friends.'

'But he's very good looking. You could have a fling.'

Izzy spat out a laugh. 'Who says I want a fling?'

'Well, you're not that old.'

Now it was John's turn to laugh. 'That's told you.'

With a huff, Izzy turned to him. 'Me and the child' – Jeanette giggled at that – 'are here to pick up the turkey, venison and sausages.'

'Coming right up. I'll go get it for you. Anything else?'

Izzy looked around the festive atmosphere of the shop. 'I'm sure you've got lots of tempting treats that I'm going to walk out with.'

'I've got lots of tempting treats,' he said with an outrageous wink.

She rolled her eyes and grinned at him. She'd realised he was a seasoned flirt. One of those chancers that tried it on with anyone new. He wasn't someone to take seriously. 'I'm sure you have but I've got a list.'

'She's really hot on lists.' Jeanette nodded. 'Lists for everything.'

'I like to be organised.'

'I'll leave you be while I go and get the bird for you. I'll have it at the front desk.'

'He's nice,' said Jeanette as he wandered off. 'You ought to ask him out, if you don't fancy Ross.'

At times like this, Izzy was clearly reminded that Jeanette

was only eighteen. This must be what it was like to have a younger, annoying sister.

'Thanks for the advice.' John had had his chance and blown it. Was it something about her? Good old dependable Izzy, everyone's friend until something more sparkly, more glamorous came along?

'Well, you're not getting any younger. Oh look, those chocolate penguins look nice. You could put them on the chocolate log, they'd look dead cute.'

Izzy was very glad of the change of subject.

'You should buy some of this smelly stuff,' said Jeanette, pointing to a selection of fragrant candles and an oil diffuser with sticks. 'Scottish Pine and Cranberry, very Christmassy. I bet Mrs Carter-Jones will expect this sort of thing.'

'Mrs Carter-Jones is very demanding.'

'I ken but she's paying for it. Money doesn't seem to matter to the woman.'

Izzy put several into the shopping basket, wincing at the cost of each of them, but Jeanette had a point, it was the sort of small touch that guests remembered. She always liked it when restaurants and bars had nice scented liquid hand soap.

It was very hard to remember her strict budget when there were so many delicious things on offer and she succumbed to some tiny sugar paste snow-dusted fir trees, which would go on top of the Christmas cake, some loganberry gin liqueur in the prettiest shaped glass bottle, as well as the double cream, whisky truffles and smoked bacon that were on her list. Thank goodness the castle had plenty of storage as the fridge was going to be chock full once she'd also collected the meat.

'Miss McBride.'

At the tart tone Izzy looked up from the cellophane-wrapped bag of cinnamon sticks and dried orange slices she'd just picked up but didn't need. 'Mrs McPherson, how are you?'

'I'm well.' Her dark, beady eyes stared hard at Izzy. With an ingratiating smile and looking about her as if the groceries might be bugged, she leaned towards Izzy and asked in a loud whisper, 'There's a rumour Rod Stewart's flying in for Hogmanay?'

'Not to my knowledge,' said Izzy, suppressing a giggle.

'So, it is the Beckhams, then,' crowed the postmistress with a fervent gleam in her eye. 'It was them or Rod. Shame, I'm partial to a bit of sing-song.'

'What?' asked Izzy, the image of Mrs McPherson doing a duet with Rod Stewart short-circuiting her brain. She was also horrified that such extravagant rumours were circulating.

Mrs McPherson tapped her nose. 'I know you canna tell me. Dinna worry. I'll no say a word. The secret's safe with me, hen.' With a serene smile, she picked up her wicker shopping basket and drifted away down the aisle.

Izzy watched her go as Jeanette giggled behind her.

'Here you go,' said John, nudging the turkey at the front desk. 'Don't forget to take the giblets out.'

'I won't,' said Izzy, thinking of all the things she needed to remember. She'd add it to the Christmas Day list. She just had to remember to do that.

'It'll feed plenty. So then there'll be turkey curry all round for when your guests get snowed in.' He paused and squinted up at the sky through one of the high Velux windows. 'The snow's due in the next couple of days. They're saying there could be up to twenty inches in less than twenty-four hours. The castle'll be cut off, but at this time of year, I don't need to say make sure you've got supplies in.'

'As long as the castle's not cut off before Christmas Eve, I don't—' Before she could finish she was interrupted by a yell from the other side of the shop.

'John, do you know where Mrs McPherson's order is? I canna find it.'

He huffed out an irritated sigh. 'I have to do every bluidy thing round here,' he muttered before striding off. 'Merry Christmas to ye. Hope you have a good one and Rod's in fine singing voice,' he called over his shoulder.

Izzy rolled her eyes. Mrs McPherson had a lot to answer for.

Just as she and Jeanette had loaded their shopping into the boot of the car, her mobile rang and, juggling her car keys, she answered it without registering who was calling.

'Izzy, it's Duncan. There's a mon here to see ye. Xanthe says he's called Philip.'

Chapter Nineteen

I zzy's heart was pounding as she walked into the castle, holding her head high. She'd made the short drive back as sedately as possible, deliberately not rushing, although her hands had trembled on the wheel. Philip could wait. She was not going to rush back. Though she couldn't deny their meeting in Edinburgh had been on her mind. Until of course that kiss with Ross.

Her mother's peal of laughter rang out from the morning room and for a moment Izzy hesitated, a small part of her wanting to at least run up and put on a quick coat of mascara.

'I'll take the shopping through,' said Jeanette, her eyes alight with curiosity. Izzy had barely spoken on the journey home; inside her head it was like a gale blowing on bin collection day, random thoughts flying like empty crisp packets through her brain.

'Thanks,' she said absently, following the sound of her mother's voice to the library, which was the current project. At the door she waited for a moment, still wondering what had brought Philip all this way.

'I can't believe you got a taxi from Fort William, darling. It must have cost a fortune. You must stay the night.'

She heard Philip's voice respond in a low murmur but didn't catch every word. 'It's … Izzy … feelings … forgive me.'

Forgive him. Could she? Her breath caught in her throat and a burst of hope ricocheted in her chest like a pinball wheel; crazy, random and manic. Had Philip come to tell her he loved her? And what about Ross? She couldn't stop thinking about that kiss but what did it mean to him? Was he really busy or just avoiding her?

She pushed open the door, a tremulous smile on her face.

'Izzy, darling. Look who's here.'

Philip stood beside Xanthe, a shy smile on his face, the bright winter sun coming in through the window catching his blond hair.

'Hi, Iz.' He held out both hands.

'Philip,' she said, not moving from the doorway, as a stray thought struck her. How had she never noticed before that he had sloping shoulders?

He paused before walking across the room. 'Iz, sorry to burst in on you but I…' His eyes sought hers.

She swallowed.

'I really needed to see you. I haven't been able to stop thinking about you since I saw you the other day.'

Xanthe clapped her hands. 'Isn't that lovely? Now come sit down, Izzy. I've been telling Philip all about the work we've been doing to the castle. You'll have to give him the grand tour and he's very taken with your walnut and coffee cake.' She waved a hand at the coffee table, where the empty cups and cake plate sat. Izzy frowned as another irrelevant thought popped into her head. *The cake was meant for Ross.*

Like a feeble, hen-witted idiot she nodded and sat down.

'It's delicious. I don't remember you baking before. Although just as well.' He patted his flat stomach. 'You've always been a feeder.'

Izzy stared at him. Had she? More often than not Philip had invited himself to her flat for dinner. But when she invited him, he was always busy doing other things.

He laughed. 'I hear you were in Fort William, if I'd realised I'd have cadged a lift instead of getting a taxi from the station.'

'Philip,' Izzy said, her head finally clearing at the mention of Fort William. There was a car full of shopping to unload, which she should be doing instead of leaving it to Jeanette. 'What are you doing here?'

Xanthe tutted. 'He's come to see you. Honestly.' She rolled her eyes conspiratorially at Philip. 'I think perhaps I should leave you two to it.'

'I think you should,' muttered Izzy.

Xanthe gave Philip a kiss on the cheek. 'So lovely to see you, it's so romantic surprising us like this. I'll see you later.' With that she tripped out of the room on her kitten heels, leaving behind a strong waft of her trademark Guerlain perfume.

Philip immediately stood and moved to sit beside Izzy.

'Darling—'

Izzy let out an involuntary laugh. "Darling" coming from him sounded so … so ridiculous.

Philip frowned. 'What?'

'Sorry,' she said, spluttering slightly. 'It just sounded' – she lifted her shoulders – 'well, you know. Odd.'

He narrowed his eyes. 'There's nothing odd about travelling for four hours to see you.'

She sighed. 'Why didn't you tell me you were coming?' She thought about her lists. 'It's really not a good time.'

Philip recoiled. 'Izzy! I've come all this way to see you. I've missed you. Really missed you.'

She nodded, not really knowing what to say to that. There were so many other things to think about, like whether Jeanette was putting the shopping away in the right places – the vegetables for Christmas Day should go in the second fridge in the pantry, along with any other items that needed to be kept separately. Would she know that the beef was for Christmas Eve? – and whether Ross would ever kiss her again.

Her hands plucked at the fabric of her jeans. One pot of cream was for the soup but the other one needed to be put in the other fridge. Was Ross avoiding her, after that wits-scattering kiss?

'Izzy. I made a terrible mistake with Antonia. Getting engaged like that so quickly.'

'That was a year ago,' said Izzy, frowning.

'I know but it took me a while to realise what was missing in my life. It was you. Iz, you know me so much better than anyone else. Antonia just didn't get me. You…' He smiled at her, his eyes seeking hers. 'You've always put up with my flaws and weaknesses. You understand the whole man.' Izzy frowned again. But what about her? Everything he was saying was about him. What about them being together was good for her?

The door opened and Philip looked up, his face immediately a mask of distaste. 'What's he doing here?'

Izzy turned to find Ross standing in the doorway, those broad shoulders framed by the entrance.

'Sorry,' he said in a brusque voice, 'didn't realise there was anyone in here.' For a moment he stared at Izzy, those blue eyes too perceptive by far. Her brain short-circuited and she stared at his lips because she couldn't seem to do anything else. He waited, a clear invitation for Izzy to speak if she wanted to but she couldn't find the words, her brain had been sucker punched by a completely new realisation. When she didn't say anything, he nodded and left.

'He lives here,' said Izzy in a quiet voice. It was obvious Ross had come to see if she needed rescuing. Doing something for her, just like he so often did. That was what friends did. They got up in the middle of the night to empty buckets. They gave people lifts to Edinburgh even though it could potentially expose their secret. They carried you when your feet were frozen.

Like Philip had said so many times, she knew him better than anyone else and she knew with absolute clarity that he would never have done any of those things for her. He only wanted her when he needed her. She was useful to him, nothing more.

'Do you love me, Philip?'

The classic mouth-dropping-open surprise told her everything as he struggled to say anything.

'I … well, of course. We've known each other for ever. You know I do.'

She stood.

'Where are you going?'

'To phone for a taxi to take you back to Fort William.'

'What! Don't be silly. What's this about? Not saying the words?'

'No,' said Izzy, giving him a blinding smile, everything clicking into place. 'But I'm just so busy. I haven't got time for you today or tomorrow or the day after. Give me a call in the New Year and perhaps we can go out for a meal in Edinburgh or something.'

'Izzy! You can't do this to me.'

'Do what?'

'Leave me high and dry when I've come all this way to see you.'

She gave a laugh and shook her head. 'Philip, we've always been friends and that's all it will ever be. I'm sorry it took us both so long to realise that.' She felt she was being more than generous, letting him off so gently.

He'd left her high and dry so many times, not least of all when he'd so callously announced his engagement to another woman. It had been cowardly because he'd known how she felt about him, but she wasn't about to follow his lead and be unkind to him; that wasn't her way. 'You deserve to find the right woman who loves you as much as you love her.'

Philip swallowed, hard. She watched his Adam's apple dip and then he looked up with a sad smile. 'When did you get to be so wise?'

She shrugged.

'Are you sure I can't stay? You won't change your mind?'

'Philip, I'm calling that taxi.'

'Won't you at least give me a hug for old time's sake?' He moved in before she could push him away.

The door opened again and this time it was Duncan, who

gave Philip a ferocious glare. 'Looking for Xanthe, have you seen her?'

Izzy had a hard job biting back her smile. The day Duncan voluntarily went looking for Xanthe was the day pigs went flying over the battlements.

Philip kissed her on the forehead as Duncan retreated.

'Thanks, Izzy. And if you change your mind, you know where I am.'

'I'm not going to change my mind. Now, you can help me put all these books back on the shelves while you wait for that taxi.'

'Do I have—'

'Yes, you do,' said Izzy sharply before grinning at him. He'd got away with far too much and it was as much her own fault as his. Now, if she wanted something from him, she'd ask.

Chapter Twenty

'Thanks, Izzy,' said Jim, flopping down into his usual seat at the kitchen table. 'I'm starving.'

'You're always starving,' said Jeanette as she laid the table. 'It's a good job Izzy is teaching me to cook.'

Izzy winced; the term 'cook' was a generous one. The other girl was still a liability in the kitchen.

'Smells grand, lass. Has your friend gone?' Duncan's eyes bored into hers with blatant curiosity and a touch of uncertainty.

'He's gone and he's *just* a friend,' she said.

'That's guid then, lassie.' Duncan beamed at her. 'You deserve the best and I could tell that whey-faced wee whippet was nae the man for you.'

Izzy's heart clenched in her chest, touched by his obvious relief.

'Don't worry,' she said, patting his hand; he wasn't one for hugs. 'I'm not going anywhere.'

'Guid,' he said gruffly. 'Want a hand dishing up?'

With a gentle smile, she nodded. 'That would be lovely, Duncan. Can you put the parmesan on the table?' Izzy strained the pasta then filled the heated plates with spaghetti. There was even one for Ross in the unlikely event he turned up while they were all there.

With a satisfied sniff, she spooned the rich Bolognese sauce over the pasta and Duncan handed the first four out. 'You going to put this one in the oven for… Ross! You're here. Just in time. Come sit down, lad.'

'Hello, stranger.' Jim nudged a chair with his foot, pushing it out for Ross. 'Take the weight off.'

Huh? thought Izzy. Unlike Jim, who'd been painting in the final rush to get the last two rooms ready, Ross had been sitting on his backside all day. She gave him a narrowed-eyed assessment. To be fair, he did look tired and his hair was even more rumpled than usual. It almost looked as if he'd put in a hard day's work.

'Working hard, lad?' asked Duncan once everyone was sitting at the table.

'Yeah,' said Ross, 'but I've almost finished. I'm trying to get the first draft done by Christmas, so I can help with the Carter-Joneses. Sorry I've not been around much to help.'

'You're a guest. You don't need to help.' Izzy's words tumbled out more sharply than she'd meant them to. 'Jeanette, can you pass me the pepper? Does anyone want anything to drink?'

Ross gave her a long look but didn't say anything as general conversation took over around the table. Every now and then, Izzy would look up to find Ross's eyes on her, studying her. Each time she looked back at her food and ignored him.

'That was great, thanks, Iz.' Jim pushed his plate away and rolled his shoulders. 'I can't decide whether to go back and finish another wall this evening or try and get it all done tomorrow.'

'I could help you tomorrow,' said Ross before Izzy could reply.

'You don't have to do that,' she said at exactly the same moment as Jim said, 'That would be brilliant. We'll get it done in no time.'

She folded her arms and sat back with a mutinous expression on her face as the two of them discussed their plan of action for the next day.

Duncan gave her a sympathetic wink, misreading the reason for her displeasure. 'Leave 'em to get on with it. If the lad wants to help, let him.'

Ross could help if he wanted but he shouldn't expect her to be falling over him with gratitude. She'd had enough of men blowing hot and cold to last her a lifetime. One minute he was kissing her and then the next he'd barely spoken to her for two days. She was done with that. Seeing Philip today had shown her that she deserved so much more than being someone's afterthought.

She got up and began to tidy the kitchen.

'Let me help,' said Jeanette.

'No, you go and relax. You haven't seen Jim all day, you'll be getting withdrawal symptoms,' she teased.

Jeanette grinned and dragged Jim off to their rooms up in the attic. Izzy was so focused on loading the dishwasher, she didn't notice that Duncan had slipped off and it was now just her and Ross.

'Sent him packing, then?'

'He's gone, yes.'

'He didn't stay long. I thought he'd come to propose or something. The big gesture, turning up unannounced.'

Izzy smiled. 'Something like that, but we agreed that we're better off being friends and I feel really good about that.' She shot him an impish grin. 'Besides, he had a bloody cheek turning up like that and expecting me to drop everything for him when it's only a few days before Christmas. I made him help me put the books back on the shelves in the library while he was waiting for his taxi.'

Ross laughed. 'You didn't. Poor chap came all this way and you put him to work.'

'Too right I did. There's still so much to do.'

'Which reminds me, I've done you a wine list,' he said, pulling a sheet of folded paper out of his pocket.

'Oh.'

'I should have given it to you earlier. Jeanette says you've been shopping already.'

'Christmas Eve is four days away,' she pointed out.

'Sorry, I lost track of time.'

'Really?' she said briskly and gave him a pointed look, making him aware that she knew he'd been avoiding her.

He winced. 'Izzy.'

It was her turn to raise an eyebrow. He owed her an apology or at the very least an explanation.

He stepped towards her and put a hand under her chin. 'I'm sorry.'

She lifted her face and his eyes locked on hers, the blue giving her an unexpected jolt.

'You should be,' she said, folding her arms, waiting to hear what he had to say. She was done with vacillating men.

'I'm sorry,' he repeated.

And she knew from the husky timbre of his voice that he was apologising for much more. She blinked at him, wary and stupidly hopeful. It *was* stupid. Hadn't she learned anything?

As she was battling between logic and emotion, his hand slipped around her waist and he gently tugged her towards him, his eyes never leaving hers. The move was so slow, the intent so clear, she could have moved if she really, really wanted to, but she was mesmerised by the soft apology and thoughtful concern in his gaze.

He tugged again, pulling her that last inch towards him, and cupped her face before gently kissing her, his thumb sliding along her cheekbone. The move completely melted the last of the rickety defence around her heart and her lips opened beneath his.

'I really am sorry,' he murmured against her lips. 'I … I needed some time to think. When I realised Xanthe's your mother, it completely threw me.'

She pulled back. 'I can't help who my mother is.'

'I know. It's just, she's very…'

'Loud?' asked Izzy with a touch of ice in her words. 'She's also kind, enthusiastic and she's *my* mother and I love her.'

'I know. I'm sorry, she reminds me of someone.' He shook his head as if trying to dislodge a memory.

'What exactly are you sorry for?' she asked, because it clearly wasn't just about her mother.

'For kissing you and then abandoning you.'

'Why did you?'

He lifted his hand to her face again. 'That kiss floored me.'

The words left her speechless. It wasn't what she was expecting at all.

'Do you want to get some fresh air?' he asked suddenly.

'Yes.'

Five minutes later they were bundled up against the night air, walking down towards the loch. Above them the sky was clear, filled with thousands of pinpricks of distant light, but over on the horizon, lit up by the moon, was a bank of clouds, hovering with menace like invaders lurking on the border.

'There'll be a heavy frost in the morning,' said Izzy.

'More snow's on the way. You can feel the nip of it in the air. A special type of coldness.'

'Well, it had better stay away until our guests have arrived.' A snowstorm was the last thing they needed. 'It can snow on Christmas day and then we'll have a white Christmas. That'll please—'

'McBride, I didn't come out here to talk about the weather.'

'You called me Izzy before.'

'I did.' He stopped and put his hands on her waist again, cradling her hips. 'I meant what I said earlier. I'm sorry I've been avoiding you. I've been trying to pretend that I could ignore you – the attraction – but when I kissed you, it was something else. I'm … not good at relationships. I try and avoid drama and intense emotion at all costs. Of course, I've had relationships, but I like to keep them on an even keel.' He stopped and his mouth curved in a wry smile. 'That kiss threw me off a cliff.'

'Oh.' The words punched into her and all she could do was stare up at him, her lips parted in surprise, her eyes filled with wonder. 'Oh,' she said again because she needed to say something but it appeared that the power of speech had completely escaped her.

Men didn't say things like that, did they? Not to women like Izzy. She was the good friend next door, sort of girl. So, it was a good job that he kissed her again.

Butterflies soared and danced in her stomach, swooping and diving, as her blood fizzed in her veins like Alka-Seltzer on speed. The touch of his lips just as intoxicating as the words '*threw me off a cliff*', which reverberated over and over through her brain.

Joy, excitement, exhilaration – all whooshed through her, loosening the lid that had secured the feelings she'd been trying to keep in check for the last few days. The relief and happiness made her giddy. This man felt the same way about her as she did about him. After years of chasing hope, of unrequited feelings, it was a revelation.

At some point, snow began to fall, but they were so wrapped up in each other, it went unheeded until a large flake slid its way between them, landing on Izzy's nose. She sighed and pulled back. Ross's black hair was already covered in a fine layer of white.

'We're in danger of turning into snowmen if we stay here any longer,' said Ross with a rueful smile.

'It would be a good way to go,' replied Izzy a touch dreamily, her lips tingling.

He hooked an arm through hers. 'Come on, let's go and warm up. I feel a hot toddy coming on.'

'Mmm, I like the sound of that.'

Curled up in front of the fire, next to Ross, with a tumbler of whisky, Izzy watched the flames dancing in the hearth, licking and curling at the logs, which crackled and spat. She sighed with rare contentment. She seemed to have been operating at a hundred miles an hour for the last month and it was a relief to rest her head against his shoulder. Since they'd come in they hadn't said much but as always with Ross, his silence was companionable and restful. She didn't feel the need to have to talk.

'This is nice,' he murmured, his arm around her shoulder stroking her forearm.

'You said that about our first kiss.' She looked up, serious now. 'And then you said you were "thrown off a cliff". I'd say you're a master of understatement.'

He sighed and turned to face her.

'It doesn't sound very grown up for a thirty-five-year-old man if I say I panicked, does it?'

She considered that for a minute. 'I'm not sure. I guess it depends on how you respond to the panic.'

'Badly, obviously. I withdrew, tried to go back into my cave.' He kissed her cheek. 'After Nicole, I've made it my mission to ensure my life is on an even keel. I think that's why I've kept my writing identity a secret. I panicked because I'd lulled myself into a false sense of security. I felt so comfortable with you – no drama, no histrionics.' He laughed. 'That's why it was such a shock. And that doesn't sound very complimentary, does it? But that instant explosion... I mean, I wanted to kiss you, been wanting to for a while but I didn't expect that...' He shook his head, his brow wrinkling in confusion. 'I'm not a great romantic. I don't do big gestures or PDAs.' He pulled a face. 'I've seen too much of it when it didn't mean anything. So when I kissed you... Like I said, it completely threw me. I am sorry.'

The quiet, sincere admission jolted her. That she, ordinary Izzy McBride, could have such an impact on gorgeous, successful, self-assured Ross Strathallan. A little ember of feminine satisfaction burned fierce and bright in her heart. No, on the face of it, his words weren't very romantic, but they were heartfelt and honest.

Philip had been very good at the romantic touches – candlelit dinners, surprise weekends away, extravagant flowers – but now she knew they'd been strategic, designed to reel her back in when he'd been distant or absent for a while.

'You're forgiven, on the understanding you don't do it again. That's why I sent Philip packing today. He was my on-off boyfriend for years. We met at university and he never quite made up his mind if he wanted to be with me or not. I loved him, so I put up with the crap.' She took his hand and smiled up at him. 'You could say, I facilitated his crap.'

Ross winced. 'We're only human. And I suspect he knew.'

She nodded. 'He admitted as much today, although I'd already realised what a real friend is.' She kissed Ross's cheek. 'It's someone who thinks about you, cares about you and offers unconditional help because they can see that you need it.'

'I hope that we're going to be so much more than friends.'

Izzy nodded, a little shy. 'I'd like that.'

Chapter Twenty-One

'**P**hew!' said Ross, steering the car up the drive back to the castle the next morning, the boot full of clanking bottles. 'We made it.'

'Thanks so much. I know you would rather have stayed in bed this morning.' Izzy peered out at the snowy landscape, the feathery snowflakes curling down around them.

'Hello?' He glanced at her, a wolfish grin lighting his face. 'Wouldn't you?'

Her heart fizzed for a second, full of memories of the previous night. She wriggled in her seat, her nerve endings still tingling from his attention. For someone who said he didn't do big emotion, he certainly knew how to make a girl feel good. From the moment he'd kissed her by the fire, she'd felt as if she were his sole focus and when Ross focused on something, he was very single-minded. When he'd led her by the hand up to his bedroom, she hadn't hesitated because he wasn't the only one who'd fallen off a cliff.

Despite the wonderful dancing butterflies in her chest,

every now and then, when she thought about the heavy dump of snow forecast for later that afternoon, her stomach contracted. She crossed her fingers in her pocket. *Please, please, please let the Carter-Joneses get here.* She didn't dare think about the money they'd spent on food and wine, let alone the refurbishments. Although to be fair, the castle looked fit for a king. She sighed as they slithered round the final bend. 'Thank goodness we made it.'

'Yes, I'm not sure I could have carried you and the wine this time.'

She smiled at him but still asked, 'Do you think the roads are going to be okay?'

'Well, if they're not, we've got enough wine to withstand a siege let alone being snowed in.' She suspected Ross had deliberately misunderstood her question to reassure her, as if it was unthinkable that their guests wouldn't make it. She followed his lead.

'And if the food is terrible, we can get the guests so drunk they won't remember it.' She forced a smile and then noticed the strange car parked outside the castle. 'Oh God, do you think that's them?' She pointed to a sleek Jaguar estate. 'They're not due for a few days yet. Maybe they decided to beat the weather.' She began gathering up her things. 'I was going to welcome them and do it all properly,' she wailed.

'I'm sure Xanthe...' He stopped and squinted at the car, frowning.

'Don't even say it. Oh God. Xanthe.' Izzy closed her eyes, imagining her mother's idea of a welcome, and was already scrabbling to open the car door. 'She'll probably have made them carry their own cases in, shown them to their rooms and bounced on the bed, telling them how comfy the mattresses are, and not even thought of offering them refreshment after a long drive. They're coming from Edinburgh. They must have set off early.'

Ross laid a hand on her arm. 'Breathe, McBride. Breathe.'

'Yes. Breathe. It's going to be fine.'

'They've come to a genuine Scottish castle with a white Christmas to boot. The rooms all look perfect, the food is going to be excellent and like you said, worst comes to the worst, we'll get them pissed. You've got me, Jeanette, Jim and Duncan on side. We're a team. It will be fine.'

Despite his words, as soon as the car drew to a halt, she hopped out of the door and, leaving Ross to bring the wine in, she scurried inside, almost tripping over the suitcase that had been abandoned in the porch. With her heart beating rapidly, a mixture of nerves and apprehension, she hurried into the main hall. The fire was laid but there were no welcoming flames as she'd planned but thankfully the garland of fir branches wound around the spindles and banister of the staircase, decorated with alternating red velvet and satin tartan bows, made the room look festive, along with the artfully draped sprigs of holly above the picture frames, which Izzy knew she couldn't have achieved in a million years. Left to her, they'd have looked like random drunken twigs that had been abandoned to their fate.

On the mantelpiece above the fire were a row of fat white candles surrounded by fir cones, which had been spray-painted gold. It was tasteful and striking without being too much. Izzy felt a little pang of relief, the tension leaking out of her like a deflating balloon. First impressions would be favourable. This looked like everything you might expect from a Scottish castle.

A distant shriek of laughter rang out from the corridor leading to the kitchen as Ross came in carrying a box of wine bottles.

'They're in the kitchen?' Izzy shook her head in disbelief and headed that way closely followed by Ross.

At least Xanthe had offered the guests refreshments, thought Izzy as she pushed open the door to find Xanthe and a middle-aged couple sitting around the table with a plate of shortbread biscuits and mugs of tea. The woman didn't look the least bit like Izzy had expected Mrs Carter-Jones to look. She'd imagined someone quite smartly dressed but a bit matronly. This woman had white-blonde hair tipped in purple cut in a short crop with longer gelled curls on top and she wore a denim smock accessorised with a brilliant rainbow-coloured silk scarf and stripy tights in mustard, green and orange along with faded red leather shoes reminiscent of Cornish pasties.

'Izzy!' Her mother greeted her as if she'd been gone for days instead of a couple of hours. 'Come and meet Alicia and Graham.'

'Hello,' said Izzy as brightly as she could, wondering why on earth Xanthe had brought them in here. Admittedly, with the big pine table, the dresser filled with earthenware crockery and the Rayburn it was cosy, but her mother had put all that effort into making the sitting room look beautiful. 'Nice to meet you. I hope—'

'Mum! Dad!' Ross put the box of wine down with a thunk. 'What are you doing here?'

The woman stood up, beaming from multi-pierced ear to multi-pierced ear. Izzy wasn't sure she'd ever seen quite so many earrings on one person before. 'Ross!' Her raspy smoky-voiced yell outdid Xanthe's usual volumes by several decibels. 'My baby.'

Izzy cringed at the utter mortification on Ross's face as Alicia launched herself at him, the folds of her voluminous smock and the tails of her scarf flying, her arms outstretched.

Ross reared back. 'Dear god, Mother. I'm thirty-five.'

'You'll always be my baby,' she said, throwing her arms around him in an extravagant hug. 'Oh. You big lug, come here, give me a hug.'

Ross gave her a stiff embrace, patting her on the back.

She kissed him on both cheeks and then stepped back to assess him. 'You've been working out, young man. I can feel muscles.'

'You can't feel muscles. I'm the same as I've always been.'

'Buff. Your father's never been buff in his life, have you, Graham?' she called over to her husband, to whom Ross bore a strong resemblance.

'No, dear,' he said, catching Izzy's eye and giving her the ghost of a wry smile. Suddenly Izzy knew exactly who Ross had been talking about when he said that Xanthe reminded him of someone and that he was used to people like her.

'What are you doing here?' asked Ross again.

'They've come for Christmas,' crowed Xanthe, clearly rather pleased with herself.

'But…'

'I mentioned to Alicia that you were staying here and she said you weren't coming home for Christmas and she hadn't seen you for ages. Well, there's plenty of room here, so I invited her and Graham to come and stay for the week.' Xanthe folded her hands on the table as if expecting a pat on the back.

'You *mentioned* to Alicia?' Izzy folded her arms in an 'and-what-were-you-up-to' stance.

'Didn't I tell you, darling?' Xanthe said with breezy nonchalance. Izzy narrowed her eyes at her mother in silent challenge. They both knew full well Xanthe hadn't said a word.

'There was a piece on Alicia's website that I thought would look perfect in the Rose room. I decided to make an enquiry.' Xanthe's blithe tone didn't fool Izzy for a moment. Her bloody mother had seized on the tenuous link of Ross staying here and had contacted Alicia.

'So here we are,' trilled Alicia. 'When I heard it was a castle, well, I wasn't going to say no. I popped the turkey in the freezer, packed up and we set off. And what a marvellous place you have, Xanthe. It's so kind of you to invite us.'

'Very kind,' muttered Izzy, mainly to herself because Xanthe and Alicia were far too busy having a mutual gush-in to hear.

'It's so wonderful to meet you. I absolutely adore your work.'

'That reminds me. Graham, the car.' Alicia clapped her hands in a chop-chop, imperious gesture.

He rose and clapped a hand on Ross's back as he passed him. 'Good to see you, son.'

'You too, Dad,' he said, his mouth curving into a gentle smile that warmed Izzy's heart. The quick, silent communication between the two men said so much about their relationship.

'So Ross, Xanthe tells me you're writing a book. Why didn't I know about this? What about your work at the university? Have they fired you?'

'No, Ma, I'm on sabbatical.'

'Writing a book. What sort of book and why didn't you tell me? I mean a book. That's so exciting. What's it about? Am I in it?'

'No. How's the latest exhibition going?'

'The gallery in London is making excessive demands, I'm exhausted.' She turned to Xanthe. 'You have no idea how much hard work is involved in being an artist, you know, it really takes it out of one.' When she dragged the back of her hand across her forehead, Izzy had a hard time keeping her face straight. 'So it was so lovely of you to invite us here for a rest. I hear you're a fantastic cook, Izzy.'

'Er, well, I'm not sure about fantastic but I'll do my best,' said Izzy, ready to strangle her mother. So now there were eighteen for lunch. 'Invited anyone else, Mother?'

Alicia squealed and Izzy did a double take. She was Xanthe's kindred spirit.

'Oh Xanthe, you don't look old enough to be Izzy's mother. I had you pegged as sisters.'

'I like you even more, Alicia. And darling, for the love of God, please don't call me "Mother", it's so aging.'

'Don't even think about it, Ma,' said Ross, at the suddenly thoughtful expression on Alicia's face.'

'Spoilsport.' She pouted with a good-natured grin.

Graham came back into the room carrying a parcel wrapped in black tissue paper and a wide violet chiffon ribbon tied in an extravagant bow. He gave it to Alicia who duly presented it to Xanthe. 'A small gift for our very generous hostess.'

Xanthe's eyes widened. 'For me?' She clutched her chest.

Izzy wanted to laugh; the two of them were like a pair of 1940s matinee idols.

Tugging at the bow, she opened the parcel. 'Oh, my goodness. Alicia!' She gasped. 'It's beautiful. Stunning. Oh Alicia, you've made my day, my year, my life.' Tears shimmered in Xanthe's eyes as she said with a choked voice, 'I've always wanted a piece of your art but I could never have afforded it. That's so kind of you. Look, Izzy.' She held up the irregular shaped piece of turquoise glass, which shimmered with a range of blues and golds. It was spectacular and very typical of the work that Xanthe had admired for many years. Izzy felt a little bubble of emotion at her mother's pure joy, knowing how much the stunning piece of art would mean to her, as well as feeling a touch of guilt for judging her so harshly. Her mother really had been a fan of Alicia's work for many years. No wonder she'd jumped at the chance to get to know her.

'That is fabulous,' said Izzy, going over and dropping a kiss on her mum's cheek. 'I know how much you'll treasure it.'

'I know exactly where I'm going to put it. In the sitting room on the shelf in the alcove.' Xanthe jumped to her feet, clutching the glass piece to her chest and holding her other hand out to Alicia. 'Come. Come see what you think. And it's much nicer in there. We'll all go. Izzy, why don't you let us know when lunch will be served?'

The minute the two women left, the atmosphere in the room thinned a little, like flat Champagne missing its effervescent bubbles. Graham raised his eyebrows at his son and smiled. 'I'd best go keep an eye on them. Double trouble, who knows what they'll get up to.'

'You're a brave man, Dad.'

'Years of practice,' he said, with a mischievous smile that lit up his face and further emphasised the resemblance between father and son.

Izzy cocked her head at Ross once his father had left the room. 'So that's your mother.'

'Yup. That's my mother.'

'She doesn't know about Ross Adair, then.'

'No.' He shuddered. 'Can you imagine? I'd never get any peace. She'd tell everyone, everywhere we went.'

'I think she might be even louder than my mother.' Izzy suddenly burst into giggles. 'What were you thinking, coming here? Out of the frying pan and into the fire.'

'I didn't think it mattered when I first came, I planned to stay holed up in my room the whole time but' – he smiled at her – 'then there were other attractions.'

Izzy shot him an arch look. 'My coffee and walnut cake?'

'That and the mince pies.'

He moved forward and put his arms around her. 'And this,' he said, lowering his lips.

Izzy melted into the embrace, still consumed by the crazy fireworks that went off every time his lips touched hers. It was crazy, the fizz of attraction, but at the same time the sense of calm that being with him brought. He was the safe harbour despite the storm.

Chapter Twenty-Two

I zzy smiled as she reread the WhatsApp message with advice on the best way to ice her Christmas cake. When all this was over, she was going to have to send a large bunch of flowers to Fliss and something liquid to Jason. They'd both been lifesavers over the last few weeks. She arranged the fir trees in one corner of the square Christmas cake among the snowy peaks of thick white icing that now covered the cake. Simple but effective, exactly as Fliss had suggested.

'You're just in time to lick the bowl,' she said as Jeanette burst into the kitchen, knowing the younger woman had a very sweet tooth.

'Ace.' Jeanette swooshed her finger around the bowl, scooping up a great dollop of icing. 'Yum! And that looks fantastic, much nicer than a boring shop-bought one.' She circled the cake, her arms behind her back, just about holding back a grin.

'What?' asked Izzy, carrying the icing-covered utensils over to the sink.

'I spoke to my mum.' The words tumbled out. 'And it was fine. She cried.'

'Oh, Jeanette, that is brilliant.' Izzy dropped everything and threw her arms around Jeanette. 'Well, not that she cried, obviously, but that you've spoken.'

'It was your mum that finally convinced me to do it. Said how sad she'd be if the two of you weren't talking and she couldn't imagine not spending Christmas with you.'

Izzy paused, a little surprised. 'Xanthe said that?'

'Yeah, she said since your gran died, it had always been the two of you, that you're the two musketeers, and it wouldn't be Christmas without you. It got me thinking. I've never had Christmas away from Mum before.' Jeanette scrunched up her face. 'After that I couldn't stop thinking about her and then Jim said I should ring her as well. So I did.'

'And I take it, it went well,' said Izzy, studying Jeanette's flushed but happy face.

'I did get it in the neck for running away but I think she was so pleased that I called, she's forgiven me. Anyway, I hope it's okay – your mum said it was – but she's driving up the day after Christmas to spend New Year with us. She'll be no trouble and she can stay up in our little sitting room.'

'Don't be daft,' said Izzy immediately – because what else could she say? Jeanette and Jim were part of her family now. 'She can't stay up there.' Izzy laughed with mild hysteria because after all, seriously, what was one more? The numbers were already totally out of hand. 'But you're going to have to up your game on the potato peeling. We're already up to eighteen as it is.'

'No. Mrs Carter-Jones hasn't added more, has she?'

'No, Ross's parents turned up this morning.'

Jeanette's eyes performed dinner plate impressions. 'His parents? Here? Did he ask you?'

Izzy laughed again, telling herself she needed to get a grip, she was starting to lose it.

'No. He knew nothing about it. Xanthe invited them. Wait until you meet Alicia, his mum. I think her and Xanthe are actually secretly related.'

'What do you mean?'

'You'll see, soon enough. But it means preparing another room. We're going to have to do some room re-allocation and emergency cleaning.' Izzy cast a despairing look around the kitchen.

'Don't worry. I'll do the cleaning. Jim can help me when him and Ross have finished wallpapering the Salmon room. By the time the Carter-Joneses get here, everything will be ship-shape.'

'Thanks, Jeanette. Although if any more people turn up, I'm going to need another turkey.'

'Hey, it's okay, we've got this. Honest, Izzy. You know me and Jim will do anything for you. You saved us. We would have had to go home and even though Mum's come round, it's on our terms.'

Jeanette's phone beeped and she took it out of her back pocket. 'Oh God. What does Mrs Carter-J want now?'

She cackled in delight as she read the message. 'What sort of candles do you provide? They must be organic.' She held up a hand which Izzy obligingly high-fived. 'Told you.'

'You did. Well done. You can put them out now. I've been hiding them from Xanthe. I wouldn't put it past her to light all of them in one go if she got hold of them.'

'You're so mean about her. She's wonderful.'

'She is wonderful but a bit unreliable sometimes.'

'Wait 'til you meet my mum, she's *very* reliable. Not like yours at all. Xanthe is so much fun.'

'So you've said before. Come on, we need to crack on. I've got gravy to make.' Jason had recommended making the gravy in advance as a time-saving method, using a recipe that Adrienne at the cookery school had taught them.

As she chopped onions and peeled vegetables, drizzling olive oil and sprinkling herbs over chicken wings, she kept looking out the window, hoping each time to find that the snow had ceased falling, but every time the pale grey sky was exactly the same; there had been no let-up of the whirling blizzard of snowflakes for hours.

Once the roasting dish was stowed in the oven, she turned her thoughts to dinner for eight that night. Luckily she'd planned to make two lasagnes – one to freeze for later – so she had plenty of ingredients and it was as easy to make one big one as it was to make two. That with a salad and garlic bread would be perfect.

As she took the mince out of the fridge, she eyed the large piece of venison, which had become her bête noire. Maybe she should have practised making a Wellington before. It was a bit too late now.

This time tomorrow the guests would be here and she'd have to put into practice everything she'd learned during those weeks in Ireland. It was all going to be fine. Providing they got here.

At five-thirty, Xanthe marched into the kitchen. She'd changed into a scarlet dress with white piping and red suede boots.

'You're a few days early, Mother Christmas,' said Izzy, sliding the lasagne and the foil-wrapped French stick filled with garlic butter into the oven to cook.

'Oh, I've got another outfit for Christmas Day but I thought as Alicia and Graham were here, we'd have drinks in the lounge. So why don't you go up and put a dress on for a change? Make yourself look pretty.' The matching red fascinator bobbed as Xanthe grabbed her by the elbow and tried to steer her towards the door.

'I'm fine as I am,' said Izzy.

'No, you've been working far too hard. I'll lay the table while you go and freshen up.'

Izzy frowned at this unnatural concern, which wasn't like Xanthe.

'I thought we'd eat in here, save the dining room for tomorrow night.'

'Excellent idea, darling. Go on, off you go. I know where the knives and forks are.' She flapped her hands as if Izzy was a chicken that needed shooing away.

'Okay,' she said. There wasn't anything to do until the lasagne was cooked and it would be nice to spend some time out of the kitchen for a change and to sit down on one of the plump sofas, although she might fall asleep if she wasn't careful.

'Don't take too long. I've got Graham on drinks duty. I've told everyone to be there by quarter to six, so you'd better be quick.'

'Yes, Xanthe.' Judging by her mother's immaculate makeup, the lipstick the exact same shade as her dress, someone had allowed themselves more than fifteen minutes to get ready. Izzy might be a low maintenance sort of gal but she did like to dress up and make an effort sometimes. Fifteen minutes felt like a stretch but she resolved to do her best.

She still had quite a few dresses from her event management days, including a couple of go-to little black dresses, which her mother described as funeral chic. Knowing that donning one of them would elicit exactly that comment, she took a blue velvet dress from her wardrobe instead. Without being vain, she knew that it complemented her red hair and flattered her shape, hugging her curvy figure in all the right places. She was never going to be, and didn't want to be, a stick insect. After a super quick shower, she applied a barely there lipstick, a single coat of mascara and a spritz of perfume. 'You'll do,' she told herself in the mirror, tugging out her usual ponytail and dragging a brush through the long curls.

'Well, look at you,' said Ross, catching sight of her at the top of the stairs. Her eyes widened. Well, look at him. He'd changed into smart black trousers and a white shirt that was open at the neck and – wonders would never cease – it looked as if he'd brushed his hair, although she did wonder how long it would be before the usual forelock of wild hair fell forward.

He saw her quick glance. 'Don't you start. My mother's already telling me I need a haircut.'

'I was thinking it looked unusually smart.'

'It won't last.'

'I figured as much.' She smiled at him.

'You look gorgeous, by the way. I like the dress.'

'Thank you.' She stroked her hand down the skirt, enjoying the luxurious feel of the velvet. 'Once upon a time I used to look quite smart.'

'I can't imagine you anywhere but the castle. It suits you. Do you think you'll stay?'

'I think so, unless I sell it, I suppose.'

He did a quick double take. 'Sell it?'

'If it doesn't pay its way, I'll have to. That's why so much is resting on the Carter-Joneses.'

'I didn't mean that. Who owns the castle?'

'I do.'

He burst out laughing. 'And Xanthe plays Lady of the Manor. I honestly thought she was the one who inherited it.'

'Nope, Great Uncle Bill left it to me … which, I might add, did not go down terribly well. Although I can see why he did.' She shook her head. 'I love my mother but she doesn't have a bean of common sense. If things were left to her the place would fall down around her and she'd end up living in one room with cats, trying to keep it going rather than sell it. She's always wanted to live here. I couldn't deny her that. The only way I could think of keeping it was to open it up as a hotel.'

'So your great uncle left it to you but no money.'

'That's it, although he said things would take care of themselves. He counted on me being the practical one.'

'Heavy burden.'

Izzy shrugged. 'It is, but now, having lived here, I really don't want to leave.'

They'd reached the bottom step and both of them stopped. 'I'm sure this week is going to go perfectly, the Carter-Joneses will sing your praises to all their rich friends and you'll be booked up for months. It's looking fantastic.' He held up a hand. 'And don't you dare say anything about food. You've been feeding us for the last few months and you've not poisoned us and no one has died of malnutrition.'

'There's a difference between everyday cooking and Michelin star. The Carter-Joneses sound so dif—'

'Up themselves. In which case, don't worry. You'll either please them or you won't but there's no point second guessing anything right now. You deserve a drink and a break. Come on.'

———

Even if they hadn't known where to find Xanthe and Alicia, their joint whoops and cackles would have alerted the nearest zookeeper. When Izzy and Ross walked into the room, the two of them were sitting side by side on one of the sofas, their screeches of mirth sounding like a pair of hyaenas who'd been at the laughing gas.

'Can I get you a drink, love?' asked Graham, with that long-suffering smile of his. 'I think those two have just about left a glass of Prosecco in the bottom of the bottle.'

'They look like they're having a good time,' said Izzy.

'Your mother is quite a character,' he said, filling a glass for her. 'I've not known Alicia to take to someone quite so quickly.' He gave her the sort of wholesome smile that reached his eyes. 'They're two peas in a pod.'

'I hope you don't feel left out,' said Izzy.

'God, no.' He laughed. 'I'm delighted Alicia has found a friend.' He winked. 'Gives me a break.'

Ross rolled his eyes but didn't say anything.

Duncan walked in on bandy legs and sent the two women a suspicious glare and stalked over to join the rest of the group.

'What's going on?'

'Duncan, this is Ross's dad, Graham, and that's his mum, Alicia.'

He muttered a couple of hellos and took the bottle of beer that Ross offered him. Duncan was a creature of habit.

'So what time do these guests arrive tomorrow?' asked Duncan, as Jeanette and Jim walked into the room and joined them, after brief introductions to the two newcomers.

'Mrs Carter-J said they expected to be here at about four p.m.,' said Jeanette, consulting her phone.

'Great,' said Jim. 'I'll bank the fire in the hall in readiness and be ready to serve the welcome drinks.'

'I'll put my kilt on,' said Duncan.

'Me too,' said Jim.

'And me,' said Ross.

'Well, if you can't beat 'em, join 'em,' said Graham. 'I'll put mine on too.'

Izzy grinned at them. 'That'll set the scene beautifully. And then, while they're drinking, Jim and Duncan can take their cases up. We can show them round and then tell them that dinner will be at six-thirty.'

'And are you all organised for dinner?' asked Ross with a teasing smile.

'I have my lists,' said Izzy, patting her notebook, which was never far from her hand at the moment.

'I'm looking forward to dinner,' said Graham. 'Xanthe tells me you're a Cordon Bleu chef.'

Izzy's drink went down the wrong way. 'No, she's exaggerating. Please god, don't say she said that to the Carter-Joneses.'

Jeanette pulled a face.

'She didn't.'

With worry shining in her eyes, Jeanette nodded. 'She did, I'm afraid.'

'Why didn't you tell me?' Izzy squeaked.

'Because it would have made you panic, like you're doing now,' said Jeanette.

'I'm not panicking,' said Izzy, knocking back the rest of her Prosecco in one quick slug. The warmth hit her stomach with a punch of heat that spread out like a mushroom cloud. She sucked in a noisy breath. 'Okay, I am panicking.'

'McBride, breathe,' said Ross. 'You can do this.'

'I can't. Oh God. I have to. I feel sick.' She really did. All along her biggest worry was the food. She wasn't a professional. She'd been on a six-week cookery course to improve her basic skills. The expectation had been that she'd serve breakfast and a hearty comfort-food dinner to guests who wanted to stay in a castle. Never in the plan had there been an ambition to be a five-star luxury hotel.

The next morning, Izzy woke early and headed into the kitchen to spend the morning making another partan bree, which she planned to serve as a starter with home-made bread rolls. After that, she'd serve roast beef with dauphinoise potatoes with green beans, shallots, garlic and toasted almonds. The food would be okay but her presentation skills left much to be desired. It was all about the ingredients, she told herself. The beef had been locally sourced, the potatoes were from the farm shop and very fresh and the beans would be blanched so that they'd be perfectly crisp with that lovely nutty flavour.

She prepared as much as she could including the cranachan dessert, soaking the raspberries in a touch of whisky and toasting the oats.

After she'd done everything she could in advance, she and Jeanette raced around, checking and double checking that all the rooms were perfect. Xanthe had given Graham and Alicia one of the newly decorated rooms and Izzy hoped that the Carter-Jones party were all couples. Worst came to the worst, she'd give up her room.

By two o'clock her nerves jangled with anxiety as she looked out at the steady snowfall, but with so much to do, she couldn't afford to stop and think about anything. At quarter to four, they all gathered in the hall while Jim, resplendent in kilt complete with smart ghillie brogues, ceremoniously lit the fire. Jeanette wore one of Izzy's plain black dresses with a tartan sash matching his kilt, while Duncan wore his own plaid along with the Strathallan men who wore matching kilts. Izzy wore her best black dress along with smart black heels, which were for show only; the minute she was back in the kitchen she'd be back in her DMs.

'Of course, there's no guarantee they'll be here on time,' said Izzy. 'The weather's still atrocious.'

'I've had no word from Mrs Carter-J. Surely she'd let us know if they were running late.' Jeanette flicked a tiny fleck of lint from the sleeve of her dress.

'True,' said Izzy. Now that she had nothing to do, her nerves intensified. She sat down on the sofa nearest the fire, within reach of the Edinburgh glass decanter filled with a ten-year-old malt from Bill's collection. Cut glass tumblers, shined and polished by Jeanette, glistened in the firelight, the golden orange flames magnified by the crystal.

After half an hour, Izzy's knees were noticeably jittering up and down, so Ross suggested that they all went back to work. 'I'll keep a look out and let you know when they arrive.'

'That sounds like a good plan,' said Izzy, anxious to get back to the kitchen. 'I can always put dinner back a bit if they're really late.'

They dispersed and Izzy, back in the kitchen, consulted her list for the day. Oh shit, she'd forgotten to take the oats out of the oven and they were burned to a crisp.

As she railed at herself, she stopped, hearing an unusual noise that was getting louder. She peered out of the window at the same moment Jeanette came running into the kitchen, closely followed by Xanthe and Alicia.

'They've come by helicopter,' shrieked Xanthe.

'It's landing on the front lawn,' Jeanette squeaied.

'It's quite extraordinary,' added Alicia. 'I don't think I've seen anyone arrive by helicopter, anywhere.'

All the nerves jumped up into Izzy's throat threatening to strangle her.

'Okay, action stations, everyone.' This was it. What they'd been preparing for, for the last six weeks.

Twenty-five thousand pounds to the rescue.

Xanthe, Alicia, Jeanette, Jim, Duncan and Izzy crowded onto the front steps and, obviously alerted by the noise, Ross and his father joined them. They watched as three figures emerged from the helicopter, two jumping down and ducking below the rotor blades to scurry towards the castle carrying holdalls. The third person, well bundled up in a white puffer coat that made them almost blend into the snow, tugged at a huge grey suitcase, which then tumbled out of the helicopter, landing almost on top of them. They began dragging the case across the top of the snow like an unwieldy sled, bowed double beneath the updraft of the helicopter rotors. Izzy frowned as the figures drew closer. It looked as if it were only the younger Carter-Joneses. The sound of the helicopter engine began to increase, the noise quite deafening, and the blades spun faster as it began to rise up into the sky, whipping up the snow in a mini blizzard as it took off. Two of the figures waved madly to the pilot and then, noticing the woman battling with the suitcase, one of them went over to help her. The three of them began plodding through the knee-deep snow towards everyone on the steps.

'Tits and teeth, everyone,' said Xanthe. 'Yoohoo, welcome to Kinlochleven Castle.'

'Do that and you'll scare them off,' muttered Ross.

'Don't be mean, darling,' said Alicia, nudging her son in the ribs.

Xanthe waved but Izzy frowned as the three people drew up.

The first two were waving at her, huge grins on their faces.

Izzy blinked. It couldn't be.

'Hey, Izzy. Surprise!'

'We thought we'd come and help you.'

'Fliss! Jason! Oh my God. What are you doing here?'

As Jason launched himself at her, Fliss joined in and they ended up in a giggling group hug.

'I don't believe it,' said Izzy for the third time.

'The Avengers are here. We've come to save Christmas lunch,' said Jason, beaming at her.

Fliss nudged him. 'We've come to offer our assistance. And

we've brought sleeping bags, so hopefully you don't mind putting us up.'

'A stable will do,' added Jason cheerfully.

With a roll of her eyes, Fliss groaned. 'You're so not funny.'

'Oh guys, it's so good to see you.' Izzy thought she might just burst into tears. Both of them were seriously good cooks. Jason was a bit of a genius in the kitchen and Fliss was no slouch but she was also fantastic at presentation. With the two of them on her side, she might just pull this off.

'Er, hello.' A voice intruded and Izzy turned to see the woman in the white coat and everyone else staring at her.

'Sorry,' said Izzy.

'This is Hattie,' said Fliss. 'She bagged a lift with us from Edinburgh Airport. Jason's boss offered us a lift to Edinburgh and then the pilot said he'd bring us on as he was heading this way and Hattie overheard and said she was coming here too. Small world, eh?'

'Hi, Hattie, I'm Izzy.' Izzy nodded at the woman who was probably about the same age as her. She had a Snow White complexion, with tendrils of dark hair escaping from her faux fur Russian style hat.

'Hi, I'm sorry I've tagged along but I was told it would be okay to join the family party. I hope that's not going to be too much of a problem. If it is, I can sleep on a sofa or something.'

'Oh, you're one of the Carter-Joneses,' said Izzy, suddenly twigging.

'Yes. I'm Harriet. Are they here yet?'

'No, they haven't arrived. They are due at some point today.' Suddenly remembering this was a guest, Izzy realised this wasn't quite the choreographed welcome she'd planned. 'Oh I'm so sorry. And don't be silly, of course, we've got a room for you.' She swallowed, mentally running through the rooms on the second floor trying to work out which one they could spruce up in record time. 'Come on in. Jim will take your case.'

'Let me take your coat,' said Jeanette, stepping forward.

Hattie wriggled out of the full-length, voluminous coat, which was soaked around the hem. 'Thank you. It's the most impractical coat known to man,' she said as she handed it over, 'but my flatmate insisted I'd need it and now I'm glad. Did you know it's flipping freezing in a helicopter? Not that I've ever been in one before. Scary Mary until you get used to it. Not that I'm complaining. It got me here. Thanks, guys, for the lift. That was a lifesaver. I'd never have got here otherwise.'

Izzy smiled; she liked Hattie Carter-Jones immediately. Something inside her eased a little. Surely if she was this friendly and unassuming the rest of the family must be the same?

'Come and sit down by the fire. Would you like a glass of whisky to warm you up?'

'That sounds heavenly. I'd bloody love one. Sorry, language and all that. But it's been a right old performance getting here. It was all very last minute. I missed my flight to Edinburgh. I should have been here yesterday. I was going to meet the family at the hotel and then drive up here with them but when I heard Fliss and Jason talking to the helicopter guy in the café, I couldn't believe my luck –especially when everything has been so shitty for the last few days – I asked for a lift.'

Izzy led her over to the big leather sofa beside the fireplace, inviting Fliss and Jason to join them.

Duncan picked up the decanter on the tray and poured three whiskies.

'Wow, this place is amazing. Is that a real sword up there?' Hattie asked as she sank into the Chesterfield and gazed up at the Claymore.

'It certainly is,' said Duncan with bloodthirsty enthusiasm as he handed her the tumbler of whisky. 'Used at the battle of Culloden, it was. Lots of blood on the steel.'

Izzy gave him a quick glance, realising he'd stepped into the role of old castle retainer.

Hattie's eyes widened. 'Next you'll be telling me the castle is haunted.'

'Funny you should say that…' Xanthe started.

'There are no ghosts,' said Izzy firmly, giving her mother a quelling glance.

Xanthe huffed out a sigh, muttering to Alicia, 'She's no fun,' and then the two of them decamped to the living room.

'So, Hattie, are you the Carter-Joneses' daughter?'

'God no! I'm nothing like Gabby. We're the poor relations.' Then she realised that perhaps she was being indiscreet. 'I'm the niece. Alexander is my dad's brother.' She smiled but there was a touch of misery in her eyes as she added, 'They took pity on me and invited me because … because I was going to be on my own for Christmas,' she finished with a brittle smile. 'I'd better text them, find out where they are.'

The unease crept back and Izzy took a slug of whisky, feeling it burn down her gullet. At least she had Fliss and Jason on her team now, although where she was going to put them, she had no idea. They might have to share a twin room up in one of the turrets that had seen better days and wasn't that well heated. Jason she wasn't so worried about, he was a rough diamond, but Fliss … well, she was used to the finer things. From her cut-glass accent, Izzy had always suspected she came

278

from quite a wealthy background. She probably had more in common with the Carter-Jones clan than anyone else here.

'Why don't I show you to your room?' suggested Izzy, 'and then you can get yourself settled.'

Jim had left Hattie's suitcase at the bottom of the stairs and reappeared as if by magic.

'Can you take Hattie's case up to the Rose room?' she said, deciding that Hattie deserved one of the better rooms.

Chapter Twenty-Three

'What are we going to do?' Xanthe wailed, rushing into the kitchen. 'We don't have enough room around the table for everyone. There are only sixteen chairs, even if I could squeeze in a few extra place settings. But that will ruin the look because there's only enough matching china for sixteen.'

'We'll manage,' said Izzy, ever more grateful that the cooking cavalry had arrived.

'I was thinking, your new friends and Jeanette and Jim and Duncan can eat in here.'

Izzy, already stressed by trying to work out where she could put everyone, whirled on her mother. '*You* invited Alicia and Graham. They're not paying guests. Why should they take precedence?'

'You can't expect someone like Alicia to eat in the kitchen. Besides, Ross is paying and he'd expect his mother and father to be seated with him.'

'I don't believe you,' said Izzy, irritation losing the battle over her normal diplomacy. 'Fliss and Jason are my friends and they've come to help, so they will be sitting down in the dining room, as will Jeanette, Jim and Duncan because they live here.'

'Don't be difficult, darling.'

'I'm not being difficult.'

'Yes, you are.'

'No, I'm not.' Izzy threw the tea towel down and threw open the fridge door. 'You're impossible, Mum. Inviting all these people. The Carter-Joneses were supposed to be four people, then it was six and then it was eight and now it's ten or possibly eleven, I'm not sure where Hattie fits in. Then you invited Alicia and Graham. I'm surprised you haven't invited Mrs McPherson. Tell you what, why not the whole flaming village?'

'Oooh, keep your hair on. I think you're getting a little bit tired and testy, Isabel McBride.' And before Izzy could say another word, her mother had stalked out, quivering with indignation.

Izzy sank into one of the chairs, putting her head in her hands. It was very rare for her to blow up at Xanthe, usually because it was a pointless exercise, but she really had had enough. As well as tonight's meal to cook, she still had all the stocking presents to wrap. She'd decided that she would leave them all beneath the Christmas tree in the sitting room, so that the Carter-Joneses could sit in there after breakfast. In her head she went over what she'd bought, trying to reallocate some of the gifts to the newcomers so that everyone had a little something. Luckily she had plenty of stockings; her mother had bought her a new one every year when she was a child and they'd hung the old ones around the flat as decorations.

'Everything all right?'

Izzy looked up into Ross's sympathetic face.

'I heard shouting.'

Izzy screwed up her face, hoping he hadn't heard what she'd said. She didn't want him to think that his parents were unwelcome. 'Sorry. I needed to vent. My mother is the absolute end sometimes. She ignores whatever she doesn't want to hear.'

'I can relate to that. My mother is exactly the same. Do you think they were separated at birth?'

'It's a distinct possibility.' Izzy rubbed at her temple. 'And there's no sign of the Carter-Joneses, I'm worried they might have got stuck somewhere.'

'That would make life easier, wouldn't it?'

She sighed heavily. 'In some ways, but you know how much I'm relying on their money. I can't charge them if they're not here.'

'True.' He looked at his watch.

'I'm going to hold dinner until seven-thirty, hopefully they'll be here by then.'

Just then a hesitant Hattie appeared in the doorway. 'Can I have a word?'

'Course you can. Is everything all right with your room?'

'Yes! It's a gorgeous room. That wallpaper, it's to die for. No, it's … erm…' She tugged at her lip with her teeth, her hand making agitated movements. 'I've heard from my mum. They're, they've decided … not to come.' She said the words in a rush.

'Pardon?' said Izzy, masking her utter confusion in politeness. Not quite sure she'd heard correctly. 'Did they get stuck in the snow?'

'No. They never set off. They're having such a great time in Edinburgh. They've decided to stay.'

'They're not coming … at all? Or not until Christmas Eve?'

'They're going to an old friend of my Uncle's on Christmas Day and staying with him until Boxing Day. I'm so sorry.' Hattie moved awkwardly from one foot to the other.

'They're not coming,' repeated Izzy.

Hattie shook her head. 'I'm sorry.'

'It's not your fault,' said Izzy slowly, still trying to get her head around it. Shit, she'd been banking on that money. The deposit was long gone. She felt sick. And a little light-headed. She grasped the corner of the dresser to hold her up. Ross moved beside her, placing a hand in the small of her back. She'd spent a fortune on food and wine.

'It's bloody rude,' said Hattie suddenly. 'I'm so embarrassed, I could kill them. It isn't like them. I don't know what's happened.'

'No worries,' said Izzy, pasting a bright smile on her face while inside she was having a mini meltdown. She threw a quick glance at Ross, who gave her a reassuring smile.

'Is it okay if I stay?' Hattie asked in a small voice.

'Oh my God, I'm so sorry,' said Izzy, realising that the poor girl had been abandoned by her entire family. 'Of course you can.'

'I'm sure I can join in with the other guests,' said Hattie with forced cheer.

Izzy looked down at her hands for a moment. 'Actually, there are no other guests.'

'Oh no! Who are all those people? Are they family? Oh god, I'm intruding. I've just foisted myself on you.'

'Don't be silly. You're not intruding at all. In fact, you're the only person that's turned up that was expected. I seem to have ended up with a houseful of people, half of whom weren't invited anyway.'

'Me being the first of them,' said Ross, indicating himself with both thumbs.

'So you're not going to be any trouble, as long as you don't mind fitting in with everyone and going with the flow. It's not as if I don't have enough food.' At least it wasn't going to waste.

'Really?' Hattie's brows creased with worry.

'Yup, welcome to the mad house!'

'I'll pitch in and help. I'd rather anyway. I'm very good at peeling potatoes.'

'You've got yourself a job.'

'Why don't I start now, if I'm not in the way?'

Leaving Hattie with a mound of potatoes to peel, chatting to Ross, who was making cups of tea for Xanthe and his parents, Izzy left the kitchen carrying the ironing board. No one questioned her and she carried it up to her bedroom before she did a quick redistribution of rooms, moving Fliss and Jason from the dingy room on the third floor, giving them each a separate guest room. After all the hard work she'd put in over the last couple of months, someone should enjoy the beautiful new rooms.

Craving a bit of peace and quiet, with one big job to do before she had to start cooking this evening's dinner, she slipped back into her bedroom and sat down on the silky bedspread in an autumnal shade of russet. She put her head in her hands. What the heck was she going to do now? The two thousand pounds she'd spent on food and wine would be invoiced to the Carter-Joneses whether they liked it or not. The deposit was non-refundable but there would still be a shortfall on what she and Xanthe spent on getting the place ready and the profit she'd banked on making. The roofing contractor was booked in for the second week of January. How was she going to pay for that? Suddenly it all seemed too much and involuntary tears began to leak their way down her cheeks despite her best attempts to stop them. It was no good. There was too much to think about, too much to do, and her head ached with the effort of trying to work out what she could do to fix it all.

The gentle creak of the door made her look up. Ross stood in the doorway. 'You okay?'

'I'm trying to be.'

'Worrying about money?'

She nodded and he crossed to come and sit on the bed beside her, putting an arm around her shoulder. 'I don't know what I'm going to do. I was banking on the Carter-Jones clan to save us and spreading the word, recommending us to their rich friends.'

'There'll be other guests. You're all ready to go now.'

'Providing the roof stays intact.'

'Look, you can't do anything about them not coming now. But you can throw the best possible Christmas party and get Xanthe to Instagram the shit out of it. Is your website up and running yet to take bookings?'

'No.' Izzy sighed. 'I got a friend to set me up with a WordPress template and I made a start but I've not had time to give it any attention or get to grips with it.'

'Well, I know someone who can pay for his supper by

sorting it out for you. My dad, believe it or not, is a bit of a whiz on a computer. It'll give him a chance to escape from Mum for a while.'

'But it's Christmas.'

'Yes. You know lots of people get divorced immediately after Christmas because they end up spending too much time together? I suspect that's how my dad has survived this long; he has a man cave and a dozen interests that keep him out of the house. One of which is computers, so he'll probably fall on his knees to give thanks to you.

'And you can get Xanthe and my mum to style the pictures for you and to take them all so that you've got a bank of images of happy, smiling people having the time of their lives sitting down in the baronial dining room with the most amazing feast.'

'You've got it all worked out,' she said, searching her pockets for a tissue.

'Here.' He handed over a monogrammed handkerchief.

'Seriously? It looks like it's never been used. I don't know anyone who uses hankies.'

'You do now. My gran used to put them in my stockings every Christmas. I've a stack of them. I always carry one, just in case.'

'In case of a damsel in distress?'

'To be honest, it's the first time it will have been used.'

Izzy blew her nose with a loud and very unladylike trumpet. 'Thank you. Consider the handkerchief well and truly christened. And thank you, Granny.' It also reminded her that she needed to make a start on wrapping the stocking gifts. The good news was that they could be redistributed and she'd have enough to give to Fliss, Jason and poor Hattie whose family had abandoned her.

'I suggest that we celebrate Christmas, give everyone a jolly good time and then, when it's over, we look at what we can do to raise the cash for the roof. I could give you a loan.'

'No! No way. I couldn't do that.'

'All right, you can talk to the bank. Get a small business loan or something. There are ways and means.'

'You're right. I've been pinning my hopes on that money so much, thinking it would turn everything around. To lose it when I've put so much effort into making this week something special, it's a real blow.'

'You've still got a house full of people, none of whom are guests now, with the exception of Hattie, who doesn't strike me as the sort who expects to be waited on. Why not relax, go with it and enjoy yourself?'

'You're right. As long as no one else turns up.'

'Now what can I do to help?'

'Are you any good with Sellotape and wrapping paper?'

Five minutes later, they were sitting on the floor in her bedroom surrounded by shopping bags and Izzy had set up the ironing board.

Ross eyed it quizzically.

'It's for wrapping the presents. The perfect space to roll out your paper. Honestly, once you've used an ironing board, you'll never look back.' She pulled forward the first bag of presents that she'd picked up in Edinburgh and began allocating them.

'You wrap stocking presents?' he asked.

'Yes, always have done,' said Izzy. 'Another family tradition. What do you think of this for your mum?' She held up several packs of lace handkerchiefs. 'I'll give her a set and one each for Hattie and Fliss. Does your dad like fudge?'

'Does he ever.' Ross gave her a cheeky wink. 'I do, too.'

She gave him a severe look, holding back a smile. 'These are gifts from Santa, he hasn't left you any here.' She'd hidden another pack for him in a different bag at the back of the wardrobe.

Izzy began to create little piles of presents for each of the inhabitants of the castle. Mrs Carter-Jones had given her a generous budget; there was no point wasting it. Ross was right, she should worry about money later, although it was easier said than done.

When she'd finished dividing them up, each person had quite a nice selection and she was pleased that she'd made the effort to buy original and thoughtful presents. All of the golfing gifts went on Graham's pile, Hattie had her own gifts plus additional ones that had been earmarked for her aunt and her mother. Jason and Fliss received all of Mrs Carter-Jones's foodie gifts. It was perfect. The rest of Hattie's mother's gifts were evenly spread between Fliss and Jeanette, so that after a bit of juggling everyone had the same number of little gifts.

'I'm not sure Duncan really wants a stuffed Highland terrier,' said Ross picking it up from the pile.

'Well, who else can I give it to? He's got one less present than everyone else. Everyone has to have the same.'

Ross laughed and pulled her forward for a quick kiss. 'If you say so.'

'It's the Christmas stocking rules,' insisted Izzy. 'My mum

used to drive herself nuts every year. She'd always say she'd just got the same number of things for me and Gran and then find something she'd bought ages ago for Gran, so would have to go out and get something else for me. Then she'd count up again and I'd got more than Gran.'

'I seem to recall hearing this from my mum about me and my sisters' stockings.'

'See, it's a thing.'

'Tell you what, I've got a head torch that was an extra for my dad. I could add it to Duncan's stocking.'

'Brilliant.' Izzy beamed at him. 'Go and get it and we can start wrapping. I love Christmas morning when everyone unwraps their stocking presents. We'll put the stockings around the fireplace and hand them out after breakfast in the sitting room.

'Now it's almost here, I can hardly wait. We're going to have a wonderful day. A proper Christmas with friends and family. Just like it should be.'

Chapter Twenty-Four

'Are you nearly ready?' said Xanthe, marching into Izzy's bedroom.

Izzy, who was putting the finishing touches to her make-up, almost stabbed her eye with the mascara brush.

'Hello, Mum, do come in.' The sarcasm was lost on Xanthe, resplendent in a fuchsia pink number that seemed to be made up entirely of frills. On her head she had a matching sequinned cap, which clashed with the fresh hair dye job of fire-engine red. As she settled herself on the bed, the ruffles of fabric quivered like an animated feather duster.

'Oh, sweetie, aren't you going to put a dress on?'

Izzy looked down at her black trousers and smart lacy top with a few bits of sparkly glitter.

'What's wrong with this?'

'You're such a gorgeous girl, you ought to show off your assets a bit more.'

'My assets?'

'You know, look a bit more womanly.'

Izzy stared at her mother. Where had this come from?

'I thought this was quite dressy.' She indicated her clothes. 'Don't forget, I'll be spending a lot of time in the kitchen.'

'Yes, but you can still be the belle of the ball too, darling. You're really very pretty.'

'Thank you,' said Izzy, deadpan.

'And you ought to make a bit more effort. You're not getting any younger, you know.'

'I've got other things on my mind at the moment. What with Christmas and a houseful of people expecting to be fed and watered over the next few days.'

'But the Carter-Joneses aren't coming, darling. You can relax now.'

Izzy raised a single eyebrow and refrained from mentioning the financial repercussions of their guests not turning up. She couldn't bear to think of it any more. Ross was right, she was going to enjoy Christmas and worry about it next week. 'Have you forgotten the small matter of twelve people to provide breakfast, lunch and dinner for, over the next couple of days?'

Xanthe shrugged her shoulders. 'You'll manage, you always do. I thought we'd have a little drinky before dinner tonight in the drawing room. Six o'clock sharp. Don't be late and do put a dress on, darling.' With that she swanned out.

Izzy shook her head and studied herself in the mirror. Maybe putting on a dress for a change wouldn't be so bad. It wasn't as if she didn't have quite a few. She did love a dress, they just hadn't been the most practical thing of late.

'Darling, don't you look gorgeous. I've made, or rather I got Graham to make, them – he's a marvel with a cocktail shaker – we're having porn star martinis. I got those lovely boys at the farm shop to drop in some passion fruit. John was very disappointed he didn't see you, wasn't he, Alicia?'

'Yes,' replied Alicia in that overly sparkly fashion that suggested she was playing a part. She was no actress. 'You look lovely, Izzy, doesn't she, Ross?' Alicia nudged her son, none too gently.

'She looks very *nice*,' said Ross, with a quirk to his lips.

'Nice? Darling, that's no sort of compliment.' Alicia shook her head.

Izzy and Ross exchanged a private smile.

'Here you go,' said Graham, presenting Izzy with a beautiful coupe glass full of sparkling liquid and half a passion fruit floating in it.

'Thank you.'

'Aren't these glasses just darling?' said Xanthe, holding them up to the light.

'They are. Do you know, I've been thinking about creating a glassware line. These are lovely, are they vintage?'

'Yes. There are lots of glasses dating back from goodness knows when in the cupboards. I've had a fabulous time finding them all, it's like discovering treasure every day. Although we haven't found the real treasure – we've looked everywhere for it.'

'Real treasure?' Alicia was almost quivering with obvious excitement.

'Yes,' squealed Xanthe. 'There's a fortune hidden in sapphires somewhere in the castle. We've been looking for it everywhere but we haven't found it yet.'

'Did you hear that, Graham?' Alicia prodded her husband with a hard finger before turning back to Xanthe. 'He's got a metal detector. We could help you look.'

'The metal detector is at home,' he replied.

'Yes, but you use one. You know how to look for things.'

'Of course I do, dear.' His mild voice made Izzy laugh to herself as she and Ross caught each other's eyes once more.

Not this again. Izzy had been hoping that her mother had given up the search and finally accepted that the sapphires were long gone.

'That would be marvellous. Some fresh eyes might spot something we haven't. We've searched the house from top to bottom. I even had an expert in and he couldn't find them. But they must be somewhere.'

Alicia rubbed her hands. 'Wouldn't it be wonderful if we found them? Graham, we'll start looking tomorrow. In the meantime. I would love to see the glasses. Can you show me?'

'Yes, of course,' said Xanthe. The two women were halfway to the door when Xanthe turned around. 'Graham, you should come too.'

'Yes, you should,' said Alicia, going back and hooking an arm through his. 'Ross and Izzy can keep each other company.' There was a coy lift to her lips. 'Don't do anything we wouldn't.'

She and Xanthe giggled like a pair of schoolgirls on a sugar high.

A few seconds later, Ross and Izzy were left alone and both of them burst out laughing.

'What are they like?' asked Izzy.

'Both mad as hatters,' said Ross with a despairing shake of his head. 'I'm convinced Dad only copes because Mum takes herself off to her studio and she gets pretty wrapped up in her art. Then it's peaceful, although she forgets to eat. She can be out there all night when the muse strikes her. Dad fends for himself and takes her sandwiches. It works for them. I can't imagine anything worse.'

'Do you think the two of them are up to something?' asked Izzy.

'Those two will always be up to something. I'm going to do some work, while I can.'

'Me too.'

'Give us a shout if you need any help.'

'Are you kidding? I'm not sure I'm going to be able to move in the kitchen. With Jason and Fliss here, I can put my feet up. They're both amazing cooks.'

With a touch of ceremony, Izzy placed the glistening roast beef in the centre of the kitchen table, while Fliss put down a dish of golden, layered potatoes and a bowl of vivid green beans scattered with toasted almond slices. Everyone was squashed in around the table, sitting on a mish-mash of chairs.

Jason had brought out his own, very precious knives and began to carve slices of the beef, the outside crispy and caramelised, the inside succulent and slightly pink in the middle. As he placed slices on each plate, Fliss poured over a silky smooth red wine gravy that she'd made, before handing them out.

Izzy sat back and listened to the cheerful chatter and clink of cutlery and crockery as everyone served themselves, passing dishes around the table, helping each other.

Xanthe raised a wine glass filled with the Australian Shiraz that Ross had suggested would go well with the meal.

'To Izzy, the hostess with the mostess.'

'To Izzy,' everyone chorused. Then the low-grade chatter ceased as they all tucked in and soft groans and murmurs of appreciation filled the room. Izzy smiled to herself; there was nothing quite like feeding people. And she thought, a few moments later, with a mouthful of beef and the delicious rich gravy, there was nothing quite like eating good food. She glanced around the table, relishing the obvious enjoyment and appreciation on everyone's faces with a small glow of pride and satisfaction. This was what life was about. Eating and sharing food together, something that her mentor, Adrienne, had talked a lot about, and now, with *her* kitchen full of an eclectic mix of people, most of whom she'd never met before coming to the castle, she understood. This was what she wanted to do. Look after people, make them feel welcome at the castle and give them a break from their real lives. Time to recharge and reflect.

'These Yorkshire puddings are delicious,' said Graham, taking another one and holding it up on his fork like a prized trophy.

'Is that your third one?' asked Alicia, reaching over Jeanette who was sitting beside her and patting his tummy.

'It's Christmas,' he grumbled.

'It's Christmas every day where you and Yorkshire puddings are concerned,' said Alicia.

'They are very good, Izzy,' said Xanthe, as if she was surprised by that fact. 'You're going to make someone a wonderful wife. Do you like Yorkshire puddings, Ross?'

Izzy nearly spat her wine out. Had her mother really just said that?

'Aye, I'm quite partial to them.' He took a sip of his wine, his face suddenly blank.

'Did you hear that, Izzy? Ross likes Yorkshire pudding.'

Izzy rolled her eyes. 'He also likes mince pies.'

'You make a lovely mince pie, doesn't she, Jeanette?'

'Mmm,' said Jeanette, looking confused. 'She's a very good cook.'

'Do you mind not talking about me as if you were trying to sell me off to the highest bidder?' said Izzy through gritted teeth.

'Izzy. What are you talking about? Alicia has had a lovely idea. She's going to make some glasses inspired by the ones here and call them the Kinlochleven collection. Isn't that a wonderful idea? We can do lots of Insta together. Have you seen Alicia's page? It's amazing.'

'I can't wait to start,' said Alicia, and then she and Xanthe were off, talking about plans and ideas. To be fair to both of them, they were very creative and really bounced off each other.

Jeanette picked up a forkful of dauphinoise potatoes and sighed as she inhaled the scent of garlic and butter. 'These are so good, Izzy. Do you think you could teach me how to cook a proper roast? I'm so useless in the kitchen and I want to keep improving. And not,' she shot Jim a stern look, 'to please my husband, but for my own satisfaction.'

Izzy liked her attitude, a far cry from Xanthe's outdated comments, which to be honest were out of character. She narrowed her eyes at her mother before turning back to the younger girl.

'Of course,' said Izzy. 'Cooking a roast is easy, it's all about timing. You just shove everything in the oven.'

Jason spluttered. 'Don't let Adrienne hear you say that. What ever happened to slow food? Good ingredients?'

'All the ingredients around here are good,' said Izzy. 'I've made sure I've sourced the main ingredients from the local farm shop.'

'I have to say, this beef is excellent,' said Fliss. 'And you've cooked it to perfection. Nice and pink in the middle and so tender.'

'Do you think your mother could be any more obvious?' asked Ross in a low voice, as he was loading the dishwasher and she was getting the dessert plates out from the cupboard.

'My mother?' She gave a quiet laugh, turning back to look at the tableful of people who were all engrossed in conversation. 'I think she and your mother are in it up to their necks, don't you?'

'Sadly, yes,' he said, a scowl on his face. 'Brings back all those awful teenage memories. She was the most embarrassing mother at my school. She always managed to make a spectacle of herself. Scarred me for life.' Despite his dry tone, Izzy got the distinct impression that there was a kernel of truth to his words about his teenage days. Xanthe had been equally embarrassing back in the day, but Izzy had worn it like a badge of honour. Her friends all adored Xanthe and thought she was the coolest mum in town.

'I avoided telling her about girlfriends at that age, which I was right to do. She really messed things up for me once. I was seeing this girl at school and I really liked her. Unfortunately, my mother got it into her head that I was perfectly suited to one of her friend's daughters and inveigled a set-up with this second girl. She kept inviting her round for dinner and before I knew it, thanks to Mum, it was all over the neighbourhood that this girl was my girlfriend. Girl number one was very upset and accused me of two-timing her, and girl number two believed my mum's propaganda and thought my intentions were serious and she wouldn't take no for an answer. In the end they teamed up together and both dumped me, making sure everyone knew I was an unfaithful dick. I was the most unpopular boy in school. From then on, I wouldn't tell her anything or let her interfere in my love life. Today feels like history repeating itself.'

Unlike Ross, she chose to find the funny side of it. 'It's like being in one of those Regency novels where the best friends' dowager duchess mothers are determined to marry their offspring off to one another.'

'All the more reason to not let them know about us. There is no way I'm letting my mother select my future wife, let alone any other relationship. Now you understand why I don't tell her about my books. I dread to think what she'd do with that information. Probably make glass interpretations of the covers. Blood and gore everywhere.' He shuddered.

The words 'lighten up' danced on the tip of her tongue but she could see the irritation lining his face and decided to let them stay right there. She turned to watch him stalk back to his seat, a little saddened that he didn't feel he could share his success with his mother and that he found her so difficult. Xanthe had her faults but Izzy never doubted that her mother was a hundred per cent behind her. It had been the two of them against the world for a long time.

The dessert was greeted with suitable appreciation and Izzy grinned, aware that the pavlova she'd whipped up was actually very easy to make, not that she was going to share that with anyone. Using the passion fruit had been a stroke of genius. *Thank you, Jason.*

'That was a wonderful meal, Izzy. Thank you. You're an excellent cook,' said Alicia, patting her gently rounded stomach. 'You'll make...'

If she said she'd make someone an excellent wife, Izzy would brain her with the nearest saucepan.

'...a real go of this place, I'm sure.' Clearly Alicia had thought better of saying it, although her eyes came to rest on her son with a thoughtful gaze. He shot her a wary glance as if waiting for her next comment.

'Ross is like his father, he forgets to eat when he's absorbed in something.'

'I don't think Izzy has ever forgotten to eat, have you? Which is as well because I'm useless in the kitchen, aren't I, darling? She took over cooking Christmas lunch the year after we had baked beans on toast. Can you believe, I forgot to get the turkey out of the freezer?' Xanthe let out a gale of laughter, making light of what at the time had been a disaster.

'I forgot to switch the oven on one year,' declared Alicia with a wide grin. 'Popped the bird in and we all went out for a walk. We got back expecting lovely smells to come wafting from the kitchen. Nada. Nothing. Do you remember, Ross? You were so cross. Remember that, Izzy – when he's hungry he turns into hangry man.'

Ross's jaw clenched and then he bit into one of the after-dinner chocolate mints with a distinct snap of his teeth.

'We always used to go to the Toby Carvery on Christmas Day. My mum can't cook for toffee,' piped up Jeanette, much to Izzy's relief, although she wasn't sure if the other girl was aware of the tension or not.

'Us too,' chimed in Jason. 'Me, Mum and me sisters.'

'Do I even want to know what a Toby Carvery is?' asked Fliss, the teasing smile in her eyes taking the sting out of her words.

'You mean to tell me you've never been for a *roastmas* at a Toby Carvery?' asked Jason, almost spitting out his lager in disbelief. 'Fu... For a posh bird you don't get out much, do you?'

'I get out plenty, thank you very much.' She gave him a playful nudge in the ribs.

'You haven't lived. When we get back, I'm taking you straight round there. Mind you, you'll have to put in some training. There's a knack to it, isn't there, Jeanette?'

'There is,' she said. 'Jim's brilliant, he can get more on his plate than anyone else I know.'

'I have absolutely no idea what you're talking about,' said Fliss with a bemused shake of her head.

'It's an as much as you can eat roast dinner buffet,' explained Jason. 'You have to get your money's worth. I pile the roasties, put the veg on the bottom, drape the meat over them, pour on the gravy, balance the Yorkshire puds on the top and then you hold on to 'em with your chin.'

'Don't even think about it, Graham, remember your cholesterol,' said Alicia, tuning in to the conversation.

'No, dear,' he said, a wicked twinkle dancing in his blue eyes.

'Does anyone want any cheese?' asked Izzy, rising to her feet.

'You sit down,' said Jeanette. 'Even I can get cheese and biscuits onto the table. Jim will help me stack the dishwasher.'

'Let me help,' said Hattie. 'I'll do the dishwasher while you do the cheese.'

'If we're having cheese, we have to have port. Did you get any, Izzy?' asked Xanthe.

Thankfully she had and it was down in the cellar, as she hadn't planned on opening it until Christmas Day but now that the Carter-Joneses weren't coming it didn't matter so much.

'I'll go down and get it.'

'You've got a proper cellar. How wonderfully creepy,' said Alicia. 'Ross, you should go with Izzy, protect her from any ghosts.'

'We should get some ghost hunters in, you know,' said Xanthe. 'I bet loads of people died here. Specially down in the cellars. They were probably dungeons back in the day. We could do ghost tours, that would draw people here. Everyone loves a good ghost story.'

'I don't,' said Izzy with a quick shudder, now not so keen on going down to the cellar.

'I'll go,' said Ross, rising to his feet.

'It's not easy to find the wine rack, it's a bit of a warren down there. I'll go.'

'I'll have to come with you, then.' He sounded resigned to the idea and shot his mother a mutinous look as if to say he was doing it out of duty rather than at her suggestion.

The cellar was dimly lit with an ancient lightbulb that cast more shadows than light and Izzy wished she'd brought the heavy-duty torch from the scullery. Ross followed in her wake, but he hadn't said a word since they'd left the kitchen.

'You okay?' she asked, wending her way through the vaulted ceiling cellar and ducking under the arches between each small room. Duncan had helped find her way around down here those first two weeks she'd visited the castle. Thankfully, the way to the wine rack had an easy guide: left, left, right, right.

'Fine,' he said in that cool, calm tone of his that gave absolutely nothing away.

She had a feeling he wasn't fine at all; the chaos of his mother and Xanthe combined was obviously affecting him. He'd chosen to escape from his mother's overpowering personality while she'd learned to live with Xanthe's loud volume, high drama lifestyle.

They arrived at the wine rack and Ross whistled.

'You didn't tell me you had all this down here.'

'To be honest, I was worried it was all so old it might be like vinegar. I didn't want to rely on it.'

Ross reached forward and removed a dusty bottle, squinting in the weak light at the label.

'French. Bordeaux. 1959.'

'Is that a good year?'

'I haven't got a clue. But it's worth checking this out. You never know, they might be valuable.'

'I'd have to pay someone to come and look at them.'

'You could photograph each bottle and do some internet research.'

'That's not a bad idea.' For some reason, she noted the *you*. In recent weeks, he'd used *we* a lot.

'Right, where's this port then?'

'Up there on the right. Two bottles. We might as well take both of them up.'

They returned to the stairs but, when they reached the door at the top of the steps, it was closed. Izzy grasped the handle to open it, assuming it had blown shut or something but to her surprise the door was stuck fast.

She tried again, this time shoving her shoulder against it but the door didn't shift.

'Bugger, the door's stuck.'

'Let me try.'

Ross put the port on a shelf on the wall beside them and stepped in front of her, taking the handle and tugging. He rattled the door for a few seconds before pulling his phone out of his pocket and shining the torch at the door frame. 'For fuck's sake,' he said. 'It's not stuck, it's bloody locked.'

'It can't be. Who would lock us in? Everyone knew we were down here.'

He gave her a searching look. 'Who do you think?'

'What? You think someone did it on purpose?' asked Izzy in disbelief.

'Well, hello. Two matchmaking mamas, giggling away together. I'm no detective, but I got the distinct impression that the two of them were keen for us to spend time together. It's just the sort of thing they would do.'

'What are we going to do?'

'Call them.' He tapped at the phone screen. 'Damn, I can't get a signal. Can you?'

She had one bar on her phone but it wasn't sufficient for the call to her mother to connect. 'No, I'm not getting anything. Now what?'

'Wait until they decide to let us out, I suppose.'

Izzy hammered on the door again and yelled. 'Hello! Is anyone there? Xanthe!' She waited and listened. Nothing. No give-away giggles or footsteps. She banged again and called even louder.

'You're wasting your time,' said Ross as he began to go back down the stairs.

'Where are you going?'

'To get a bottle of wine.'

'What, now?'

'Yes. I guess they'll let us out in their own good time – let's hope they come to their senses before tomorrow morning because I really don't want to spend a whole night down here. In the meantime, I'm going to have a drink and at least we get a break from their comments.'

'We haven't got any glasses.'

He glared up at her. 'Straight from the bottle will do.'

'God, what are they like?' She stomped down the steps after him. Today might just be the day she finally strangled her mother. This had one of her harebrained ideas written all over it.

Ross didn't wait for her and walked through the cellar rooms back to the wine rack where, using the torch on his phone, he selected a bottle and grabbed the handy corkscrew hanging from a hook. Then he marched back through to the middle room, which had a couple of old chesterfield armchairs in one corner. She followed him and sank into the chair beside him as he deftly opened the bottle and took a swig from it. He didn't offer it to her and she almost didn't ask. His granite-faced expression wasn't exactly encouraging.

'Are you going to share that?'

With a twist to his mouth, he offered it to her but she decided she didn't want any.

'You're all right. Hopefully they'll let us out before long. At least we've got seats and wine.' She gave him an encouraging smile. 'It could be a lot worse.'

He stared at her for a minute, his eyebrows drawn tight below his furrowed brow.

'Could it?'

'Yes,' said Izzy. 'We know it's not for ever, they'll come and let us out eventually. We're not going to die of hypothermia or anything. The hot water pipes run along the ceiling so this part is okay.' She was trying to be practical and positive, but while it wasn't frigid, it was hardly warm. She reached over and patted his hand. 'We can always keep each other warm.'

He withdrew his hand. God, he was more pissed off than she'd realised. Their predicament was annoying but it was temporary.

'We'll be okay.'

His look was quizzical and he didn't say anything for a moment before shaking his head. 'Sorry, Izzy. This isn't okay. It feels like we're being manipulated, having our hands forced. You know, making more of something before we even know what it is ourselves. We don't know each other that well and already they're talking about marriage. You've seen what they're like.'

'I know it isn't okay, but we'll get out soon and then we'll give them a severe talking to.'

He raised an eyebrow. 'A severe talking to. Your mother and my mother?' He took a quick swig of his wine. 'I think perhaps we should call it quits before anything goes too far, while we still can and while we can still be friends. Before they get carried away and start planning a wedding and believing their own fantasy. I'm a big boy, it's not like I can't put my foot down and say no, but I'm not prepared to put up with the drama, them interfering and thinking they know best. For the time being I think we should just be friends. Maybe we can explore things later on...'

'Friends,' said Izzy, nodding, feeling the familiar sensation of a rug being pulled from beneath her feet. *Friends.* Where had she heard that before? Izzy swallowed, wishing she'd got a bottle of her own. She'd been down this road before and she'd wasted too much time wishing things were different.

With one finger she stroked at the fabric of her dress, which was stretched over her knee, not trusting her vocal cords, which had tightened like ivy tendrils around a tree.

She shrugged. 'If that's what you want,' she said dully.

'Given the situation, I think it's for the best.'

She nodded as disappointment swamped her, followed by a quick spurt of anger. His only saving grace was that at least he'd come up with the 'friends' line a few months in, instead of leading her on for three years.

'I understand,' she said stiffly, getting up from the chair.

'You do?' He sounded relieved.

'Yes. You're a coward.'

'I beg your pardon?'

She gave him a sardonic smile. 'Don't use my mother or your mother as an excuse. You don't want a relationship with me, I get that, but don't blame them.'

'I'm not blaming them.'

'No, you're not, but you are using them as an excuse for your decision. You need to own it. You're too scared to have a relationship with me.'

'That's nonsense. Of course I'm not scared.'

'Yes, you are. You said it yourself. The first time we kissed, you said it terrified you.'

His mouth firmed. 'That doesn't mean I'm scared.'

'Yes, it does. You're scared of too much emotion. You said that before too.'

'I'm not scared of emotion. Like I said before, I've seen too much of it with my mother when it didn't mean anything. It's all noise and fury, no substance. Those feelings can't be relied on, they change. They're not reliable. I don't do drama.'

'I'm not going to argue with you,' said Izzy. She'd humiliated herself with Philip on more than one occasion. If Ross wanted to be friends, that was his call, but he'd backed off once before and she'd given him the benefit of the doubt. Not this time.

She walked off and left him, her head held high. When she reached the top of the stairs, to her relief, the door had mysteriously opened itself again. What a surprise.

Finding the kitchen empty but tidy, she paused in the corridor and could hear her mother's tinkling laugh coming from the sitting room. Firming her mouth in a flat line, too dispirited to face Xanthe that night, she crossed the hall and ran lightly up to her bedroom, closing and locking the door.

Chapter Twenty-Five

DECEMBER 23

S he refused to be upset by Ross. Friends was *fine* with her.
She tapped an egg smartly on the side of the bowl with a sharp snap, scooping out the golden yolk into a second bowl and the white into a third.

She could do *friends*.

Another sharp crack.

She'd bloody done *friends* for three years.

The second yolk joined the first.

Crack again.

She was bloody brilliant at being *friends*.

So brilliant he wasn't going to know what hit him. She'd give him sodding, bloody, flaming *friends*.

She slammed a fourth egg. Bugger. She'd completely smashed it, the yolk bleeding orange into the white, rendering it useless for the meringue she was making.

She stared down at the mess. She was an idiot. Hadn't she learned anything? She should have followed her gut instinct and kept her distance from him. That stupid sizzle of sexual attraction had led her astray. Sex was responsible for a lot of things.

'Is that egg upsetting you?'

Izzy turned to find Hattie lurking in the doorway and gave a half-laugh, realising she was glaring at the contents of the bowl like a deranged lunatic.

'No, I got a bit heavy-handed. I was cross with myself. How are you? Did you sleep well?'

'Yes. I did. Best sleep I've had since…' Her voice trailed off before she said in a quiet voice, 'In ages.' She glanced away looking out of the window. 'Difficult to believe a blizzard was raging yesterday. It looks gorgeous out there today.'

Izzy followed her gaze to the blue sky and brilliant sunshine that bounced off the pure white and coated the lines of the landscape. A new day. Very different to yesterday. She smiled with irony to herself. A day to make a fresh start.

'Want a scrambled egg for breakfast?' she asked Hattie.

Hattie laughed. 'I don't mind if I do. You look like you're busy, why don't I make it?'

'Are you sure? I won't say no, I want to get this done.' She pointed out where everything was, grateful that she could carry on.

'What are you making?'

'I'm making a Christmas meringue wreath for Christmas Day which I'll decorate with loganberries, blueberries, raspberries and pomegranate seeds. That's for anyone who doesn't like Christmas pudding and brandy butter.'

Hattie groaned with heartfelt enthusiasm. 'That sounds delicious.' Then, with an impish grin, she asked, 'Are we allowed to have a little bit of both?'

Izzy laughed. 'It's Christmas Day, you can have whatever

you like.' She gave Hattie's too slim form a speculative glance. 'You can afford the calories.'

'Yeah, well, let's just say misery is the best diet on the planet,' Hattie said with a rueful twist to her lips. 'And don't feel sorry for me. I'm fine. Don't want to talk about it.'

'Fair enough,' said Izzy. 'I understand that.' She completely did. The last thing she wanted to do was talk about Ross to anyone. In fact, she didn't even want to talk *to* him.

As Hattie pottered about making her breakfast, Izzy grabbed a bottle of whisky and poured a generous slug over some frozen raspberries in one pan while she warmed some honey in another.

Hattie peered over from her side of the cooker. 'Looks interesting, what are you making with that?'

'I'm using the leftover egg yolks to make a cranachan ice cream. I'm cooking the raspberries in a dram of whisky.'

'A dram?' Hattie grinned. 'Or a few drams? And what's cranachan? Don't forget I'm a sassenach.'

'So ye are,' said Izzy, broadening her accent with a laugh. 'Cranachan is a traditional Scottish dessert made of oats, raspberries, honey and cream, so this is a variation. I've whipped up egg yolks and I'm going to stir in the honey and I'll mix that with whipped cream and a little whisky. I've got some oats toasting in the oven and I'll layer the cream and egg mix with the raspberries, starting with a layer of the toasted oats. And then pop the whole lot in the freezer in a bread loaf tin. It's a nice light dessert and I thought we could have it on Boxing Day after a nice, spicy turkey curry.'

'You've got it all planned.'

'Planned to the nth degree.' And as she'd got all the food in readiness, there was no point deviating. Izzy grinned. 'With a little help from my friends. Fliss and Jason have been sending me recipe ideas for weeks. I'm so grateful they've come to help, even though your relatives aren't coming now, but it will be good practice for when we do open.'

Hattie's face fell. 'God, I'm so sorry about them. Honestly, they're lovely people. I know Auntie Jessie was really excited about coming here but I guess the snow spooked her. She can be a bit of an anxious Annie. But it's unlike her to let—'

'Look what we found in the attic.' Xanthe and Alicia burst into the kitchen each wearing pith helmets. Even though Izzy wasn't feeling particularly charitable to either of them, she couldn't help laughing at the sight of them.

'Aren't these great?' screeched Xanthe, wobbling her head from side to side. 'I seem to recall Bill mentioning that one of his ancestors had been a friend of Dr Livingstone. Just imagine, he might have worn one of these.'

'What, Bill?' asked Izzy.

'No, Dr Livingstone.' Xanthe shook her head impatiently, nearly dislodging the hat.

Izzy stared at the pair of them in matching utilitarian khaki jumpsuits and both immaculately made up. Mascara and lipstick aside, they looked as if they were about to go on an expedition up the Amazon.

Izzy rolled her eyes. 'What are you up to?' Did she really want to know?

'We're going sapphire hunting. Working from the top down,' announced Xanthe. 'We thought we'd dress the part.'

'Of course, you did,' murmured Izzy.

'But first we need coffee.' Xanthe moved off to the coffee machine and inserted a pod, completely oblivious to the fact that Hattie had been about to make herself a coffee. 'It's going to be a long day but we're going to be methodical about it and search every room. One by one.'

'Yes,' said Alicia.

'How was last night?' asked Xanthe with an arch smile. 'You disappeared. Early night, was it?'

Izzy narrowed her eyes, refusing to give anything away. 'Not particularly. Do you want some breakfast? I've got some nice smoked back bacon from the farm shop.'

'Oooh, Graham would love bacon and eggs,' piped up Alicia. 'I'll let him know.'

'Why don't I make them?' suggested Hattie, looking a little bemused by Alicia and Xanthe.

Alicia had already disappeared, presumably to tell her husband, and Xanthe followed her like an obedient puppy.

'Are you sure?' Izzy wiped her hands on a tea towel while crossing to the fridge to retrieve the smoked back bacon she'd bought in the farm shop.

'Of course, I'm sure you've got tons to do. Do you want some?'

'No, thanks.' Her appetite appeared to have shrivelled up and died. All she could face this morning was a strong black coffee.

Even the scent of frying bacon didn't change her mind, although the smell drew in Jim and Jeanette. Then Duncan and Graham appeared along with Fliss and once again the kitchen was full of people but, Izzy thought, with sudden warmth in her chest, that was the way she liked it. These people had all come to mean so much to her in such a short space of time. That was what happened when you all pulled together towards a common goal. They'd achieved so much and the castle was ready to go.

She'd survive this latest disappointment; it only confirmed her view that she wasn't the sort of girl that men ever got serious about, but this time she had a focus.

By two o'clock, the turkey was stuffed, the potatoes were peeled and parboiled. Jason had taken charge of the Christmas pudding, which was now being steamed for the requisite eight hours. The kitchen smelled of a delightful mix of dried fruit, sugar, and nutmeg.

'Try this, Izzy.' He offered her a taster of the brandy butter he'd made.

'Wow, that's got a kick.'

'Secret ingredients. Orange zest and stem ginger.'

'Interesting, can I try?' said Fliss, and without waiting for his answer, she dug a teaspoon into the bowl. 'Mmm, that is good. I must remember that.' She whipped out a notebook from the pocket of her apron and made a quick note.

'Remember I want the credit on that one,' said Jason.

'Yeah, right. You always want the credit. Move over, I need to get these on to boil.' Fliss was making mini bagels and had coiled the dough into small donut shapes, ready to boil before they were baked. Although not strictly Scottish, they'd agreed that they'd make the perfect foil for the local smoked salmon and crowdie that Izzy planned to serve for breakfast.

The three of them wove in and out of each other as they cooked, sharing hints and tips, with Jason and Fliss exchanging their usual insults and banter. The two of them were unlikely friends as Fliss spoke with a cut-glass English accent while Jason was pure East End London but they'd bonded over a love of food and cooking while in Ireland on their course.

'It is so good of you both to give up your Christmas to come here,' said Izzy. 'I can't thank you enough.'

'No sweat, Iz,' said Jason. 'My mum and younger sisters are at my older sister's playing grandma and aunties with my new niece.' He shuddered. 'Too much oestrogen all round for my liking.'

'Jason, you can't say things like that,' protested Fliss.

'I just did. Besides, why are you here?'

Fliss grinned at him. 'Didn't fancy the testosterone triplets on a family ski trip.' She shuddered. 'Skiing is no fun when it's so damned competitive. Three of my brothers just want to hurl themselves down black runs, drink beer and beat their chests, and the other one is somewhere up the Amazon exploring the rainforest. So not my idea of fun.'

'And cooking for a house party is?' teased Izzy.

'In a castle? In Scotland? With no relatives? Hell, yes,' said Jason. 'Besides, I hadn't done my Christmas shopping.'

'Jason!' cried Fliss, outraged. 'You're so useless.'

'What? I don't know what girls like. What did you buy your brothers?'

Fliss smirked. 'Beer and football shirts. Easy.'

Izzy smiled to herself. In her cache of stocking fillers, she had just the perfect gifts for both Jason and Fliss. She was going to enjoy seeing everyone open their stockings.

Duncan stomped in. 'Any soup, lass? Those bluidy women are going to be the death of me.'

'I'll get you some, Duncan,' said Fliss, wiping her hands on her apron. 'I made some this morning. It's French onion.' Fliss had taken a bit of a shine to the old man and within minutes was fussing round him, setting out a bowl of piping hot soup and a couple of freshly made poppy-seed-dusted rolls.

'How's the treasure hunting going?' asked Izzy, as she expertly rolled out the pastry under Jason's supervision. She was preparing the venison wellington for the following day and he'd made a mushroom paté, which she was waiting to cool before she spread it on the pastry along with a layer of prosciutto to wrap around the joint of venison that Jason was currently searing in a large frying pan.

'Gah!' Duncan filled his mouth with a spoonful of soup. 'They've been banging and tapping in every room. They're not going to find anything. I reckon Bill sold them long ago. He always said he kent where they were. If he still had them, he'd a left them to you for the upkeep of this place. He was no stupid.'

'At least it's keeping them out of trouble,' observed Izzy.

'Those two invented trouble,' said Duncan. 'By the way, where's Ross today? I've no seen him.'

Izzy gritted her teeth and focused on her pastry.

'He's a handsome one,' said Fliss. 'Is he taken?'

Duncan glowered at her. 'I've a mind that he's interested in our Izzy.'

She held up her hands. 'Okay.'

'He's not,' snapped Izzy.

Duncan eyed her with concern.

'Xanthe and Alicia seemed quite keen to hook the two of you up together,' replied Fliss.

'Xanthe and Alicia live in fantasy land,' said Izzy. 'Ross and I are just friends.'

'Ah, right,' said Fliss nodding. 'The old "just friends" scenario.'

'There's no scenario. That's how it is.' Izzy tilted her chin as if daring anyone to say any more. Thankfully Alicia and Xanthe reappeared at that moment.

Xanthe sank wearily into a chair at the table. 'I'm bamboozled. We've looked everywhere.'

'Not everywhere,' said Alicia, the light of battle in her pale blue eyes. 'We haven't looked here or in the cellars.'

'I'd be careful you don't get locked in the cellars,' said Izzy with a touch of venom. 'That door is rather dodgy.' She gave her mother a meaningful stare. 'I'd hate for you to get stuck down there and miss Christmas Day.'

Both women exchanged uneasy glances.

'Have you seen Ross today?' asked Alicia with a mind-blowing lack of humility.

Izzy ignored the question.

'Nae,' said Duncan. 'The lad must be working, although I thought he said he'd finished for the holidays.'

'Poor boy. He works so hard. I hardly ever see him.' Alicia's face saddened and she stared out the window. 'I think I'll drag him out for some fresh air with his old mother.'

'That's a good idea,' said Xanthe. 'Izzy, you're looking a bit peaky. Have you been outside today?'

'No, I haven't,' snapped Izzy, glaring at her mother. 'And forget it. Ross and I are not interested in each other, okay?'

Her mother reared back, looking affronted. 'I don't know what you mean.'

'You know exactly what I mean. I don't need you meddling in my love life.'

'But darling, you don't have a love life.'

'And Ross would be perfect for you,' added Alicia.

Izzy put her hands on her hips and stared at the two

women. They were both gazing up at her with such earnest expressions that she burst out laughing, even though inside her heart felt very heavy. 'You two are incorrigible. Leave it. And I don't want to hear any more about it.'

'I don't know what you mean,' said Xanthe with an aggrieved sniff. 'And if you aren't interested in each other, then what's the problem in going for a walk?'

'There is no problem but I'm busy.'

'You ought to take a break,' said Jason, ignoring Fliss's jab to his ribs. 'We're pretty much organised. There's not much more to do today.'

'Aye lass, it's braw out there. Gorgeous day. You don't want to be stuck inside.'

'Whose side are you on?' Izzy rounded on Duncan who sat with an imperturbable smile on his face.

'Yours o' course, lassie. But you need to get some fresh air. This place will drain ye if ye let it. Bill always said that this place was as much about the land as the building. To survive here you have to have a love of the land.'

Izzy narrowed her eyes at the old man. Since when had he turned into a philosopher?

Thing was, now that it had been mentioned, she longed to get outside and go for a walk in the crisp snow while the sun was shining. 'I'll get out when I've finished doing this. Have you put the serving spoons on the table in the dining room, Xanthe?'

'I'll do it when we get back from our walk.'

'I'm not going for a walk.'

'Oh darling, I never see you. We can have some mother-daughter time.'

'I see you every day.'

'You know what I mean. Besides, I want to talk to you. We haven't had a proper chat for ages.' Xanthe gave her a guileless, cheerful smile.

Izzy sighed. 'Okay. I'll go for a walk with *you*.'

Her mother beamed. 'Lovely, I'll go dig out my wellington boots and my hiking socks.'

Clad in several layers, snow boots and a pair of sunglasses, Izzy met her mother on the doorstep of the castle, relieved to see that she was on her own.

Xanthe hooked her arm through Izzy's. 'Isn't this lovely? Just the two of us.'

Izzy squeezed her mother's arm. 'It is and I meant to say thank you for all the work you've done on the rooms. They do look amazing.'

'I know,' said Xanthe. 'But I'm having second thoughts about living here, you know.'

'You are?' Izzy's voice pitched in surprise.

'Not for me, but for you. You're still so young. Isolating yourself out here. When are you going to meet people?'

'You mean a man.'

'Don't look like that. You could get a manager in to run the place and go back to Edinburgh or Glasgow. Or you could sell the place. I wouldn't mind so much. I realise I've been a bit selfish, putting so much responsibility on you. I just always wanted something better for you. I thought living in a castle would be wonderful but it's a lot for a young woman when you still have so much to do in life. And I didn't think about how expensive it would be. Duncan told me about the roof. I'm sorry Izzy, darling. I've not been the best mother. I could sell the flat in Glasgow, you know.'

'No, you could not,' said Izzy, touched by her mother's rare introspection. 'It's yours. It's an asset for the future. Especially if this all goes tits up.'

'Yes, but darling, do you really want to stay here in the middle of nowhere?'

Izzy thought for a moment, looking at the distant skyline of snow-covered hills watching a bird of prey crest the horizon, the sun sparkling on the snow crystals. 'I don't think I could leave now. I love it here. I feel like I've found my place. I love having a kitchen full of people. With Jim, Jeanette and Duncan, it's like a whole new family. I've found what I want to do.' She'd found a purpose and liked looking after people.

They walked on, both lost in thought. The world was quiet, the sounds deadened by the layer of snow around them. *Yes*, thought Izzy. She could stay here. This was what she wanted to do. She'd enjoyed her trip to Edinburgh when she'd gone with Ross but this was home in a way that nowhere else had ever been.

'Look! It's Alicia. Yoohoo! Alicia!' Then her mother added, 'And Ross.'

Izzy shot her mother a reproachful glare. Xanthe held up her hands. 'I didn't. This is just a coincidence.' Then, with an impish grin, she said, 'Maybe it's meant to be.'

'And maybe it isn't,' growled Izzy.

Xanthe floundered through the snow towards Alicia and Ross. 'Isn't this wonderful?' She and Alicia greeted each other as if they hadn't seen each other in days rather than a mere half an hour.

'It's glorious,' said Alicia. 'I'm thinking about expanding

my idea for a new collection. I could call it the Kinlochleven Castle Winter Collection.' Izzy followed her mother, feeling her spirits drop as she pasted a resigned smile on to her face.

'Hello,' she said to Ross when she caught up with him and his mother. Alicia and Xanthe had already abandoned them, talking like a pair of parakeets, squawking and shrieking about the light, the colours and how inspiring it all was. Ross stood facing her.

'Sorry,' said Izzy. 'I don't think this was planned.'

'No matter,' he said. 'How are you?'

'I'm fine,' said Izzy in a pert voice. Did he think she was heartbroken or something? Arrogant git. 'You?'

'Good. Lovely day.'

'It is.'

Ahead of them they could hear the two women's animated chatter bouncing from the still water of the loch.

'I've never known my mother take to someone quite like she has to Xanthe.'

'Same. Xanthe has lots of friends but no one she's close to. She really likes your mum.'

'They are exhausting though.'

'They are but they're not doing anyone any harm.'

He shrugged.

They fell into step beside each other in awkward silence.

'How's the book coming along?'

'The first draft is finished.'

'So will you be leaving after Christmas?'

Ross dug his hands into his pockets and carried on walking for several steps. 'I'd like us to be friends but I'll understand if you'd rather I left.'

Izzy swallowed. Did she want him to stay? Part of her did and another part of her wasn't sure that she could bear it.

'I need to think about it,' she finally admitted.

'I've made a mess of things. I'm sorry.'

She shrugged. It was as much her fault as his. She'd fallen into the same old pattern of falling for someone and mistaking how they felt about her because she couldn't believe they didn't feel the same way.

'Let's chalk it up to experience,' she said without bitterness. 'It was a fling.'

He reached out and touched her arm, an expression of pain crossing his face. 'I'm sorry.'

'Yes, you keep saying that,' she said, shaking off his hand. Why did he make it sound as if it were out of his control? Bloody men.

She stomped forward towards the loch, its edges blurred by the snow and her vision clouded with stupid, self-pitying tears. There were sections that had iced over and it was difficult to see where the water ended and the land began but she wanted to put some distance between them. She refused to let him see that she was hurt. It wouldn't achieve anything, only further pile on the humiliation.

A loud crack reverberated under her foot and she stopped dead, looking down.

'Izzy!' Ross yelled.

Beneath her feet the snow began to separate, black water surging up through the cracks. Icy cold swept over her feet and too late she realised she'd stepped out onto the ice hidden under the snow. Before she could turn to go back to safety, the surface disintegrated and for a second she teetered on the edge. Then she was falling, her body already recoiling against the certain cold. The water clawed at her thighs, her waist and then circled her chest with an iron grip. With a panicked gasp at the sheer icy temperature, she felt her lungs freeze. Fingers of ice trickled down her neck as she bobbed in the water, weighted by her heavy layers. She went under. Water went up her nose, into her mouth, and she could taste the peaty earthiness as her teeth went into shock. Cold. So cold. It took her breath away. The whole world was ice and her brain had frozen too. Every muscle had tensed and she couldn't seem to get control of her limbs. The loss of control terrified her and something forced her to move. With a sudden burst of panic she forced herself upwards.

'Izzy! Izzy!' She heard Ross shouting but her mind was in chaos. 'Grab the branch.'

She was only a couple of metres from the edge and as the water ran over her head, the icy chill frosting her face, she saw him waving a large branch towards her. She could barely feel her hands but she reached out, twigs snapping as she tried to grasp it. Her hands wouldn't work. With a desperate heave she wrapped her arms around the branch, like a koala hugging a tree.

'Izzy! Izzy! Izzy!' Her mother's cries filled the air, shrill and hysterical.

'Hold on, McBride.' The lines on Ross's face were taut with strain as he heaved the branch back. 'Come on. I've got you.'

She hugged the branch harder as Ross pulled her waterlogged body towards him. Her feet touched the bottom and she scrambled towards the bank. Ross grabbed one of her flailing arms and pulled her out, hauling her up against him. Her teeth chattered so hard she was in danger of biting her tongue and she couldn't feel her hands.

'Take her clothes off,' commanded Alicia, already peeling her own coat off. 'We need to get her warm and dry. Xanthe, your scarf.'

Izzy stood unable to do anything as Ross peeled off her coat. Xanthe went to work on the zip of her trousers, as Alicia pulled off her jumper and undershirt in one go and began drying her with the scarf. In seconds Izzy was naked, standing barefoot on Ross's scarf, déjà vu clamouring at the sight of her feet and the green wool scarf together again. The two women rubbed her briskly before enveloping her in Alicia's big down coat.

'I'll go back to the house and get an electric blanket switched on, on one of the beds,' said Xanthe. 'We need to get her warmed up as quickly as possible. Ross, do you think you can carry her?'

The warmth of Alicia's coat was bliss on Izzy's skin as Ross scooped her in his arms. She closed her eyes as her body betrayed her by settling into his hold.

'It's all right, Izzy. We've got you.'

She stared up at him, shock a stranglehold on her body. His blue eyes were creased with worry and concern and she heard an odd mumbling and realised it was her trying to speak but she had no idea what she was trying to say and her lips were so numb she couldn't actually form any words. It was as if she were divorced from herself. All she could feel was cold. Cold everywhere. Her hair heavy and wet, ice seeping into her skull.

'Hat.' Alicia snatched Ross's woollen beany hat from his head and stuffed it on Izzy's, pulling it down almost to her nose, covering her ears. The sudden warmth was a momentary reprieve that she could focus on but she couldn't stop the violent shivers that had taken over her body.

'It's okay, Izzy. We'll get you back to the house and warmed up in no time.' Xanthe grabbed her hand and forced her own gloves onto her trembling fingers. 'You're going to be fine.' There was a crack in Xanthe's voice, as if she were trying to reassure herself as much as Izzy.

Izzy tried to speak to her mother but there was a numbness to everything as she fought through cotton wool trying to make sense of her situation. But some primeval response had taken charge and she was reduced to a shaking wreck, unable to do any more than mutter gibberish.

Chapter Twenty-Six

I zzy burrowed into the blessed warmth of her bed. Warm. She was warm. The memory of the grip of icy water lit up her brain and she snuggled back. Disjointed memories floated. Alicia drying her hair with fierce blasts from the hairdryer. Xanthe urging her limbs into pyjamas. Ross carrying her into bed and tucking her in tight like a mummy. She closed her eyes, revelling in the heat that she could feel under the sheets. An electric blanket. She shivered again, despite being warm. The cold. It had been so unrelenting. So terrifying. She didn't want to wake up properly. She wasn't even sure where she was but she knew that she didn't want to leave this cosy burrow.

When she surfaced again, this time her mind had sharpened, casting off the blurry edges.

She kept her eyes closed because it was too much effort to lift the lids.

'Mum was amazing,' she heard Ross say. 'She completely took charge, knew what to do. Whereas I didn't have a clue.'

'She's a smart woman,' said Graham, with a definite touch of pride.

'I know,' said Ross with a sigh. 'But…'

There was a silence and Izzy waited, instinctively aware that he wanted to say something important.

'How do you do it, Dad?'

His dad gave a small chuckle. 'I give thanks every day that I found your mother. I know you find it hard and when you were younger, embarrassing. She's a force to be reckoned with, but do you know what? She's majestic. An amazing, talented, passionate, full-spirited woman.'

'But the drama. It's never-ending. Don't you worry that she's like Icarus, she'll fly too close to the sun one day?'

Graham laughed again. 'But, son, she can fly.'

There was a silence and Izzy's heart missed a beat. What a gorgeous thing to say.

Neither man spoke for a few minutes and Izzy could feel the weight of the silence in the room, as if both of them were thinking about that simple, heartfelt statement.

Finally Graham asked, 'Do you remember your grandmother? She was the original dour Scot. I think the word was invented for her. Life for her was a joyless affair. She never saw the good, the positive. She was a mean-spirited misery of a woman who I swear drove my father into an early grave. When I met your mother, she was the sunlight. I envied her that ability to fly, unfettered, free. To find the joy in life. I fell in love with her joie de vivre. She's a happy soul. Always finds the good in people. She's interested in people, fascinated by things. Life is an adventure to her.' Izzy heard the squeak of his chair as Graham relaxed back, the rustle of his clothes as if he were crossing his legs.

'Yes, she's loud, oblivious to other people sometimes and dives down the most obscure rabbit holes that can drive you insane. There are times where I have no idea what she's talking about or where she's going with an idea but she's never selfish or unkind. Sorry, son, I know you find her difficult but her art, her warmth, her generosity of spirit brings great pleasure to people. I decided a long time ago that those people who find her embarrassing, well ... that's their problem. Not hers.'

What a lovely, lovely man, thought Izzy. There was so much love and sincerity in his words. She wondered if her father would have put up such a spirited defence of Xanthe, had he lived. It saddened her that she'd never know and neither would her mother.

'You mean, my problem,' said Ross in a subdued voice.

Graham huffed out a sigh. 'It's only a problem if you choose to see it that way. I know you've stayed away since you went to university. Wanted your independence. Didn't want your mother interfering.'

'Has it been that obvious?'

'Only to me. Your mother misses you, but like I said, she has a tremendous capacity to see the good in people and she also believes that everyone should be free to do what they need to do in life. That's her great gift, she lets people be who they are because she is who she is. You're a grown man, you have your own life to lead.' Graham paused and there was silence in the room for a moment before he said in a lower, more serious voice, 'But I wonder if perhaps you still see your mother through those teenager eyes. I'm not saying you haven't grown up but I'm saying that by staying away so much, you've not given yourself the chance to view your mother through adult eyes.'

Izzy kept herself still, wishing that she'd made her awareness known earlier. This was weighty father–son stuff and she felt like an intruder but she didn't want to interrupt what was obviously a rare moment between the two of them. It also felt important.

'I never thought about it like that.' She heard Ross shifting, the movement making the chair creak as his feet scuffed the wooden floorboards. 'It's not that I don't love her.'

'Of course you do, she's your mother, but you don't see the person she is, only the mother you think she should have been. But think again. You were never neglected, she might have been self-absorbed and wrapped up in her art but she always loved you.'

'And you,' Ross said, as if in sudden revelation, 'picked up the slack.'

Izzy, peeping through half-lidded eyes, saw Ross shake his head with a tender expression in his eyes.

'We used to go fishing. A lot. And you'd always make me Marmite sandwiches and pack a couple of cans of Irn-Bru. I used to love those trips.'

'Your mother hates fishing. It was guaranteed peace and quiet.'

'Doesn't the constant noise and chaos get to you?'

'I developed tactics for dealing with it. Why do you think I have such a well-stocked shed? And such a low golf handicap. But I promise you, dealing with the noise and chaos, as you call it – though I prefer to see it as spontaneity and enthusiasm – is worth it for everything else that your mother has brought into my life. You being one of the best things. She loves you, son, and she's not stupid, she knows you find her irritating. It grieves her but she can't change who she is.'

'She knows. Shit. That's awful.' Ross dropped his head into his hands. 'I've been an idiot. She and Xanthe were so practical down at the lake when it came to it, when there was an emergency.'

'Aye, neither of them are fools. Not my words, son, but you needed to have your eyes opened.'

'Why didn't you say anything before?'

'Because I wasn't sure you'd listen. But I think things have changed now.'

'I'm not sure how, but yes, I see it now.'

'It's probably to do with falling in love. Maybe it's your turn to jump off a cliff, take flight and see where it takes you.'

Izzy quickly blinked her eyes shut. She didn't want to hear any more so with an incoherent mumble, she stretched and moved, fluttering her eyes as if she'd only just woken up.

'Izzy?'

'Mmm,' she murmured, opening her eyes. Sunlight poured into the room, beams streaming through the diamond leaded panes. With a wince she levered herself up, her body leaden with surprising weariness.

'How are you feeling?' Ross leaned over her, his blue eyes filled with something that made her heart flip over.

'I'll leave you to it,' said Graham and slipped quietly away, giving a fond, fatherly smile that for some reason made her want to cry.

'Tired.' The word slurred on her tongue, which seemed to be too heavy to lift. She struggled to sit up, her limbs lethargic, like disobedient children refusing to obey her.

'Here, let me help you.' Gently he pulled the pillows from behind her and propped them up so she could fall back onto them.

He reached for a flask beside the bed and poured steaming liquid into a mug. 'Have some tea.'

She took the offered drink and took a thankful slip, feeling the delicious heat of the black tea course down her throat. 'Mmm, thanks,' she said, as the lassitude weighing her down lifted and her mind started clearing. She took another long draught, feeling the hot tea warming as it slipped down.

'Are you warm enough?'

She nodded, suddenly shy as she remembered being naked by the loch. Now she was wrapped in flannel pyjamas, her feet in lovely, soft, woollen socks. She shivered.

'Do you want another blanket?' asked Ross.

She shook her head. 'No, I'm okay. Just remembering. I was so cold.'

'You were.'

'Thank you. For pulling me out.' With a wince, she remembered him shouting, telling her to grab the branch, the terror in his eyes. Him carrying her. Him tucking her in. That barely there kiss he'd dropped on her forehead. No, she closed her eyes, she didn't want to remember that. Maybe she'd imagined it. He hadn't had any choice but to help her. It didn't mean anything and now he was probably feeling sorry for her and guilty that he'd upset her.

He reached for her hand. 'I'm sorry, Izzy.'

'Nothing to be sorry for. My fault. I wasn't looking where I was going.'

'I meant I'm sorry for making such a mess of things. Trying to deny what I was feeling.'

She shrugged and looked away, out of the window. She could see the loch, its serene gunmetal surface looking calm and benign. With a shudder she remembered the icy bite of its clutches and the shock of the cold wrapping itself round her with the strength of an iron cage. Her stomach lurched at the sickening memory of her utter impotence.

'It's fine, Ross.' She refused to look at him. She couldn't do this. Not now. If she looked at him, she knew she'd cry. She loved him but he didn't get to feel sorry for her. He didn't need to say things for the wrong reasons just to make her feel better.

'No, Izzy. It isn't. I got it wrong. I panicked. It wasn't your mum or my mum – it was me. You were right, I *was* being a coward, denying my feelings. Izzy, I think I might be falling in love with you.'

Too little. Too late. And a little voice in Izzy's head shrieked *Think? Might?* No, that wasn't good enough. He had to know. But she couldn't wait for him to make up his mind. Like Graham said, he had to jump off the cliff.

He spoke again. 'I couldn't handle the strength of the emotion. It knocked me sideways and then when you fell in the loch, I felt it again.'

She turned to him. He would never be fully in. He'd always be running scared. She'd played this game before with Philip. Every time she put some distance between them, he'd come running back. Too scared to lose her but not enough in love with her to step over the edge and make the commitment. Ross was the same. She wasn't going to let her heart be lifted up and then dropped, over and over.

'I made a mistake, Izzy.'

With a small sad smile, she shook her head, 'No, you didn't.'

A frown puckered his forehead. 'What do you mean?'

'You were right. We should just be friends. I don't want someone who's scared of love, who's going to back off

333

whenever the feelings threaten to overwhelm them or they think they're being manipulated into something. I want someone who's all in. Not someone who thinks they *might* be in love. Someone who's prepared to throw themselves off a cliff. You're not that person, Ross.'

She turned her head away. 'I need to sleep now.'

He stood up and she didn't dare look at him. Instead, she closed her eyes and pulled the blanket up to her chin, waiting until she heard the bedroom door click shut. Only then did she allow the tears to slip down her cheeks. She hadn't been lying when she said she wasn't going to change her mind; she loved him but she wasn't going to accept second best. This time she deserved more.

Chapter Twenty-Seven

'Y ou can't,' protested a voice outside Izzy's bedroom door. 'Izzy won't mind,' replied Xanthe in her usual blithe way. People rarely stopped her from doing what she wanted.

'See, Graham,' said Alicia. 'Izzy won't mind.'

'I think the poor girl needs to get some rest.'

Despite herself, Izzy's lips twitched. Incorrigible didn't begin to describe those two.

'She's been in bed all of yesterday afternoon and all morning. It's Christmas Eve.' Izzy put her phone down and considered feigning sleep to teach her mother a lesson but figured it would do no good. What on earth were they up to now?

Seconds later, Xanthe sailed into the room. 'Darling, how are you feeling? We thought we'd come and keep you company for a little while. You don't mind if Graham checks the panelling and the bathroom?'

Graham gave her an apologetic smile before saying with a

firm air, 'Or we can come back another time when you're feeling better.'

She smiled at him. He was such a lovely man and it wasn't his fault his son's emotions were buried deeper than the earth's core.

Alicia was very lucky to have Graham, who clearly adored her and wasn't ashamed to show it, in spite of her eccentric tendencies. It was a shame Xanthe had never met anyone after Izzy's father. They might have balanced out some of her excesses.

'No, it's fine. You go ahead.' To be honest, she was glad to see other people, it took her mind off brooding about Ross. She'd done the right thing, even if it didn't feel like the right thing at the moment.

'I still think it's a fool's errand,' he muttered.

'I heard that, Graham,' said Alicia before plonking herself down next to Izzy on the bed. 'How are you, dear? Your colour's a lot better. Poor thing, you gave us all quite a turn. Not sure me or your mother have been quite so successfully upstaged before.' She laughed. 'Although you handled it very well. No crying or screaming. You and Ross are so well matched. Both as cool as cucumbers.'

Izzy frowned, seeming to recall that while Ross had pulled her out, it had been Alicia that had been barking orders at everyone. There'd been no flapping or hand-wringing on her part at all.

'I know you're cross with him at the moment but he's a good boy really.'

Izzy's eyes widened.

'Oh don't worry, he doesn't tell me anything.' Her face

softened. 'But I know my son, even if he thinks I'm a lunatic. I'm sorry we teased you so much, I could see how much he liked you and … Xanthe and I foolishly thought giving him a nudge would help. I rather think that's backfired spectacularly on us.'

'What's he said?' asked Izzy, rather shocked that Ross would have said anything to his mother.

Alicia let out a cackle. 'Darling girl, you think he would confide in me? He'd rather dig out his own innards with an ice-cream scoop. But he's been in a foul mood ever since he left your room yesterday. What on earth did you say to him?' She grinned. 'Although it's always good to keep these boys on their toes.'

Izzy's mouth pinched tight. There was no way she was going to tell Alicia a thing. Ross would never forgive her for that.

'Ah, look at that. I admire your loyalty to him. I'll have to prise it out of the darling idiot myself.' She stood up and shook her voluminous tunic out. 'Any joy, Graham?'

Graham, who'd been in the bathroom, came out and shook his head.

'Nothing here,' came Xanthe's muffled voice from beneath the bed. Izzy leaned down. 'What are you doing?'

'I thought they might be under the bed.'

Izzy stared at her mother with a perplexed frown.

'You never know, they might be in a secret compartment.'

'They might,' Izzy agreed gravely.

'We'll leave you in peace,' said Alicia. 'Come on, Xanthe, I've had an idea.' The two of them disappeared as quickly as they'd arrived.

'Why does that fill me with foreboding?' asked Graham, with a smile that defined long suffering as he plodded after the two women. 'See you later.' He gave a wave and left.

Izzy huffed out a long sigh, suddenly feeling lonely. This morning she'd had quite a few visits – Jason and Fliss, bearing the most divine mince pies and little iced gingerbread shapes that they made to hang on the tree, Jeanette with a large mug of tea and Duncan with a lunch tray for her. All of them had been at great pains to reassure her that everything was under control. She didn't need to taste Jason's amazing lobster bisque or Fliss's rye bread rolls to confirm that was the case. Contrarily, the one person she would have liked to see kept his distance, exactly as she'd told him to.

In a cowardly way, she was rather glad of an excuse to stay up here, although Ross had probably retreated to his room, away from everyone else. She was dreading Christmas Day, when she'd have to pretend everything was normal. In a way she almost wished Fliss and Jason weren't here to help. She could have skulked more in the kitchen and avoided Ross. But no, big girl pants were required. She was going to have to pull them up and get on with it. She was Izzy McBride, that was what she did.

At five o'clock, when Izzy was heartily sick of her own company, Jeanette popped her head around the door. 'Hey, Izzy, how are you doing?'

'I'm fed up and bored.'

'Good,' said Jeanette. 'Xanthe says you have to come down

for Champagne cocktails at six. You can't possibly stay up here on your own on Christmas Eve. She made Jim promise to carry you down the stairs if need be.'

'Poor Jim.'

'He's terrified of your mother. I don't know why, she's so sweet. Anyway, do you think you might come down? I'll help you get dressed and everything.'

Izzy snorted. 'I'm quite capable of getting dressed. I'm absolutely fine. I only agreed to stay in bed for today because Xanthe said if I didn't, she'd call the doctor out.'

Much as Izzy hated being stuck upstairs away from her kitchen on such a busy day, she had dozed for quite a lot of the time, probably in response to the shock of yesterday's adventure, but now she had no more excuses to hide away and after all this preparation and angst, she was *not* going to miss Christmas. And she was not going to miss out on Champagne cocktails.

She swung her legs over the bed. 'I'll get up and have a shower.' She was going to have to face Ross at some point and she was going to make sure she looked her best. Show him what he was missing. Warrior princess mode was required.

Half an hour later, she was up and dressed with freshly washed hair and looked and felt human again. Energised by her shower, she made an effort with her hair and left the red curls to tumble down her back for a change instead of being bundled up in her usual messy bun. Okay, she was making quite a bit of effort. She even put on some lip gloss and then wiped it off because that was trying too hard. Then she put it back on because it was Christmas Eve and she and Xanthe had always dressed up for Champagne cocktails on Christmas Eve. She tilted her chin in the mirror. Dressing up was tradition. Nothing whatsoever to do with showing anyone what they'd thrown away.

'Izzy, you're just in time,' said Fliss, who was lifting a bowl out of the fridge when she arrived in the kitchen. 'I've made some sugar syrup for the sugar rims on the glasses. Xanthe has found the most amazing Champagne flutes. Very plain but very elegant. Aren't they beautiful?' She nodded towards the cluster of long-stemmed glasses that were waiting on the side. 'Xanthe wants to 'gram them before we serve them. She's set up a shot on the table with pine cones and candles. You didn't inherit her artistic talents, then.'

Izzy shook her head. It was a standing joke that her presentation skills were terrible.

'Did you get the edible glitter? I can't find it.'

'I hid it from Xanthe after I used it last time.'

'Good shout, she'd have found a way to use it.'

Izzy retrieved the golden glitter and sprinkled a good amount in a flat saucer of sugar.

'Here we go,' said Fliss, picking up the first glass and dipping it into the sugar syrup before dipping it into the sugar and glitter.

Izzy beamed. 'It looks amazing. Everyone was very impressed when I did it on the whisky sours when we decorated the tree. I'd never have thought of doing that before you suggested it.'

'I'm a genius,' said Fliss with a smug smile.

'In your own head,' grumbled Jason, pulling a tray of sausage pinwheels from the oven and sliding them onto a flat plate. They were the neatest little pinwheels Izzy had ever seen. She was so glad the other two had come.

'You're not going to serve those like that, are you?' she scolded.

'They're frigging sausage pinwheels. It's Christmas Eve. We'll do the fancy stuff tomorrow.'

'No,' said Fliss, smacking him on the hand. 'We do it properly. You serve food with love, remember.'

'It is served with love. I bloody love a sausage pinwheel.'

Fliss put her hand on her hip and tutted.

'You two don't get any better,' said Izzy with a laugh.

Jason immediately put an arm around Fliss. 'We love each other really.'

'Ew, get off me,' said Fliss. 'You big oaf.'

'See. I'm the brother she always wanted.'

'I've got four brothers already. I do not need another one.'

'Okay, besties.'

Fliss shuddered. 'I've never used that word in my life. You're just Jason.'

He pulled a mournful face. 'No one appreciates me.'

'You'd be appreciated a whole lot more if you put those on a nice plate, chopped up a few cherry tomatoes and added some watercress to give it some proper care and attention.'

'Henpecked, I am,' muttered Jason, but Izzy noticed he did exactly as Fliss suggested.

'What goes in these Champagne cocktails, then?' asked Fliss.

'It's a family recipe passed down from my great gran.

We've had these for as long as I can remember. Put a sugar lump in the bottom of the glass, a few drops of Angostura bitters on the sugar lump and then pour chilled brandy into the bottom of the glass and top up with Champagne. My grandad, when he was alive, was always in charge of making these.' With a smile Izzy thought of her grandad, a quiet man who'd died before his time. He'd always read her stories and taken her on walks, pointing out all the birds. She hardly thought of him these days but Christmas always brought back those rare, bittersweet memories.

'Ah, that's lovely. Family traditions are wonderful. At Christmas at home, my mum always used to leave a plate of crackers and cheese and port for Father Christmas. I always wondered why we didn't leave a mince pie out and poor Rudolph didn't get a carrot like everyone else. Took me and my brothers years to twig the connection between my grandad hating mince pies and being partial to cheese and port before bed.' Fliss giggled, lost in her own memories for a moment.

'My mum used to crack open the tin of Roses on Christmas Eve. We were lucky if there were any left on Christmas Day, except for the coffee creams. None of us liked them.'

'I love a coffee cream,' said Fliss.

'You would, you're posh.'

'I think it's time we took these through, don't you?' said Izzy with a stern look at both of them.

They laughed and this time Fliss with a mock punch to Jason's ribs said, 'We love each other really. He's my bestie.'

Everyone was assembled in the drawing room when Izzy, Jason and Fliss came through. The room shimmered with the glow of golden fairy lights across the mantelpiece and flickering candles on all the windowsills were reflected back in the dark glass. The curtains had been left open and outside the snow lit up the evening landscape, making it feel even cosier inside. Xanthe had done a beautiful job in here. The Christmas tree glistened in the light, the silver and gold baubles twinkling. The simplicity of the decoration enhancing the overall warmth of the décor.

'Merry Christmas Eve, one and all,' called Xanthe as soon as the glasses were handed out, raising her glass in a toast.

'Thank you for having us,' said Hattie lifting her glass in response. 'Especially me.'

'Yes,' said Graham. 'Thank you to Izzy and Xanthe for being such generous hosts and inviting us to stay.'

'It's a pleasure,' said Xanthe with bountiful aplomb, which made Izzy grin to herself and automatically look around to catch Ross's eye. He would have understood the irony. But there was no sign of him and despite everything she'd told herself, she felt a small hiss of disappointment, like the puncture of a tyre. How contrary was she? But surely if he had proper feelings for her, if he thought he might love her, he would have put up more of a fight. His absence proved what she'd suspected all along – that he didn't feel for her what she felt for him.

'Cheers, Izzy,' said Jim with a defiant grin.

'Aye, lass,' added Duncan. 'Thanks for turning this place into a proper home. You've made me verra welcome and ye didn't hae to.'

Izzy blushed.

'Yes, thank you, Izzy,' said Xanthe, crossing the room and putting her arm across Izzy's shoulders. 'For allowing me to live my dream. You're the best daughter a woman could have.'

Izzy blinked. It was rare her mother claimed kinship like that.

'Of course I'm the best, I'm the only one you've got,' joked Izzy, refusing to allow the lump in her throat to get the better of her.

A sudden hush alerted her to the arrival behind her, like atmospheric pressure affecting a barometer. She turned to find Ross striding into the room towards her, carrying the Claymore on his shoulder with deadly purpose, his eyes focused on her, sharp and intent. No one else existed. His kilt flared at the knee as he moved and the white linen shirt gaped, revealing a smooth, broad chest. Her mouth went dry as all her Jamie Fraser fantasies turned into dust at the sight of Ross's brawny shoulders and strong neck. Stunned, she stared back at him. Her skin pinpricked in awareness, tiny electrical jabs buzzing across her scalp, her neck, the palms of her hands.

The world shrank to just him.

'Izzy McBride, I need you to come with me.'

The room fell completely silent apart from the crackle of the flames behind her. His gaze never left her face. Her heart thudded so hard she could almost hear her pulse pounding through her body. When he slowly held out his left hand, she took it. There was a hushed silence as she allowed him to lead her from the room, the sword balanced on his right shoulder.

The candles on the mantelpiece in the great hall had been lit and flames leaped and danced in the grate, casting a soft, warm glow around the old wood-panelled walls. Ross swung the sword down from his shoulder, the tip to the ground, and stopped in front of her, backlit by the fire and the candles. Her lips parted, more in awe at the sight of him haloed by the flames behind him, but she waited for him to speak, waited for the weight of his words.

With one hand atop the sword and the other loose by his side, she watched as he drew in a breath. 'Izzy McBride, I love you.' His husky voice sent a white-hot flash through her. Surprise, exultation, amazement and shock collided like an explosion. His gaze didn't waver from her face.

'No *might* or *think* about it,' he declared. 'I'm throwing myself off the cliff.' She saw his hand shake where it grasped the Claymore. 'With a weighted backpack and no safety helmet or parachute.'

Then he dropped to one knee, still holding the sword.

'So fair art thou, my bonnie lass,
So deep in luve am I;
And I will luve thee still, my dear,
Til a' the seas gang dry.'

She swallowed, dumbstruck.

'Ross? W-what…?' was all that Izzy could manage.

'I love you.'

'B-but this…' she murmured.

'I thought I would make a grand gesture, so that you would know how I feel. So that you never doubt it.'

'Well, as gestures go, this is pretty big.' She gave him a tremulous smile.

'Is it enough to convince you that I've been an idiot and that I've come to my senses?'

'I think so.'

'Not good enough, Izzy McBride. I want someone who's all in. Not someone who thinks they might be in love. Someone who's prepared to throw themselves off a cliff,' he said with a teasing twinkle in his eyes that was underpinned by a touch of uncertainty.

She laughed, recognising her own words. 'Okay then, lead me to the clifftop.'

'Oh for God's sake, Izzy, kiss the mon,' called Duncan.

Izzy and Ross both turned to find everyone peering through the doorway at them.

'Don't keep him in his misery. The poor beggar's been dribbling after ye for weeks. He was just too stupid to ken it.'

Ross wrinkled his nose. 'He's got a point.'

'Yes, Izzy, you're not getting any younger and let's face it, you're not awash with offers.'

Izzy laughed. 'Thanks, Mother.'

'She's got a point, too,' agreed Ross.

'And I'm starving,' called Jim.

'You've eaten a whole tray of pinwheels,' complained Jeanette.

'I can't decide if this is terribly romantic or terribly unromantic,' said Izzy, stepping forward to stroke Ross's face, her heart bursting at the tenderness softening his eyes. 'I wasn't expecting an audience.'

'Me neither. Maybe you could kiss me and decide after that,' he said. 'Or maybe I could scoop you up and carry you out to the kitchen because I really don't want an audience while I ravish you. I'm never going to be big on drama but I can do it if I have to.'

She leaned in and kissed him. The sword fell to the floor with a clatter as he slipped his arms around her and hauled her against his big, hard body. Who needed Jamie Fraser when you had your very own Ross Strathallan?

'Now, can we get out of here?' he muttered.

'Yes.'

'By the way, I think I've found your sapphires.'

Chapter Twenty-Eight

CHRISTMAS DAY

'Oh no!' wailed Izzy and then started to giggle. Nothing was going to upset her today. She dropped the heavy tray on the counter top.

'Something wrong?' asked a low voice as a pair of arms slid around her waist. She turned to kiss Ross, tasting coffee on his breath.

'It won't go in.' Her eyes danced with mischief.

'I didn't hear any complaints last night.'

Izzy giggled again, the laughter bubbling up like Champagne. Happiness fizzed through her and she was almost convinced little sparks danced from her skin. 'I meant the turkey. It's too big for the oven.' Despite the potential disaster, she couldn't take it seriously.

'Oops,' said Ross, staring at the twenty-four-pound bird nestled in a large roasting tin.

She prodded the butter-slathered pimply skin with a disconsolate finger as her bottom lip quivered with mirth. 'I can't believe this. All the planning and it never occurred to me to check the oven was big enough.'

'You mean you didn't put it on the list?'

She nudged him with a playful elbow. 'No, I didn't.' She sighed. 'I'm going to have to cut it up. I guess it will cook quicker that way.'

'Tell you what. Let's have another coffee and then we'll think about the best plan of attack.'

She grinned at him. 'We' sounded so much better than 'you'.

She sat down at the table while he replaced her mug on the Nespresso machine and popped in another pod. As she listened to its familiar buzz, her head ticked through various options. She could butcher the whole thing, something she'd learned to do in Ireland, then cook the breast, the wings and the legs separately, but Adrienne had always insisted that cooking on the bone enhanced the flavour of the meat and she'd wanted today to be perfect.

When Ross placed the coffee in front of her, she took a cautious sip and sighed.

'There's one thing I could do. I could chop it in two.'

Ross raised an eyebrow, smiling slightly. 'And then superglue it back together once it's cooked?'

She nodded. 'Funny but it might work.'

'Right. Would you like me to get the axe from Duncan's tool shed?'

'Axe?' Izzy straightened. 'I was thinking a saw, but actually, an axe is probably better.'

Ross stared at her and cleared his throat. 'I was joking.'

'Oh God, this is ridiculous, isn't it? It's straight out of

situation comedy territory.' She began to laugh. His lips twitched.

'Just a bit.'

'But I can't think what else to do. If I cut it in half through the top, I can perhaps put it back together and hide the join with bacon strips when I carry it in.'

'Are you going to be able to do that?'

'No idea, but what's the worst that can happen?'

'You could chop your hand off.'

'You've already demonstrated you're good with a chopper,' Izzy said, her eyes dancing again. 'You can do it.'

He swooped in for a quick kiss before saying, 'You want me to take an axe to the turkey?'

'What else do you suggest? I need to get it in the oven and I also need to start preparing breakfast. I told everyone to be down by nine and I'm not even dressed yet.'

'You're making enough noise to wake the dead,' said Jason, coming into the room bleary-eyed and clutching the front of his head. 'Merry Christmas.'

'Merry Christmas.'

'Och, aye, that whisky stuff is strong,' Jason groaned.

'Only if you drink half a bottle,' said Ross, exchanging a quick look with Izzy. They'd left Graham, Fliss, Jason and Jim to it last night.

'Wasn't me,' he complained. 'It was Fliss. I was helping her.'

'The two of you were arguing about who can hold their drink best,' pointed out Ross. 'Honestly, the pair of you.'

'They're always like this,' said Izzy, with a shake of her head. 'Let me guess, Fliss drank you under the table again?'

'Effing right she did. For a posh bird, she can down it.' He peered at the turkey. 'Shouldn't that be in the oven by now?'

'Yes, but there's a slight problem. It's too big to go in the oven.'

Jason sniggered. 'That's a bummer.'

'It's all right, Ross is going to cut it in two with an axe.'

'No bloody way.' Jason shook his head. 'Seriously?'

'Well, what do you suggest?' asked Izzy, with a trace of belligerence, because seriously she needed to find a solution like half an hour ago.

'Spatchcock it, of course.'

'Of course,' repeated Izzy with a roll of her eyes. 'What does that even mean?'

Jason began to rifle through the drawers and then, with a shout, held up a pair of short, blunt-nosed scissors. 'Brilliant. Poultry shears. Let me, lady and gentleman, show you how to spatchcock a turkey.'

Wielding the shears, Jason gave them a quick butchery masterclass, cutting the backbone out of the turkey and flattening it on to a bigger baking tray.

'Thank you so much,' said Izzy, very grateful that he was here and the Carter-Joneses weren't.

'Glad to be of service. Now, have you got any paracetamol? I've got a banging headache. Whoever said whisky was the water of life flamin' lied.'

'Merry Christmas, Izzy,' said Jeanette, skipping down the last few stairs into the hall with Jim at her heels. 'Look what Jim bought me.' She held out a hand to show off a pretty silver bangle. 'And my mum sent us some money as a belated wedding gift for a honeymoon. I'm so happy that she's forgiven me.' Jeanette's face glowed with happiness.

'Aw, that's wonderful, Jeanette.' Izzy gave her a hug. 'Happy Christmas. Come and have a glass of Bucks Fizz.' Ross and Jason had been quite insistent that they all met in the hallway for drinks before breakfast. Despite his hangover, Jason cheerfully stood in the centre of the room, serving Bucks Fizz to everyone as they arrived.

'Merry Christmas!' Alicia's voice boomed from the gallery above and then she came gliding down the stairs in a full-length red tartan taffeta dress with a black bodice. She greeted Xanthe with a hug and they exchanged their familiar parakeet shrieks of love, approval and amazement, before Alicia turned to Izzy. 'Happy Christmas, darling, you looked positively blooming. You obviously had a good night.'

'Mother,' protested Ross, although his mouth twitched as he rolled his eyes.

'Thanks, Alicia,' said Izzy with an awkward laugh, hoping she wasn't blushing too much.

'Where's Fliss?' asked Jeanette, looking around anxiously, making indiscreet signals to Jim and Duncan who were making equally indiscreet 'what?' signals back to her.

'I'm here,' said Fliss, appearing in a beautiful pink silk dress, having taken off her apron.

'Good, we're all here.' Jeanette tapped the side of her glass, bringing to mind an officious pixie.

When everyone quieted, she lifted her glass. 'I'd like to propose a toast to our amazing hostess, Izzy, who has made us all feel so at home. She's so kind, generous and welcoming and I don't know of many other people who would have taken in two waifs and strays and then given them a job. Even before we came to live in the house, you were kind. Didn't say anything about us camping on your land. Said we could help ourselves to wood. So we did...' She gave Jim and Duncan an extremely unsubtle go-do-something hard stare and as they slipped out of the front door, there was one of those awkward no-one-knows-what-to-do silences for a couple of seconds. Then, to everyone's immediate relief, they staggered back into the room carrying the most beautiful log bench with a big red ribbon tied around the back rest.

'Merry Christmas, Izzy!' yelled Jeanette. 'Thank you for giving us a home and a chance ... well, we can't thank you enough.'

Duncan and Jim put the bench down in front of Izzy.

'Jim made it,' Jeanette said proudly.

Izzy reach out to touch the soft satin finish of the pale bench seat, which had been highly polished, contrasting with the weathered bark edge details on the back and the arms. 'It's lovely,' she said, feeling tears welling up in her eyes before scooping Jeanette in a hug, slopping her drink all over the floor. 'It is lovely, thank you. Thanks, Jim, it's amazing. Did you really make this?'

'Aye.' He came and gave her a hug too.

Izzy wiped at her mascara. 'I'm not going to have any make-up left at this rate.'

Everyone laughed and they settled into small groups, chatting as Jason, Fliss and Graham tried the bench out, admiring the workmanship and patting the seat.

After a breakfast of smoked salmon, bagels and cream cheese – although Duncan refused to eschew his usual porridge, even if it was Christmas Day, and Jason opted for a bacon bagel butty, which he claimed was a guaranteed hangover cure – Izzy hurried back to the kitchen to begin the day's work and the castle's inhabitants dispersed to get ready for the main event, Christmas lunch.

With Jason and Fliss helping her, the preparations all went smoothly and for the first time in what felt like months, Izzy was finally able to relax.

'I think we deserve another glass of champers,' said Fliss, as she checked her watch. The turkey was out of the oven, resting under a coat of tin foil and a pile of tea towels, the meat juices had been added to the gravy bubbling on the hob and the vegetables both in the oven and on the top were a few minutes away from being done. 'We're almost there.'

'I'm getting used to this stuff,' said Jason, as he poured glasses for the three of them. 'Although I'll always like my lager.'

'You're such a pleb,' teased Fliss.

'Better than being a stuck-up madam,' Jason teased back.

'I was going to say how glad I am that you're here,' said Izzy with a laugh. 'You've made today go so much easier. To the three musketeers. Thank you for rescuing me.'

'It's just practice, you'll be fine by next Christmas,' said Fliss with a comforting smile.

'If it weren't for you two, I might not have made it through this Christmas, let alone next,' Izzy replied with feeling.

Izzy carried the turkey through to the dining room as if she were leading a triumphant procession, the crisp golden skin glistening on the big antique platter. Around the meat were kilted soldiers, little bacon-wrapped chipolatas, along with balls of her home-made haggis stuffing and a second of sausage meat, which smelled of orange and chestnut. Behind her, Fliss carried two tureens of amber-edged roast potatoes, steaming slightly. Following her, Jeanette held a tray bearing three large jugs of gravy. Bringing up the rear was Jason carrying honey-roasted parsnips with chilli, carrots cooked in star anise and butter, and peas and asparagus in herbs.

Xanthe had lit all the candles in the room and the fire glowed with a welcome orange warmth. The table was *Downton Abbey* immaculate, the glow of the candles reflected by the polished silver cutlery. In vast Champagne buckets, burnished with age, bottles of wine were waiting on ice while sets of crystal glasses had been placed at each setting for water, red and white wine. Ross, as promised, performed his wine waiter duties diligently and had already filled the glasses.

Izzy took her place at the head of the table, Ross on her left and Jeanette on her right with Fliss and Jason next to them. At the opposite end of the table her mother waved at her and gave her a double thumbs-up.

Jason began to carve the turkey and Fliss handed out the plates with Izzy urging everyone to fill them. 'Don't forget there's bread sauce, cranberry sauce, stuffing, sage and onion, haggis and sausage meat.'

'Mmm, yum,' said Jeanette and then looked at her husband. 'If you want a decent Christmas lunch ever again we might have to stay here for ever.'

He laughed.

The minute everyone's plates were full, Xanthe jumped to her feet and lifted her wine glass.

'A toast to Izzy, my darling daughter. Thank you for making my dreams come true. This is officially The Best Christmas Ever. Happy Christmas, Izzy.' Everyone around the table rose to their feet and lifted their glasses chorusing, 'Happy Christmas.'

Duncan's voice was the loudest of all as he wiped his eyes, Graham sitting next to Alicia caught his wife's hand and they exchanged a touching look, Jeanette gave Jim a smacking kiss on the cheek and Jason and Fliss grinned at each other. Hattie looked on with a gentle smile and Izzy smiled back at her, conscious the girl was on her own. To her delight, Hattie grinned back and nodded, saying, 'It might be the best Christmas ever.'

Izzy swallowed back a lump in her throat and beamed at everyone, tears blooming in her own eyes. This was what Christmas was about. The company of good friends and family. Sharing food and love around a table. Ross laid his hand over hers and gave it a little squeeze. Something warm blossomed in her chest. This was home and these people were family.

'You're amazing, do you know that?' said Ross to her in a quiet undertone.

'I had a little help from my friends,' she replied, grinning at him, happiness radiating from every pore.

'Yes, but you get the friends you deserve.'

Overhearing, Fliss smiled at them. 'That's a very good saying and very apt.'

Izzy waved a hand over her face. 'Shh, I'm getting emotional.'

'Nothing wrong with that,' said Ross with a wink.

She widened her eyes at him and laughed.

'Crackers!' yelled Xanthe. 'Everyone needs to pull their crackers and you have to wear your hats.'

Duncan groaned and muttered but Izzy noticed he put on his purple paper crown along with everyone else.

After two hours of joy, during which everyone chatted, ate, laughed and celebrated with good food, good wine and wonderful company, Izzy was touched that Alicia insisted that she, Xanthe and Graham did the tidying, leaving the others to stay at the table and enjoy a glass of port.

'Your mother's actually very practical, you know,' Izzy observed to Ross, as she watched Alicia carrying several plates in true silver service style.

'So I'm realising. I had a good long heart-to-heart with her while you were cooking up a storm this morning. Dad told me a few home truths the other day and I realised that I've maybe not been very fair to her.' He leaned forward and kissed her before saying, 'Falling in love changes your perspective on things.'

Izzy simply smiled, deciding not to tell him she'd overheard his conversation with his dad.

'Shall I be Father Christmas?' Xanthe asked, her voice brimming with excitement and the indigo feather on today's fascinator quivering in support. Dressed in a matching figure-hugging, indigo blue velvet dress, she looked resplendent. There was no other word for it.

Having finished the washing up, she'd marched into the dining room complete with flamingo pink, feather-trimmed rubber gloves to invite everyone into the drawing room and they were now assembled on the sofas and chairs while a fire burned in the hearth and the fairy lights winked and flashed on the Christmas tree.

Overnight a number of wrapped parcels had appeared under the tree as well as the stockings.

'This one is for you, Izzy,' said Xanthe, her eyes sparkling. 'Go on, open it. I can't wait for you to see it.'

Feeling a little self-conscious with all eyes on her, Izzy took the present. 'Let me give you one.'

'I've already seen it,' Xanthe said, reaching for Izzy's parcel.

'I hope you haven't been peeking,' said Izzy, who had put the present under the tree at the very last minute because her mother couldn't be trusted with surprises.

'Who, me?' Xanthe grinned as she portrayed dramatic indignation, putting her hand on her heart. 'Jeanette, you can come and be parcel elf. This one is for Alicia.' Jeanette duly distributed the presents as Xanthe pulled them out from underneath the tree. 'This one's for Ross. This one's for Graham.' Xanthe had bought everyone a little gift to go along with the Scottish tablet that Izzy had made. The tablet was all beautifully wrapped in pockets of cellophane tied up with coils of gold, silver and green ribbon.

Once everyone had a gift, Xanthe declared they could be opened. With great enthusiasm she ripped into the neat square parcel from Izzy, removing the box. 'Oooh,' she squealed. 'It's a hat box.' She lifted the lid and pulled out a raspberry colour felt hat with an asymmetric brim and a feather pin on the front. 'Izzy!' She gulped and then promptly burst into tears. 'This is beautiful. You darling. I love it. Look, isn't it beautiful?' She ran over to Izzy and scooped her into a big hug. 'Thank you, sweetheart.'

'That's okay, Mum.'

'You know me so well.' Xanthe, wiggling her bottom and nestling like a broody hen into the small space between Izzy and Duncan, looped her arm around Izzy's shoulder, sniffing as she said, 'Thanks for putting up with me. I love you.'

'I love you too, Mum,' said Izzy before adding with a grin, 'I knew you'd like it.'

'Now open yours. You're going to love it.'

Izzy had no doubt she would. Xanthe had impeccable taste and always managed to find just the thing you never thought you needed.

She lifted the heavy parcel onto her knee and teased the paper off slowly as Xanthe complained the whole time about how slow she was being. Inside the parcel was a clothbound box set of Diana Gabaldon's complete *Outlander* series.

'Mum, these are gorgeous.' She stroked the spines. 'Where ever did you find them? Thank you.'

'My pleasure, darling. I ordered them from America. I know how much you love Jamie Fraser.'

Izzy smiled and glanced quickly at Ross, who smirked at her. She might have told him about her Jamie Fraser fantasies the night before.

'Now, Graham,' said Xanthe, bossy as always. 'Let's see what you got.'

'Thanks, Xanthe,' said Jeanette, a fake bright smile on her

face as she held up an enormous Christmas jumper complete with furry reindeer antlers and a flashing red nose.

'Oh blast!' spat Xanthe crossly. 'That one's for Jim. He must have yours.'

'Do you think?' asked Jim, who had squeezed himself into the tiny matching jumper and thrust his left hip out in a classic model pose. Everyone burst out laughing.

'I've got one more present for people,' said Xanthe, handing out book-shaped parcels. 'Here you go. This is for you and Jeanette, this is for you, Hattie – sorry, Izzy, I gave her yours but I know you've read them all – one for Alicia and Graham and one for Duncan.'

As they unwrapped their parcels, Izzy's eyes shot to Ross's in disbelief. Xanthe had given them all a Ross Adair book.

'Thank you, I've no read any o' these,' said Duncan. 'I like a good crime thriller.'

'You can read it first, Jim,' said Jeanette, 'so you can tell me if there are any scary bits.'

'How thoughtful, Xanthe,' said Alicia. 'Graham and I love books.'

'That's all right.' She sat back on her heels with a smug, cat-like smile, before adding, 'And Ross can sign them all.'

Izzy's funny half-hiccough-cum-strangled-gasp drew all eyes to her.

'What, darling? Didn't you know?'

'What do you mean?' asked Alicia.

'You didn't know either?' asked Xanthe, her eyes seeking out Ross, who was studying the cornice. Izzy's hand crept into his and she gave it a supportive squeeze.

'Know what?' Alicia asked.

Graham began to laugh. 'Is it true?'

Ross gave a surreptitious nod.

'Is what true?' asked Alicia. 'I do wish you'd tell me what's going on. Why would Ross sign these books?'

'Ross Adair is Ross Strathallan,' explained Graham gently. 'Our son.'

'Really?' Alicia's face was a picture. 'Are you?' She turned to Ross.

He nodded.

She beamed. 'Thank god for that. Imagine how embarrassing it's been having to admit that my son is a dusty old history professor. Gosh, I wish you'd told me sooner. I've had to put up with Margaret Baxter telling me that her son is a successful taxidermist. A thriller writer is much more exciting. I can't wait to tell her.'

'How did you know, Xanthe?' asked Izzy.

'Mrs McPherson told me, of course. That woman knows everything except the importance of check-ups at the dentist. Honestly, Alicia, you should see her teeth. But she does sell some incredible wool in the post office. I've been planning to do some knitting.' As Xanthe and Alicia entered into an in-depth conversation about needles and stitches, everyone else went back to looking over their presents.

Izzy's thoughtful stockings went down well with everyone, especially Hattie, who had no family or friends around her but had received gifts from everyone, including a set of glass tile coasters from Alicia and a drawstring toilet bag from Xanthe, which she'd made using upcycled fabrics and deep russet tassels that had once adorned the old dining room curtains.

'This is wonderful, Xanthe. You're so talented,' said Alicia, admiring the scarf that she'd made, again from a patchwork of upcycled fabrics, each end patterned with a hotch-potch of pretty buttons.

Xanthe beamed. 'Yes, I'm thinking of setting up an arts and crafts co-operative in one of the barns.'

'You are?' Izzy blinked; her mother never ceased to surprise her.

'Well, once the house is up and running, I won't have anything to do,' she said with blithe disregard to the work that would need to go into looking after guests. 'You've got Jeanette to help you and so I thought Jim and Duncan could help fit out the end barn and I could invite local crafts people to exhibit and sell their wares. I could probably get one of those arts grants and Jim could sell his benches and make other furniture.'

'You've got it all worked out.' Izzy had to admire her. Xanthe never let anything get in the way of a good idea, and it was definitely a good idea.

'You're not the only pretty face around here, darling.'

'And Ross and I have one last present,' said Izzy, standing up. 'Or rather, an announcement.'

'Oh my God, Alicia. We're going to be grandparents,' Xanthe exclaimed.

Izzy groaned while Ross put his hand over his eyes and ducked his head.

'No, Mother. We know where the sapphires are.'

Xanthe screamed as everyone started talking at once.

'You found them.'

'Where?'

'How did you find them?'

'When did you find them?'

Ross held up a hand. 'Why don't you all come into the hall?'

With puzzled frowns everyone rose to their feet and followed Izzy and Ross into the hall. The two of them stood in front of the fireplace, beneath the Claymore.

'So, lassie, where are they?' asked Duncan, a slight touch of challenge in his voice, as if he didn't believe her.

Izzy held back a smirk. 'In plain sight.'

'What do you mean?' Xanthe's plaintive voice asked.

'Where's the best place to hide something?'

'In plain sight,' said Graham, scanning the walls of the hall. Izzy nodded and everyone began looking around the room while she and Ross exchanged a private smile.

'So where are they?' Xanthe yelled, her impatience escaping her. 'Put us out of our misery.'

Ross turned and lifted the Claymore down from the wall. 'I wondered what that idiot Gregory was blathering on about when he talked about the knobs on the handle. I assumed he was spouting his usual rubbish.' He lay the sword down on the oak sideboard and beckoned everyone over, pointing to the small oval lumps adhered to the handle.

'Those are the sapphires?' Xanthe wrinkled her nose.

'They've been disguised,' explained Ross. 'Someone's glued them on and painted over them.'

'Bill. The sneaky beggar,' said Duncan. 'He always said he kent where they were. I thought it were pride talking.'

'It explains why he said the Claymore shouldn't ever pass out of the family,' said Izzy.

'Well, they're not as pretty as Isabella's necklace,' said Xanthe with a pout. 'Sorry, Izzy. I thought they were going to be fabulous jewels. I'm quite disappointed.'

'I'm not. I'm looking at a new roof.'

'Tsk, tsk.' Xanthe's fascinator bobbed in disapproval. 'I don't know where you get it from. Always so practical.'

Ross slipped an arm around Izzy's waist and whispered in her ear, 'Thank goodness,' before kissing her softly on her neck. 'With our gene pool, we're going to need all the help we can get. I'm not sure we'll ever have a quiet life but somehow I think I can cope.'

'Oh, this is typical,' Hattie's voice suddenly rang out. 'You'll never believe it, my aunt and uncle want to know if they can come here for Hogmanay, arriving the day after tomorrow.'

Izzy began to laugh. 'Of course, they can. The more the merrier.'

She was pretty sure she'd be able to show them the finest Scottish hospitality. After all, how could she fail? She had her family and friends around her.

Six months later...

Hattie gulped as she watched Luc strip off his T-shirt. OMG, he had abs – real life abs. A six-pack instead of a six-pound bag of potatoes. She couldn't take her eyes off them. He looked like a flipping male model in all his six-foot-three gorgeous glory.

Thank goodness she was wearing sunglasses and could pretend that she wasn't looking at him.

With one quick fluid movement he dived into the cool blue water, swimming like a sleek seal for a good half length of the pool before surfacing with a shake of his head. Should she acknowledge him, she wondered? The last thing she wanted was to engage in conversation with him when she was sitting here in her matronly, baggy Marks and Spencer swimming costume. She looked down and tugged at the faded orange and pink pattern. When had she stopped caring? When had she stopped wearing a bikini for goodness' sake?

Hattie watched Luc swimming with an easy front crawl, his biceps bunching with each stroke. She indulged in a little heartfelt sigh to herself. He really was an absolute Adonis and he probably knew it. What's more she could bet that his girlfriends would wear fabulous, tiny bikinis and sport nearly all-over-body golden tans not manky old swimsuits like this one where the lycra had given up the ghost in strategic regions.

She closed her eyes and tried to block out the vision of Luc, which worked just fine until everything went quiet. When she opened her eyes, he was hauling himself out of the pool, lifting that awesome body up over the edge in a definite show of very masculine strength.

With water running off him, the droplets glistening in the sunshine like crystals, he walked straight towards her, with that confident easy swagger and roll of the hips that made her think of cowboys.

'Bonjour, Hattie.' As usual he dropped the H from her name which was charming without him even trying.

'Hi,' she said, trying to be cool, but there was a giveaway squeak in her voice. God, she'd turned into a guinea pig overnight.

'Nice costume,' he said with a lift of one decidedly rakish brow. If they were still looking for a new James Bond, he'd got that look nailed.

'Do you think so?' she asked brightly, wanting to cover herself up.

'No, it's hideous.' He gave her a wicked smile. 'Why bother? No one's here.'

'Apart from you.'

'I won't mind, if you don't.'

She blushed and picked up her book. Luc always managed to make her feel very gauche and inexperienced, which was bloody irritating because she was a grown woman and she'd had sex plenty of times, thank you very much. Although looking at him, she suspected his sort of sex was very different to the type she was used to or rather not used to anymore. Chris hadn't been that interested for the last eighteen months.

'What are your plans today?' she asked in a desperate attempt to hold a normal conversation.

He shrugged, a proper Gallic, lazy shrug. He had very nice broad shoulders... and there she went again. Objectifying the poor man.

'I have no plans. It's a day off from the vines. I thought perhaps...' he paused and his eyes rested on her face. '...I might seduce you.'

Pardon! Hattie managed out a strangled gasp, even more grateful for the sunglasses that protected her outraged stare. What on earth did she say to that?

Find out what happens next with Hattie and Luc in

The French Champagne Chateau

Available to preorder now and on sale in 2023

Acknowledgments

This book was inspired by the most beautiful wedding of very dear friends, Lesley and Richard. Thanks guys for inviting me to the most joyous, romantic ceremony I've ever been to. It was a handfasting on the beach in brilliant spring sunshine in the stunning location of Crear, Tarbert in Argyll opposite the Isle of Jura. Driving up there along Loch Lomond past Loch Fine to Argyll, full of magnificent scenery, remains one of my favourite journeys. After this glorious trip, I just knew I had to set a book in Scotland.

This is my 20th book and I've written a few of these acknowledgements now, so forgive me if you've seen these names before but each one of them plays a very important part in my writing life. Huge thanks to my dear author friend, Donna Ashcroft, we talk constantly and usually know each other's characters almost as well as our own. I'm also very grateful that I have my Party Peeps, Bella Osborne, Philippa Ashley, Darcie Boleyn and Sarah Bennet who keep me sane, offering support and brilliant advice.

Extra special thanks to my family, Nick, Ellie and Matt, who have absolutely no sympathy when I tell them that the latest book is dreadful – they've heard it all before.

Thank you to Broo Doherty, my amazing super-agent – I couldn't have a better person on my side (although she doesn't have any sympathy either when I tell her my book is dreadful). Equal thanks to Charlotte Ledger, my editor, officially the nicest person on the planet (she does sympathise when I tell her my book is dreadful and then makes them so much better with her brilliant editorial skills).

I'm incredibly grateful to the amazing Rights Team at HarperCollins, Zoe, Agnes, Aisling, Sarah, Sam and Rachel who sell my books all around the world and are unfailingly enthusiastic about every one of them and also to the fabulous One More Chapter Team, Emma, Sara, Jennie and Bethan.

And a huge thank you to each and every reader, without you, I wouldn't have the best job in the world. Thank you for buying my books, sharing reviews and contacting me.

ONE MORE CHAPTER

One More Chapter is an
award-winning global
division of HarperCollins.

Sign up to our newsletter to get our
latest eBook deals and stay up to date
with our weekly Book Club!
<u>Subscribe here.</u>

Meet the team at
<u>www.onemorechapter.com</u>

Follow us!
@OneMoreChapter_
@OneMoreChapter
@onemorechapterhc

Do you write unputdownable fiction?
We love to hear from new voices.
Find out how to submit your novel at
<u>www.onemorechapter.com/submissions</u>